David Singmaster

~~1998~~ c 2000

The Dead Hand

and Other Uncollected Stories

The R. Austin Freeman
Omnibus Edition
Volume 9

The Dead Hand

and Other Uncollected Stories

R. AUSTIN FREEMAN

Omnibus Edition Volume 9

Edited and Introduced by
Douglas G. Greene
and Tony Medawar

THE BATTERED SILICON DISPATCH BOX
1999

For photocopies of various stories we are grateful to Freeman scholar, David Ian Chapman, and to Jack Adrian, who knows more about popular literature during Freeman's lifetime than any other living human being.

Canadian Cataloguing in Publication Data

Richard Austin Freeman (1862-1943)
    The Collected Writings of Richard Austin Freeman

    ISBN 1-55246-084-3 Volume 1
    ISBN 1-55246-086-X Volume 2
    ISBN 1-55246-088-6 Volume 3
    ISBN 1-55246-090-8 Volume 4
    ISBN 1-55246-092-4 Volume 5
    ISBN 1-55246-094-0 Volume 6
    ISBN 1-55246-096-7 Volume 7
    ISBN 1-55246-098-3 Volume 8
    ISBN 1-55246-066-5 Volume 9 (The Dead Hand and Other Uncollected Stories)
    ISBN 1-55246-082-7 Volume 10 (In Search of Dr. Thorndyke)
    ISBN 1-55246-170-X Volume 11 (The Anthropologist at Large,
                                    Thorndyke Scholarship & Pastiches)
    ISBN 1-55246-100-9 The Set of Volumes 1-11
    ISBN 1-55246-102-5 Electronic Edition

First Printing in Canada February 1999

All Inquiries and Orders;
George A. Vanderburgh, *Publisher*
THE BATTERED SILICON DISPATCH BOX™

E-Mail: gav@gbd.com

420 Owen Sound Street
P. O. Box 204,   P. O. Box 122
Shelburne, Ontario   Sauk City, Wisconsin
CANADA L0N 1S0   U.S.A. 53583-0122
Fax (519) 925-3482   *Fax:* (608) 643-5080

*C*ontents

Contents

Introduction

1. THE MECHANIC OF CRIME AND DETECTION

Of the many writers of detective stories who followed in the immediate wake of Sir Arthur Conan Doyle, Richard Austin Freeman (1862-1943) stands out not only as a fine writer but as a technician and plotter of the highest order. In the words of Raymond Chandler, "Austin Freeman ... has no equal in his genre."[1] His novels and many short stories mark the first stage in the maturing of the detective story and the replacement of Sherlock Holmes's detection by deduction by a more linear narrative wherein an actual or apparent crime is seen to take place and is then solved by science. Of course, there would be other developments, such as the emergence of the psychological mystery, but the inverted mystery and a focus on the forensic investigation of crime, Freeman's principal hallmarks, have earned him a solid place in the pantheon of the genre.

Detective stories that begin from the perspective of the criminal are now not uncommon, for example the *Columbo* television mysteries of Richard Levinson and William Link, but before 1908 they were all but unknown. Tradition dictated that the purpose and sole object of any detective story should be the identification and punishment of the guilty party, working backwards from the crime, but Freeman believed that readers would relish the chase more if it were seen from both sides. His approach was mainly to set a challenge to his readers by showing them the commission of a crime, from the perspective of the criminal, and afterwards show step by step how a cast-iron solution could be built from the smallest and most obscure of clues, even if their significance could be determined only by a detective with a good deal of specialist knowledge.

Such a detective was Dr. John Evelyn Thorndyke, unquestionably one of

---

[1] Letter to Hamish Hamilton, quoted in *Raymond Chandler Speaking*, ed. Dorothy Gardiner and Katherine Sorley Walker (1962).

iii

the very greatest of all fictional detectives. As Holmes is to the Victorian Age, Thorndyke is *the* Edwardian detective and, like the work of Conan Doyle, the Thorndyke mysteries are a valuable portrait of the manners and style of the Edwardian age, with even the atmosphere and setting of the later novels – written many years after the First World War – having more in common with that earlier time than the period in which they are ostensibly set.

Thorndyke is methodical, logical, precise and correct – at all times and in all senses of the word. He may rightly be considered even more omniscient than Holmes, with whom he has often been compared. But Thorndyke is the more compassionate of the two men and, when needed, more resolute and rigorous. He may be less imaginative than Holmes and less given to inspiration but the plain fact is that Thorndyke has little need for such qualities. The man is simply too damned clever and his talent and technical abilities are unparalleled – "practical wizardry"[1] to quote the term used by John Dickson Carr. Thorndyke is the complete investigator, an amalgam of the police officer, the legal reasoner and, above all, the scientific expert. He has an extraordinarily comprehensive and preterhuman knowledge of the minutiae of almost every field of matters animal, vegetable or mineral. Not for Thorndyke any armchair ratiocination or cunning disguise to accumulate evidence from garrulous grooms and talkative servants, simply the meticulous collation of evidence and equally careful and mechanical reconstruction of the facts, identifying initially unseen links and uniting disparate threads to form a web of compelling evidence. With Holmes there might sometimes be a margin of error but for Thorndyke there is never any possibility of error and, once reached, his conclusions are seldom if ever in any serious doubt.

Some have considered this thoroughness a failing, such as Ronald Knox who censured Freeman for his "a tendency to an undue laboriousness of

---

[1]   John Dickson Carr. "The Jury Box." *Ellery Queen's Mystery Magazine*, June 1973.

detail,"[1] but for others the principal pleasure of his stories is the profusion of detail and the methodical and leisurely nature of the investigations. Freeman rarely allows Thorndyke to lecture the reader and he is for the most part a good-humoured companion to his readers as well as to his fictional colleagues. Yet his perfection as an investigative machine renders Thorndyke vulnerable to one criticism that is difficult to refute. Notwithstanding Freeman's protest that Thorndyke is "quite normal,"[2] this is quite plainly not true. He is not normal. His omniscience is simply incredible and it is sometimes difficult to reconcile the occasional glimpses of genuine humanity and heroism with his sometimes cold and unemotional stance. Although the various younger men who narrate his cases often marry and develop emotionally, Thorndyke remains unchanged. As he was at the time of his first case, *The Red Thumb Mark* (1907), he is the same at the time of his last, *The Jacob Street Mystery* (1942), and, in a letter written in 1938, Freeman commented that Thorndyke had "stopped growing old some years ago and now remains stationary at about 50."

Throughout his long career, the focal point is his barrister's lodgings in King's Bench Walk in the Temple, a timeless warren of old buildings hunched on the edge of the City of London. Thorndyke's world is essentially masculine, detached and assiduously private with only his dextrous and highly skilled manservant Nathaniel Polton and (unlike Sherlock Holmes) there is no one who could have been, for Thorndyke, "always *the* woman." Freeman's own thoughts on his character were set out in a radio broadcast, "Meet Dr. Thorndyke," which is included in this volume.

---

[1] Ronald Knox. "Mystery Stories." *Encyclopedia Britannica* (14th Edition, 1929)

[2] R. Austin Freeman, "Meet Dr. Thorndyke," included in this volume.

2. UNCOLLECTED DETECTION AND CRIME

Thorndyke appears in a total of 40 short stories and novellas[1] and 21 novels,[2] and there is also an unpublished variant text of *The Eye of Osiris* (1911), the novel that many regard as Thorndyke's finest investigation.[3] Only one item in which Thorndyke is known to appear has not previously been collected and that omission is put right with this volume. "The Dead Hand" (*Cassell's*, October and November 1912) is a two-part inverted detective story. Instead of including it in one of his collections of Thorndyke stories, Freeman decided that the plot was strong enough to use as a novel, *The Shadow of the Wolf* (1925). Although the murderer's bad luck seems monumental, the scientific investigation and, as in Freeman's first stories, the sea setting are very effective.

Thorndyke was immensely popular – Freeman appears even to have sold the rights for the use of his name in advertisements – but he was not Freeman's only memorable creation. In Professor Humphrey Challoner, the anti-hero of the episodic novel *A Savant's Vendetta* (1914), Freeman pre-empted Brian Garfield's *Death-Wish* (1972) by nearly sixty years, setting a clever but essentially "ordinary" man against an anarchist and criminal underclass after the brutal murder of his wife. Challoner's ruthlessly single-minded quest for the murderer was first published as a serial and he later appeared in a single short story, "The Mystery of Hoo Marsh" (*Pearson's*, March 1917), which shows him in a still darker light. This story is collected for the first time in this volume and in it Challoner has yet to

---

[1]   The novellas were subsequently expanded to novels: *The Mystery of 31 New Inn* (1912) and *The Shadow of the Wolf* (1925). The first novella was collected in *The Best Dr. Thorndyke Detective Stories*, ed E.F. Bleiler (1973); the second in this volume.

[2]   *The Mystery of Angelina Frood* (1924) is effectively a plaimpsest of the most celebrated unfinished detective story, Charles Dickens' The Mystery of Edwin Drood (1870), which Freeman considered "superb."

[3]   Several affectionate and thoroughly enjoyable pastiche investigations have been published, among them *Dr. Thorndyke's Dilemma* (1976) by John Dirckx, and *Goodbye, Dr. Thorndyke* (1972) by Norman Donaldson, author of the biography *In Search of Dr. Thorndyke* (1971).

locate his wife's murderer. Impelled by "a certain spirit of mischief," he is distracted from the vendetta by a group of perhaps surprisingly trusting anarchists. Freeman was deeply interested in eugenics, as he showed in articles such as "The Menace of the Sub-Man" and "Segregation of the Fit,"[1] and one cannot help feeling that in Challoner there is a glimpse of Freeman as eugenist, taking direct action with respect to those unfit for society.

In addition to the last stories of Thorndyke and Challoner, this collection includes two little known puzzles, both in a rather lighter vein than "The Mystery of Hoo Marsh." One is "The Sign of the Ram," first published in the issue dated 20 May 1911 of a little-known periodical *Everybody's Weekly*; Freeman would go on to use the central feature of "The Sign of the Ram" in the Thorndyke short story "The Case of the White Footprints," and he could well have seen himself as the unnamed doctor who narrates the story.[2] The other story, "The Mystery of the Seven Banana Skins," was published in *Everyman* over two issues dated 1 and 8 December 1933 where it was re-discovered by Stephen Leadbeatter, that most forensic of Freeman's admirers. It would appear to be Freeman's last published short story but it is set in April 1915 and surely belongs to an earlier phase of Freeman's career; in contrast to the omniscience and flawlessness of Dr. Thorndyke, Horatio Gobler's "constructive study" of the crime is utterly mistaken while the true explanation of the body and the bananas is quite ridiculous and extremely funny.

3. OTHER UNCOLLECTED TALES AND ESSAYS

Freeman had begun writing short stories during the late 1890's after an illness he contracted as a physician in Africa prevented him from practicing medicine on a fulltime basis. His first tale – at least the earliest that has so far been identified – is "The Resurrection of Matthew Jephson," published in the September 1898 issue of *Cassell's*. It was the first of at least thirteen sea stories by R. Austin Freeman. Such settings were of course very popular in the Late Victorian and Edwardian periods, with W. Clark Russell being

---

[1] Perhaps mercifully, the ominously titled "Hitlerism on Appro." has yet to be traced.

[2] Freeman was born in April 1862, under Aries, the sign of the ram.

perhaps the most successful of all; Conan Doyle has Dr. Watson praise one of his novels. Other writers come to mind, such as Rudyard Kipling whose *Captains Courageous* was published only a year or so before "The Resurrection of Matthew Jephson," Robert Louis Stevenson and, perhaps the most direct influence on Freeman, W.W. Jacobs. Though best known for a single tale of supernatural terror, "The Monkey's Paw," Jacobs' entertaining short stories often have a humorous bent and his popularity may have encouraged Freeman's Bill Jakins stories. These were written in two groups published in *Cassell's* between 1900 and 1904 and in *Nash's* in 1909 and 1910. A seaside rogue, Jakins is similar to Romney Pringle, a crook whom Freeman and Dr. John James Pitcairn under the joint pseudonym of "Clifford Ashdown" had created for *Cassell's* at the same time as the early Jakins tales. Pringle, however, plans out his crimes, while Jakins goes for the main chance, and often gets bitten in the process. Most of the Jakins stories involve a bit of crime, and some like "The Sleuth-hounds" (recently discovered by Jack Adrian) even have some haphazard investigation.

Freeman's other sea stories also often feature crime, including "The Ebb Tide" (*Cassell's*, February 1903), which is one of the best of his early stories. "By the Black Deep" (*Windsor*, April 1903) – whose attribution to "R. Austin Freeman and Ashdown Piers" clearly identifies Pitcairn as co-author – is also a crime story, as is, at least at the sentimental conclusion, "A Question of Salvage" (*Cassell's*, September 1916).

Freeman can certainly not be accounted one of the great masters of the sea story, but his tales are always well constructed, lively, and full of a salty flavor. It is more difficult to be positive about his stories of comedy and romance. When they include crime, as in "A Suburban Autolycus" (*Cassell's*, November 1904) and "A Woman's Vengeance" (*Pall Mall*, October 1912), they still work well, but his straight comic stories like "Under the Clock" (*Royal*, July 1901) and "Ye Olde Spotted Dogge" (*Cassell's*, April 1904) are rather lumbering. Several of his stories concern a charming romance, most obviously a portion of "A Woman's Vengeance" and the whole of "Ruth" (*Ladies World*, December 1912), a story whose publication was doggedly tracked down by another Freeman enthusiast, Jo Crosland Boyle. Of course, besides the splendid scientific detection, there is in many of Freeman's Dr. Thorndyke novels, especially *The Eye of Osiris*, a restrained yet heartfelt Edwardian romance story. Certainly, Freeman could be sentimental in these romantic plots and sub-plots but there is also a sturdiness, a commitment to the relationships he describes that makes them immensely attractive.

Finally, this collection also includes "The Art of the Detective Story," in which Freeman mounts a stout defence of such stories and provides a "technical" analysis of their structure; and two pieces on actual crimes but not, alas, Freeman's musings on an infamous poisoning in Croydon, England which seems to have been published in pamphlet form but which has yet to be located. "The Cleverest Crime – In Fact or Fiction" concerns the crime on which Freeman based the Thorndyke short story "The Case of Oscar Brodski" and, while he never based any mystery on the events he described in the article, "The Peasenhall Mystery," his explanation of the terrible death of Rose Harsent is that used in John Dickson Carr's sinister story "Blind Man's Buff."

4. *STILL LOST STORIES*

Happily, albeit frustratingly, it has recently been established that Freeman wrote a number of other stories and serials which have yet to be discovered, having perhaps been published long ago in some obscure and long-forgotten magazine or newspaper. The available records give only titles and, unless they are located, one can only speculate as to what they might concern. Some would appear to be serials, such as "A Crusader's Misadventures," "The Adventures of Jack Osmond,"[1] and "The Adventures of Corporal Sims," but *The King's Secret* could well be a novel. Among the lost short stories are "The Haarschneide Machine," "The Auchtermuchtie Burglary," "The Gun Runner," "*La Belle Anglaise*" and "The Cavern." These and some of the other manuscripts that are known to have been offered for publication may of course have been accepted and published under different titles. As an example, David Ian Chapman, the Freeman expert and editor of *John Thorndyke's Journal*, has suggested that one lost title, "The Horologist at

---

[1] David Ian Chapman has suggested that this might be the original title of *A Certain Dr. Thorndyke* (1927) in which a John Osmond is the central character.

Large," could be the novel in which *Mr. Polton Explains* (1940) and it is certainly reasonable to conclude that *The Surprising Experiences of Mr. Shuttlebury Cobb* (1927) was the eventual title of the apparently lost work, *The Surprising Experiences of Solomon Pike*, but "A Corpse in the Case" could fit any number of Freeman's Thorndyke stories.

Then there is the unsolved riddle of "Jack Wylde," the author of a number of mystery stories for teenagers during the 1920's which draw on some of Freeman's Thorndyke stories, but opinion is sharply divided as to whether Freeman himself was Wylde.[1] Certainly, the name is an obvious pseudonym with its play on the name of the duplicitous eighteenth century criminal Jonathan Wild. Yet the stories could simply be the work of an unscrupulous plagiarist and, at this distance of time, it is impossible to be certain either way.

Today, R. Austin Freeman is unjustly neglected. Until the publication of The Battered Silicon Dispatch Box's omnibus volumes, his work has been hard to come by and, like other luminaries of the Golden Age, he and his important contribution to the history of the detective story are not widely recognised. The aim of bringing together his previously uncollected short stories in this volume, together with Freeman's thoughts on the detective story and on certain actual crimes, is certainly not to present the best of his work – for that the reader is advised to locate and read not only the classic *The Eye of Osiris* but also *A Silent Witness* (1914) and *The Cat's Eye* (1923). We, nevertheless, hope to provide a broad and enjoyable overview, ranging from romances of the sea and the soul to the final outrage of that hunter of criminals, Humphrey Challoner, and the last perhaps the very last – of the chronicles of a certain Dr. Thorndyke.

– Tony Medawar and Douglas G. Greene

Cyberspace, November 1998

---

[1]   See "Was Jack Wylde really R. Austin Freeman?" by W.O.G. Lofts and Derek J. Adley, *The Armchair Detective*, August 1974, and "Jack Wylde – the Man, the Myth and the Mandarin" by David Ian Chapman, *John Thorndyke's Journal*, Issue 2, Summer 1991.

Detection and Mystery

Dr. Thorndyke by H.M. Brock

The Dead Hand

I. How It Happened

ABOUT half-past eight on a fine, sunny June morning, a small yacht crept out of Sennen Cove, near Land's End, and headed for the open sea. On the shelving beach of the cove two women and a man, evidently visitors (or "foreigners," to use the local term), stood watching her departure with valedictory waving of cap or handkerchief, and the boatman who had put the crew on board, aided by two of his comrades, was hauling his boat up above the tide-mark.

A light, northerly breeze filled the yacht's sails and drew her gradually seaward. The figures of her crew dwindled to the size of dolls, shrank with the increasing distance to the magnitude of insects, and at last, losing all individuality, became mere specks merged in the form of the fabric that bore them.

On board the receding craft two men sat in the little cockpit. They formed the entire crew, for the *Sandhopper* was only a ship's lifeboat, timbered and decked, of light draught and, in the matter of spars and canvas, what the art critics would call "reticent."

Both men, despite the fineness of the weather, wore yellow oilskins and sou'-westers, and that was about all they had in common. In other respects they made a curious contrast — the one small, slender, sharp-featured, dark almost to swarthiness, and restless and quick in his movements; the other large, massive, red-faced, blue-eyed, with the rounded outlines suggestive of ponderous strength, a great ox of a man, heavy, stolid, but much less unwieldy than he looked.

The conversation incidental to getting the yacht under way had ceased, and silence had fallen on the occupants of the cockpit. The big man grasped the tiller and looked sulky, which was probably his usual aspect, and the small man watched him furtively.

The land was nearly two miles distant when the latter broke the silence.

3

"Joan Haygarth has come on wonderfully the last few months, getting quite a fine-looking girl. Don't you think so, Purcell?"

"Yes," answered Purcell, "and so does Phil Rodney."

"You're right," agreed the other. "She isn't a patch on her sister, though, and never will be. I was looking at Maggie as we came down the beach this morning and thinking what a handsome girl she is. Don't you agree with me?"

Purcell stooped to look under the boom, and answered without turning his head: "Yes, she's all right."

"All right!" exclaimed the other. "Is that the way –"

"Look here, Varney," interrupted Purcell. "I don't want to discuss my wife's looks with you or any other man. She'll do for me or I shouldn't have married her."

A deep, coppery flush stole into Varney's cheeks. But he had brought the rather brutal snub on himself and apparently had the fairness to recognise the fact, for he mumbled an apology and relapsed into silence.

When next he spoke he did so with a manner diffident and uneasy, as though approaching a disagreeable or difficult subject.

"There's a little matter, Dan, that I've been wanting to speak to you about when we got a chance of a private talk."

He glanced rather anxiously at his stolid companion, who grunted, and then, without removing his gaze from the horizon ahead, replied: "You've a pretty fair chance now, seeing that we shall be bottled up together for another five or six hours. And it's fairly private unless you bawl loud enough to be heard at the Longships."

It was not a gracious invitation. But if Varney resented the rebuff he showed no sign of annoyance, for reasons which appeared when he opened his subject.

"What I wanted to say," he resumed, "was this. We're both doing pretty well now on the square. You must be positively piling up the shekels, and I can earn a decent living, which is all I want. Why shouldn't we drop this flash note business?"

Purcell kept his blue eye fixed on the horizon and appeared to ignore the question; but after an interval and without moving a muscle he said gruffly: "Go on," and Varney continued:

"The lay isn't what it was you know. At first it was all plain sailing. The notes were first-class copies and not a soul suspected anything until they were presented at the Bank. Then the murder was out, and the next little tap that I made was a very different affair. Two or three of the notes were spotted quite soon after I had changed them, and I had to be precious fly, I can tell you, to avoid complications. And now that the second batch has come in to the Bank, the planting of fresh specimens is going to be harder still. There isn't a money-changer on the Continent of Europe that isn't keeping his weather eyeball peeled, to say nothing of the detectives that the Bank people have sent abroad."

He paused and looked appealingly at his companion. But Purcell, still minding his helm, only growled "Well?"

"Well I want to chuck it Dan. When you've had a run of luck and pocketed your winnings it is time to stop play."

"You've come into some money, then I take it?" said Purcell.

"No, I haven't. But I can make a living now by safe and respectable means, and I'm sick of all this scheming and dodging with gaol everlastingly under my lee."

"The reason I asked," said Purcell, "is that there is a trifle outstanding. You hadn't forgotten that, I suppose?"

"No, I hadn't forgotten it, but I thought that perhaps you might be willing to let me down a bit easily."

The other man pursed up his thick lips and continued to gaze stonily over the bow.

"Oh, that's what you thought?" he said; and then after a pause: "I fancy you must have lost sight of some of the facts when you thought that. Let me just remind you how the case stands. To begin with, you start your career with a little playful embezzlement, you blue the proceeds and you are mug enough to be fond out. Then I come in. I compound the affair with old Marston for a couple of thousand, and practically clean myself out of every penny I possess, and he consents to regard your temporary absence in the light of a holiday.

Now, why do I do this? Am I a philanthropist? Devil a bit. I'm a man of business. Before I ladle out that two thousand, I make a business contract with you. I have discovered how to make a passable imitation of the Bank of

England paper; you are a skilled engraver and a plausible scamp. I am to supply you with paper blanks, you are to engrave plates, print the notes, and get them changed. I am to take two-thirds of the proceeds; and although I have done the most difficult part of the work, I agree to regard my share of the profits as constituting repayment of the loan.

"Our contract amounts to this: I lend you two thousand without security — with an infernal amount of insecurity, in fact — you 'promise, covenant, and agree,' as the lawyers say, to hand me back ten thousand in instalments, being the products of our joint industry. It is a verbal contract which I have no means of enforcing, but I trust you to keep your word, and up to the present you have kept it. You have paid me a little over four thousand. Now you want to cry off and leave the balance unpaid. Isn't that the position?"

"Not exactly," said Varney. "I'm not crying off the debt; I only want time. Look here, Dan; I'm making about three fifty a year now. That isn't much, but I'll manage to let you have a hundred a year out of it. What do you say to that?"

Purcell laughed scornfully. "A hundred a year to pay off six thousand. That'll take just sixty years and as I'm now forty-three, I shall be exactly a hundred and three years of age when the last instalment is paid. I think, Varney, you'll admit that a man of a hundred and three is getting past his prime."

"Well, I'll pay you something down to start. I've saved about eighteen hundred pounds out of the note business, You can have that now, and I'll pay off as much I can at a time until I'm clear. Remember, that if I should happen to get clapped in chokee for twenty years or so, you won't get anything."

"I'm willing to take the risk," said Purcell.

"I daresay you are," Varney retorted passionately, "because it's my risk. If I am grabbed, it's my racket. You sit out. It's I who passed the notes, and I'm known to be a skilled engraver. That'll be good enough for them. They won't trouble about who made the paper."

"I hope not," said Purcell.

"Of course they wouldn't, and you know I shouldn't give you away."

"Naturally. Why should you? Wouldn't do you any good."

"Well, give me a chance, Dan," Varney pleaded. "This business is getting on my nerves. I want to be quit of it. You've had four thousand; that's a hundred per cent. You haven't done so badly."

"I didn't expect to do badly. I took a big risk. I gambled two thousand for ten."

"Yes; and you got me out of the way while you put the screw on poor old Haygarth to make his daughter marry you."

It was an indiscreet thing to say, but Purcell's stolid indifference to his danger and distress had ruffled Varney's temper.

Purcell, however, was unmoved. "I don't know," he said, "what you mean by getting you out of the way. You were never in the way. You were always hankering after Maggie, but I could never see that she wanted you."

"Well, she certainly didn't want you." Varney retorted. "And, for that matter, I don't think she wants you now."

For the first time Purcell withdrew his eye from the horizon to turn it on his companion. And an evil eye it was, set in the great, sensual face, now purple with anger.

"What the devil do you mean?" he exclaimed furiously; "you infernal, sallow-faced, little whipper-snapper! If you mention my wife's name again I'll knock you on the head and pitch you overboard."

Varney's face flashed darkly, and for a moment he was inclined to try the wager of battle. But the odds were impossible, and if Varney was not a coward, neither was he a fool. But the discussion was at an end. Nothing was to be hoped for now. Those indiscreet words had rendered further pleading impossible.

The silence that settled down in the yacht and the aloofness that encompassed the two men was conducive to reflection. Each ignored the presence of the other. When the course was altered southerly, Purcell slacked out the sheets with his own hand as he put up the helm. He might have been sailing singlehanded. And Varney watched him askance, but made no move, sitting hunched up on the locker, nursing a slowly-matured hatred and thinking thoughts.

Very queer thoughts they were. He was following out the train of events that might have happened, pursuing them to their possible consequences. Supposing Purcell had carried out his threat? Well, there would have been a pretty tough struggle, for Varney was no weakling. But a struggle with that solid fifteen stone of flesh could end in only one way. No, there was no doubt; he would have gone overboard.

And what then? Would Purcell have gone back to Sennen Cove, or sailed alone into Penzance? In either case, he would have had to make up some sort of story; and no one could have contradicted him whether the story was believed or not. But it would have been awkward for Purcell. Then there was the body. That would have been washed up sooner or later, as much of it as the lobsters had left. Well, lobsters don't eat clothes or bones, and a dent in the skull might take some accounting for. Very awkward this — for Purcell. He would probably have had to clear out; to make a bolt for it, in short.

The mental picture of this great bully fleeing in terror from the vengeance of the law gave Varney appreciable pleasure. Most of his life he had been borne down by the moral and physical weight of this domineering brute. At school, Purcell had fagged him; he had even bullied him up at Cambridge; and now he had it fastened on for ever, like the Old Man of the Sea. And Purcell always got the best of it. When he, Varney, had come back from Italy after that unfortunate little affair, behold! the girl whom they had both wanted (and who had wanted neither of them) had changed from Maggie Haygarth into Maggie Purcell. And so it was even unto this day. Purcell, a prosperous stockjobber now, spent a part of his secret leisure making, in absolute safety, these accursed paper blanks, which he, Varney, must risk his liberty to change into money. Yes, it was quite pleasant to think of Purcell sneaking from town to town, from country to country, with the police at his heels.

But in these days of telegraphs and extradition there isn't much chance for a fugitive. Purcell would have been caught to a certainty, and he would have been hanged, no doubt of it. The imagined picture of the execution gave him quite a lengthy entertainment. Then his errant thoughts began to spread out in search of other possibilities. For, after all, it was not an absolute certainty that Purcell could have got him overboard. There was just the chance that Purcell might have gone overboard himself. That would have been a very different affair.

Varney settled himself composedly to consider the new and interesting train of consequences that would thus have been set going. They were more agreeable to contemplate than the others, because they did not include his own demise. The execution scene made no appearance in this version. The salient fact was that his oppressor would have vanished; that the intolerable burden of his servitude would have been lifted for ever; that he would have been free.

It was mere idle speculation to while away a dull hour with an uncongenial companion, and he let his thought ramble at large. One moment he was dreamily wondering whether Maggie would ever have listened to him, ever have to come to care for him; the next, he was back in the yacht's cabin, where hung from a hook on the bulkhead the revolver that the Rodneys used to practice at floating bottles. It was usually loaded, he knew, but, if not, there was a canvas bag full of cartridges in the starboard locker. Again, he found himself dreaming of the home that he would have had, a home very different from the cheerless lodgings in which he moped at present; and then his thoughts had flitted back to the yacht's hold, and were busying themselves with the row of half-hundredweights that rested on the timber on either side of the kelson.

When Varney had thus brought his mental picture, so to speak, to a finish, its completeness surprised him. It was so simple, so secure. He had actually planned out the scheme of a murder, and he found himself wondering whether many murders passed undetected. They well might if murders were as easy and as safe as this — a dangerous reflection for an injured and angry man. And at this critical point his meditations were interrupted by Purcell, continuing the conversation as if there had been no pause:

"So you can take it from me, Varney, that I expect you to stick to your bargain. I paid down my money, and I'm going to have my pound of flesh."

It was a brutal thing to say, and it was brutally said. But more than that, it was inopportune — or opportune, as you will, for it came as a sort of infernal doxology to the devil's anthem that had been, all unknown, ringing in Varney's soul.

Purcell had spoken without looking round. That was his unpleasant habit. Had he looked at his companion, he might have been startled. A change in Varney's face might have given him pause; a warm flush, a sparkle of the eye, a look of elation, of settled purpose, deadly, inexorable — the look of a man who has made a fateful resolution.

It was so simple, so secure! That was the burden of the song that echoed in Varney's brain.

He glanced over the sea. They had opened the south coast now, and he could see, afar off, a fleet of black-sailed luggers heading east. They wouldn't be in his way. Nor would the big four-master that was creeping away to the west, for she was hull down already, and other ships there were none.

There was one hindrance, though. Dead ahead the Wolf Rock Lighthouse rose from the blue water, its red-and-white ringed tower looking like some gaudily painted toy. The keepers of lonely lighthouses have a natural habit of watching the passing shipping through their glasses, and it was possible that one of their telescopes might be pointed at this very moment. That was a complication.

Suddenly there came down the wind a sharp report like the firing of a gun, quickly followed by a second. It was the explosive signal from the Longships Lighthouse, but when they looked round there was no lighthouse to be seen — the dark-blue, heaving water faded away at the foot of an advancing wall of vapour.

Purcell cursed fluently. A pretty place, this, to be caught, in a fog! And then, as his eye lighted on his companion, he demanded angrily: "What the devil are you grinning at?"

For Varney, drunk with suppressed excitement, snapped his fingers at rocks and shoals; he was thinking only of the lighthouse keeper's telescope and of the revolver that hung on the bulkhead. He must make some excuse presently to go below and secure that revolver.

But no excuse was necessary. The opportunity came of itself. After a hasty glance at the vanishing land and another at the compass, Purcell put up the helm to gybe the yacht round on to an easterly course.

As she came round, the single headsail that she carried in place of jib and foresail shivered for a few seconds, and then filled suddenly on the opposite tack. And at this moment the halyards parted with a loud snap; the end of the rope flew through the blocks, and, in an instant, the sail was down and its upper half trailing in the water alongside.

Purcell swore volubly, but kept an eye to business. "Run below, Varney," said he, "and fetch up that coil of new rope out of the starboard locker while I haul the sail on board. And look alive. We don't want to drift down on to the Wolf."

Varney obeyed with silent alacrity and a curious feeling of elation. It was going to be even easier and safer than he had thought. He slipped through the hatch into the cabin, quietly took the revolver from its hook, and examined the chambers.

Finding them all loaded, he cocked the hammer and slipped the weapon carefully into the inside breast pocket of his oilskin coat. Then he took the coil of rope from the locker and went on deck.

As he emerged from the hatch, he perceived that the yacht was already enveloped in fog, which drifted past in steamy clouds, and that she had come up head to wind. Purcell was kneeling on the forecastle, tugging at the sail, which had caught under the forefoot, and punctuating his efforts with deep-voiced curses.

Varney stole silently along the deck, steadying himself by mast and shroud, softly laid down the coil of rope, and approached. Purcell was quite engrossed with his task; his back was towards Varney, his face over the side, intent on the entangled sail. It was a chance in a thousand.

With scarcely a moment's hesitation, Varney stooped forward, steadying himself with a hand on the little windlass, and softly drawing forth the revolver, pointed it at the back of Purcell's head at the spot where the back seam of his sou'wester met the brim.

The report rang out but weak and flat in that open space, and a cloud of smoke mingled with the fog; but it blew away immediately, and showed Purcell almost unchanged in his posture, crouching on the sail, with his chin resting on the little rim of bulwark, while behind him his murderer, as if turned into bronze, still stood stooping forward, one hand grasping the windlass, the other still pointing the revolver.

Thus the two figures remained for some seconds motionless like some horrible waxworks, until the little yacht, lifting to the swell, gave a more than usually lively curvet; when Purcell rolled over on to his back, and Varney relaxed the rigidity of his posture like a golf-player who has watched his ball drop.

Purcell was dead. That was the salient fact. The head wagged to and fro as the yacht pitched and rolled, the limp arms and legs seemed to twitch, the limp body to writhe uneasily. But Varney was not disturbed. Lifeless things will move on an unsteady deck. He was only interested to notice how the passive movements produced the illusion of life. But it was only illusion. Purcell was dead. There was no doubt of that.

The double report from the Longships came down the wind, and then, as if in answer, a prolonged, deep bellow. That was the fog-horn of the lighthouse on the Wolf Rock, and it sounded surprisingly near. But, of course, these signals were meant to be heard at a distance. Then a stream of hot sunshine, pouring down on deck, startled him, and made him hurry. The body must be got overboard before the fog lifted.

With an uneasy glance at the clear sky overhead, he hastily cast off the broken halyard from its cleat and cut off a couple of fathoms. Then he hurried below, and, lifting the trap in the cabin floor, hoisted out one of the iron half-hundredweights with which the yacht was ballasted.

As he stepped on deck with the weight in his hand, the sun was shining overhead, but the fog was still thick below, and the horn sounded once more from the Wolf and again it struck him as surprisingly near.

He passed the length of rope that he had cut off twice round Purcell's body, hauled it tight, and secured it with a knot. Then he made the ends fast to the handle of the iron weight.

Not much fear of Purcell drifting ashore now. That weight would hold him as long as there was anything to hold. But it had taken some time to do, and the warning bellow from the Wolf seemed to draw nearer and nearer. He was about to heave the body over when his eye fell on the dead man's sou'wester, which had fallen off when the body rolled over.

That hat must be got rid of, for Purcell's name was worked in silk on the lining and there was an unmistakable bullet-hole through the back. It must be destroyed, or, which would be simpler and quicker. lashed securely on the dead man's head.

Hurriedly, Varney ran aft and descended to the cabin. He had noticed a new ball of spunyarn in the locker when he had fetched the rope. This would be the very thing.

He was back again in a few moments with the ball in his hand, unwinding it as he came, and without wasting time he knelt down by the body and fell to work.

And every half minute the deep-voiced growl of the Wolf came to him out of the fog, and each time it sounded nearer and yet nearer.

By the time he had made the sou'wester secure the dead man's face and chin were encased in a web of spunyarn that made him look like some old-time, grotesque-vizored Samurai warrior.

Varney rose to his feet. But his task was not finished yet. There was Purcell's suit-case. That must be sunk too, and there was something in it that had figured in the detailed picture that his imagination had drawn. He ran to the cockpit where the suit-case lay, and having tried its fastenings and found it unlocked, he opened it and took out a letter that lay on top of the other contents. This he tossed through the hatch into the cabin, and, having closed and fastened the suit-case, he carried it forward and made it fast to the iron weight with half a dozen turns of spunyarn.

That was really all, and indeed it was time. As he rose once more to his feet the growl of the foghorn burst out, as it seemed, right over the stern of the yacht, and she was drifting stern foremost, who could say how fast. Now, too, he caught a more ominous sound, which he might have heard sooner had he listened — the wash of water, the boom of breakers bursting on a rock.

A sudden revulsion came over him. He burst into a wild, sardonic laugh. And had it come to this, after all? Had he schemed and laboured only to leave himself alone on an unmanageable craft drifting down to shipwreck and certain death? Had he taken all this thought and care to secure Purcell's body, when his own might be resting beside it on the sea-bottom within an hour?

But the reverie was brief. Suddenly, from the white void over his very head, as it seemed, there issued a stunning, thunderous roar that shook the deck under his feet. The water around him boiled into a foamy chaos, the din of bursting waves was in his ears, the yacht plunged and wallowed amidst clouds of spray, and for an instant a dim, gigantic shadow loomed through the fog and was gone. In that moment his nerve had come back. Holding on with one hand to the windlass he dragged the body to the edge of the forecastle, hoisted the weight outboard, and then, taking advantage of a heavy lurch, gave the corpse a vigorous shove. There was a rattle and a hollow slash, and corpse and weight and suit-case had vanished into the seething water.

He clung to the swinging mast and waited. Breathlessly he told out the allotted seconds until once again the invisible Titan belched forth his thunderous warning. But this time the roar came over the yacht's bow. She had drifted past the rock then. The danger was over, and Purcell would have to go down to Davy Jones' locker companionless after all.

Very soon the water around ceased to boil and tumble, and as the yacht's wild plunging settled down once more into the normal rise and fall on the long swell, Varney turned his attention to the refitting of the halyard. But what was this on the creamy, duck sail? A pool of blood and two gory imprints of his own left hand! That wouldn't do at all. He would have to clear that away before he could hoist the sail, which was annoying, as the yacht was helpless without her headsail, and was evidently drifting out to sea.

He fetched a bucket, a swab, and a scrubbing-brush, and set to work. The bulk of the large bloodstain cleared off pretty completely after he had drenched the sail with a bucketful or two and given it a good scrubbing. But the edge of the stain where the heat of the deck had dried it remained like a painted boundary on a map, and the two hand-prints — which had also dried, though they faded to a pale buff — continued clearly visible.

Varney began to grow uneasy. If those stains would not come out — especially the hand-prints — it would be very awkward, they would take so much explaining. He decided to try the effect of marine soap, and fetched a cake from the cabin, but even this did not obliterate the stains completely, though it turned them a faint, greenish brown, very unlike the colour of blood. So he scrubbed on until at last the hand-prints faded away entirely, and the large stain was reduced to a faint green, wavy line, and that was the best he could do — and quite good enough, for the faint line should ever be noticed no one would suspect its origin.

He put away the bucket and proceeded with the refitting. The sea had disengaged the sail from the forefoot, and he hauled it on board without difficulty. Then there was the reeving of the new halyard, a troublesome business involving the necessity of his going aloft, where his weight — small man as he was — made the yacht roll infernally, and set him swinging to and fro like the bob of a metronome. But he was a smart yachtsman and active, though not powerful, and a few minutes' strenuous exertion ended in his sliding down the shrouds with the new, halyard running fairly through the upper block. A vigorous haul or two at the new, hairy rope sent the head of the dripping sail aloft, and the yacht, was once more under control.

The rig of the *Sandhopper* was not smart, but it was handy. She carried a short bowsprit to accommodate the single headsail and a relatively large mizzen, of which the advantage was, that by judicious management of the mizzen-sheet the yacht would sail with very little attention to the helm. Of this advantage Varney was keenly appreciative just now, for he had several things to do before entering port. He wanted refreshment, he wanted a wash, and the various traces of recent events had to be removed. Also, there was a letter to be attended to. So that it was convenient to be able to leave the helm in charge of a lashing for a minute now and again.

When he had washed, he put the kettle on the spirit stove, and while it was heating busied himself in cleaning the revolver, flinging the empty cartridge-case overboard, and replacing it with a cartridge from the bag in the locker. Then he picked up the letter that he had taken from Purcell's suitcase and examined it. It was addressed to "Joseph Penfield, Esq., George Yard, Lombard Street," and was unstamped, though the envelope was fastened up. He affixed a stamp from his pocket-book, and when the kettle began to boil, he held the envelope in the steam that issued from the spout. Very soon the flap of the envelope loosened and curled back, when he laid it aside to mix himself a mug of hot grog, which, together with the letter and a biscuit-tin, he took out into the cockpit. The fog was still dense, and the hoot of a steamer's whistle from somewhere to the westward caused him to reach the foghorn out of the locker, and blow a long blast on it. As if in answer to his treble squeak came the deep bass note from the Wolf, and unconsciously he looked around. He turned automatically, as one does towards a sudden noise, not expecting to see anything but fog, and what he did see startled him not a little.

For there was the lighthouse — or half of it, rather — standing up above the fog-bank, clear, distinct, and hardly a mile away. The gilded vane, the sparkling lantern, the gallery, and the upper half of the red and white ringed tower, stood sharp against the pallid sky; but the lower half was invisible. It was a strange apparition — like half a lighthouse suspended in mid-air — and uncommonly disturbing, too. It raised a very awkward question. If he could see the lantern, the light-keepers could see him. But how long had the lantern been clear of the fog?

Thus he meditated as, with one hand on the tiller, he munched his biscuit and sipped his grog. Presently he picked up the stamped envelope and drew from it a letter and a folded document, both of which he tore into fragments and dropped overboard. Then, from his pocket-book, he took a similar but unaddressed envelope from which he drew out the contents, and very curious those contents were.

There was a letter, brief and laconic, which he read over thoughtfully. "These," it ran, "are all I have by me, but they will do for the present, and when you have planted them I will let you have a fresh supply." There was no date and no signature, but the rather peculiar hand-writing was similar to that on the envelope addressed to Joseph Penfield, Esq.

The other contents consisted of a dozen sheets of blank paper, each of the size of a Bank of England note. But they were not quite blank, for each bore an elaborate watermark, identical with that of a twenty-pound banknote. They were, in fact, the "paper blanks" of which Purcell had spoken. The envelope with its contents had been slipped into his hand by Purcell, without remark, only three days ago.

Varney refolded the "blanks," enclosed them within the letter, and slipped letter and "blanks" together into the stamped envelope, the flap of which he licked and reclosed. "I should like to see old Penfield's face when he opens that envelope," was his reflection as with a grain smile, he put it away in his pocket-book. "And I wonder what he will do," he added, mentally, "however, I shall see before many days are over."

Varney looked at his watch. He was to meet Jack Rodney on Penzance Pier at a quarter to three. He would never do it at this rate, for when he opened Mount's Bay, Penzance would be right in the wind's eye. That would mean a long beat to windward. The Rodney would be there first, waiting for him. Deuced awkward, this. He would have to account for his being alone on board, would have to invent some lie about having put Purcell ashore at Mousehole or Newlyn. But a lie is a very pernicious thing. Its effects are cumulative. You never know when you have done with it. Now, if he had reached Penzance before Rodney he need have said nothing about Purcell — for the present, at any rate, and that would have been so much safer.

When the yacht was about abreast of Lamorna Cove, though some seven miles to the south, the breeze began to draw ahead and the fog cleared off quite suddenly. The change in the wind was unfavourable for the moment, but when it veered round yet a little more until it blew from east-north-east, Varney brightened up considerably. There was still a chance of reaching Penzance before Rodney arrived; for now, as soon as he had fairly opened Mount's Bay, he could head straight for his destination and make it on a single board.

Between two and three hours later the *Sandhopper* entered Penzance Harbour, and, threading her way among an assemblage of luggers and small coasters, brought up alongside the Albert Pier at the foot of a vacant ladder. Having made the yacht fast to a couple of rings, Varney divested himself of his oilskins, locked the cabin scuttle, and climbed the ladder. The change of wind had saved him after all, and, as he strode away along the pier, he glanced complacently at his watch. He still had nearly half an hour to the good.

He seemed to know the place well and to have a definite objective, for he struck out briskly from the foot of the pier into Market Jew Street, and from thence by a somewhat zig-zag route to a road which eventually brought him out about the middle of the Esplanade. Continuing westward, he entered the Newlyn Road along which he walked rapidly for about a third of a mile, when he drew up opposite a small letter-box which was let into a wall. Here he stopped to read the tablet on which was printed the hours of collection, and then, having glanced at his watch, he walked on again, but at a less rapid pace.

When he reached the outskirts of Newlyn he turned and began slowly to retrace his steps, looking at his watch from time to time with a certain air of impatience.

Presently a quick step behind him caused him to look round. The newcomer was a postman, striding along, bag on shoulder, with the noisy tread of a heavily-shod man, and evidently collecting letters. Varney let him pass; watched him halt at the little letter-box, unlock the door, gather up the letters and stow them in his bag; heard the clang of the iron door, and finally saw the man set forth again on his pilgrimage. Then he brought forth his pocket-book and, drawing from it the letter addressed to Joseph Penfield, Esq., stepped up to the letter-box. The tablet now announced that the next collection would be at 8.30 P.M. Varney read the announcement with a faint smile, glanced again at his watch, which indicated two minutes past four, and dropped the letter into the box.

As he walked up the pier, with a large paper bag under his arm, he became aware of a tall man, who was doing sentry-go before a Gladstone bag, that stood on the coping opposite the ladder, and who, observing his approach, came forward to meet him.

"Here you are, then, Rodney," was Varney's rather unoriginal greeting.

"Yes," replied Rodney, "and here I've been for nearly half an hour. Purcell gone?"

"Bless you, yes; long ago," answered Varney.

"I didn't see him at the station. What train was he going by?"

"I don't know. He said something about taking Falmouth on the way; had some business or other there. But I expect he's gone to have a feed at one of the hotels. We got hung up in a fog — that's why I'm so late; I've been up to buy some grog."

"Well," said Rodney, "bring it on board. It's time we were under way. As soon as we are outside, I'll take charge and you can go below and stoke up at your ease."

The two men descended the ladder and proceeded at once to hoist the sails and cast off the shore-ropes. A few strokes of an oar sent them clear of the lee of the pier, and in five minutes the yacht *Sandhopper* was once more outside, heading south with a steady breeze from east-north-east.

II. The Unravelling of the Mystery

OMANCE lurks in unsuspected places. We walk abroad amidst scenes made dull by familiarity, and let our thoughts ramble far away beyond the commonplace. In fancy we thread the ghostly aisles of some tropical forest; we linger on the white beach of some lonely coral island, where the cocoa-nut palms, shivering in the sea-breeze, patter a refrain to the song of the surf, we wander by moonlight through the narrow streets of some southern city, and hear the thrum of the guitar rise to the shrouded balcony; and behold! all the time Romance is at our very doors.

*　　*　　*　　*　　*　　*　　*

It was on a bright afternoon early in March, that I sat beside my friend Thorndyke on one of the lower benches of the lecture theatre of the Royal College of Surgeons. Not a likely place this to encounter Romance and yet there it was, if we had only known it, lying unnoticed at present on the green baize cover of the lecturer's table. But, for the moment, we were thinking of nothing but the lecture.

The theatre was nearly full. It usually was when Professor D'Arcy lectured; for that genial *savant* had the magnetic gift of infusing his own enthusiasm into the lecture, and so into his audience, even when, as on this occasion, his subject lay on the outside edge of medical science. To-day he was lecturing on marine worms; standing before the great blackboard with a bunch of coloured chalks in either hand, talking with easy eloquence — mostly over his shoulder — while he covered the black surface with those delightful drawings that added so much to the charm of his lectures.

I watched his flying fingers with fascination, dividing my attention between him and a young man on the bench below me, who was frantically copying the diagrams in a large note-book, assisted by an older friend, who sat by him and handed him the coloured pencils as he needed them.

The latter part of the lecture dealt with those beautiful sea-worms that build themselves tubes to live in; worms like the *Serpula*, that make their shelly or stony tubes by secretion from their own bodies; or, like the *Sabella* or

Terebella, build them up with sand-grains, little stones, or fragments of shell.

When the lecture came to an end, we trooped down into the arena to look at the exhibits and exchange a few words with the genial professor. Thorndyke knew him very well, and was welcomed with a warm handshake and a facetious question.

"What are you doing here, Thorndyke?" asked Professor D'Arcy. "Is it possible that there are medico-legal possibilities even in a marine worm?"

"Oh, come!" protested Thorndyke. "Don't make me such a hide-bound specialist. May I have no interest in life? Must I live for ever in the witness-box, like a marine worm in its tube?"

"I suspect you don't get very far out of your tube," said the professor, with a smile at my colleague. "And that reminds me that I have something in your line. What do you make of this? Let us hear you extract."

Here, with a mischievous twinkle, he handed Thorndyke a small, round object, which my tend inspected curiously as it lay in the palm of his hand.

"In the first place," said he, "it is a cork; the cork of a small jar."

"Right," said the professor. "Full marks. What else?"

"The cork has been saturated with paraffin wax."

"Right again."

"Then some Robinson Crusoe seems to have used it as a button, judging by the two holes in it, and an end of what looks like cat-gut."

"Yes."

"Finally, a marine worm of some kind — a *Terebella*, I think — has built a tube on it."

"Quite right. And now tell us the history of the cork or button."

"I should like to know something more about the worm first," said Thorndyke.

"The worm," said Professor D'Arcy, "is *Terebella Rufescens*. It lives, unlike most other species, on a rocky bottom, and in a depth of water of not less than ten fathoms."

It was at this point that Romance stepped in. The young man whom I had noticed working so strenuously at his notes had edged up alongside, and was staring at the object in Thorndyke's hand, not with mere interest or curiosity, but with the utmost amazement and horror. His expression was so remarkable that we all, with one accord, dropped our conversation to look at him.

"Might I be allowed to examine specimen?" he asked; and when Thorndyke handed it to him, he held it close to his eyes, scrutinising it with frowning astonishment, turned it over and over, and felt the frayed ends of cat-gut between his fingers. Finally he beckoned to his friend, and the two whispered together for a while, and watching them I saw the second man's eyebrows lift, and the same expression of horrified surprise appear on his face. Then the younger man addressed the professor.

"Would you mind telling me where you got this specimen, sir?"

The professor was quite interested.

"It was sent to me," he said, "by a friend, who picked it up on the beach at Morte Hoe, on the coast of North Cornwall."

The two young men looked significantly at one another, and, after a brief pause, the older one asked:

"Is this specimen of much value, sir?"

"No," replied the professor, "it is only a curiosity. There are several specimens of the worm in our collection. But why do you ask?"

"Because I should like to acquire it. I can't give you particulars — I am a lawyer, I may explain — but, from what my brother tells me it appears that this object has a bearing on — *er* — on a case in which we are both interested. A very important bearing, I may add, on a very important case."

The professor was delighted.

"There, now, Thorndyke," he chuckled. "What did I tell you? The medico-legal worm has arrived. I told you it was something in your line, and now you've been forestalled. Of course," he added, turning to the lawyer, "you are very welcome to this specimen. I'll give you a box to carry it in, with some cotton wool."

The specimen was duly packed in its box, and the latter deposited in the lawyer's pocket; but the two brothers did not immediately leave the theatre. They stood apart, talking earnestly together, until Thorndyke and I had taken our leave of the professor, when the lawyer advanced and addressed my colleague.

"I don't suppose you remember me, Dr. Thorndyke," he began; but my friend interrupted him.

"Yes, I do. You are Mr. Rodney. You were junior to Brooke in *Jelks* v. *Partington*. Can I be of any assistance to you?"

"If you would be so kind," replied Rodney. "My brother and I have been talking this over, and we think we should like to have your opinion on the case. The fact is, we both jumped to a conclusion at once, and now we've got what the Yankees call 'cold feet.' We think that we may have jumped too soon. Let me introduce my brother, Dr. Philip Rodney."

We shook hands, and, making our way out of the theatre, presently emerged from the big portico into Lincoln's Inn Fields.

"If you will come and take a cup of tea at my chambers in Old Buildings," said Rodney, "we can give you the necessary particulars. There isn't so very much to tell, after all. My brother identifies the cork or button, and that seems to be the only plain fact we have. Tell Dr. Thorndyke how you identified it, Phil."

"It is a simple matter," said Philip Rodney. "I went out in a boat to do some dredging with a friend named Purcell. We both wore our oilskins as the sea was choppy and there was a good deal of spray blowing about; but Purcell had lost the top button of his, so that the collar kept blowing open and letting the spray down his neck. We had no spare buttons or needles or thread on board, but it occurred to me that I could rig up a jury button with a cork from one of my little collecting jars; so I took one out, bored a couple of holes through it with a pipe-cleaner, and a threaded a piece of cat-gut through the holes."

"Why cat-gut?" asked Thorndyke.

"Because I happened to have it. I play the fiddle, and I generally have a bit of a broken string in my pocket; usually an E string — the E strings are always breaking, you know. Well, I had the end of an E string in my pocket then, so I fastened the button on with it. I bored two holes in the coat, passed the ends of the string through, and tied a reef-knot. It was as strong as a house."

"You have no doubt that it is the same cork?"

"None at all. First there is the size, which I know from having ordered the corks separately from the jars. Then I paraffined them myself after sticking on the blank labels. The label is there still, protected by the wax. And lastly there is the cut-gut; the bit that is left is obviously part of an E string. "

"Yes," said Thorndyke, "the identification seems to be unimpeachable. Now let us have the story."

"We'll have some tea first," said Rodney. "This is my burrow." As he spoke, he dived into the dark entry of one of the ancient buildings on the south side of the little square, and we followed him up the crabbed, time-worn stairs, so different from our own lordly staircase in King's Bench Walk. He let us into his chambers, and, having offered us each an armchair, said:

"My brother will spin you the yarn while I make the tea. When you have heard him you can begin the examination-in-chief You understand that this is a confidential matter and that we are dealing with it professionally?"

"Certainly," replied Thorndyke, "we quite understand that."

And thereupon Philip Rodney began his story.

"One morning last June two men started from Sennen Cove, on the west coast of Cornwall to sail to Penzance in a little yacht that belongs to my brother and me. One of them was Purcell, of whom I spoke just now and the other was a man named Varney. When they started, Purcell was wearing the oilskin coat with this button on it. The yacht arrived at Penzance at about four in the afternoon. Purcell went ashore alone to take the train to London or Falmouth, and was never seen again dead or alive. The following day Purcell's solicitor, a Mr. Penfield, received a letter from him bearing the Penzance postmark and the hour 8.45 P.M. The letter was evidently sent by mistake — put into the wrong envelope — and it appears to have been a highly compromising document. Penfield refused to give any particulars, but thinks that the letter fully accounts for Purcell's disappearance — thinks, in fact, that Purcell has bolted."

"It was understood that Purcell was going to London from Penzance, but he seems to have told Varney that he intended to call in at Falmouth. Whether or not he went to Falmouth we don't know. Varney saw him go up the ladder on to the pier, and there all traces of him vanished. Varney thinks he may have discovered the mistake about the letter and got on board some outward-bound ship at Falmouth; but that is only surmise. Still, it is highly probable; and when my brother and I saw that button at the museum, we remembered the suggestion and instantly jumped to the conclusion that poor Purcell had gone overboard."

"And then," said Rodney, handing us our tea-cups, "when we carne to talk it over we rather tended to revise our conclusions."

"Why?" asked Thorndyke.

"Well, there are several other possibilities. Purcell may have found a proper button on the yacht and cut off the cork and thrown it overboard — we must ask Varney if he did — or the coat itself may have gone over or been lost or given away, and so on."

On this Thorndyke made no comment, stirring his tea slowly with an air of deep preoccupation. presently he looked up and asked. "Who saw the yacht start?"

"I did," said Philip. "I and Mrs. Purcell and her sister and some fishermen on the beach. Purcell was steering, and he took the yacht right out to sea, outside the Longships. A fog came down soon after, and we were rather anxious, because the Wolf Rock lay right to leeward of the yacht."

"Did anyone besides Varney see Purcell at Penzance?"

"Apparently not. But we haven't asked. Varney's statement seemed to settle that question. He couldn't very well have been mistaken, you know," Philip added with a smile.

"Beside," said Rodney, "if there were any doubts, there is the letter. It was posted in Penzance after eight o'clock at night. Now I met Varney on the pier at a quarter-past four, and we sailed out of Penzance a few minutes after to return to Sennen."

"Had Varney been ashore?" asked Thorndyke.

"Yes, he had been up to the town buying some provisions."

"But you said Purcell went ashore alone."

"Yes, but there's nothing in that. Purcell was not a genial man. It was the sort of thing he would do."

"And that is all that you know of the matter?" Thorndyke asked, after a few moments' reflection.

"Yes. But we might see if Varney can remember anything more, and we might try if we can squeeze any more information out of old Penfield."

"You won't," said Thorndyke. "I know Penfield and I never trouble to ask him questions. Besides, there is nothing to ask at present. We have an item of evidence that we have not fully examined. I suggest that we exhaust that, and meanwhile keep our own counsel most completely."

Rodney looked dissatisfied. "If," said he, "the item of evidence that you refer to is the button, it seems to me that we have got all that we are likely to get out of it. We have identified it, and we know that it has been thrown up on the beach at Morte Hoe. What more can we learn from it?"

"That remains to be seen," replied Thorndyke. "We may learn nothing, but, on the other hand, we may be able to trace the course of its travels and learn its recent history. It may give us a hint as to where to start a fresh inquiry."

Rodney laughed sceptically. "You talk like a clairvoyant, as if you had the power to make this bit of cork break out into fluent discourse. Of course, you can look at the thing and speculate and guess, but surely the common sense of the matter is to ask a plain question of the man who probably knows. If it turns out that Varney saw Purcell throw the button overboard, or can tell us how it got into the sea, all your speculations will have been useless. I say, let us ask Varney first, and if he knows nothing, it will be time to start guessing."

But Thorndyke was calmly obdurate. "We are not going to guess, Rodney; we are going to investigate. Let me have the button for a couple of days. If I learn nothing from it, I will return it to you, and you can then refresh your legal soul with verbal testimony. But give scientific methods a chance first."

With evident reluctance Rodney handed him the little box. "I have asked your advice," he said rather ungraciously, "so I suppose I must take it, but your methods appeal more to the sporting than the business instincts."

"We shall see," said Thorndyke, rising with a satisfied air. "But, meanwhile, I stipulate that you make no communication to anybody."

"Very well," said Rodney, and we took leave of the two brothers.

As we walked down Chancery Lane, I looked at Thorndyke, and detected in him an air of purpose for which I could not quite account. Clearly, he had something in view.

"It seems to me," I said tentatively, "that there was something in what Rodney said. Why shouldn't the button just have been thrown overboard?"

He stopped and looked at me with humorous reproach.

"Jervis!" he exclaimed, "I am ashamed of you. You are as bad as Rodney. You have utterly lost sight of the main fact, which is a most impressive one. Here is a cork button. Now an ordinary cork, if immersed long enough, will soak up water until it is water-logged, and then sink to the bottom. But this one was impregnated with paraffin wax. It can't get water-logged, and it can't sink. It would float for ever."

"Well?"

"But it *has* sunk. It has been lying at the bottom of the sea for months, long enough for a *Terebella* to build a tube on it. And we have D'Arcy's statement that it has been lying in not less than ten fathoms of water. Then, at last, it has broken loose and risen to the surface and drifted ashore. Now, I ask you, what has held it down at the bottom of the sea? Of course, it may have been only the coat, weighted by something in the pocket; but, there is a much more probably suggestion."

"Yes, I see," said I.

"I suspect you don't — altogether," he rejoined, with a malicious smile. And in the end it turned out that he was right.

The air of purpose that I noted was not deceptive. No sooner had we reached our chambers, than he fell to work as if with a definite object. Standing by the window, he scrutinised the button, first with the naked eye, and then with a lens, and finally laying it on the stage of the microscope, examined the worm-tube by the light of a condenser with a two-inch objective. And the result seemed to please him amazingly.

His next proceeding was to detach, with a fine pair of forceps, the largest of the tiny fragments of stone of which the worm-tube was built. This fragment he cemented on a slide with Canada balsam; and, fetching from the laboratory a slip of Turkey stone, he proceeded to grind the little fragment to a flat surface. Then he melted the balsum, turned the fragment over, and repeated the grinding process until the little fragment was ground down to a thin film or plate, when he applied fresh balsam and a cover-glass. The specimen was now ready for examination; and it was at this point that I suddenly remembered I had an appointment at six o'clock.

It had struck half-past seven when I returned, and a glance round the room told me that the battle was over — and won. The table was littered with trays of mineralogical sections and open books of reference relating to geology and petrology, and one end was occupied by an outspread geological chart of the British Isles. Thorndyke sat in his armchair, smiling with bland contentment, and smoking a Trichinopoly cheroot.

"Well," I said cheerfully, "what's the news?"

He removed the cheroot, blew out a cloud of smoke, and replied in a single word:

"Phonolite."

"Thank you," I said. "Brevity is the soul of wit. But would you mind amplifying the joke to the dimensions of intelligibility?"

"Certainly," he replied gravely. "I will endeavour to temper the wind to the shorn lamb. You noticed, I suppose, that the fragments of rock of which that worm-tube was built are all alike."

"All the same kind of rock? No, I did not."

"Well, they are, and I have spent a strenuous hour identifying that rock. It is the peculiar, resonant, volcanic rock known as phonolite or clink-stone."

"That is very interesting," said I. "And now I see the object of your researches. You hope to get a hint as to the locality where the button has been lying."

"I hoped, as you say, to get a hint, but I have succeeded beyond my expectations. I have been able to fix the locality exactly."

"Have you really?" I exclaimed. "How on earth did you manage that?"

"By a very singular chance," he replied. "It happens that phonolite occurs in two places only in the neighbourhood of the British Isles. One is inland and may be disregarded. The other is the Wolf Rock."

"The rock of which Philip Rodney was speaking?"

"Yes. He said, you remembered, that he was afraid that the yacht might drift down on it in the fog. Well, this Wolf Rock is a very remarkable structure. It is what is called a 'volcanic neck,' that is, it is a mass of altered lava that once filled the funnel of a volcano. The volcano has disappeared, but this cast of the funnel remains standing up from the bottom of the sea like a great column. It is a single mass of phonolite, and thus entirely different in composition from the sea-bed around or anywhere near these islands. But, of course, immediately at its base, the sea-bottom must be covered with decomposed fragments which have fallen from its sides, and it is from these fragments that our *Terebella* has built its tube. So, you see, we can fix the exact locality in which that button has been lying all the months that the tube was building, and we now have a point of departure for fresh investigations."

"But," I said, "this is a very significant discovery, Thorndyke. Shall you tell Rodney?"

"Certainly I shall, But there are one or two questions that I shall ask him first. I have sent him a note inviting him to drop in to-night with his brother, so we had better run round to the club and get some dinner. I said nine o'clock."

It was a quarter to nine when we had finished dinner, and ten minutes later we were back in our chambers. Thorndyke made up the fire, placed the chairs hospitably round the hearth, and laid on the table the notes that he had taken at the late interview. Then the Treasury clock struck nine, and within less than a minute our two guests arrived.

"I should apologise," said Thorndyke, as we shook hands, "for my rather peremptory message, but I thought it best to waste no time."

"You certainly have wasted no time," said Rodney, "if you have already extracted its history from the button. Do you keep a tame medium on the premises, or are you a clairvoyant yourself."

"This is our medium," replied Thorndyke, indicating the microscope standing on a side-table under its bell glass. "The man who uses it becomes to some extent a clairvoyant. But I should like to ask one or two questions if I may."

Rodney made no secret of his disappointment.

"We had hoped," said he, "to hear answers rather than questions. However, as you please."

"Then," said Thorndyke, quite unmoved by Rodney's manner, "I will proceed; and I will begin with the yacht in which Purcell and Varney travelled from Sennen to Penzance. I understand that the yacht belongs to you and was lent by you to these two men?"

Rodney nodded, and Thorndyke then asked:

"Has the yacht ever been out of your custody on any other occasion?"

"No," replied Rodney, "excepting on this occasion, one or both of us have always been on board."

Thorndyke made a note of the answer and proceeded:

"When you resumed possession of the yacht, did you find her in all respects as you left her?"

"My dear sir," Rodney exclaimed impatiently, "may I remind you that we are inquiring — if we are inquiring about anything — into the disappearance of a man who was seen to go ashore from this yacht and who certainly never came on board again? The yacht is out of it altogether."

"Nevertheless," said Thorndyke, "I should be glad if you would answer my question."

"Oh, very well," Rodney replied irritably. "Then we found her substantially as we had left her."

"Meaning by 'substantially'?"

"Well, they had had to rig a new jib halyard. The old one had parted."

"Did you find the old one on board?"

"Yes; in two pieces, of course."

"Was the whole of it there?"

"I suppose so. We never measured the pieces. But really, sir, these questions seem extraordinarily irrelevant."

"They are not," said Thorndyke. "You will see that presently. I want to know if you missed any rope, cordage, or chain."

Here Philip interposed.

"There was some spun-yarn missing. They opened a new ball and used up several yards. I meant to ask Varney what they used it for."

Thorndyke jotted down a note and asked: "Was there any of the iron-work missing? Any anchor, chain, or any other heavy object?"

Rodney shook his head impatiently, but again Philip broke in.

"You are forgetting the ballast-weight, Jack. You see," he continued, addressing Thorndyke, "the yacht is ballasted with half-hundredweights, and, when we came to take out the ballast to lay her up for the winter we found one of the weights missing. I have no idea when it disappeared, but there was certainly one short, and neither of us had taken it out."

"Can you," asked Thorndyke, "fix any date on which all the ballast-weights were in place?"

"Yes, I think I can. A few days before Purcell went to Penzance we beached the yacht — she is only a little boat — to give her a scrape. Of course, we had to take out the ballast, and when we launched her again I helped to put it back. I am certain all the weights were there then."

Here Jack Rodney, who had been listening with ill-concealed impatience, remarked:

"This is all very interesting, sir, but I cannot conceive what bearing it has on the movements of Purcell after he left the yacht."

"It has a most direct and important bearing," said Thorndyke. "Perhaps I had better explain before we go any further. Let me begin by pointing out that this button has been lying for many months at the bottom of the sea at a depth of not less ten fathoms. That is proved by the worm-tube which has been built on it. Now, as this button is a waterproofed cork, it could not have sunk by itself, it has been sunk by some body to which it was attached, and there is evidence that that body was a very heavy one."

"What evidence is there of that?" asked Rodney.

"There is the fact that it has been lying continuously in one place. A body of moderate weight, as you know, moves about the sea-bottom impelled by currents and tide-streams, but this button has been lying unmoved in one place."

"Indeed," said Rodney with manifest scepticism. "Perhaps you can point out the spot where it has been lying."

"I can," Thorndyke replied. "That button, Mr. Rodney, has been lying all these months at the base of the Wolf Rock."

The two brothers started very perceptibly. They stared at Thorndyke, they looked at one another, and then the lawyer challenged the statement.

"You make this assertion very confidently," he said. "Can you give us any evidence to support it?"

Thorndyke's reply was to produce the button, the section, the test-specimens, the microscope, and the geological chart. In great detail, and with his incomparable lucidity, he assembled the facts, and explained their connection, evolving the unavoidable conclusion.

The different effect of the demonstration on the two men interested me greatly. To the lawyer, accustomed to dealing with verbal and documentary evidence, it manifestly appeared as a far fetched, rather fantastic argument, ingenious, amusing, and entirely unconvincing. On Philip, the doctor, it made a profound impression. Accustomed to acting on inferences from facts of his own observing, he gave full weight to each item of evidence, and I could see that his mind was already stretching out to the, as yet unstated, corollaries.

The lawyer was the first to speak. "What inference," he asked, "do you wish us to draw from this very ingenious theory of yours?"

"The inference," Thorndyke replied impassively, "I leave to you; but perhaps it would help you if I recapitulate the facts."

"Perhaps it would," said Rodney.

"Then," said Thorndyke, "I will take them in order. This is the case of a man who was seen to start on a voyage for a given destination in company with one other person. His start out to sea was witnessed by a number of persons. From that moment he was never seen again by any person excepting his one companion. He is said to have reached his destination, but his arrival there rests upon the unsupported verbal testimony of one person, the said companion. Thereafter he vanished utterly, and since then has made no sign of being alive, although there are several persons with whom he could have safely communicated.

"Some eight months later a portion of this man's clothing is found. It bears evidence of having been lying at the bottom of the sea for many months, so that it must have sunk to its resting place within a very short time of the man's disappearance, The place where it has been lying is one over, or near, which the man must have sailed in the yacht. It has been moored to the bottom by some very heavy object; and a very heavy object has disappeared from the yacht. That heavy object had apparently not disappeared when the yacht started, and was not seen on the yacht afterwards. The evidence goes to show that the disappearance of that object coincided in time with the disappearance of the man; and a quantity of cordage disappeared, certainly, on that day. Those are the facts in our possession at present, Mr. Rodney, and I think the inference emerges automatically."

There was a brief silence, during which the two brothers cogitated profoundly and with very disturbed expressions. Then Rodney spoke.

"I am bound to admit Dr. Thorndyke, that, as a scheme of circumstantial evidence, this is extremely ingenious and complete. It is impossible to mistake your meaning. But you would hardly expect us to charge a highly respectable gentleman of our acquaintance with having murdered his friend and made away with the body, on a — well — a rather far-fetched theory."

"Certainly not," replied Thorndyke. "But, on the other hand, with this body of circumstantial evidence before us, it is clearly imperative that some further investigations should be made before we speak of the matter to any human soul."

Rodney agreed somewhat grudgingly.

"What do you suggest?" he asked.

"I suggest that we thoroughly overhaul the yacht in the first place. Where is she now?"

"Under a tarpaulin in a yard at Battersea. The gear and stores are in a disused workshop in the yard."

"When could we look her over her?"

"To-morrow morning, if you like," said Rodney.

"Very well," said Thorndyke. "We will call for you at nine, if that will suit."

It suited perfectly, and the arrangement was accordingly made. A few minutes later the two brothers took their leave, but as they were shaking hands, Philip said suddenly:

"There is one little matter that occurs to me. I have only just remembered it, and I don't suppose it is of any consequence, but it is as well to mention everything. You remember my brother saying that one of the jib halyards broke the other day?"

"Yes."

"Well, of course, the jib came down and went partly overboard. Now, the next time I hoisted the sail, I noticed a small stain on it; a greenish stain like that of mud, only it wouldn't wash out, and it is there still. I meant to ask Varney about it. Stains of that kind on the jib usually come from a bit of mud on the fluke of the anchor, but the anchor was quite clean when I examined it, and besides, it hadn't been down on that day. I thought I'd better tell you about it."

"I'm glad you did." said Thorndyke. "We will have a look at that stain to-morrow. Good-night." Once more he shook hands, and then, re-entering the room, stood for quite a long time with his back to the fire, thoughtfully examining the toes of his boots.

We started forth next morning for our rendezvous considerably earlier than seemed necessary. But I made no comment, for Thorndyke was in that state of extreme taciturnity which characterised him whenever he was engaged on an absorbing case with an insufficiency of evidence. I knew that he was turning over and over the facts that he had, and searching for new openings; but I had no clue to the trend of his thoughts until, passing the gateway of Lincoln's Inn, he walked briskly up Chancery Lane into Holborn, and finally halted outside a wholesale druggist's.

"I shan't be more than a few minutes," said he; "are you coming in?"

I was, most emphatically. Questions were forbidden at this stage, but there was no harm in keeping one's ears open; and when I heard his order I was richer by a distinct clue to his next movements. Tincture of Guaiacum and

Ozonic Ether formed a familiar combination, and the size of the bottles indicated the field of investigation.

We found the brothers waiting for us at Lincoln's Inn. They both looked rather hard at the parcel that I was now carrying, and especially at Thorndyke's green canvas-covered research case; but they made no comment, and we set forth at once on the rather awkward cross-country journey to Battersea. Very little was said on the way, but I noticed that both men took our quest more seriously than I had expected, and I judged that they had been talking the case over.

Our journey terminated at a large wooden gate on which Rodney knocked loudly with his stick; whereupon a wicket was opened, and, after a few words of explanation, we passed through into a large yard. Crossing this, we came to a wharf, beyond which was a small stretch of unreclaimed shore, and here, drawn well above high-water mark, a small, double-ended yacht stood on chocks under a tarpaulin cover.

"This is the yacht," said Rodney. "The gear and loose fittings are stored in the workshop behind us. Which will you see first?"

"Let us look at the gear," said Thorndyke, and we turned to the disused workshop into which Rodney admitted us with a key from his pocket. I looked curiously about the long, narrow interior with its prosaic contents, so little suggestive of tragedy or romance. Overhead the yacht's spars rested on the tiebeams, from which hung bunches of blocks; on the floor a long row of neatly-painted half-hundredweights, a pile of chain-cable, two anchors, a stove, and other oddments such as water breakers, buckets, mops, etc., and on the long benches at the side, folded sail, locker cushions, side-light lanterns, the binnacle, the cabin lamp, and other more delicate fittings. Thorndyke, too, glanced round inquisitively, and, depositing his case on the bench, asked, "Have you still got the broken jib halyard of which you were telling me?"

"Yes," said Rodney, "it is here under the bench." He drew out a coil of rope, and flinging it on the floor, began to uncoil it, when it separated into two lengths.

"Which are the broken ends?" Thorndyke asked.

"It broke near the middle," said Rodney, "where it chafed on the cleat when the sail was hoisted. This is the one end, you see, frayed out like a brush in breaking, and the other –" He picked up the second half and, passing it rapidly through his hands, held up the end. He did not finish the sentence, but stood with a frown of surprise staring at the rope in his hands.

"This is queer," he said, after a pause. "The broken end has been cut off. Did you cut it off, Phil?"

"No," replied Philip. "It is just as I took it from the locker, where I suppose, you or Varney stowed it."

"The question is," said Thorndyke, "how much has been cut off. Do you know the original length of the rope?"

"Yes. Forty-two feet. It is not down in the inventory, but I remember working it out. Let us see how much there is here."

He laid the two lengths of rope along the floor and we measured them with Thorndyke's spring tape. The combined length was exactly thirty-one feet.

"So," said Thorndyke, "there are eleven feet missing, without allowing for the lengthening of the rope by stretching. That is a very important fact."

"What made you suspect that part of the halyard might be missing as well as the spunyarn?" Philip asked.

"I did not think," replied Thorndyke, "that a yachtsman would use spunyarn to lash a half-hundred-weight to a corpse. I suspected that the spunyarn was used for something else. By the way, I see you have a revolver there. Was that on board at the time?"

"Yes," said Rodney. "It was hanging on the cabin bulkhead. Be careful. I don't think it has been unloaded."

Thorndyke opened the breech of the revolver, and dropping the cartridges into his hand, peered down the barrel and into each chamber separately.

"It is quite clean inside," he remarked. Then glancing at the ammunition in his hand, "I notice," said he, "that these cartridges are not all alike. There is one Curtis and Harvey, and five Eleys."

Philip looked with a distinctly startled expression at the little heap of cartridges in Thorndyke's hand, and picking out the odd one, examined it with knitted brows.

"When did you fire the revolver last, Jack?" he asked, looking up at his brother.

"On the day when we potted at those champagne bottles," was the reply.

Philip raised his eyebrows. "Then," said he, "this is a very remarkable affair. I distinctly remember on that occasion, when we had sunk all the bottles, reloading the revolver with Eleys, and that there were then three cartridges left over in the bag. When I had loaded I opened the new box of Curtis and Harvey's, tipped them into the bag and threw the box overboard."

"Did you clean the revolver?" asked Thorndyke.

"No, I didn't. I meant to clean it later, but forgot to."

"But," said Thorndyke, "it has undoubtedly been cleaned, and very thoroughly. Shall we check the cartridges in the bag? There ought to be forty-nine Curtis and Harvey's and three Eley's, if what you have told us is correct."

Philip searched among the raffle on the bench and produced a small linen bag. Untying the string, he shot out on the bench a heap of cartridges which he counted one by one. There were fifty-two in all, and three of them were Eley's.

"Then," said Thorndyke, "it comes to this: since you used that revolver it has been used by someone else. That someone fired only a single shot, after which he carefully cleaned the barrel and reloaded. Incidentally, he seems to have known where the cartridge bag was kept, but did not know about the change in the make of the cartridges. You notice," he added, looking at Rodney, "that the circumstantial evidence accumulates."

"I do, indeed," Rodney replied gloomily. "Is there anything else that you wish to examine?"

"Yes. There is the sail. You spoke of a stain on the jib. Shall we see if we can make anything of that?"

"I don't think you will make much of it," said Philip. "It is very faint. However, you shall see it."

He picked out one of the bundles of white duck, and, while he was unfolding it, Thorndyke dragged an empty bench into the middle of the floor under the skylight. Over this the sail was spread so that the mysterious mark was in the middle of the bench. It was very inconspicuous; just a faint, grey-green, wavy line like the representation of an island on a map. We all looked at it attentively for a few moments, and then Thorndyke said, "Would you mind if I made a further stain on the sail? I should like to apply some re-agents."

"Of course, you must do what is necessary," said Rodney. "The evidence is more important than the sail."

Accordingly Thorndyke unpacked our parcel, and as the two bottles emerged, Philip read the labels with evident surprise, remarking: "I shouldn't have thought the Guaiacum test would have been of any use after all these months."

"It will act, I think, if the pigment is there," said Thorndyke; and as he spoke he poured a quantity of the tincture — which he had ordered diluted to our usual working strength — on the middle of the stained area. The pool of liquid rapidly spread considerably beyond the limits of the stain, growing paler as it extended. Then Thorndyke cautiously dropped small quantities of the Ether at various points around the stained area and watched closely as the two liquids mingled in the fabric of the sail. Gradually the Ether spread towards the stain, and, first at one point and then another, approached and finally crossed the wavy grey line, and at each point the same change occurred; first, the faint grey line turned into a strong blue line, and then the colour extended to the enclosed space, until the entire area of the stain stood out, a conspicuous blue patch.

Philip and Thorndyke looked at one another significantly, and the latter said, "You understand the meaning of this reaction, Mr. Rodney; this is a bloodstain, and a very carefully washed bloodstain."

"So I supposed," Rodney replied, and for a while we were all silent.

There was something very dramatic and solemn in the sudden appearance of this staring blue patch on the sail, with the sinister message that it brought. But what followed was more dramatic still. As we stood silently regarding the blue stain, the mingled liquids continued to spread; and suddenly, at the extreme edge of the wet area, we became aware of a new spot of blue. At first a mere speck, it grew slowly as the liquid spread over the canvas into a small oval, and then a second spot appeared by its side.

At this point Thorndyke poured a fresh charge of the tincture, and when it had soaked into the cloth, cautiously applied a sprinkling of Ether. Instantly the blue spots began to elongate, fresh spots and patches appeared, and as they ran together there sprang out of the blank surface the clear impression of a hand — a left hand, complete in all its details excepting the third finger, which was represented by an oval spot at some two-thirds of its length.

The dreadful significance of this apparition and the uncanny and mysterious manner of its emergence from the white surface impressed us so that for a while none of us spoke. At length I ventured to remark on the absence of the impression of the third finger.

"I think," said Thorndyke, "that the impression is there. That spot looks like the mark of a finger-tip, and its position rather suggests a finger with a stiff joint."

As he made this statement, both brothers simultaneously uttered a smothered exclamation.

"What is it?" he asked.

The two men looked at one another with an expression of awe. Then Rodney said in a hushed voice, hardly above a whisper, "Varney, the man who was with Purcell on the yacht — he has a stiff joint in the third finger of his left hand."

There was nothing more to say. The case was complete. The keystone had been laid in the edifice of circumstantial evidence. The investigation was at an end.

After an interval of silence, during which Thorndyke was busily writing up his notes, Rodney asked, "What is to be done now? Shall I swear an information?"

Thorndyke shook his head. No man was more expert in accumulating circumstantial evidence; none was more loath to rely on it.

"A murder charge," said he, "should be supported by proof of death and, if possible, by production of the body."

"But the body is at the bottom of the sea!"

"True. But we know its whereabouts. It is a small area, with the lighthouse as a landmark. If that area were systematically worked over with a trawl or dredge, or, better still, with a creeper, there should be a very good chance of recovering the body, or, at least, the clothing and the weight."

Rodney reflected for a few moments.

"I think you are right," he said at length. "The thing is practicable, and it is our duty to do it. I suppose you couldn't come down and help us?"

"Not now. But in a few days the spring vacation will commence, and then Jervis and I could join you, if the weather were suitable."

"Thank you both," replied Rodney. "We will make the arrangements, and let you know when we are ready."

It was quite early on a bright April morning when the two Rodneys, Thorndyke, and I steamed out of Penzance Harbour in a small open launch. The sea was very calm for the time of year, the sky was of a warm blue, and a gentle breeze stole out of the north-east. Over the launch's side hung a long spar, secured to a tow-rope by a bridle, and to the spar were attached a number of creepers-lengths of chain fitted with rows of hooks. The outfit further included a spirit compass, provided with sights, a sextant, and a hand-lead.

"It's lucky we didn't run up against Varney in the town," Philip remarked, as the harbour dwindled in the distance.

"Varney!" exclaimed Thorndyke. "Do you mean that he lives at Penzance?"

"He keeps rooms there, and spends most of his spare time down in this part. He was always keen on sea-fishing, and he's keener than ever now. He keeps a boat of his own, too. It's queer, isn't it, if what we think is true?"

"Very," said Thorndyke and by his meditative manner I judged that the circumstances afforded him matter for curious speculation.

As we passed abreast of the Land's End, and the solitary lighthouse rose ahead on the verge of the horizon, we began to overtake the scattered members of a fleet of luggers, some with lowered mainsails and hand-lines down, others with their black sails set, heading for a more distant fishing-ground. Threading our way amongst them, we suddenly became aware that one of the smaller luggers was heading so as to close in on us. Rodney, observing this, was putting over the helm to avoid her when a seafaring voice from the little craft hailed us.

"Launch ahoy there! Gentleman aboard wants to speak to you."

We looked at one another significantly and in some confusion; and meanwhile our solitary 'hand' — seaman, engineer, and fireman combined — without waiting for orders, shut off steam. The lugger closed in rapidly and of a sudden there appeared, holding on by the mast-stay, a small, dark man who hailed us cheerfully:

"Hullo, you fellows! Whither away? What's your game?"

"God!" exclaimed Philip, "It's Varney. Sheer off, Jack! Don't let him come alongside."

But it was too late. The launch had lost way and failed to answer the helm. The lugger sheered in, sweeping abreast of us within a foot; and, as she crept past, Varney sprang lightly from the gunwale and dropped neatly on the side bench in our stern sheets.

"Where are you off to?" he asked. "You can't be going out to fish in this baked potato can?"

"No," faltered Rodney, "we're not. We're going to do some dredging — or rather –"

Here Thorndyke came to his assistance. "Marine worms," said he, "are the occasion of this little voyage. There seems to be some very uncommon ones on the bottom at the base of the Wolf Rock. I have seen some in a collection, and I want to get a few more if I can."

It was a skilfully-worded explanation, and I could see that, for the time, Varney accepted it. But from the moment when the Wolf Rock was mentioned all his vivacity of manner died out. In an instant he had become grave, thoughtful, and a trifle uneasy.

The introductions over, he reverted to the subject. He questioned us closely, especially as to our proposed methods. And it was impossible to evade his questions. There were the creepers in full view; there was the compass and the sextant, and presently these appliances would have to be put to use. Gradually, as the nature of our operations dawned on him, his manner changed more and more. A horrible pallor overspread his face, and a terrible restlessness took possession of him.

Rodney, who was navigating, brought the launch to within a quarter of a mile of the rock, and then, taking cross-bearings on the lighthouse and a point of land, directed us to lower the creepers.

It was a most disagreeable experience for us all. Varney, pale and clammy, fidgeted about the boat, now silent and moody, now almost hysterically boisterous. Thorndyke watched him furtively and, I think, judged by his manner how near we were to the object of our search.

Calm as the day was, the sea was breaking heavily over the rock, and as we worked in closer the water around boiled and eddied in an unpleasant and even dangerous manner. The three keepers in the gallery of the lighthouse watched us through their glasses, and one of them bellowed to us through a megaphone to keep further away.

"What do you say?" asked Rodney. "It's a bit risky here with the rock right under our lee. Shall we try another side?"

"Better try one more cast this side," said Thorndyke; and he spoke so definitely that we all, including Varney, looked at him curiously. But no one answered, and the creepers were dropped for a fresh cast still nearer the rock. We were then north of the lighthouse, and headed south so as to pass the rock on its east side. As we approached, the man with the megaphone bawled out fresh warnings, and continued to roar at us until we were abreast of the rock in a wild tumble of confused waves.

At this moment Philip, who held the tow-line with a single turn round a cleat, said he felt a pull, but that it seemed as if the creepers had broken away. As soon, therefore, as we were out of the backwash into smooth water, we hauled in the line to examine the creepers.

I looked over the side eagerly, for something new in Thorndyke's manner impressed me. Varney, too, who had hitherto taken but little notice of the creepers, now knelt on the side bench, gazing earnestly into the clear water, whence the tow-rope was rising.

At length the beam came in sight, and below it, on one of the creepers, a yellowish object, dimly seen through the wavering water.

"There's somethin' on this time," said the engineer, craning over the side. He shut off steam, and, with the rest of us, watched the incoming creeper. I looked at Varney, kneeling on the bench apart from us, not fidgeting now, but still, rigid, pale as wax, and staring with dreadful fascination at the slowly-rising object.

Suddenly the engineer uttered an exclamation. "Why, 'tis a sou'wester, and all laced about wi' spuny'n. Surely 'tis Hi! steady, sir! My God!"

There was a heavy splash, and as Rodney rushed forward for the boat-hook I saw Varney rapidly sinking head first through the clear, blue-green water, dragged down by the hand lead that he had hitched to his waist. By the time Rodney was back he was far out of reach; but for a long time, as it seemed, we could see him sinking, sinking, growing paler, more shadowy, more shapeless, but always steadily following the lead sinker, until at last he faded from our sight into the darkness of the ocean.

Not until he had vanished did we haul on board the creeper with its dreadful burden. Indeed, we never hauled it on board; for as Philip, with unsteady hand, unhooked the sou'wester hat from the creeper, the encircling coils of spunyarn slipped, and from inside the hat a skull dropped into the water and sank. We watched it grow green and pallid and small, until it vanished, as Varney had vanished. Then Philip turned and flung the hat down in the bottom of the boat. Thorndyke picked it up and unwound the spunyarn.

"Do you identify it?" he asked, and then, as he turned it over, he added. "But I see it identifies itself." He held it towards me, and I read in embroidered letters on the silk lining, 'Dan Purcell.'

The Sign of the Ram

It was a pleasant little party that I joined, on my first evening at Lowestoft, at Dr. Power's dinner-table, and rather an odd one too. The pleasantness was imparted by my genial host and his wife and their two comely daughters; the oddity by their guest, an old acquaintance of Dr. Power's in his "wander-years." For Mr. James Kwamin Brewe was a gentleman of colour — a negro, in fact — a native of Cape Coast, where he practised as a barrister; and, though a perfectly civilised, educated man, displayed an outlook on life that was unusual.

"Mr. Brewe has come over to brush up his legal knowledge in the Courts," Power explained to me.

Brewe laughed boisterously.

"I came away," said he, "to avoid our rainy season, and dropped into your 'silly season.' There's nothing to do and nothing to see."

"Oh, come now," said Mrs. Power, "you've seen a very wonderful thing to-day — a millionaire's wedding presents. We took Mr. Brewe," she continued, addressing me, "up to Willowdene, a big house belonging to a Mr. Renshaw. His daughter is about to marry a very rich Chicago gentleman — a Mr. Mifflin — and the wedding presents are set out in the billiard room."

After dinner, Dr. Power took me into the surgery, and formally handed over the practice, as he was travelling up to London by the last train.

I went to bed, confident of am undisturbed night. Great, therefore, was my surprise and indignation when, about two o'clock, I was roused by the coachman, who acted as night porter.

"Hallo!" I sang out, sitting up in bed. "What's the matter?"

"Message from Willowdene, sir. Mrs. Renshaw's took worse. Their dogcart's a-waiting."

The latter fact afforded more satisfaction to him than to me, and, as I shuffled into my clothes, I heaped maledictions on the agent who had given me Power's practice.

Nevertheless, the brisk drive along the dark road was not unpleasant, and when I jumped down on to the gravel drive, grasping the emergency bag, I was wide awake and eager to do my principal credit. An elderly man received me in the hall and conducted me up the broad staircase.

"You haven't been long, doctor," he said. "It's a shame to drag you out at this hour, but my wife is in great pain. Perhaps Dr. Power has told you about her?"

"Yes; she has been suffering from an attack of gastralgia, I understand," was my guarded reply.

Power had, in fact, been rather vague, and when I came to examine the patient, I found my own diagnosis no triumph of precision. The one obvious fact, however, was that the poor lady was suffering intensely, and I judged that a quarter of a grain of morphine would meet the immediate necessities of the case, while the diagnosis could be considered with more precision on the morrow.

I administered the dose, and, as I repacked my bag, watched the deep satisfaction the rapid operation of this "gift of God," as it was named in the days when the resources of the physician were fewer and more prized. Gradually the lines of suffering faded from the worn face, the restless twitchings and turnings ceased, and in a few minutes the patient sank into a quiet sleep.

"Thank God for that!" said Mr. Renshaw, softly opening the door to let me out.

He led the way along the corridor which crossed the main staircase to the other side of the house, and, preceding me into the smoking-room, lit the gas.

"It was very good of you to come so quickly," he said, as he handed me my tumbler and the cigar-box, "and I hope you will be able to do something permanent for my wife. We shall be having a wedding here in a day or two."

"So I have heard," I said, "and the fame of the presents had reached me already."

"Yes," said Mr. Renshaw; "they are very splendid and costly — absurdly so, I think. But the old man — the bridegroom's father — has a weakness for diamonds, and he has let himself go. Come and see them, they are in the billiard-room close by."

"Isn't it rather unsafe," I asked, as we walked down the corridor, "to leave them at night in this remote part of the building?"

"Bless you," he answered, "they are not left! My head gardener, Gannet, is on guard with a revolver, and all the lights turned on."

At this moment we heard the sound of a window shutting softly, and Mr. Renshaw started forward.

"Now, what the deuce is that?"

He strode to the door, rapped loudly with his knuckles, and threw it open. Then he drew back with an exclamation, for the room was in total darkness.

"What is the meaning of this, Gannet?" he demanded angrily. But not a sound came from the dark room.

Without waiting, he groped forward into the darkness, and then I heard a stumble, followed by a cry of alarm.

"A light! A light, for God's sake!" he shouted, and, as I struck a wax match, I saw him stooping over the prostate form of a man. He snatched the vesta from my hand and, running to a bracket, lit the jet. Instantly the bright light flooded the room, showing us a litter of empty jewel-cases and the body of the gardener stretched on the floor.

Mr. Renshaw darted to the window, flung it up, and leaned out. "There he goes!" he shouted. "Give me the revolver! Quick!"

But by the time I had picked up the pistol and taken it to him, the burglar had vanished.

"Curse those diamonds!" muttered Renshaw. "I wish I had never seen them. Do what you can, doctor, for the poor old fellow while I go after the scoundrel!"

The eastern sky was pallid with the dawn, when a long-drawn breath, followed by unbroken silence, told us that sturdy Tom Gannet had gone forth into the unknown. I drew a sheet over the corpse, and taking Mr. Renshaw gently by the arm, led him from the room. Outside the door, the police superintendent — Bowles, by name — was waiting, and as we emerged he inquired, in a business-like tone:

"How is the gardener, sir?"

"He is dead," I answered.

The officer made a note of the fact, and then remarked:

"One of my men has found some footprints leading to the river. I should like to take the doctor's opinion on them. You see," he continued, as we came out into the grounds, "there's a patch of clay by the river, half-dried; that is to say, it is soft, but not sticky. Now a man seems to have crossed that patch twice, coming from the river first, and then going back to it; but we can't be sure it is the same man, because the first set of prints are those of boots, whereas the returning prints are of bare feet. However, there are similar foot-prints, though less distinct, on the flower-beds under the billiard-room window — boots and bare feet."

"No stockings?" asked Mr. Renshaw.

"No shoes or stockings," replied the officer; "but there's nothing very remarkable in that. The queer thing is that he doesn't seem to have had any little toes."

"No little toe on either foot!" exclaimed Mr. Renshaw. "But that is most astonishing! I can't imagine any accident by which a man could lose *both* little toes. It must have been a deformity, or perhaps a disease."

"Exactly," said the officer. "That's what I want to know. What do you say, doctor?"

"I agree with Mr. Renshaw," I replied, "that it could hardly be a case of injury, and I should dismiss the idea of deformity; but there are several diseases by which a man might lose both his little toes. Rejecting senile gangrene, as we are evidently dealing with an active and vigorous man, there remain three well-known affections, all of which might produce these conditions."

"What are they?"

"They are Raynaud's disease, frostbite and ergotism."

"I know frostbite," said the officer, "but I've never heard of the other two. What are they like?"

"Raynaud's disease," I explained, "is an obscure affection of the blood-vessels, which is characterised by periodic attacks, during which the fingers or toes become wasted and tapered at the ends, and, occasionally, one or more actually dies, and, of course, drops off."

"What sort of people does it attack?"

"Oh, all sorts of people!"

"Then it's no use to us," said the officer promptly. "Tell us about ergotism, doctor. Ergot is a drug, isn't it? Men don't take it habitually, do they?"

"Not intentionally," I replied. "Ergot is a parasitic fungus which attacks the ears of rye, causing the disease of grain known as 'spurred rye.' People who eat bread made from 'spurred' grain become affected with chronic ergot poisoning. This happens in the countries where rye is the staple food, and extensive epidemics have occurred."

"But what are the effects of ergot poisoning?" the officer asked, rather eagerly.

"Primarily, it causes a contraction and, ultimately, obliteration of the small arteries, so that the blood supply is gradually reduced, and finally cut off altogether. Naturally, as in Raynaud's disease and in frostbite, it is the outlying parts of the body that suffer most. When the circulation is failing, the effects of its failure will appear first, and with most intensity, in the little toes, other things being equal."

"This is very interesting," said Mr. Renshaw, glancing at the superintendent, who was, however, deep in thought, "but I don't see how it helps to discover the murderer."

"I think it helps us very materially," I answered. "It is evident the person most likely to be frostbitten is a person living in a country with a very cold climate, and a person most likely to suffer from ergotism is one living in a country where rye is the staple food. But it happens that the countries where rye is eaten are also countries having a very cold climate — Russia and Poland, for instance."

The superintendent looked at me with strong approval. "The fellow's a Russian or a Pole or a Finn, or else he's a sailor," he announced. "Sailors often get frostbitten."

"He may be both," I said, and the superintendent again approved; but at this moment we arrived at the spot, over which a constable stood on guard.

One set of footprints led from a point on the river-bank towards the house, and these had been made by the boots of a man — medium-sized boots, but in no way distinctive, though every brad was visible in the impressions. The other set of prints led from the direction of the house to the point on the river-bank from which the other foot-prints started; and there was no doubt as to the absence of the little toe, for the impressions were so perfect that every fold and crease of the skin was visible even to the papillary ridges.

"We can't say for certain that both sets of prints are from the same man," the superintendent remarked, "but there can't be much doubt. The boots would have fitted the bare feet. I imagine he took off his boots to climb up the ivy, and when you disturbed him, he climbed down, picked them up, and legged it barefooted."

"You think then that he climbed the ivy and entered by the billiard-room window?" Mr. Renshaw asked.

"No, no, sir; he couldn't have done that with Gannet there. He entered by the landing window, tapped at the billiard room door, and, when Gannet opened it, he knocked the poor fellow down with a blow of the case-opener."

"No doubt you're right," said Mr. Renshaw; "and, if so, that favours the idea of a sailor. But he seems to have come from the river. Is there any sign of a boat?"

"Yes, sir; some sort of boat has been here. Looks like the long counter of a clinch-built sailing-boat, moored stern-on to the bank; but she must have been a queer-looking craft, and pretty easy to spot if we can find her."

He led us to the waterside where, at the point to which the two sets of footprints converged, the impression of the boat was plainly visible on the earth of the bank.

"Don't some of the Russian and Scandinavian vessels carry a canoe-shaped jolly-boat?" I said. "A keelless boat with a long beak at the stern?"

The superintendent looked down eagerly at the impression. "Yes! By Jove, sir, that's it!" he exclaimed. "What they call a 'pram' — a thing like half a banana. I must make inquiries of the harbour-master and see if there are any foreign craft in the port."

"And meanwhile," said I, "those footprints are precious. We ought to take plaster moulds of them. Is there any plaster of Paris in the house?"

"Yes," said Mr. Renshaw; "by a lucky chance we have just got in a supply to repair a ceiling. I'll send up for some at once."

A couple of bags of plaster with a large basin and a kitchen spoon were presently brought down, and I proceeded to mix the plaster with water and fill up the deep footprints with the creamy liquid.

"Wouldn't it be as well to take a mould of the boat, too?" I suggested, and, the superintendent approving, I poured a supply of liquid plaster on the impression on the bank.

While the plaster was setting firmly, I paid my morning visit to Mrs. Renshaw (who was now awake and quite free from pain); then, having taken up the moulds, appropriating a pair from the bare feet for my own use, I drove back into Lowestoft to make my report to the coroner.

Within an hour of my return I had finished the morning's business, and, was now free for an hour or two. Naturally, my steps strayed in the direction of the harbour, and, as I approached, my eye caught the tall masts of a brig that lay alongside the quay, discharging blocks of ice on to a flat cart. I strolled past the vessel and stooped to read the name on her wide, flat counter; and had just made out the words "Anna, Archangel," when I felt a light touch on my shoulder, and turned sharply to find the superintendent regarding me with a grim smile.

"I thought I should find you here, doctor," said he. "Looks as if we'd struck the right thing, doesn't it? But I don't see her pram anywhere, do you? Here, Johnny!" he continued, addressing a tow-haired seaman, "what's become of your pram?"

"Der bram haf gone to Oulton Broad."

"Oh," said the other significantly; "and where's the skipper?"

"Der schgibber haf gone to Oulton Broad, too," was the reply. "He schday ad der Atmiral Hotel."

"Oh," said the superintendent, still more significantly, "then I think we will go to Oulton Broad, eh, doctor?"

We set off at a brisk walk for the station. We had just taken our tickets and were proceeding up the platform, when we overtook Mr. Brewe.

"So you're off?" I said, as he greeted me with unnecessary effusiveness.

"Yes," he replied; "back into harness to-morrow." Then, with a side-glance at the superintendent: "Anything up?"

I told him briefly what had happened.

"Just my luck," he exclaimed, "to be leaving just when the sport is going to begin."

He gave me his card, and I was promising to look him up in town, when the guard blew his whistle and the superintendent dragged me into the carriage.

The landlord of the "Admiral" was standing at the door when we arrived, and he greeted the superintendent with respectful geniality: "Can I do anything for you?"

"Yes," said Bowles. "You've got a Russian skipper staying here, haven't you?"

"Yes, Captain Popoff. Came up yesterday in his pram."

"What's he doing here?"

"Got some business with the yacht-builders."

"Why did he come in the pram? Why didn't he walk, or take the train?"

"Brought a lot of gear in her — blocks and stuff — for the builders."

"Where was he last night — say, from twelve to four?"

"In bed, I reckon. He turned in about eleven and got up at six. Like to see him? He's in the coffee-room writing letters."

The officer nodded, and we were duly ushered into the room, where Captain Popoff sat at a table writing. Superintendent Bowles introduced himself, and the captain, with a shipmaster's curtness, demanded his business. Now Bowles was an intelligent man, and believed in direct and straightforward methods. Accordingly, he gave the captain a brief account of the robbery, and hinted at his suspicions.

"But what has this to do with me?" demanded Popoff, in excellent English and an indifferent temper; "you don't think I did it, do you?"

Bowles's answer was in the Scottish manner.

"Where was your pram last night?"

"Where I left it, I suppose."

"I should like to have a look at it," said Bowles, whereupon the skipper swept up his papers into the writing-case, and, inviting us to "come on, then," stumped out of the room.

The *Anna's* pram was floating alongside the landing-stage, and, as we approached, the captain eyed her critically. "Someone's been meddling with her," he said. "I made the painter fast with a clove-hitch; now it's made fast with a round turn and two half-hitches."

We stood in a row on the narrow stage, stooping over he little boat; and presently Bowles stepped into her, closely scrutinising the thwarts, the gunwale and the floor.

"Nothing to lay hold of here," he said discontentedly; "not a trace." Finally he lifted out the bottom-boards and groped in the crevices of the planking, and then, suddenly, he stood up with some tiny object between his finger and thumb. "What do you make of this?" he said, exhibiting his treasure to me in the palm of his hand. It was a small piece of wire, doubled sharply on itself and having the free ends curved backwards towards the doubled end, the whole thing being about the fifth of an inch long.

"Bit of brass wire," said the skipper. "Looks like part of a hook from a lady's dress."

"Not brass," said Bowles. "It's gold, yellow native gold. Part of a clasp, I should say."

He stepped up on to the stage and looked earnestly at the skipper, who returned a defiant stare.

"Well," he demanded, "do you think it's me?"

"I think it's someone from your ship."

"Would you know him if you saw him?" asked the captain.

"I should know his feet, if I saw them bare," was the reply.

Without a word, Popoff sat down on the landing-stage, and, tearing off his boots and socks, rolled over on his back and thrust his feet aloft towards the superintendent.

"Are those the feet?" he demanded aggressively.

A momentary glance showed that they were not, for both little toes were in full evidence, each enriched by a goodly corn.

"No, they're not," said Bowles, with a grin of vexation, "so there's nothing against you, captain."

"Very well," said Popoff: "then you come down and look over the brig."

As we approached the vessel, Popoff ran on ahead to roar out instructions to his men. The effect was magical. By the time we had descended the ladder, the entire crew, numbering eight, all told, was ranged along the deck, barefooted and with their trousers rolled up to the knees.

The superintendent and I, with the captain — himself barefooted — walked slowly down the line, beginning with the mate and ending with the "doctor," a pale and lanky youth who still grasped the potato that he had been peeling.

Then Bowles looked me blankly in the face.

"Well, I'm hanged!" said he. For a full complement of sixteen toes had scattered his hopes to the winds.

"Not here?" asked the captain sarcastically.

Bowles shook his head sadly, and as we retired up the ladder towards the grinning smack-boys, we were impelled by a *vis a turgo* of derisive howls from the deck.

And so this very promising clue petered out, leaving the police as much in the dark as ever. When, at the end of my week, I returned to town, I carried with me the plaster casts of a pair of bare feet, an electrotype facsimile of the little gold object — made by a local typefounder — and the earnest exhortation of Superintendent Bowles to "think over the matter and let him know if anything occurred to me."

Back in my rooms in London, I did think the matter over — frequently, but without result. In my walks abroad, in my visits to the hospital, at the restaurants where I lunched, and in the bed wherein I slept, the problem continually recurred to my mind.

And thus it happened that, on a certain day, when I was browsing, catalogue in hand, in an upper gallery of the Hunterian Museum, suddenly I halted with a start. On the shelf before me stood a jar, a huge oval jar containing two human feet.

It was not the mere presence of a pair of feet that caused my sudden excitement, nor was it their strange dusky colour, which might have been due to prolonged immersion in spirit. It was the fact that each of the feet was destitute of a little toe. Feverishly, I turned over the leaves of the catalogue until I found the number of the specimen, and then I read: "The feet of a Western African negro affected with ainhum. Both the little toes have separated. On the plantar surface of the right foot, between the great and second toes, is a mature chigger or sand-flea (*Pulex penetrans*) in its cyst, and both feet exhibit cicatrices of old cysts."

Ainhum! What the deuce was ainhum? I made straight for the library, where, taking a work on "Tropical Diseases" down from the shelf, I ran my eye down the index. Ah! Here it was. "Ainhum — A disease affecting the dark-skinned races, especially common in West Africa.... A furrow or constriction forms at the base of the little toe, and, gradually deepening, leaves the digit hanging by a narrow pedicle. This ultimately snaps and the toe drops off. Both little toes are commonly affected, and, much more rarely, the other toes may be attacked...."

I shut the book with a snap, and hurried away in an ecstasy of sudden enlightenment. The cast of the footprint, which I had frequently examined, showed a number of small scars at the bases of the toes, the possible origin of which had puzzled me not a little. Now I understood. They were chigger scars; and the footprint had been made not by a Russian or Pole, but almost certainly by a negro.

I was hurrying home to send off a letter that should rejoice the heart of Superintendent Bowles, when I suddenly bethought me that Brewe had been in Lowestoft for some time. Now, if there had been a negro in the neighbourhood, Brewe might have seen him, and might even be able to give us his name and description. It was worth trying, only, of course, I must approach the matter cautiously. Brewe had invited me to call on him, and, since his rooms were in Bedford Place, hard by, why not call now?

The resolution was no sooner formed than acted upon, and, twenty minutes later, I found myself following a faded page-boy up the broad staircase of the Bloomsbury boarding-house. Mr. Brewe received me with boisterous geniality, and for some time his flow of conversation prevented me from opening the subject which had brought me to his rooms. And then, on a sudden, I determined not to open it at all, for I had seen something that sent my thoughts flying in a new direction.

On my host's little finger, showing conspicuously against the dusky skin, was a ring — a very curious ring, of deep yellow native gold, ornamented with a raised pattern of some kind.

"That is rather a striking ring that you are wearing, Brewe," I said. "You didn't get that in England, I'll swear."

"Not much," laughed Brewe. "Your English jewellers are more sparing with their gold. This is the pure, native metal — made at Ogua — Cape Coast, as you call it — by a poor benighted African, from gold washed in a calabash from the surface soil. Look at it; it isn't a bad piece of work for a savage."

He handed it to me.

A very curious object it was, rude and clumsy in workmanship, and yet handsome and striking, displaying in its design the unerring decorative instinct of the barbaric workman. It was a flat band with raised edges, the space between which was filled with strange cabalistic figures.

"Is there any meaning in this design?"

"Yes," replied Brewe. "This is what is called a Zodiac ring; the figures are the signs of the Zodiac. They are not very correct, I imagine, but they form the traditional Cape Coast design."

I turned the ring thoughtfully in my fingers, trying to recognise the rudely executed signs, and then, suddenly I started, for the turning of the ring had brought into view a blank space from which one of the "signs" was missing. I looked at the spot more closely. Two tiny fragments of the missing figure struck up from the surface, but they gave no clue to its shape. Then I examined the adjacent characters; I had learnt the signs of the Zodiac once. Had I forgotten them?

The second character to the left of the space was a zigzag line — the conventional representation of water all the world over. That must be Aquarius. Then the character next to the blank space on the left was formed of two horizontal lines with looped ends, one above the other. They must be the two fishes — Pisces. I looked to the right of the space. The first character was a circle surmounted by a half-circle. Could that be the bull's head — Taurus? Yes, surly, for the next figure consisted of a pair of vertical lines, clearly the twins — Gemini.

Then the missing sign must be Aries — the Ram. Now, how was Aries represented? I cudgelled my brains for some moments, and then it came to me in a flash. Of course! It was a vertical line for the head with a downward curve on each side at the top to represent the horns. In fact, it was precisely like the little gold object that we had found in the pram.

I had a facsimile of that object in my card-case. If I could only get a chance–

Fortune — in the disguise of a seedy page-boy — knocked at the door. Brewe hurriedly excused himself, and I heard him run down the stairs. In an instant my card-case was open, the little metal object between my finger and thumb. A glance at it showed two tiny hollows corresponding to the two projecting fragments on the ring, and when I laid it in the vacant space, the two projections fitted snugly into the little recesses, and the Zodiac ring was complete.

"I'm awfully sorry," said Brewe, when he burst into the room a minute later, "but there's a man come to see me on business, and I can't very well put him off."

"Certainly not," I replied, rising, and handing him back the ring. "Besides, I only dropped in for a few minutes' chat."

"But you'll come and see me again?" he said, holding out his hand.

And as I shook it, feeling rather like Judas Iscariot, I mumbled inarticulately, and backed towards the door.

From Bedford Place I proceeded at a trot to Holborn Post-office, whence presently issued a telegram addressed to Superintendent Bowles, and worded thus:

"Believe I have found the man. Come to my rooms and bring all casts."

The incomplete chain of evidence was made perfect by the contents of J.K. Brewe's dispatch-box. Like many another amateur, Brewe had found it easier to commit a robbery than to dispose of the booty, and the entire "swag" — as Bowles called it — was recovered when he was arrested.

Bowles himself is now chief constable in an adjacent borough, and reveres me as the instrument of his promotion. As for Brewe, he reposed until lately under the flagstones of the narrow, barred passage in Newgate known as Birdcage Walk — excepting his feet, which, enshrined in a colossal glass jar, may be seen in the museum of St. Margaret's Hospital even unto this day.

The Mystery of Hoo Marsh

I T IS, I believe, impossible for a really intelligent person who is brought continuously into contact with any class of object to avoid developing an interest, and more or less specializing therein. I can even imagine a perfectly sane man becoming interested in postage stamps or Staffordshire figures if they should be persistently kept within his field of vision.

I mention the matter as explaining the rather odd interest in the natural history of the criminal of which I became conscious after some years spent in search for a particular offender.

I was in pursuit of the unknown, but identifiable, wretch, who had robbed me of my beloved wife by an unprovoked murder; and in that pursuit the criminal population of London passed in review before me by tens, by scores, in the little barber's shop in Whitechapel that I rented for the purpose.

And thus it was that my attention began to occupy itself with the affairs of Mr. Fritz Meyer and his friend, Hans Schneider.

It was a Thursday afternoon, usually a rather slack time with me, when a customer stalked into the empty shop, and, flinging himself into the operation chair, gruffly uttered the monosyllable, "Shave."

I had covered his face with lather, and had just taken up the razor, when the door opened quietly, and a small, shabby man entered and, catching up a newspaper, subsided into a chair and began to read.

My clients, I may mention, were mostly inveterate newspaper readers, and had a habit of holding the paper so that it screened their persons from the knees upwards; which was what the present visitor did; but as, from time to time, I glanced towards him, I caught a pair of beady eyes, just above the edge of the paper, scanning the customer in the chair with eager and inquisitive suspicion.

The operation finished, I laid aside the razor and whisked the cloth off my client. Instantly the beady eyes vanished behind the newspaper; the patient rose from the operating chair, and, standing before the mirror, carefully arranged his moustache, and put on his hat with scrupulous exactness; then, slapping down the fee on the marble washstand, he stalked out of the shop without a word.

As the door closed, the newspaper was lowered, and the little, shabby man stole noiselessly over to the operating chair.

"Know anything about that bloke, Mr. Vosper?" he asked.

I invested him in the mantle of his predecessor (Vosper was the *nomme de guerre* that I had had painted over the shop-front.)

"Nothing whatever, Mr. Towler," I replied.

Mr. Towler leered round at me admiringly.

"You never knows nothing, Mr. Vosper," said he.

"I mind my own business, Mr. Towler," I replied.

"You do so," he agreed. "The cops don't get much out of you, I guess."

Now this was perfectly true.

My quarrel with the criminal class was a personal one, and I did not choose to complicate matters by taking the police into my confidence; a fact which was recognised with deep appreciation by my clients.

"Not," Mr. Towler continued after a pause, "that I've git anything to say for coves like that one what's just gone out. These here anarchists is a pack of silly asses. What's the sense of burstin' a crib if you don't pouch nothin' out of it?"

"What makes you think that man is an anarchist?"

"Think!" exclaimed Towler. "I don't think, I know. J'ever go to Ikey Morganstein's restaurant? I do sometimes; and as sure as ever I goes there, I sees this chap, Meyer, and a fat old cove named Snider a-sittin' in the back parlour along of a whole bilin' of bloomin' foreigners, a-colloguin' and a-waggin' of their chins like Madame Twoswords let loose."

Mr. Towler's reasoning was by no means conclusive, nor had I any use for anarchists. Still, I was not unwilling to collect one or two specimens of this curious type for my museum; for, as I have said, I had gradually become somewhat of a criminal fancier, and all types were of more or less interest. But were Mr. Meyer and his friends really anarchists?

It was none of my business, yet a certain spirit of mischief impelled me to look into the matter.

Now it happened that a short time previously I had met with a quite interesting book on the chemistry of high explosives, and another on the construction of submarine mines; it also happened that I had fitted up one of my superfluous rooms as a little workshop in which I could beguile the tedium of odd intervals of leisure by practising the fascinating art of turnery.

These were disconnected and irrelevant circumstances, but they occurred to me among many others when I decided to embark on a preliminary investigation.

I began by turning upon my lathe the parts of one or two small percussion detonators from the drawings in the book on mines, and these, when I had finished them, I bestowed in my trousers' pocket along with my small change. The treatise on mines I placed on a shelf in the shop, with its title towards the wall, and the hand-book on explosives, when I was not studying it, I kept in the little shop-parlour ready for use.

It was some three or four days later when an opportunity occurred for me to make the first tentative move. Glancing over the top of the window screen, I perceived Mr. Meyer and his crony, Mr. Schneider, slowly bearing down on the shop. Instantly I darted into the parlour, and, putting on my spectacles, snatched up the book on explosives, opening it at a place which I had marked with a sheet of paper, whereon I had written a chaotic mass of grouped figures in imitation of a secret cypher.

The clan of the bell announced the opening of the shopdoor. I peered through the crack of the parlour door, and, having ascertained that the newcomers were, indeed, my Teutonic friends, I dallied awhile to allow them to develop a certain degree of impatience; and then when they began, with one accord, to stamp and bang their sticks on the floor, I dashed out with the open book in my hand.

"Vy de teffel do you keep us vaiting?" Mr. Meyer demanded, dropping heavily into the operating chair.

I apologized confusedly, and, laying my book on top of the other on the shelf, but with its title outwards, began to fill a mug with hot water. As I did so I kept a furtive watch on my two customers, and was gratified to observe that both of them glanced at the book, turning their heads slightly on one side and more readily to read the title. Having filled the mug, I moved quickly to the shelf, and turned the top book over so that its title was hidden.

Then I proceeded to lather Mr. Meyer's face, keeping, however, an attentive eye upon his companions.

Mr. Schneider, though a typical German, was very unlike his friend, the lean and angular Meyer. Stout, burly, with iron-grey hair and moustache, there was about him a certain gruff, Bismarckian joviality in which hitherto the gruffness had greatly predominated. It was evident that the book had engaged his serious attention, for as he sat with a cogitative scowl on his grim, deeply-lined face, I saw his eyes wander towards it repeatedly, and at length, his curiosity overcoming his good manners — it must have been a very unequal contest — he stepped quietly across the shop, and, taking the two books from the shelf, retired to his chair. I saw him turn over the leaves of both with raised eyebrows, and run an inquisitive eye over the meaningless groups of figures on my bookmark.

After poring over these hieroglyphics for a minute or two, and, as I can confidently say, without being able to make anything of them, he restored the books to the shelf, and laughed softly.

"Why, Mr. Vosper," he exclaimed in excellent English, "I did not know that you were a man so dangerous! Is it that you will blow us all up, or have you some plan for taking off whiskers with melinite?"

I mumbled some incoherent explanation, and as at this moment Mr. Meyer, having been duly sponged and powdered, rose from his chair and tendered me a shilling, I proceeded to execute the next move.

Thrusting my hand into my pocket, I brought it out hastily, filled with small change and the little brass pieces of the detonators; the whole of which I contrived to let fall, so that pence, shillings, flanges, washers, and spindles rolled indiscriminately about the floor.

Mr. Schneider was most polite. Regardless of his weight and rotundity, he was down on his hands and knees in a moment, gathering up sixpences and detonators — especially detonators — in the most delightfully helpful manner; and even the sour-visaged Meyer did not disdain to come to my assistance. I thanked them both effusively as I took the last of the brass turnings from Meyer's hands.

"It is nothing," said Mr. Schneider, with a note of geniality which was new to me, "but I am only wondering what these strange little objects may be. You are not making a mine to blow us all up, Mr. Vosper?"

I stammered out an explanation to the effect that I was engaged in making a model engine; an explanation to which they both listened gravely, though I saw them exchange a quick glance.

The ice was broken with a vengeance. Schneider's affability was so extreme that he received the shaving-brush in his mouth twice while he was being lathered, and nearly lost the tip of his nose during the subsequent operation.

And, meanwhile, Mr. Meyer sat poring over my dummy cypher, with the naïvest curiosity and a portentous frown.

I continued with some difficulty to traverse the extensive territory of the Schneiderian countenance, with appropriate pauses for smiles and facetiæ, and secretly speculated on he next development. Its nature was much as I had anticipated. As Mr. Schneider rose from the chair he held out a shovel-like hand.

"You are a clever man, Mr. Vosper; you are thoughtful; you have *geist*. I should like to talk with you of these so interesting matters. Will you not drink a glass of beer with us at Morganstein's Restaurant?"

I began mumbling to excuse myself, urging that my business gave me very little leisure. But Schneider would listen to no refusal, and, when he and his friend had departed, it was with my promise to join them that very evening as soon as I had shut my shop.

Morganstein's Restaurant was pleasantly situated in the Mile End Road, at the corner of a narrow by-street. Various inscriptions in Yiddish were painted on the plate-glass windows, through which astonished wayfarers from the West could obtain a view of a picturesque collection of objects, which at the first glance suggested a miscellaneous gleaning from the pathological shelves of the Hunterian Museum, but were in reality articles of food.

I was evidently expected, for the white-aproned shopman, without remark, opened the parlour door, and ushered me into the Holy of Holies.

It was an unexpectedly large apartment containing a long able, around which some dozen men were seated. As I entered Schneider rose at the head of the table, and, greeting me effusively, inducted me into an empty chair at his side, hanging my hat on a peg behind me.

I noticed that the company viewed me furtively and a little suspiciously, and that my arrival had apparently put a stop to the conversation. The awkward silence, however, was almost immediately broken by the tactful Schneider.

"You shall not be afraid, my friends," said he, "of the terrible Mr. Vosper. He comes to drink a glass of beer with us, not to blow us into eternity. Is it not so, Herr Vosper? You have no bombs in your pockets, for instance."

"Bombs!" I repeated. "What should I be doing with bombs?"

"*Ach!*" said Schneider, "that is what I would like to know. But you shall not mind our little jokes; you shall drink some beer with us, or, perhaps, some Rhine wine?"

It was evident that my fame had preceded me, that I had been introduced as a man of mystery connected with the diabolical industry of bomb production. The conversation, mainly carried on in excellent English, flitted about from subject to subject, but always tended to come back to that of explosives.

Meanwhile, I continued stolidly to consume some Hunterian delicacies and lower the level in the wine-bottle, maintaining profound taciturnity and a profession of total ignorance on the subject of bombs, explosives, and other like matters.

But yet I was not too taciturn. Once or twice I allowed myself to be taken off my guard, and to let fall some technical phrase which I saw was noted with eager interest by the company.

I am not easily affected by alcohol, nor was there any reason for avoiding its effects. The more indiscreet I should be, the better my plan would work. But, as a matter of fact, I was not indiscreet at all. The effect of the unwonted stimulant was merely to beget a cheerful garrulousness, which I freely encouraged, and a spirit of humorous mischief.

In short, under cover of simulated vinous exaltation, I disgorged on the company as much of my recent reading as I could remember, expressed with the utmost technicality and confusion of language at my command.

My friends were deeply impressed, as I could judge by the profound attention with which they listened, and it was equally evident to me that none of them had any theoretical knowledge either if chemistry or mechanism. As to my hosts, the genial Schneider and saturnine Meyer, they were so pleased with me that they insisted on seeing me home.

From this time forward my shop was haunted, not only by Meyer and Schneider, but by others of the company which I had met at Morganstein's, and, though I maintained the most taciturn and unresponsive attitude, I had no difficulty in gathering what it was that they wanted of me.

For some reason which was of no interest to me, these rascals wished to get possession of a supply of bombs or infernal machines of some kind, and they wished to use me as a catspaw.

It was pretty plainly intimated that, if I would agree to manufacture and store these commodities until they were needed, I could be assured of my private satisfaction, and liberal payment to boot.

These proposals gave me abundant food for thought. Of course, I could not be in any way a party to this villainy; but yet, I seemed to perceive the chance of a haul on a scale that had been beyond my wildest dreams.

I had met fifteen of these wretches, and it appeared that they were ready to swim into my net with but the gentlest guidance. If only I could devise a net large enough to hold them, surely I should be deserving of a place amongst the greatest philanthropists of all time.

I gave the matter a good deal of consideration, but, as often happens, the real inspiration came quite by chance. I was glancing over one of the many papers that I provided for my clients, when my eye was caught by an advertisement.

It ran thus:

"Small Factory to Let on the Hoo Marshes, near Chatham, with a certain amount of Plant, including a small Motor Pump. The Premises, somewhat out of repair, lately used as a bottle factory, will be let, together with convenient landing-stage for barges, at a low rent. — Apply J. Stodder, High Street, Rochester."

I laid the paper down and reflected profoundly.

No detailed scheme presented itself, but that was of little consequence. A general plan is the really important thing, and the advertisement had given me a starting-point for further consideration.

My first proceeding was to make arrangements with an excessively discreet gentleman of the name of Salaman, who was nominally a ship chandler and marine store dealer, to receive letters for me and, if necessary, to furnish references. Next, I contracted with a fellow-barber, named Levinstein, for the use of his assistant, when required, to act as *locum tenens.*

Then, having made these arrangements, I sallied forth one morning, leaving my substitute in possession, and took the train for Rochester.

There I made my way along the high Street to an ironmonger's shop, and, having read on the fascia thereof the inscription "J. Stodder," I entered boldly, and nearly fell into the arms of a small, grey-bearded man with a very bald head and very large spectacles.

"Is Mr. Stodder at home?" I inquired.

"Very much at home, thank you," the little man replied, with a bright smile, "and entirely at your service."

"I've come to inquire about those factory premises that you advertise," said I, upon which another, and yet brighter, smile led me to infer that I was the only applicant.

"What sort of business were you thinking of carrying on?" he asked.

"Well," I replied, "it's just an experimental effort. I have devised a new kind of medicine bottle, which I have protected temporarily, and I want to see if it is possible to get it on the market."

"Then," exclaimed Mr. Stodder, grasping at the lapel of my coat, "the place will suit you down to the ground. You'll hardly want any new plant at all."

"I haven't much capital," I began hesitating, but he interrupted me with a grin.

"Neither have I. Had the confounded place on my hands for the last eighteen months, so I'm prepared to let you down easily. You'd like to see the place, I suppose?"

I replied that I should, whereupon he offered to conduct me thither as soon as he had handed over the shop to his assistant.

We had travelled nearly three miles along a level road running parallel to the river, when I perceived, away on our right, a sort of peninsula of marshy land on which were two groups of ruinous buildings, about a quarter of a mile apart.

Mr. Stodder pointed out the farther of these as the eligible premises that we were about to visit, and shortly afterwards we turned off on to a narrow track that led out across the marshes.

The building, as we approached it, took on a somewhat less ruinous aspect, but as a set-off, extensive puddles of water came into view.

Across these we made our way by means of bricks and other objects which had been laid down as stepping-stones.

"This water isn't of any consequence," said Mr. Stodder, as he inserted a key into the main door. "An hour's pumping will clear it all off, and then the windmill would keep the place dry in ordinary weather. Mind how you come."

The warning was by no means unnecessary, for as my friend opened the door, I saw that the whole of the ground floor was under water.

We entered cautiously, and by means of a number of floating planks, on which we trod like wading birds, explored the lower part of the premises.

"The place must be very damp even when it is pumped out," I remarked.

"Not at all," he replied. "There's a nine-foot sump with drainage-pipes leading into it. I'll show you."

He unlocked the door leading into a small brick chamber, and, pushing in a couple of massive planks, preceded me with extreme caution.

"Mind you don't fall overboard," said he, as I crept along the half-submerged planks. "That's the sump."

I looked down through the water, and by the dim light saw, in the middle of the brick floor, what looked like the mouth of a well, some three feet across.

"There," said Mr. Stodder, "that's nine feet deep, and the suction pipes of the windmill and the pump both go to the bottom, so when she's pumped out, you've got nine feet of well-drained soil under the building."

We came out of the sump chamber, locking it after us, and made a tour of the rest of the premises, which I examined carefully, but need not describe in detail. We explored the workrooms and offices on the upper floor, and we examined the small chimney-shaft, and the artesian well in the yard.

Finally we overhauled the little engine that worked the pump.

"I see," said I, glancing at a pile of empty tins, "that it's a petrol engine."

"Yes," he replied. "Ought to have been paraffin, but it's of no consequence. You don't often want the pump when the windmill's going. Shall we look at the landing-stage?"

I assented, and we walked down the wooden causeway to the little jetty that overhung the mud; and this brought our inspection to an end.

"Well," said Mr. Stodder, as we walked back and locked up, "what do you think of the place?"

"I think it will do," I replied, "if the rent isn't too high."

"You needn't be afraid," said he. "I should be glad enough of a tenant on almost any terms, if it was only for the chance of getting the place burnt down."

"Why? Do you want it burnt down?" I asked.

"Well," he answered, with a grin, "it's been a dead loss to me up to the present, so a trifle of insurance money would come in handy. Not that I am suggesting –"

"No, no," I said, "of course not. By the way, is this other place yours?"

As I spoke, we stopped to survey the second group of buildings, which were ruins pure and simple.

"Yes, that's mine, too," he replied. "P'raps you'd like to take it along with the other. It's a nice residential property," he added, with a smile.

He pointed to the remains of a large, square chimney-shaft, which had been fitted with a roof, a chimney-stack, and a door at the base.

"I've never seen a window in a chimney-shaft before," I remarked.

"Nor have I," he answered. "The top of this one fell down, and the foreman of he other place fitted it up as a residence. Come and have a look at it."

He unlocked the door with a key from his bunch, and we entered the eccentric residence.

The lower part, which was quite dark, save for the light that came in by the door, communicated with the single room above by a rickety ladder, which we ascended carefully until we reached a trap-door. Pushing this up, we gained admittance to a smallish, square room furnished with a single window, a ship's cabin stove, a table, a chair, and a sleeping-bunk.

"Not so bad as you'd think," said Mr. Stodder, glancing round with a cheerful smile. "Airy situation, quiet neighbourhood, and a charming view from the window."

"Yes," I agreed, as we scrambled down the ladder, "a solitary man might do worse, at any rate, for temporary quarter. So I think we'll include this in the bargain."

Mr. Stodder smiled and nodded, and then proceeded to the terms of that bargain.

"You'd like a pretty long lease," he began hopefully.

"Later, perhaps," I replied, "not now. This is an experiment, and I haven't much capital. If I can't sell my goods I shall have to shut up. What do you say to a lump sum down for a six month's trial?"

He would sooner have had a lease, naturally, but he was ready to agree to anything. In the end it was arranged that he should get the water pumped out and the windmill in working order, and that I should come down in a week's time for another inspection.

As I travelled back to the town, my ideas began slowly to crystallise. No settled plan, indeed, had yet shaped itself, but, as I sat thinking and dreamily watching the fields and hedgerows skim past the carriage window, certain mental pictures recurred with suggestive persistency, and seemed by degrees to connect themselves.

After this, events began to move more rapidly. My absence from the shop had come to the notice of my friends, Meyer and Schneider, and I found them waiting there when I returned.

As I had been at some plains to make myself presentable, I think those gentlemen were somewhat impressed by my appearance and its incongruity with my position as a Whitechapel barber. During the next few days their overtures were renewed in a more direct form, and though I still disclaimed all knowledge of the manufacture of bombs or explosives, an occasional judicious lapse of discretion drew them by degrees farther into the net.

On the day fixed, after due notice to Mr. Levinstein, I kept my appointment with Mr. Stodder, who met me at Strood, and we made our way as before to the factory. Its appearance was now much improved. After a brief look round, I expressed myself satisfied and proposed that I should come down in yet another week, pay the rent in advance, take a receipt, and assume possession, to which my very free and easy friend smilingly agreed without so much as asking my name and address.

"And, by the way," said I, "if you could have that room in the Tower of Silence made habitable, I could put up there while the factory is being fitted, and you could let me know what you have spent."

To this also he agreed, with a grin at the magniloquent title that I had bestowed on the ruined shaft, and we started off briskly towards Strood.

As we had crossed the marshes from the factory, I had observed in the distance two men advancing in our direction, but they suddenly disappeared, and though as we passed the place I scanned the hedgerows closely, no trace of them was to be seen. At Strood Station, where Mr. Stodder left me with a valedictory handshake, I found that I had three-quarters of an hour to wait for a train, for which I was not altogether sorry, since it gave me the opportunity of verifying a suspicion which those two vanishing figures had aroused. But the time passed and the train arrived without bringing any such verification; and I had just seated myself in an empty first-class compartment, deciding that I must have been mistaken, when confirmation of my suspicions appeared at the open door — a good deal out of breath and very red in the face.

"Ah, my dear friend, Mr. Vosper!" gasped Schneider, as he tumbled into the carriage, followed by Mr. Meyer, "but you are such an active man!"

Meyer joined in impatiently:

"Vot is ze good of zese lies, Mr. Fosper? Ve haf found you out."

"*Nein*, my friend," interposed Schneider, "we have found him at home. Now we are in his confidence, so we can talk business."

He accordingly proceeded to talk business, and I, assuming the attitude of having been unmasked, listened and even assented with pretended reluctance.

Briefly, Mr. Schneider's proposal amounted to this:

That I should, at my own risk, manufacture and store until wanted, some two dozen floating mines, so disguised as to be capable of being transported without arousing suspicion; that I should submit drawings and a small experimental working model; on which I should receive fifty pounds on account, a further hundred to be paid on the delivery of the whole consignment at a date to be fixed hereafter.

I made a show of demurring strongly, but eventually allowed my opposition to be borne down my Mr. Schneider.

"Your objections, my friend," said he, "are foolish. You desire satisfaction. You will get it — through us, and we shall pay you in addition. You cannot refuse. You have a bomb factory, and it would be so unpleasant if the police should get information and call to inspect your wares. Is it not so?"

I admitted gloomily that it was, and so the bargain was clinched.

I fell to work on the carrying out of my contract without delay, in order that I might earn the advance payment before I again visited Strood, for it happened that the sum, fifty pounds, was exactly what I wanted to pay Mr. Stodder — forty-five pounds rent, and five pounds for fittings and sundries — and the payment of this without drawing a cheque on my bank would extricate me from the only difficulty that I foresaw.

Having provided myself with the simple materials, I proceeded on the following day to manufacture a small quantity of blasting gelatine, a process that was simple enough and fairly free from danger on so small a scale.

And while I worked I turned over the mechanical part of the problem.

The mines had to be efficient and suitable in shape, and yet innocent in appearance. At first, this combination of qualities looked rather impossible, but here again my vivid mental picture of the factory furnished inspiration. The stack of empty petrol tins in the store rose before my mind's eye, and the problem was solved.

Nothing could be more innocent in appearance than a petrol tin, and though its rectangular shape was quite unsuitable, it would be an easy matter to bring it to the required circular section by a cage of wire or wooden hoops. For the rest, the friction tube could be inserted into the mouth of the tin, and the rotating star attached to the stopper.

It looked a perfectly efficient design, and, as appearances were all that was aimed at, that was sufficient.

I made a set of neat drawings in plan, elevation, and section; then, with a two-ounce tobacco tin, I constructed a miniature model loaded with a couple of drachms of blasting gelatine and furnished with a little friction tube and a four armed star which fitted on the spindle-square.

My friends were delighted with the drawings and eager to try the experimental model, to which end a select committee accompanied me with it, early on the following morning, to a remote part of Hackney Marshes. Arrived there, we buried it in the turf and, having fixed on the star, attached to one of the arms the end of a reel of carpet thread.

Then we retired to a discreet distance, paying out the thread as we went until we were able to shelter behind a tree. The slack of the thread having been cautiously drawn in, I gave a sharp twitch. Instantly there followed a ringing report and a little cloud of earth flew up from the neighbourhood of the mine.

My clients were jubilant, and still more so when on returning to the place where the mine had been we found a deepish, symmetrical crater upwards of three feet across.

"My friend," exclaimed Schneider shaking my hand ecstatically, "you are a genius! I shall pay you your advance this very moment, and you shall proceed immediately to make us the rest of these pretty toys."

From an obese leather wallet he extracted a cheque, and having written his name on the back of it with a fountain pen handed it to me.

I glanced at it, and, having noted that it was drawn on the London Branch of the Innsbruck Bank to the order of Herr Hans Schneider, slipped it into my pocket with even more satisfaction than my friends can have guessed, for it not only solved my difficulty, but offered me a fresh inspiration.

From that time forward, Mr. Levinstein's assistant held exclusive possession of my shop. I had something better to do now than to shave and cut hair.

My new scheme was shaping itself out with such rapidity that only a few trivial details remained, and as its completeness grew so did my interest and enthusiasm. A couple of days later I revisited Rochester, and having handed to Mr. Stodder the ill-gotten cheque received in exchange the document assigning to Herr Schneider the exclusive possession and enjoyment of all that messuage and premises known as and being the Hoo Marsh Factory, together with the ruined chimney shaft, which document Mr. Stodder was kind enough to secure for me in his excellent iron safe.

Then followed a period of feverish activity. In the first place I ordered a quantity of coal and coke and a cartload of broken glass, which I did not want, and a few carboys of sulphuric and nitric acid and acetone, together with a hundredweight of cotton wool, which I did.

I also provided myself with a coast-guard's telescope, a bicycle, and a small wireless installation, complete with transmitter and receiver, and a relay battery; and when all these commodities had been duly delivered at the factory I fell to work.

My proceedings were strictly methodical. Each day I manufactured some ten pounds of blasting gelatine, and, having made it up in a paper parcel. I lowered it carefully to the bottom of the sump. Then I filled a petrol tin with dry sawdust, and having carefully fitted it up with a dummy friction tube, removable cage of hoops and star, and a shackle for the mooring rope, placed it in one of the empty stores. This was my daily task. In the intervals of work, I busied myself in making my tower residence habitable, cycled up daily to Strood and Rochester for provisions, which I hoisted up to my rooms by means of a rope rove through a pulley that my predecessor had fixed above the window, apparently for this purpose, and planned out the erection of the wireless apparatus.

As it was finally set up, the arrangement was this: The transmitter was fixed opposite the open window of the tower, with the reflector placed so as to throw the beam on the window of the factory counting-house; while in the counting-room the other mirror was placed so as to catch the beam and focus it on the receiver.

With the receiver was connected a powerful relay battery, the use of which will appear later.

So my labours proceeded day by day for a fortnight. It was a restful and peaceful interlude. I enjoyed the quiet and solitude of the wide and lonely marshes, so refreshing after the crowded squalor of Whitechapel, and I looked with gratification on the packages of blasting gelatine which gradually accumulated in the sump.

On the fifteenth day I received a letter from Schneider, saying that a select committee would call on the morrow to inspect the work and, if possible, to fix a date for the removal of the mines.

Accordingly, on the following day, Schneider and Meyer made their appearance at the factory in company with three other rascals, and were duly shown round the works. I had thoughtfully provided the possibility of a few trifling mishaps — carefully limited, however, as to their effects — with a view to creating an appropriate atmosphere and a suitable mental state; and some of them were quite effective. A few drops of nitro-glycerine, for instance, smeared on the concrete floor nearly took the sole off the boot of a bearded Teuton named Schnitzler, whose nerves were so shattered thereby that he hastily grabbed up a handful of loose gun cotton — which I suppose he mistook for cotton wool — to wipe the sweat from his face; with the result that (as he happened to be smoking a cigarette at the time) he was a bearded Teuton no longer.

These little accidents produced an excellent effect.

When I opened the store containing the formidable array of dummy mines the conspirators held their breath, and glanced wistfully towards the factory gate. With one exception. A truculent Prussian, named Ochsenbein, showed a slight tendency to be troublesome. First, he insisted on my fitting up one of the mines for action, and fixing on the star of whiskers, which was well enough. But when he made as if he would remove the stopper to inspect the contents I uttered a yell of terror and flew out on to the marshes, where I was speedily joined by my guests.

"You have done very well, my friend, Vosper," said Schneider, wiping his face his face with a large spotted handkerchief, "we are quite satisfied. Now we can make the other arrangements, and perhaps we can talk better out here in the fresh air."

He linked his arm in mine, and led me gently along the path, away from the neighbourhood of the factory.

The arrangements that he proposed were quite simple. In a week's time, at eight o'clock in the morning, the entire gang would appear at the factory, leaving a small motor van on the road. Each man would then take a petrol tin, with the hoops and stars appertaining to it, and carry it to the van, when the whole body would make off for an unstated destination. As this had been the original arrangement, the date only having been left open, I agreed, with profound satisfaction and relief that the plan had not been altered.

"Very well, Mr. Schneider," said I, "The mines shall all be ready by that date. But you had better not be seen in a crowd near the factory. Come one at a time and ge out of sight at once. If I should not be able to be there punctually, I will leave the factory gate unlocked and I will place some refreshment in the large workroom next to the counting-house, where your friends had better wait for me. But I shall try to be there myself."

"Do you not then live in the factory?" Schneider asked.

"Bless you, no!" I exclaimed. "What! Sleep over two dozen mines? No, my friend, I have a quiet little retreat well out of range."

Schneider nodded. "*Ach!*" said he, "but you will try to meet us punctually?" And when I had made the promise, with a good conscience, he continued, drawing me apart form the others:

"There is one other little matter, Herr Vosper. When did you pay my cheque into your Bank?"

"I didn't pay it in at all," I replied. "I handed it to my landlord for the rent. He thinks it's my cheque."

"You mean that he thinks you're Hans Schneider?"

"He's quite sure of it," I replied, with a smile.

Schneider grinned sourly and remarked:

"You are a funny dog, Herr Vosper, but you are a deep dog, too. But I do not like this. My cheque has not been paid in yet, and I do not like my cheques drifting about. Who is your landlord?"

I gave him Mr. Stodder's name and address.

These he carefully noted, and then, rejecting the offer of rest and refreshment in the factory, he departed with his friends in the direction of Strood.

The days flew by in a whirl of joyful expectation, and at length the last day's work drew to a close. The sump was more than half full of the deadly explosive; the raw material was used up to the last ounce; and the output of the day's labour lay in my workroom in the form of a hugh lump of the plastic gelatine and a bucketful of superfluous nitro-glycerine.

Now came a slight deviation from the ordinary routine. First, I went up into the counting-house, which was immediately over the sump chamber, and, boring a hole through the floor, led down through it the two wires that were connected with the relay battery and the coherer of the wireless receiver. These I attached to an electric detonator, which I buried in the substance of the mass of blasting gelatine, and, making the whole up into a paper parcel, lowered it down carefully into the sump.

Then, I took the bucket of nitro-glycerine and very carefully poured it over the heap of packages in the well-like cavity, and, leaving the dripping bucket on the brink, I went out and securely locked the door of the chamber.

The finishing touch was put on in the large workroom next to the counting-house, where I set out invitingly a couple of dozen bottles of beer and a substantial lunch, the materials for which had been delivered at the factory earlier in the day.

This done, I went out, and, locking up the factory for the last time, betook myself to the Tower of Silence.

It was long before I fell asleep that night. With the setting of the sun, a breeze had arisen which grew rapidly in strength until, long before midnight, half a gale was roaring down the river valley and howling around my solitary refuge. The tower rocked alarmingly; and now I bethought me of a wide crack that I had noticed in the brick work near the base. It would be a wretched anti-climax if the crazy tower should be blown down during the night, burying me in its débris.

The wind, however, died away and the morning was calm and sunny; but the boisterous night had given me a useful hint. My intention had been to sit by the open window and at the appropriate moment to press down the Morse key of the wireless apparatus.. Now I saw that this would never do. The key would have to be operated from some safe place outside the tower; and as I brewed my morning tea, I employed myself in thinking out a simple and effective plan.

It was not a difficult problem. Among the factory stores, I remembered having seen a large ball of stout Manila twine and a number of iron screw-eyes. With these I thought I could make the necessary arrangements, and determined to bring them back with me when I went to unlock the factory gate. And this I did. Having made a tour of inspection round the factory, securely locking the counting-house and the sump chamber, I put the twine and screw-eyes in my pocket, and adding to them a small tin of tallow, made my way back to the tower.

It was now seven o'clock; time for me to make my final preparations. I began by screwing an eye into the floor immediately under the key and another close to the opening of the trap; then, cutting off a long length of twine, I tied one end to the key and passed the other through the two eyes, greasing the string thoroughly with tallow at the rubbing parts. For safety's sake I placed a double piece of blotting paper between the contact points of the key, so that I could try how the appliance worked. Next I opened the trap, dropped down the end of the string, and, descending to the ground, fixed another well-greased screw eye into the side of the ladder, and passed the string through it. It was now possible to stand well outside the tower, and by pulling the string through the open door to depress the key.

Everything was now ready, and, indeed, none too soon. For as I stood at the door and glanced back towards Strood, I was aware of a little party of men in the far distance advancing along the road.

I shut the door, and, ascending to the room above, took the blotting paper from between the points of the key, and seated myself at the open window with the telescope at my side.

Some twenty minutes passed before the men came into view from the window — which was on the opposite side of the tower to the door.

As soon as the little group appeared I focused my telescope on it, and recognised at once five of the members of the gang, including the inquisitive Ochsenbein. I watched them turn off along the marshes, cautiously approach the factory, and disappear at last through the gate.

A minute or two later another party came into sight — Schnitzler and three of his friends this time — to be followed quite shortly by yet another group.

And so my friends passed along the road, small in the distance but plain in the field of my telescope, until thirteen out of the fifteen were safely within the factory walls.

But still my little flock lacked two of its sheep, and they were bell-weathers, too. Neither Schneider nor Meyer had yet put in an appearance. I waited a minute longer, and then, beginning to grow uneasy — for delay might spoil all — I quickly descended the ladder, and, opening the door, looked out. It was lucky that I did so, for the first object that my eyes lighted on were my friends, Meyer and Schneider, bearing down upon the tower, and already but a hundred yards distant. Apparently they had discovered my retreat, and had come to fetch me; and something in their appearance suggested that they were coming in no friendly spirit. I looked steadily into their sullen faces, and instantly decided that strategy must give way to tactics. My plans would have to be modified. Closing the door, I shot the rickety bolt and scrambled up the ladder, taking the string up with me.

For a moment or two I was somewhat at a loss, but a peremptory thumping at the door and a glance at the open trap gave me the inspiration for my next move. I let down the trap, and quickly passing the string through the massive ring-bolt by which it was lifted, drew the string as tight as I dared and tied it securely to the ring.

And, meanwhile, the thumping below grew louder and developed into heavy battering. But everything was ready now. The slightest attempt to raise the trap from below would tighten the string and bring the contact points of the key together. Then from the reflector would dart forth a directed beam of aerial waves to impinge upon the second reflector in the counting-house and focus upon the receiver; the metallic grains of the coherer would fly together, admitting the powerful current from the relay battery down the wires to the detonator in the sump, and then —

The battering on the crazy door was doing its work. Loud creakings and an ominous sound of cracking woodwork told me that it was time for me to be gone.

Stepping to the open window, I grasped the two ropes that hung from the pulley, and, climbing out, prepared to let myself down. At that moment a bursting sound from below told me that the door had yielded.

Instantly I slid off the window-sill, and, letting one of the ropes slip quickly through my fingers, slid down the face of the tower.

As I reached the ground I sprang aside to get clear, keeping my eyes fixed on the factory. And even as I looked the catastrophe came. In an instant the factory walls were rent by a network of cracks, there was a flash of violet light from within, and then the factory was not, but in its place, a great, balloon-like cloud of white smoke and dust with a halo of flying fragments.

I gazed at it with joyful fascination, and was still gazing when there came a sound like the single stroke of a titanic drum, and I found myself lying on my back among the coarse grass. A moment later a strange shattering crash that shook the ground whereon I lay, and after that all was still save for a patter of fragments falling afar off.

I uncovered my face, and dislodging a couple of bricks that had rolled on to me, sat up and looked about. The factory had vanished, and the great, white cloud sailed slowly across the marshes towards the river. And my late residence? That was gone, too, and an elongated heap of bricks showed whither it had gone. I rose to my feet and walked over to the scattered heap. A battered telescope, a tea-kettle and a few splintered articles of furniture were all that remained of my late home. But my guests were there too. Mr. Meyer, with his head set at an unusual angle, was the first who came into view, stark and still among the rubbish; and then I came on the jovial Schneider — at least, I assumed that it was he, though the solid mass of brickwork that had fallen on his head threw the onus of identification on the contents of his pockets. And so my fifteen sheep were all safely gathered into the fold whereunto it would be well if all other sheep of a similar breed could be in like manner conducted.

That same night, I relieved Mr. Levinstein's assistant; and as I lathered the countenance of a notorious nark, with the tail of my eye I could read on the reverse of the paper behind which my friend, Mr. Towler, had entrenched himself, a scare head-line that announced a mysterious explosion near Rochester.

And that was the last that I ever heard of the affair.

The Mystery of the
Seven Banana Skins

O N A fine afternoon in April, 1915, Mr. Potter Higham walked thoughtfully up Fleet Street, taking an occasional glance at a sheaf of papers that he held in his hand. His profound cogitations and the pencilled notes on the papers that he held both related to a very important event looming in the immediate future — the inaugural meeting of the British Industries Defence League, which was to take place in less than an hour's time at Number 40 Bolt Court.

This meeting meant a great deal to Mr. Potter Higham. As chairman of the Amalgamated Mechanical Doll Manufacturers, he had long been harassed by the activities of the iniquitous German, who not only preceded in dumping his mechanical dolls on the English market at a price far below that at which the A.M.D.M. could produce them, but to this outrageous injury added the still more outrageous result of making a measurably superior doll to that turned out by the A.M.D.M.

But the day of reckoning was at hand. The war which to so many was to bring ruin, resentment and desolation, was, for Mr. Potter Higham and his shareholders, a heaven-sent blessing. Whatever might happen to the German in the field, he was going to be ousted from British commerce, and his exit would usher in a golden dawn for the A.M.D.M. Thenceforth they would be free to make their dolls as badly as they pleased and sell them at famine prices, secure from the competition of the grovelling Teuton. It was a glorious prospect.

Thus, with his mental vision fixed ecstatically on a Promised Land of unlimited profits and his material eyes peering over the top of the typed agenda of the meeting, he turned into Bolt Court, and headed for number 40. He knew the way well, and the foolscap sheet, while it hid the ground, allowed him to see the number over the doorway. Still preoccupied with his

75

golden visions, he was in the act of stepping into the entry when his foot encountered something, and he tripped and fell on a body which was lying just within the portal. The angry exclamation which had half escaped, changed into a cry of horror when he realized that the body on which he had fallen was a dead body, and as he hastily scrambled to his feet, the blood that smeared both his hands shouted tragedy.

Now Mr. Potter Higham was a cool and ruthless man of business. He could contemplate with callous delight the fortune that was to be extracted from the blood of a million patriots; but the blood that wetted his hands filled him with unspeakable horror. With those encrimsoned hands spread out before him, he ran down the Court into Fleet Street, whimpering like a terrified child.

Naturally, his appearance attracted attention. In a matter of seconds he found himself the nucleus of a crowd, eager, excited, interrogative. In a few seconds more that crowd had yielded two commanding personalities, the one physically gigantic and clothed in official blue, the other physically diminutive but morally colossal — in short, no less a person than Mr. Horatio Gobler, the famous journalist, especially retained by *The Trifler* as the investigator of crime.

The crowd, of course, surged up Bolt Court. But it soon surged down again under pressure from the police. A guardian constable was then stationed at each end and the Court kept clear of all unauthorized persons while those authorized proceeded to investigate the tragedy. By a constable and the journalist, Mr. Potter Higham, still trembling like a leaf and bedewed with sweat, was led back to the fatal entry in which the body still lay supine and contorted. Here, in an incredibly short time, they were joined by an inspector and the police surgeon; and when the latter had pronounced the body to be actually dead, and stated that death had apparently been caused by a stab with a large knife, the former turned his attention to Mr. Potter Higham.

"Tell us what you know about this affair," said he.

Mr. Higham told the little that he knew, and told it rather confusedly, for he did not much like the way in which the inspector looked at him.

"You don't know who he is, I suppose?" said the inspector.

"I've no idea," was the nervous reply.

"Just look at him and see if you recognise him."

Mr. Higham cast a shuddering glance at the white face with the horrible staring eyes. And as he looked, his own eyes dilated and his mouth fell open.

"God help us!" he exclaimed. "It's Mr. Scotter!"

"Who is Mr. Scotter?"

"He is — or rather was — the President of the British Industries Defence League."

"Let me see," said Mr. Gobler; "isn't that the new society that has been formed with the object of clearing all German industries out of the country?"

"That," replied Mr. Potter Higham, cautiously, "is one of its objects."

"And the principal one, I think?" the journalist persisted.

"Er, well; perhaps that is so," Mr. Higham conceded.

"Are you a member of the league?" the inspector asked.

"Yes. Mr. Scotter and I were attending here with some other gentlemen interested in British Industries in order to hold the inaugural meeting and settle the programme."

"I see," said the inspector. "Well, I suppose you have no objection to my searching you. It's a mere formality and if you consent I shan't have to detain you."

"What do you want to search me for?" Mr. Higham enquired anxiously.

"Oh, just to see if you have a large knife about you. I don't suppose you have. As I say, it's a mere formality."

The readiness with which Mr. Higham agreed made the search evidently unnecessary. Of course, he had no such knife; and when this fact had been established and his visiting card, with his London address written on it, handed to the inspector, he was allowed to depart; which he did up the stairs to await in the temporary board-room the arrival of the other members of the League. Almost at the same moment a wheeled stretcher drew up at the entry.

II

As Mr. Potter Higham disappeared up the stairs the inspector and the journalist each produced his notebook and made a rapid entry of the eye-witnesses' evidence. The police surgeon looked at his watch and remarked:

"You notice that the deceased has something in his hand?"

"I hadn't," said the inspector. "What is it?"

"Looks like a fragment of paper," was the reply; and the surgeon, stooping, disengaged, with some difficulty, from the tightly-grasping fingers (which were now seen to be deeply gashed and covered with blood) a small scrap of what looked like newspaper and handed it to the inspector, who carried it out into the brighter light and examined it, while Mr. Gobler craned eagerly over his shoulder.

"Ha!" exclaimed the latter. "The plot thickens. This is a scrap of a German newspaper."

"Looks like it," the inspector agreed, adding: "and it looks like a case for us and a scoop for you. I suppose you're going to spread yourself out?"

"I shall investigate the case certainly, and I take it that we shall work together as we usually do?"

"Yes, I don't expect that the C.I.D. will object. We know that we can trust you to be discreet and not to give away any secrets."

"You can trust me implicity," said Mr. Gobler. "And since we are to be colleagues, I suggest that, when the body has been removed, we begin the investigation without delay!"

The inspector nodded and turned to superintend the loading of the stretcher with its tragic burden. Then, as the little vehicle was wheeled away, followed by the constable and the surgeon, he looked enduringly at the journalist.

"Where do you propose to begin? This piece of paper seems to hint at a likely direction."

"It does," agreed Mr. Gobler. "But perhaps we may as well see who there is in this building."

He stepped across the entry towards the board on which was painted a list of the tenants, and was about to read it when one of the ground floor doors opened and a spectacled office boy thrust out his head and bestowed on Mr. Gobler an intimidating stare.

"You just chuck it," said the office boy.

"Chuck what?" demanded the astonished journalist.

"Ho, yus," was the cryptic reply. "Mighty innercent, you are. Think it's blooming funny, I suppose. Ought to know better at your age. What do you mean by it?"

"Mean by what, you young idiot?" exclaimed the bewildered Gobler.

"Why, stuffin' banana skins into our letter-box."

Here the youth plunged his hand into the open letter-box and drew out a banana skin, which he held aloft contemptuously for a moment and then flung out into the entry, after which he slammed the door.

Mr. Gobler picked up the skin and regarded it reflectively.

"This is rather odd, you know," said he.

"Not odd at all," dissented the inspector.

"Some damn boy –"

"Possibly," said Gobler. "But yet we must go warily. We are looking out for a clue and we mustn't pass over anything, no matter how trivial. Now, I wonder –"

He crossed to the opposite door, and, crouching down somewhat in the attitude of a jumping frog (about to jump) and endeavoured to squint through the aperture. Suddenly the door flew open and he descended on all fours (in the attitude of a frog that has jumped), on to the threshold of an office. A small, hairy man of fierce and irritable aspect confronted him and glared at the banana skin which he still grasped.

"So it's you, is it?" demanded the hairy one.

Mr. Gobler rose to the direct posture (while the inspector hurried out into the court to blow his nose) and, holding up the banana skin, began, suavely:

"Would you mind — ?"

"Yes, I should!" roared the hairy gentleman. "One's enough. What the devil do you do it for?"

He half closed the door and pointed indignantly to a wire letter-cage, in the bottom of which reposed a banana skin.

"If that's a joke, it's a dam bad joke," said he; and, with that, he whisked up the lid of the cage, fished out the banana skin, hurled it in Mr. Gobler's face, hustled the journalist out into the entry and banged the door.

As Mr. Gobler picked up the second banana skin, the inspector re-entered, wiping his eyes.

"Seemed a bit peevish," he remarked.

"Yes. Silly to get so annoyed about nothing. But now inspector, you see the importance of not disregarding trifles. One banana-skin in one letter-box might mean nothing; but when it comes to a second — you see, evidence of this kind is cumulative."

"Evidence of what kind?" demanded the inspector, with a faint grin.

"I was thinking of the calculus of probabilities," replied Gobler. "But don't let us waste time on academic discussions. I suggest that we examine all the other letter-boxes."

"Very well," said the inspector. "You fire away and I'll stand by in case anyone jibs. But you'd better put those skins in your pocket."

The enthusiastic Gobler stuffed the two items of cumulative evidence in his pocket and bounded up the stairs, while the inspector awaited developments below. The journalist was absent some time, and during that time the inspector caught, now and again, borne down from above, sounds of altercation. At length, Mr. Gobler reappeared, descending the stairs, and the officer advanced to meet him.

"Any luck?" he asked.

"I haven't met with any more banana skins," was the reply, "but I have discovered a fresh clue. The offices of the German newspaper, the *Morgenbabbler*, are on the top floor."

"Ah, I remember now. But it stopped publication when war broke out. Still, I think we had better have a look at the offices. Was there anyone there?"

"Yes. A German of sorts. But let us finish one thing at a time. I'm going to examine the letter-boxes of the other buildings."

"Right O!" the inspector said patiently. "Carry on: but I shall stay here and see that that German doesn't sneak off."

If Mr. Gobler's enthusiasm had been at all damped by his lack of success on the upper floors of number 40, it was more than revived by the results from number 41. For the first letter-box on the ground floor yielded a banana-skin and that of the opposite office produced another. As in the case of number 40, however, the investigator drew blanks on the upper floors, and he now began to suspect that it was the ground floors only that had received these mysterious offerings. And so it proved to be. In all, he collected a half-dozen banana-skins — all from ground floor letter-boxes — with which he returned triumphantly to number 40, at the entrance of which the inspector was waiting.

"Six!" he announced, proudly, holding his trophies aloft; and as he spoke, his feet flew from under him and he sat down heavily.

"Seven," corrected the inspector, pointing to a greasy stripe on the pavement and a flattened yellow and black object that was adhering to the sole of the investigator's boot. And Mr. Gobler, rising stiffly, but with unabated enthusiasm, added the seventh specimen to the body of cumulative evidence.

"Well," said the inspector, "it's a rum go; but I don't see that we're much forrarder. There, doesn't seem much connection between seven banana-skins and a murdered man."

"I'm not so sure," replied Mr. Gobler. "You will agree with me, I think, that this is, in a sense, a political crime. The murdered man was the head of this new Anti-German League and was, I should say, murdered in his official capacity, probably by a member of some German secret society."

"Quite possibly."

"Well now; have you never heard of those secret societies in West Africa — particularly the Gold Coast and Togoland — whose members leave messages at the houses of their friends or enemies by depositing simple common objects, such as a bunch of cowries, a ball of clay with a parrot's feather, and so on?"

"No, I haven't, and if I had, this isn't the Gold Coast or Togoland."

"I know; but the same kind of signals could be used as there."

The inspector shook his head. "Guess-work" said he. "You're trying to make bricks without straw — and without much clay either. Let's adjourn these banana-skins and go up and interview that newspaper chappie."

"By all means," Gobler assented. "But we won't forget the banana skins. As we build up our case we shall find that each item of evidence will drop into its place like the pieces of a jig-saw puzzle. And most fascinating it will be to fit them in."

"Very," the inspector agreed as they ascended the stairs: "and there are plenty of vacancies — in fact, the puzzle is all spaces and no pieces at present."

A sharp rap with Mr. Gobler's stick on the door of the office tenanted in more peaceful times by the editorial staff of the *Morgenbabbler* resulted in its opening and revealing a stout, elderly, careworn man, who, on observing the inspector, at once invited the two investigators to enter.

"We have just called to make a few enquiries," said the inspector. "Are you the proprietor of this paper?"

"Yes," was the reply, in excellent English, "and the editor. My name is Hans Ochsenbein. What information can I give you?"

"Well, a man has been found dead below, apparently murdered; and this was taken from his hand. What do you make of it?"

At the word "murdered," Mr. Ochsenbein became obviously uneasy and nervous; and when the inspector handed to him a fragment of blood-stained paper he became still more so.

"You want me to tell you if this is a piece of my paper," he said, as he scrutinised the repulsive-looking fragment. "That is, I fear, impossible. The type and the paper are similar to ours, but so are those of many German papers published in this country."

"You don't recognise the matter?" pursued the inspector.

"There is not enough," replied the editor. "The piece is too small. And there are no means of comparison. I have sold the whole plant and all the files and back numbers."

"Well," said the inspector, "I don't suppose it matters. By the bye, what are these premises being used for now?"

"I use this small office myself until the tenancy expires. The large room is used by some of my countrymen as a sort of club, where they meet to smoke and talk."

"Who are they?"

"They are all naturalised or registered. There is Mr. Karl Schnitzler of Whartons at number 42 –"

"Is that on the ground floor?" asked Gobler.

"Yes. Then there is Mr. Oppenheim. He is employed at number 43 –"

"Ground floor?" queried Mr. Gobler.

"Ground floor," assented Mr. Ochsenbeim. "And there is Mr. Rosenbaum."

"Who is he?"

"He is the managing director of the All British Jam Company."

"What sort of company is that?"

"Well, it is just a private company. The directors are the shareholders. There are four of them: Schmidt, Meyer, Schneider and Rosenbaum."

"Where is their factory?"

Mr. Ochsenbein smiled indulgently. "It is a secret — but it is an open secret. The factory is at Zuchesdorf."

"That is the centre of the beet district, isn't it?" said Gobler.

"Yes."

"And what tort of jam do they make?" the inspector asked.

"That I do not know," replied Ochsenbein.

"It doesn't matter," said Gobler. "A beetroot by any other name would taste as sweet. Has this company any other connections?"

"It is, in a way, affiliated with the firm of Dankwerts and Bamberger, the produce merchants of Quitta and Bagida."

"Where is Quitta?"

"It is on the Gold Coast."

"Oh, indeed!" exclaimed Gobler. "And Bagida?"

"That is in Togoland."

Mr. Gobler bestowed a significant glance at the inspector, who was clearly not a little impressed. After a solemn pause he asked:

"Have any of them been here today?"

"Yes. Schnitzler, Oppenheim and Rosenbaum were here this afternoon. They are old friends. They were all together in a factory at Little Popo."

"Where is that?"

"It is the principal town of Togoland."

Mr. Gobler's eyebrows went up and the inspector asked:

"What time did they leave?"

"Rosenbaum left about an hour ago. The other two went away soon after lunch."

"What is Rosenbaum like — to look at, I mean?"

"Well, he is rather short and rather stout, he is clean shaved, has a crop of bushy hair and wears spectacles."

"Do you know where he lives?"

"I don't, but I could easily find out."

"I wish you would and just let me know. And that, I think, is all we want to know at present." The inspector looked interrogatively at Mr. Gobler, and as the latter began to move towards the door, he wished Mr. Ochsenbein "good day" and followed his colleague out.

On the landing Mr. Gobler halted and addressed his companion impressively.

"Well, inspector: what do you think of the puzzle now? Isn't it coming together neatly?"

"It is, indeed. That was a remarkable point you made with those banana-skins. I shouldn't have given them a thought."

"Yes, it was a good point; the banana, a native of the Gold Coast and Togoland, the mystical number seven and the tracing of two out of the seven to the very doors of enemy aliens from those regions. It is all very complete: this Anti-German League — the President, too — murdered on the threshold of a house that it is a veritable nest of German secret society. The bit of paper, which almost certainly came from that meeting-place; and this man Rosenbaum with his German factory which the League would certainly snuff out. Wonderfully complete. Now we've got to collar Rosenbaum."

"There isn't much against him at present," the inspector remarked. "Certainly not enough to justify an arrest."

As he spoke, the pair came down to the entry, where a caretaker was swabbing the floor and the pavement with a mop, while a stranger stood outside and watched him intently. The latter, catching sight of the inspector, addressed him eagerly.

"I hear a man has been murdered at this house."

"Yes," was the curt reply.

"Could you tell me the exact time that it happened?"

The inspector looked at him sourly, but nevertheless answered:

"Between 3.40 and 3.45."

"Then," the stranger exclaimed, "that will have been the man."

"What man?" demanded the inspector.

"I will tell you. At 3.43 — I can be exact because I looked at my watch, which I set this morning by the post office clock — I was coming from Gough Square when I met this man coming round the corner from this Court. He was running like the devil — which was a bit queer to begin with — and he was carrying something with both hands as if it were alive — something wrapped up in newspaper. And there was blood on the paper."

"Anything else queer about the paper?" the journalist asked.

"Yes. it wasn't an English paper. It was printed in big, funny-looking type — Jewish perhaps."

"What was the man like?"

"I hardly know. My attention was taken up by the queer way he was carrying the thing, whatever it was. He seemed mighty flurried; but what he was like I couldn't say, except that he was short, punchy man and that he wore spectacles."

"That's good enough," said the inspector. "Which way did he go?"

"He shot through into Gough Square, and then I lost sight of him."

The inspector hastily took down the name and address of the witness and then the two investigators started off at a brisk pace towards Gough Square. As they turned into the Square, the journalist collided heavily with a man who was hurrying in the opposite direction.

"Hello!" exclaimed the former, looking hard at the newcomer. "Isn't your name Rosenbaum?"

"Und vot if it is?" demanded the other.

"Only this," said the inspector: "that I arrest you on suspicion of having murdered a man named Scotter in Bolt Court. Now, be careful. I must warn you that everything you may say will be taken down and used in evidence against you."

"But I haf only chust heard of zis dreadful zing!"

"Very well. Come along and see if any witness can identify you."

They return to Bolt Court and looked for their late informant. But he had already gone; and pending his re-discovery Mr. Rosenbaum, protesting and on the verge of collapse, was led away into durance.

III

Mr. Jacob Scotter was a great man. He was one of the pillars of British commerce; one of the master builders of our Empire, a maker of industrial England, and, above all, a mighty producer of dividends. He had burst upon the commercial world in the first place as the inventor of Tosher's Tasty Toothpullers — an adhesive and tenacious sweetmeat, beloved of juveniles but abhorrent to the wearers of artificial teeth — but his genius for applied chemistry and his ingenuity in the use of waste by-products, to say nothing of his abilities as a financial manipulator, had raised him to an exalted place among the magnates of industrial companies.

Yet, in spite of his greatness and his colossal wealth, Mr. Scotter was a man of simple habits, and as he walked up Fleet Street early on an April afternoon in 1915, on his way to preside at the inaugural meeting of the British Industries League, he looked about him eagerly for some kind of inexpensive nutriment. Once, at a restaurant, he had been charged half-a-crown for lunch — a misadventure that he had never forgotten. Since then he had avoided restaurants, and even teashops he had entered warily only when no baker's shop could be found.

Now Fleet Street does not abound in baker's shops, but is fairly well furnished in the matter of fruit-barrows, and one of these caught the roving eye of Mr. Scotter; a barrow piled high with rather overdue bananas, and decorated with a ticket indicating that these exotic delicacies might be acquired at the rate of one penny each or seven for sixpence. Mr. Scotter halted to reflect, with his eye on the barrow. His internal sensations suggested half-a-dozen as a satisfactory meal. Seven seemed excessive, though to be sure, the seventh involved no additional expense. Still, it seemed a waste — but perhaps a compromise might be arranged. With this idea approached the barrow and suavely opened negotiations; but his offer of fivepence half-penny for six was received with unwarrantable discourtesy, even to the use of disparaging epithets, and in the end he paid his sixpence and received seven bananas in a bag which he bestowed in the tail pocket of his frock coat.

The next proceeding was to find a quiet place in which to consume them. And behold! here was Bolt Court — actually his destination and furnished with an appropriate, almost prophetic name. He entered and looked about him. The Court was strangely quiet and secluded, in fact, at the moment, it was quite deserted. Slipping his hand into his tail pocket, he fished out number one, dextrously peeled it and consumed it with a rapidity that a pelican might have admired. But now the disposal of the skin had to be considered. It would be untidy to drop it on the pavement; besides, there would be presently six others. At this moment a postman bustled up the Court, thrusting sheaves of letters into the letter-slits as he went. Mr. Scotter listened at the first door, heard the letter-box opened from within, emptied and reclosed. Then he stepped lightly to the door and noiselessly dropped the banana-skin through the letter-slit.

Five more bananas were swiftly consumed and their skins softly let down into the most accessible letter-boxes. The seventh — and last — was more than half devoured and Mr. Scotter was edging towards the entry of number 40 (for the third time) when he heard a quick step approaching from Fleet Street. Rapidly he gulped down the remainder of the banana and bore down, with the skin in his hand, on the nearest letter-box. But he was too late. Before there it was time for him to dispose of his offering unobserved, the footsteps were close behind him. He might have retained the incriminating skin until the newcomer had passed, instead of which, in a momentary embarrassment, he dropped the skin and quickened his pace towards the entry of number 40.

He had just reached the threshold when some metallic object dropped with a clatter on the pavement immediately behind him. He halted and was in the act of turning round when he caught a muffled exclamation and the stamping of feet. For one instant he had a vision of a man staggering towards him, a man who held a newspaper bundle in his right hand. Then the man lurched against heavily, grasped his arm, as if to save himself from falling, and at the same moment Mr. Scotter felt a horrible pain in his left breast. It was but a matter of moments, for he felt himself falling; and, even as he fell, the agonizing pain faded away into unconsciousness.

Simeon Stubb held the distinguished position of carver at the Turkeycock Tavern in Fleet Street, a post of honour to which his sedate and studious aspect accentuated by a pair of concave spectacles — and the comfortable chubbiness of his somewhat short person gave due support. He was an expert carver, and like a good workman, he had a solicitous care for the implements of his craft. When therefore his favourite carving fork developed a pronounced wobble in its guard, he wasted no time, but, as soon as the grill-room emptied, bore the infirm fork to the cutlers for repair. No elaborate explanations were needed. He simply handed the fork across the counter and was turning away when the shopman remarked:

"That cook's knife that you left last week is ready if you'd like to take it with you."

Mr. Stubb decided that he would, whereupon the shopman produced and laid on the counter a great triangular-bladed knife like an overgrown Spanish dagger.

"You ought to have brought it in its leather sheath, you know," said the shopman. "These are nasty, dangerous knives to carry uncovered; and, I tell you, this one is sharp — point like a needle and edge like a razor. I'll wrap it up for you, but, all the same, you go carefully and hold the point down."

"I always am careful," said Stubb; then, as the shopman rolled the knife in a newspaper, remarked, "That's a rum-looking paper. Where did you get?"

"That," replied the shopman, "is a Hun paper — enemy alien — the *Morgenbabbler,* published in Bolt Court. But it went pop when the war broke out, and, as there won't be much demand here for German papers for the next fifty years or so, the proprietors sold the whole thing up, and my governor bought about half a ton of back numbers for wrapping. Smart of him, I call it, for paper is paper just now."

"Ah, you're right," said Stubb. "Fortunately for us, our customers provide their own wrappings for our goods. So long."

He picked the knife up carefully and went forth, holding it with the concealed point downwards. As he had to make a call in Gough Square, he crossed at the Circus end to the north side of Fleet Street and threaded his way cautiously among the crowd until he reached Bolt Court and turned in gladly out of the traffic. At the moment the court was empty, with the exception of an elderly gentleman, whose back was towards Stubb and who seemed to be taking a belated open-air lunch. Stubb noted the proceeding with disfavour, born, no doubt, of professional prejudice against unorthodox meals; and when the *alfresco luncher* dropped a banana-skin on the pavement he was positively indignant.

"There's a nasty, slovenly thing to do," he soliloquised. "Dangerous, too, if anyone should tread on it." He changed his course slightly, intending to kick it into a corner, but at this moment the knife, having bored its way through the paper, fell with a clatter on the pavement. He picked it up hastily and reinvested it in its wrapping paper, walking on slowly as he did so; and so engrossed was he with his occupation that he forgot all about the banana-skin until he fairly planted his foot on it. Instantly that foot shot away from under him. He uttered an exclamation and staggered forward, with arms outspread, right on to the elderly gentleman. The latter staggered heavily against him and grabbed his arm. For a few moments they swayed together; then the stranger fell, dragging Stubb down on top of him.

Now, the banana-skin was the sole cause of the mishap, and Stubb realised the fact. Nevertheless, he was a polite man, and, as he scrambled to his feet, he apologised profusely. But the elderly gentleman answered never a word and lay motionless as a statue. Stubb looked down at him in surprise; and the surprise turned to stony horror. For the handle of the cook's knife was sticking straight up from the elderly gentleman's waistcoat.

"God Almighty!" gasped Stubb. "I've killed the man!"

He stood for a full second staring and still as a graven image. The next moment, as he realised the awfulness of his position, he stooped, plucked out the reeking knife, wrapped it hastily in the paper, and, holding it in both hands as though it had been a venomous serpent, raced up the court, crossed Gough Square, and ran for his life by way of New Street, Nevill's Court and Fetter Lane; nor did he call a halt until he had reached the back entrance of the Turkeycock Tavern.

"That knocks the bottom pretty completely out of your 'constructive study,' as you call it," the inspector remarked, maliciously, as the coroner's jury, after listening to the evidence of Simeon Stubb and the cutler's shopman, returned a verdict of death by misadventure. "Your article in the *Trifler* will look a bit silly now."

"Not at all," retorted Mr. Gobler. "That article appeared two days ago. Who cares about a back number! It's to-morrow's issue that matters."

And, as Mr. Gobler was an expert and experienced journalist, the probability is that he knew what he was talking about.

Bill Jakins Stories

The Story of a Pram

I OFTEN LARFS w'en I thinks of it," remarked the waterman as, emerging from the hospitable portals of the "Ship and Lobster" he drew his sleeve across a countenance that wind and weather, combined with alcoholic stimulants, had toned to the colour of an underdone sirloin. He illustrated and enforced this remark by hereupon exploding into convulsions of laughter of a highly abdominal quality; and prodding his companion vigorously in what anatomists would describe as the epigastrium, and pugilists as the bread-basket, he continued:

"Two pun' ten, and all night in the jug; and the best of it was — d'ye see? — that he never knowed it was his own pram."

Here he was again overcome, and his companion, a mild-looking Norwegian, with an immense yellow beard, smiled a sickly smile, glancing round furtively for some possible means of escape; for the fact was, that he had already listened patiently to the recital of this "merry, conceited jest" three times in almost uninterrupted succession, and now the waterman showed unmistakable signs of beginning again.

At this critical moment Providence was graciously pleased to intervene. From the tiny companion-hatch of a barge that lay high and dry alongside the quay there emerged a head, and this being in due course followed by the shoulders, trunk and extremities appertaining thereto, disclosed a complete bargee, who, rolling across the deck after the manner of his kind, approached an almost perpendicular plank, up which he proceeded to walk with the ease and unconscious grace of a house-fly. Arriving at the upper end of the plank, he was confronted by the hilarious waterman, to whom he addressed himself.

"Wot are yer bustin' yerself about now, Bill Jakins?" he inquired.

Bill Jakins, controlling his mirth with a heroic effort, essayed to explain.

"I was a-tellin' Mr. Petersen here about old Bob Honeyball."

"Oozee?" queried the bargee.

"Old Bob Honeyball wot was skipper of the *Pole Star*," persisted Jakins.

"Wot *Pole Star?*" asked the bargee.

The waterman regarded the new-comer with solemn interest, hardly able to realise his incredible good fortune. Here was a man who had never heard of Bob Honeyball or even the *Pole Star!* Why, he was good for half a dozen recitals of the yarn at the least.

While this dialogue was proceeding, the Norwegian, taking advantage of the diversion, sidled stealthily along the fence until he reached a hole where several boards had fallen out. Through this hole he shot tail foremost, like a startled lobster, and immediately afterwards might have been seen striding across the marshes with the speed of a professional wobbler.

"Come and set down here, and I'll tell yer all about Bob Honeyball," said Jakins, and the bargee, following his companion, not without some misgivings, the pair seated themselves upon the housing of a prostrate mast, and the waterman commenced his story.

This story we will take the liberty of editing for the benefit of the reader:–

The dusk of a tranquil evening towards the end of September was closing in upon the summit of Windmill Hill — having already enveloped the town of Gravesend in the valley below — when Captain Robert Honeyball, knocking out his pipe upon the heel of his boot, hailed the white-aproned waiter from the interior of one of those green-painted arbours that abutted on the old windmill.

"Hi! you there! Bring us another pot of Burton. You can stow a drain more, I suppose, uncle?"

"Ah!" replied the individual addressed "just another drop, Bob."

The waiter departed barwards, and the captain leisurely refilled his pipe.

"I've brought the receipt," he observed significantly to his companion, a ruddy-faced, elderly man, arrayed in the traditional frock coat, white waistcoat and chimney-pot hat of the Trinity House pilot.

"Right," responded the latter; "then I may as well hand over the dibbs, and we shall be quits." He dived into a capacious breast pocket, and produced a canvas bag, which he passed across the table to the captain, remarking, "Count it before the waiter comes, and then give me the receipt."

Honeyball emptied the bag on to the table, and rapidly counted the little heap of gold coins; then, returning them to the bag, which he stowed in his pocket, he remarked:

"O.K., uncle, thirty pounds; here's the receipt."

The waiter now returned, and set down on the table a mighty tankard of foaming ale, from which the two men filled their glasses.

"When do you go to sea?" inquired the pilot.

"To-night, I hope," replied Honeyball. "I haven't been on board yet, but I told Simpson — that's the mate, you know — to be ready to get under way, at eleven o'clock."

"You didn't come down on the barque, then?"

"No; I left London two days ago, and arranged with Simpson that he should take on a fresh crew, and get a pilot, and bring the barque down here to wait for me, and I saw this afternoon that she was anchored off the 'Lobster.'"

"What time are you going aboard?" asked the pilot.

"I told Simpson to send a boat to the landing-stage at nine, and, as it's half-past eight now, I'd better be strolling down that way."

"I'll walk a little way with you," observed the pilot; and the two men, having conscientiously drained the tankard, emerged from the arbour.

It was now quite dusk, and, as they came out upon the grass-plot under the shadow of the windmill, a constellation of twinkling lights extended over the whole length of the anchorage.

Across the now invisible land on the Essex shore the red eye of the Mucking Lighthouse glowed; while away to the right the bright gleam of the Chapman was seen winking at stated intervals as though the little lighthouse were chewing the cud of some profound nautical joke.

From the summit of the hill our friends entered a steep, winding, narrow street, and they had not proceeded many yards down this thoroughfare when they became aware of two bay windows, which being furnished with crimson blinds, shed a warm and ruddy glow upon the narrow footway. A yet nearer approach revealed a small signboard swinging from the bough of a tree, and at the same time brought into view a figure approaching from the opposite direction.

"Well, I *am* blowed!" exclaimed the newcomer as the three men met in the ruby radiance of the parlour window; "if it ain't Bob Honeyball!"

"And why not Bob Honeyball?" inquired the captain, in whom the Burton had developed a metaphysical and speculative bent.

"Ah! and why not?" assented the other, cautiously evading the philosophic challenge. "Well, here we are," he continued, "led by Providence, so to speak, to the very front door of the Old Windmill Tavern. Shall we loobricate?"

Captain Honeyball coughed.

"The fact is," he said, "I ordered a boat to be sent to the 'Ship and Lobster' at nine o'clock."

"What of that?" cheerily demanded the new arrival — who, by the way, also belonged to the glorious company of the Trinity Pilots — "what of that?" Then, sinking his voice to a confidential growl, he added, "I tell you what: the landlord here has got some hollands that'll — that'll regular make you sit up."

"Ah!" murmured Captain Honeyball, smacking his lips; "that ain't the effect that hollands generally has on me. However, I'll step in with you for a few minutes just to have a little chat"; and the three men vanished into the doorway of the "Old Windmill," intent on investigating the commercial products of the Netherlands.

It was about this time that there emerged from the gloom that brooded over the face of the waters opposite the "Ship and Lobster" a pram (or ship's boat) containing two men, one of whom plied a pair of peculiarly stumpy sculls. Having brought their craft alongside the easternmost of the two landing-stages, they made fast the painter to a ring-bolt and strolled up on to the quay outside the tavern, and gazed about as though in search of someone.

"Don't see him nowhere," observed one of the men to the other as he peered about in the darkness.

"No," replied the other; "he vos nod gome yet."

The pair sauntered tip and down the path by the quay for some twenty minutes with growing impatience.

"Said he'd be here at nine o'clock, and here it is gone half-past," grumbled the English sailor.

"Waiting for anyone?" inquired a seedy-looking waterman who lurched up at this moment.

"Ah," replied the sailor, "we're waiting for our skipper."

"Wot ship?" asked the stranger.

"Pole Star: out there, astern of the big steamer," answered the sailor, indicating the whereabouts of his vessel. "Haven't seen anyone waiting about, I suppose?" he continued.

"Wot's yer skipper like?" queried the waterman evasively.

"Durned if I know," replied the seaman; "I never clapt eyes on him in my life. We're a new crew, we are."

"Well," said the waterman cautiously, "there was a man down 'ere about three-quarters of a hour ago, but I don't see 'im nowheres now."

"Went away to get a drink perhaps," suggested the sailor: and then, as if struck by a brilliant idea, he added, "And why shouldn't we have a drink too? Look ye here, sonny, you just keep a look out while we run in and have a tot, and we'll stand you a pint when we come out."

"Right y'are," agreed the waterman. "I'll call you if the skipper turns up, never fear." So the two sailors vanished into the tavern, while the waterman betook himself to a bench in a sheltered and obscure corner of the quay.

He had hardly settled himself, however, before Captain Honeyball made his appearance upon the quay, a walking — or rather, staggering — advertisement for the potency of the "Old Windmill's" hollands. The belated commander gazed round with a somewhat vacant expression, and then, seeing nobody, on the quay, he rolled unsteadily on to the landing-stage next to the one at which the pram was moored and, placing his hands to his mouth, emitted a husky bellow:

"Pole Star, ahoy?"

This hail awakening no response but a few faint echoes, the skipper having waited a few moments, again addressed the anchorage with a roar like that of all infuriated buffalo.

"Pole Star, AHOY!"

Here the waterman, who had emerged from his hiding-place, approached the captain stealthily.

"It's a dark night, mister," he remarked.

"'*POLE STAR*, AHOY!'"

Captain Honeyball turned round sharply.

"What's that you said?" he inquired.

"I said it was a dark night," replied the waterman.

"Well, any old fool call see that," retorted the captain irritably. "Have you seen anybody, waiting about here?"

The waterman reflected.

"There was two chaps come here about a 'our ago," he said. "They said they was a-waitin' for their skipper, but 'e never come, so they went aboard without 'im. I heard 'em say as they reckoned the mate 'ud have to take the ship to sea as the skipper 'adn't turned up."

"What ship did they belong to?" inquired Honeyball with some anxiety.

"*Polar Bear*, I think it was, or suthin' like that."

"*Pole Star*, you mean, don't you?" queried Honeyball.

"All, that was it — *Pole Star*," agreed the waterman.

"Well now, look here," said the captain earnestly, "that *Pole Star* is my ship. I'm the captain. You put me aboard of her, and I'll give you five bob. There she is, you see, quite close and handy," and he pointed to a light out in the anchorage which the waterman happened to know belonged to an iron four-master which was waiting for the ebb.

"Can't be done," replied the waterman decidedly, "but I'll tell you what I *will* do," he added; "I've just bought a new boat — she's up at the yard still, and I'm going to sell my pram. I'll let you have her cheap — dirt cheap."

"Where is she?" asked the skipper.

"There she is, made fast to that other landing-stage," replied the waterman.

"Well, you put me aboard in her, and I'll give you half a quid."

"I'll sell you that pram," pursued the waterman, ignoring the skipper's offer, "for two pun' ten, and that's giving her away, that is."

"I don't want to buy your pram," exclaimed the skipper; "I want to get aboard my ship. How much d'ye want for the trip?"

"Two pun' ten," argued the waterman, "is a purtickly ridiklus price for a good sound pram."

"I ain't going to buy your infernal pram," roared the skipper wrathfully, and then the two men were silent for a while.

"She's a-gettin' her side lights out," remarked the waterman presently, and the skipper with some difficulty managed to discern a tiny green spark just abaft the anchor light of the vessel that he fondly imagined to be the *Pole Star*.

"How much do you want for putting me aboard?" asked the skipper huskily.

"You buy my pram, and then you call put yourself aboard."

"I keep saying I don't want your pram," growled Honeyball.

"Very well," said the waterman resignedly, and there was another pause.

"The tug seems to be rangin' up alongside," observed the latter a minute later. "They'll be off to sea without yer if yer don't mind yer eye."

The skipper glared anxiously at the distant vessel, and perceived with a thrill of horror the two white lights and the green starboard light of the tug backing down upon her.

"There goes her riding light," exclaimed the waterman, and sure enough as he spoke the ship's anchor light slid down the forestay and vanished.

"Look here," said Honeyball, turning fiercely upon the waterman, "I'll give you a quid if you'll put me aboard sharp. Is that good enough for you?"

"Two pun' ten –" began the waterman.

"Oh, dry up," snapped the captain, and again silence fell upon the pair — a silence that was hardly broken by the faint echoes of sounds of revelry that stole out into the night from the parlour of the "Ship and Lobster," where at this moment some wassailer was declaring:

"For we will be jolly and drown melancholy
 With a health to each jovial and true-hearted soul."

"She's a-gettin' her anchor up now," remarked the waterman cheerfully.

The horror-struck captain listened. Faintly across the quiet river came the rhythmical "clink-clink" of a capstan pawl.

The skipper hesitated for an instant. Then dragging the canvas bag furiously out of his pocket, he picked out with trembling fingers three gold coins.

"Here you are," he said with set teeth, "here's two pound ten. Where's your pram?"

"I'll show you," said the man, seizing the money and glancing uneasily at the door of the tavern. "There she is, made fast to that landing-stage."

Without another word the captain rushed down the landing-stage, leaped into the pram, and, casting off the painter, began to scull furiously towards the vessel.

Meanwhile the waterman had turned about and started off along the path at a brisk trot.

His form had just faded into the darkness, and the sound of his footsteps were growing faint when the door of the tavern opened and the two sailors emerged. Now, as they, stepped on to the quay, the first object that met their gaze was a pram, whose single occupant was sculling wildly out towards the anchorage, while a glance at the landing-stage showed them that their boat was no longer in its berth.

"Hullo! you there! Wot are yer up to with that there pram?" roared the English mariner, and then, as the retreating figure ignored his question, he sorted out a choice little collection of nautical expletives of the most pungent quality, and fired them off with the rapidity of a machine-gun.

"Now then! what's all this row about?" shouted a man in a smart gig that was pulled swiftly towards the landing-stage.

"Are you the river police?" asked the sailor.

"Yes," replied the man who sat in the stern; "what's the row?"

"That chap there's a-making off with our pram."

The police boat instantly sheered off and started in pursuit.

"Ahoy there, you in the pram! Heave to, will you?" shouted the man in the stern. But the skipper continued to scull away like clockwork.

The swift gig, however, rowed by two men, soon overhauled the pram; and, as it approached, the man in the boat reached out with a boat-hook and caught hold of the pram's gunwale; but the captain adroitly knocked away the boat-hook, and bestowed upon the man that wielded it a smart tap on the head with the blade of the scull.

The watchers from the shore now dimly saw the shadowy forms of the two boats approach and merge into one dark mass, while sounds of strife and objurgation were heard across the face of the calm water. Slowly the boats drifted back towards the quay, bringing with them an atmosphere of disquiet until they had approached within a few fathoms of the shore, when there arose a loud shout followed by a heavy splash, and a few moments after Captain Honeyball appeared upon the beach clasped in the embrace of two very wet and very angry Thames policemen.

Now, whether the "Old Windmill's" hollands had, according to the prediction of the pilot, caused Captain Honeyball to "sit up," is uncertain, but there is no doubt whatever that it indirectly had that effect upon the river policemen, for no sooner had the captain's feet touched *terra firma* than he broke out into a display of such astonishing agility that he appeared to his affrighted captors to be possessed of as many arms as Briareus and as many legs as a centipede, all and sundry of which members he seemed desirous of planting upon the bodies of his enemies.

"'THAT CHAP THERE'S A-MAKING OFF WITH OUR PRAM'"

The Homeric conflict, however, which ensued, though glorious, was brief, and the proceedings were brought to a close by the departure townwards of the captain and his oppressors in that processional formation technically known as the "frog's march."

Late on the following afternoon the mate of the *Pole Star*, as he sat on the poop glancing over the day's news, suddenly observed his commander climbing over the bulwark on to the deck.

"Here you are at last then," he remarked, as the skipper walked somewhat sheepishly aft. "Why, we were getting quite anxious about you. What have you been doing with yourself?"

The captain winked solemnly, and tapped the side of his nose with his forefinger.

"Ah!" said the mate grinning; "been painting the town red, have you? Well, you look as if you had," with a glance at the skipper's disordered apparel. "Well, well, at your time of life too! Nice old rip, *you* are!" And he laughed indulgently.

"Tell the pilot to heave up the anchor as soon as the tide makes," said the captain, as with a genial but somewhat weary smile he descended to the cabin.

The discreet mate made no further reference to the skipper's somewhat tardy appearance on board; and as the two seamen, bearing in mind their rather protracted efforts to "drown melancholy" in the "Ship and Lobster," preserved a judicious silence, the whole matter remained, even to the actors in the tragedy, "wrop" — as Mr. Yellowplush would say — "in mistry."

"Yes," concluded the waterman, rising from the mast and following the retreating bargee, "I often larfs when I thinks of it. Two pun' ten in 'ard cash, and all night in the jug; and the best of it was — d'ye see? — that 'e never knowed it was 'is own pram."

"I tell you what it is, Bill Jakins," said the bargee, as he slowly backed stern foremost down the tiny companion way. "It's my belief that you know more than anybody else about the spending of that there two pun' ten."

And perhaps the bargee was right.

Victim of Circumstance

THE FLOOD TIDE was beginning to slacken in Gravesend Reach, and the shipping was making its preparations for the ebb. On board downward-bound barges brails were being cast off amidst the clinking of windlass pawls and the rattle of sheet-blocks; tugs began to fidget uneasily around foreign-going ships: the dock-gates stood wide agape, and already the great red funnel of an Atlantic Transport liner was creeping stealthily forward behind the long row of dock sheds.

It was at this moment that there appeared somewhat suddenly upon Tilbury Pier a small, pale clergyman in a state of extreme agitation, accompanied by a carpet-bag, two umbrellas, a holdall, and a brown paper parcel. His advent was apparently unnoticed — but only apparently, for a pair of small blue eyes set in a large red face were fixed inquisitively upon him from a height of some two inches above the deck of the pier. The owner of the eyes was perched upon the steps that lead down to the water at the east end of the pier-barge, and as the clergyman approached he leaned down and hoarsely hailed a man in a wherry that was made fast alongside.

"Look up, Bill, 'ere's a job for yer — looks like a pretty soft thing, too."

"Wot is it?" inquired the other, a little indistinctly, for his head was jammed under the half-deck, where he was attending to some trifling repairs.

"It's a devil dodger, Bill," replied the first man confidentially, and as he again inspected the approaching stranger he added, "Lord! but he *do* look a bloomin' mug! You'll make it 'arf a quid, Bill, easy."

Stimulated by these encomiums, Bill Jakins arose and crawled up the steps to examine his quarry. As his head rose above the deck and the victim hove in sight his companion whispered enthusiastically:

"Look at 'im, Bill. Ain't 'e a infant? You'll 'ave to stand me suthin' 'andsome outer this yer job."

At this moment the clergyman's eye met the watery and bloodshot orb of William Jakins, and he inquired meekly:

"Are you a waterman?"

"Am I a waterman?" echoed Jakins impatiently. "Wot else would I be? Do I look like a bloomin' ipperpottermus?"

Waiving this question with a deprecating smile, the clergyman meekly suggested it was a waterman that he was in search of, "and" he added, "I am afraid I am a little behind time, you know, so I shall ask you to very kindly use what expedition you –"

"Where d'yer want to go?" interrupted Jakins.

"To Hamburg," replied the little clergyman brightly.

"Hamburg!" exclaimed the waterman, "why yer don't suppose I'm going to row yer to Hamburg, do yer?"

"Oh! *dear* no!" the parson hastily replied. "I only want to be taken off to the ship that sails for Hamburg; let me see, I think that is the one — yes, I recognise her from the description."

He pointed, as he spoke, to a steamer that was moored to a buoy on the Gravesend side of the river, from whose ensign-staff the Italian colours fluttered.

Mr. Jakins shot a significant glance at his mat — Bob Hunkers by name; and the latter, standing behind the clergyman, winked solemnly. Then the waterman and his victim descended the little iron steps and took their place in the wherry.

"Yer can't steer, I suppose?" suggested the waterman in a tone of contemptuous pity.

"Oh! yes, I can steer fairly well. I used to go on the river a good deal some years ago."

"Well, then, take them there lines and put us as straight as yer can for that ship o' yourn."

The parson seized the lines and began to steer the lumbering wherry with the care and precision of the coxswain of a racing eight.

Meanwhile the waterman, having in a leisurely way shipped his sculls, commenced pulling with a great show of bodily execution but with surprisingly little effect on the boat, which, in fact, abandoning itself to the influence of the tide, sagged steadily stern foremost in the direction of Northfleet.

"By the way," said the parson presently as the boat crept out into mid stream, "I forgot to ask your fare."

"My fare," responded Jakins absently. "Oh, well, there ain't no call to talk about fares with an open-'anded gent like yerself. Wot'll do for you'll do for me."

"Well then, shall we say a shilling," suggested the parson pleasantly.

The waterman's face froze into an expression of horror.

"Wot was that you said?" he inquired icily.

"A shilling," repeated the passenger.

"A shilling!" shrieked the waterman, "a shilling! Why of all the darned impidence –" He was too overcome to finish the sentence.

"You can go a long way in a hansom for a shilling," remarked the clergyman in a persuasive tone.

"Then you bloomin' well go and call a 'ansom, and you can go to the bottom in it for your confounded shillin'." Having thus explained his views, the waterman unshipped, his sculls and regarded his passenger with a stony glare.

"Pray don't stop rowing," entreated the clergyman. "We can discuss this little matter as we go along."

Jakins reluctantly re-shipped his sculls, and as he slowly dipped them in the water the parson continued:

"Now what would you consider a reasonable fare for a short distance like this?"

"For forty year 'ave I used this 'ere river," said Jakins sententiously, "and never 'ave I been orferred less than five bob for a trip."

"I am afraid I can't do that for you," replied the parson. "The fact is, half-a-crown is all the silver I have — and very fortunate I am to have that, for I am indebted for my possession of it to a most odd and interesting circumstance."

"Ho?" grunted the waterman plying his sculls like a clockwork figure that has nearly run down.

"Yes," continued the parson gleefully, "a most curious circumstance. When I came to take my ticket at Fenchurch Street I found, to my surprise, that I had nothing less than a five pound note; and this the booking clerk refused most emphatically — I may say contumeliously — to accept.

"Fortunately a bystander witnessed my embarrassment, and most kindly, most generously, offered to assist me. He was so very good as to relieve me of the bank-note, and having taken my ticket for me handed me the balance

— four pounds ten in gold and half a crown, as you may see for yourself."
Here he fished the coins out of his pocket and spread them out in his hand for
the waterman's inspection.

"So you see," he concluded, "that is all I have. I can't give you what I don't
possess. You can't squeeze blood out of a stone, you know. Ha! Ha!"

"Can't I though?" muttered Jakins, "you'll see presently." And, having
sulkily pocketed the half-crown, he resumed his labours.

"Do you know," said the parson suddenly about ten minutes later (by which
time the boat had drifted some hundreds of yards in the direction of
Northfleet) "it doesn't seem to me that we are getting on very rapidly."

"Ho?" grunted Jakins.

"No. I have been watching that buoy there, and we don't seem as if we
were passing it somehow."

"You watch it carefully," said Jakins. "You'll soon see us shoot by it."

The clergyman stared fixedly at the buoy for some two minutes, and then
exclaimed in a tone of alarm:

"Why, I do believe we are going backwards!"

"Do yer?" inquired Jakins stolidly.

"I do indeed. Just look at that buoy yourself for a few moments, and I am
sure you will agree with me."

The waterman turned a fishy eye towards the buoy, and presently
remarked:

"Starn foremost it is, sure enough."

"Dear me!" exclaimed the clergyman. "Can you explain it?"

"I can," replied Jakins with exasperating composure. "It's the tide wot's a-
doin' it."

"But aren't you used to rowing against the tide?"

"Not for 'arf a crown, mister."

"Well, but haven't I explained that I have no more silver?"

"Yer 'ave," assented Jakins, "but yer can 'and me 'arf a thick 'un, and I can
give yer change when I puts yer aboard."

"Oh! but don't you think –" the parson was beginning, when his ear caught
a dismal and impatient toot from the steamer's whistle; upon which, without
more parley, he passed a half-sovereign to his tormentor.

The waterman, having pocketed the coin spat on his hands, grasped the sculls, and proceeded to give a demonstration of the power of money.

A few vigorous strokes sent the boat past the buoy, and in a very few minutes the steamer loomed right over the bows.

Her mooring rope was already cast off, and the rhythmical thump of the propeller blades was audible as the boat swept alongside; while even as the waterman grasped the rail of the accommodation ladder some hands above were gathering in the slack of the hoisting tackle.

"Now then! Look alive!" shouted Jakins as the bewildered parson, clasping his carpetbag, his umbrellas, his holdall, and his parcel, staggered on to the grating and clung to a stanchion, "mind yer don't drop them umberellas overboard."

"Perhaps you can let me have the change now," gasped the clergyman.

"Heave up!" shouted an officer on deck and as the ladder commenced to slowly ascend the terrified parson scuttled up, barking his shins at every step, and at length vanished through the gangway.

Jakins, having seen his victim fairly on board, pushed off and sculled along easily a little distance astern of the slowly moving steamer, glancing up at the gangway now and again as though he thought he had not yet seen the last of his passenger.

And he had not. In barely two minutes from the time of his disappearance the ladder was again lowered, and the parson danced out on the top stage still embracing his luggage and squawking like a young raven.

"Hillo!" bawled Jakins as this apparition met his gaze. "Wot's up now?"

"I'm on the wrong ship," bleated the unhappy clergyman.

"Well, then, come orf," responded Jakins unsympathetically.

"Hurry up there," said a voice from above; and the parson once more floundered into the wherry.

"Wot did yer want to get aboard the wrong ship for?" asked the waterman severely.

"I thought it was the Hamburg steamer; they told me to look for a steamer with a black funnel."

"Ah," remarked Jakins solemnly, "yer shouldn't go making mistakes o' this sort: they comes expensive."

"How do you mean — expensive?"

"Why I mean that in consekence o' this ere horror o' yours you've got to pay for two trips w'en one would 'a done."

"You don't mean to say you are going to charge me another fare!" exclaimed the clergyman.

"Why wot d'yer think I come a-toilin 'on this river for? D'ye suppose I'm a bloomin' phlanthrerpist?"

"No; I do not," replied the parson with emphasis. "Where is my change?"

"Wot change?" demanded Jakins.

"The change from that half-sovereign that you promised to give me when I went on board."

"Young man," said Jakins gravely. "You're intoxicated. I don't know nothin' about any change."

"I fear you are a very untruthful man," said the clergyman sadly. "How much are you going to charge for putting me on board this ship?"

"'Arf a quid," replied Jakins promptly.

"What!" shrieked the parson, "half a sovereign? I won't pay it. You shall put me on shore, and I will get another waterman."

"Please yerself," said Jakins quietly. "Ashore or afloat it's the same price — 'arf a quid."

The parson clasped his hands and sighed.

"You'd better make up yer mind slick," said Jakins. "They're haulin' down the Peter on your ship."

The parson hesitated a moment; then, realising his hopeless position, he drew forth a half-sovereign and slapped it down on the thwart in front of him. The waterman stowed the coin in his pocket with the other spoils, and struck out briskly for the Hamburg steamer.

"Thank Heaven, this is the right ship at last," sighed the passenger as he read the name on the vessel's counter while the boat swiftly rounded under her stern.

Arrived at the foot of the ladder, the parson dumped his luggage piecemeal on to the grating, and as he deposited the last package he turned to admonish the waterman.

"You are a very wicked man," he said, "a *very* wicked man, and I can only hope that your sinful heart may be –"

"Hup yer git," said Jakins, assisting his fare with a dexterous hoist; and the clergyman floundered on to the grating into the miscellaneous heap of his belongings.

Half an hour later Bill Jakins and his companion Bob Hunkers brought the wherry alongside the river stairs of the Old Amsterdam, and made the painter fast to the handrail.

"Wot's it to be, Bob?" inquired Jakins.

"Well, I think I'll begin with a go of s'rub — 'ot," replied Bob.

"Begin with s'rub, will yer? Seem to think you're in for a regler beano! You do!"

The pair made their way to the bar, where Jakins, addressing the barman jauntily, called for "two s'rubs-'ot."

The steaming liquor was presently produced and Jakins, not without a trace of pompousness in his manner, flung down on the counter one of the half-sovereigns that he had so lately acquired.

The barman rang the coin on the counter, then picked it up and examined it; then rang it again and again examined it; and at length went over to the window, where he subjected it to a minute scrutiny.

Presently he returned and passed the coin back to Jakins.

"Won't do," he remarked.

"Wot d'yer mean?" Jakins asked indignantly.

"Snide," said the barman stolidly.

"Git out!" exclaimed Jakins, examining the coin incredulously, "that 'arf quid's all right; but still, if yer don't like it I can give yer another — there! wot d'yer think of that one;" and he pushed the second half-sovereign across to the barman.

The latter took up the coin, inspected it, rang it on the counter, and handed it back.

"Won't do," said he.

"Won't do!" shouted Jakins. "Why yer don't mean to say there's anything wrong with it?"

"Rank bad un," said the barman impassively.

"Durn me if this ain't a pretty fine go," growled Jakins, as with a rueful face he drew out the half-crown and sheepishly placed it on the counter.

"Look 'ere," said the barman sharply, "this is coming it a bit too thick, this is"; and fixing the half-crown in a notch of the coin-tester he bent it nearly double as though it were made of putty. Then he retired abruptly into the parlour behind the bar.

The two longshoremen regarded one another in silence for some time, sipping, their shrub thoughtfully.

"Well, this 'ere's a corker, this is," said Jakins presently, "a living corker: and I ain't got another stiver, Bob so you'll have to pay."

"Me 'ave to pay," exclaimed Hunkers in pathetic tones, "w'en I come in 'ere to be treated. Nice sort of thing that is too."

"Two shrubs — eightpence," said the barman who had just returned from the parlour.

Hunkers dived into his pocket and brought out a single handful of coppers, which he counted out painfully and with a sorrowful countenance.

"There, that leaves me 'igh and dry, that do," he complained; and then the two men resumed the consumption of shrub, condoling with one another upon their misfortune.

Their condolences were, however, cut short by the appearance of a stranger in a black coat with white metal buttons, who entered the bar softly, and looked about. as if in search of someone.

"That's 'im." said the barman pointing at Jakins.

"That's 'oo?" queried Jakins in a tone of alarm.

"You've got to come along o' me," said the policeman, laying a persuasive hand on the waterman's shoulder.

"Wot for?" said Jakins.

"What for? Why for a-pitchin' a snide acrost the counter of the Old Amsterdam that's what for."

"Them there coins was paid to me by a parson — a regler sky-pilot — wasn't they, Bob Hunkers?" protested Jakins appealing to his friend for corroboration.

"Oh, I dare say," said the constable with a grin. "P'raps it was the Archbishop of Canterbury, wasn't it? You come along quiet now."

"But I tell yer it's all a mistake," persisted the terrified waterman.

"Ho yes, *I* know," said the policeman wagging his head, "they always say that. You come along."

"But I assure you, swelp me –"

"Come along."

And he went along.

The Great Tobacco "Plant"

MONG the axioms with which the wisdom of our forefathers has enriched us none obtains more universal acceptance among the prudent than that which assures us that walls have ears. The statement is, of course, to be understood in a strictly metaphorical sense and does not imply the existence of actual visible and tangible auricular appendages, except such as may be attached to the heads of human eavesdroppers; but even with this necessary limitation there is one class of wall to which the generalization is not applicable — to wit, the river-wall. This immunity from the common vice of walls in general is to be ascribed to the fact that the river-wall is traversed by passengers along its summit, so that both sides can be simultaneously seen and the presence of invisible listeners thus rendered impossible.

It was, no doubt, a judicious consideration of these facts that induced a pair of watermen on a certain summer evening to take their way along the narrow path on the riverwall that stretches eastward from the town of Gravesend, for there was in their aspect and manner something secret and stealthy. They trudged on in silence until they had left the 'Ship and Lobster' — the last outlier of the town — some two hundred yards behind, when one of them spoke.

"'Ere y'are, Jakins, this'll do. You can speak yer mind 'ere safe enough without you're a-going to holler so that they can hear you out in the anchorage."

"Yes," replied Jakins, "this seems a nice quiet spot for a chat."

He looked round on the vacant marshes and the anchorage thinly sprinkled with vessels, and continued —

"Now, about this yer business wot I said I had to tell yer about; it's wot them shop blokes call a 'good line,' and it ought to bring in something worth while and no risk to speak of."

"What's the lay?" inquired the other suspiciously.

"Wot 'ud yer say to 'baccy?"

"I should say 'It ain't good enough for Bob Hunkers' — that's what I should say. Terbaccer! and in this yer town of Gravesend too, with that old weasel Hawkins at the head of the customs. Didjever hear of anyone as caught old Hawkins a-napping?"

Jakins serenely lighted his pipe.

"Wot you say, mate, is purfectly right," he agreed. "I ain't a-goin' for to make no excuses for this 'ere man 'Awkins. I admits 'is inquisitiveness and officiousness is a public scandal; but still I say it's a good line."

"Did you ever catch old Hawkins a-napping?"

"Not me, nor no one else. 'E don't nap, don't old 'Awkins, not 'e; but *'e goes to church*, and then the others does the nappin' for 'im."

"I don't believe it can be done, Bill," said Hunkers, but with less decision in his manner.

"It 'as been done," replied Jakins, "and it's been done pretty often."

"Oh?" said Hunkers with awakening interest.

"Yes, and I'll jest tell yer 'ow the trick's worked. Sunday morning at eleven o' clock 'Awkins toddles into the parish church with 'is Bibles and 'is prayer-books as 'oly as a cherybim on a tombstone. About the same time one or two 'ard-worked watermen gets into their boat, and by way of a little 'oliday paddles away down the reach to 'ave a look at the Ovens buoy. Now while they're higzamining that buoy and so improving their minds, wot do they see a-steamin' up the Lower Hope but the Netherland boat *Van Tromp*, and they've 'ardly time to get out of the way when round the Ovens she comes. Just as she passes the buoy, they see the steward run into the starboard alleyway and heave something overboard — something heavy with a line made fast to it.

"Curiosity indooces them to row up to the place w'en the steamer 'as passed and there they find a batten floating with twenty fathom of lead-line bent on to it, and w'en they 'auls in the lead-line, to their astonishment they finds 'alf a 'undredweight of baccy at the other end, done up in a watertight package. They gets the package on board and opens it and finds the baccy made up into small parcels of about four pounds each, so they pulls round Coal'us Point and goes ashore near East Tilbury with the baccy stowed under their weskits and in their pockets, and looks in on a friend where they 'ides the stuff away until they wants it to run up to London. Then they paddles back just in time to meet the old gentleman a-comin' 'ome from church."

Bob Hunkers pondered awhile on this scheme and then said –

"Well, where do I come in, in this? What do you want me to do?"

"I'll tell yer," replied Jakins. "My bit comes off next Sunday, and this time we shall 'ave to run it rather close. The wind being probably easterly and the tide running up strong, the *Van Tromp* will make Coal'us Point soon after eleven, and so with the tide dead agin us we ought to get an early start. Now wot I propose is that we get under way about ten and pull easily down the reach, so as to be a good 'arf way to the Ovens by eleven. Then your part comes in. You wait about outside the old man's 'ouse until you see 'im come out all figged out for church with 'is gold-top cane, and 'is prayer-books and Bibles: and as soon as you see 'im fairly under way you make us a signal."

"How can I make you a signal and you halfway down to the Ovens?"

"I'll higsplain to yer," said Jakins a little pompously. "Yer know Sam Brightman's got a noo suit of sails to 'is boat?"

"I know that."

"Red tan mains'l and white duck mizen."

"That's right."

"Well, Sam Brightman's in this job and 'e'll leave 'is boat with 'er painter fast to the Terrace Pier on Sunday. Now as soon as you've made sartain that the old bloke ain't a-goin' to neglect 'is religious dooties you just hook it off to the Pier, jump into that boat, 'oist sail and put 'er straight for the Essex shore and get the sun on the starboard side of them noo sails so as we can see 'em from where we are."

"But 'spose the old cove don't go to church?"

"W'y then yer stops ashore and we shall know that it ain't no go."

Hunkers reflected. Certainly the task as far as he was concerned seemed tolerably free from risk, and promised a very fair profit, so after mature deliberation he decided to stand in with the smugglers.

The Jubilee clock had just chimed the half hour after ten, and the bells in the various church steeples, accepting the announcement as official, had begun to call their respective congregations to worship, when Bob Hunkers, sauntering up the quiet sunny street, took up a not-too-conspicuous position commanding a view of a green-painted door set in a high redbrick wall.

Selecting a conveniently situated post he assumed an attitude of dignified repose and, with great deliberation, filled a clay pipe of a somewhat swarthy complexion from a tin tobacco box.

He had, however, hardly blown a half dozen puffs of smoke into the softly stirring air when the green door opened and there emerged from it a fresh-looking elderly lady and a pair of tall, strapping girls.

Hunkers watched the new comers inquisitively out of the corner of his eye, as they turned in the direction of the parish church and noted that they had not closed the door after them, a fact which was presently accounted for by the appearance of a small, brisk, elderly man in unexceptionable Sunday attire, who carried, perhaps a little ostentatiously, a prayer-book and Bible, and displayed to its best advantage a fine gold-headed malacca cane. Slamming the door after him with an air of absolute finality, the old gentleman stepped actively up the street until, turning a corner, he abruptly disappeared from view. Almost at the same moment Bob Hunkers, 'shaking off dull sloth,' put his pipe into his pocket and started off at a sharp trot.

The red tan mainsail and snowy mizzen of Sam Brightman's boat glistened gaily in the sunlight as they glided out from the anchorage into the fairway by the Essex shore, and carried a joyful message to the watchers down by the Ovens buoy.

But not to them alone.

High up under the roof of the tall customs building is a room in which stands, on a firm tripod, a telescope of portentous size and exceptional power. To the eye-piece of this instrument, on the present occasion, was applied a keen grey eye, the property of a small, brisk, elderly gentleman, who was ensconced in a heavy leather-covered chair. On another chair close by was a chimney-pot hat, a prayer-book and a Bible, while leaning against it was a stout malacca cane with a gold top.

For nearly a quarter of an hour the elderly gentleman continued to gaze through the telescope with unabated interest. Suddenly he rose from his chair, and stepped through a door-way on to a gallery at the back of the house immediately below the flagstaff, cast off the signal halyards from their cleat and lowered the flag.

For some minutes he stood on the gallery anxiously scanning the anchorage, until presently a small launch emerged from behind a Swedish barque. Then he again hoisted the flag and returned to his vigil at the telescope.

It was a full quarter past eleven by Sam Brightman's new gun-metal watch when the anxious smugglers, hovering around the Ovens buoy, beheld a yellow-funnelled steamer sweep round Hope Point and turn up the Lower Hope.

"That's 'er, sure enough," exclaimed Jakins with suppressed excitement, and, then looking round, he added, "I suppose it's all right and the coast clear?"

"There's a launch coming down," said Brightman, shading his eyes with his hand.

"Where away?" inquired Jakins, catching up a battered binocular and pointing it up Gravesend Reach. "Oh, I see 'er; she's a stranger — white funnel with a red top — seems to 'ave a lot of wimmen aboard — some bloomin' Cockney pleasure party, I expect. Well, we'll keep our eye on 'er, although she needn't interfere with out little business." He turned to look at the steamer creeping up the Lower Hope and looming larger every minute.

"Now then," he said, "it's time we begin to pull down to meet 'er. Give way, Sam, and keep a look-out as she passes."

The drum of the steamer's propeller came up on the breeze, mingled with the hoarse murmur of the parted water as it foamed away from her bows. Higher and higher rose the black hull until it seemed to tower over the boat. Suddenly a dark object appeared, suspended by a line over the ship's side, and slid down until it disappeared into the water. Immediately after a small billet of wood, to which the end of the line was attached, was flung overboard, and then, as the steamer swept by with a roar, a man was seen to step out from the shadow of the alleyway and wave his arm to the occupants of the boat.

"Heave ahead, Sam," shouted Jakins. "I saw the batten floating just now when the steamer's wash turned it over. Ah! there it is," and he stood up, holding the yoke-lines taut that he might steer with the more precision.

A couple of minutes' pulling brought the boat alongside the batten, and Jakins was just stooping over to catch hold of the line that was fast to it, when Sam Brightman exclaimed in a warning voice:

"Hold hard a minute, Bill. Hadn't we better let that launch give us the go-by first?"

Jakins scowled at the little vessel, which was now a quarter of a mile distant and presenting her port bow to them, and said:

"Oh, she's all right; she won't come nowheres near us. Besides, I tell you they're only a lot o' bloomin' Cockneys. There!" he added triumphantly, as the blatant voice of a concertina struggled up the wind; "didn't I tell yer so?"

"All right, Bill," said Brightman a trifle uneasily; "let's get the stuff on board and clear out of this."

Without more loss of time Jakins fished up the line with a boat-hook, and a few steady pulls brought the submerged package to the surface.

Brightman now lent a hand, and the two men heaving together, the tarpaulin-covered bundle was tumbled all dripping into the stern sheets.

"Now, my boy," said Jakins gleefully, "get to yer oars, and we'll have this ashore before you can say 'knife.'"

"Hullo!" exclaimed Brightman, "what's that infernal launch up to now?"

The vessel in question, having altered her course, had now come within two hundred yards of the boat, and was making as if to pass between it and the Essex shore.

"Never you mind 'im," said Jakins gruffly. "Jest you row on and don't take no notice." That was all very well; but the occupants of the launch were disposed to be so excessively companionable that it was a course not easy to adopt. Having got to shoreward of the boat, the launch gradually edged up until only a few yards separated the two vessels.

"Look out there!" protested Jakins. "You'll be aboard of us if yer don't mind."

On a side seat of the little launch, with their backs to the smugglers, sat three ladies of massive proportions attired in showy blouses and colossal hats. Opposite them was a man in a blazer and straw-hat, who, with the aid of a concertina and a loud brassy voice, regaled his fair companions with that once-popular melody, "Did you ever catch a weasel asleep?" while lounging over the rail, at the starboard bow, was another blazer-clad gentleman, who regarded the smugglers languidly through an eye-glass.

"Nice fresh morning," observed the latter, ignoring Jakins's protest.

"We can see that for ourselves," replied Jakins curtly. "You sheer off, or you'll be a-capsizin' of us."

The launch was now alongside, and the man in the eye-glass, leaning over the rail, inquired confidentially:

"I say — have you found him?"

"Found 'im!" exclaimed Jakins. "Found 'oo?"

"Why, Bowden, the man who was drowned off Purfleet. I thought I saw you hauling a body on board."

"Now you sheer off," said Jakins in a wrathful tone; "else someone'll be lookin' for your body."

At this moment the launch bumped against the boat, and as the two vessels touched, the man with the eye-glass whipped up a boat-hook and adroitly fished up the boat's painter which he immediately belayed to a cleat inside the rail.

The smugglers rose together with a shout, and then stood speechless and gaping. For, as they rose, the three ladies also stood up, disclosing the astonishing fact that, in the place of the flowing draperies proper to their sex, each wore a pair of blue cloth trousers of a distinctly nautical cut. While Jakins was yet staring stupidly at this alarming apparition, the fair things turned, and one of them (on whose face grew a sandy moustache) stepped smartly over into the boat, and, regardless of the welfare of the blue cloth trousers, quickly took a seat on the contraband package.

Jakins sank to a thwart with a groan, while the intruder, still seated on the package, having removed his hat and with it a wig, composedly peeled off a voluminous blouse, displaying the hated uniform of his Majesty's Customs.

Bob Hunkers, beating slowly to windward against the strong tide, was just stretching out towards the Ovens buoy, when there appeared round Coalhouse Point a small launch towing what looked like a waterman's wherry in which were three or four men. To Hunkers's experienced eye there was something familiar in the aspect of these figures, and when at the launch's mast-head he descried a blue flag with some white device, a sudden pang of terror shot over him. In a moment his helm was put hard up, and his boat scudded up the reach with a flowing sheet as fast as wind and tide would carry her.

Beyond the Dreams of Avarice

THE AFTERNOON sun shone brightly on the little lawn that stretches from the river front of the "Clarendon" down to the water's edge, and on two elderly gentlemen who sat together at a small table supporting two tumblers filled with a clear effervescent liquid. They were engaged — that is to say, the elderly gentlemen were engaged — in earnest conversation, which one of them, a small, thin, irascible-looking man with a yellowish-brown face and a white moustache interrupted at intervals by rising from his chair and peering with screwed-up eyes up Gravesend Reach in the direction of Northfleet, concluding his survey by dropping back into his seat with an impatient grunt.

"I always said," observed his companion after one of these excursions, "and I will always maintain that these Indian appointments are a mistake; the life is pleasant enough, I admit, and the pay is good, but what? — what, I ask you, can compensate for a damaged liver?"

The little man grunted, and snatched a mouthful from his tumbler.

"Now, for instance," pursued the other, "look at me" (the little man turned a scornful grey eye upon him). "Why, bless you, I can't swallow a mouthful of — of anything that's worth swallowing, don't you know, but I feel it at once — here — and there." He prodded himself as he spoke, first under the wing rib, and then endeavoured to reach his shoulder blade, but the rotundity of his figure rendering this impossible, he indicated the spot with the crook of his umbrella.

"Yes," continued the sufferer, regardless of the contemptuous expression that was gathering upon his little friend's yellow face, "the most trifling thing does it; a bit of toasted cheese, a morsel of potato salad –"

"Ha!" snorted the short gentleman.

"Yes, indeed," continued the unsuspecting invalid, "or a little prawn curry or a scrap of mango chutne –"

"Yes, yes," burst in the little man, "or a few horse chestnuts, or a dozen or so of tenpenny nails. Bah! my dear Morton! Shall I tell you what you are? You are an ass! A self-indulgent, gormandising booby," and here the small gentleman in his irritation seized his companion's tumbler and drained it at a draught.

"What would you recommend me to do?" inquired Mr. Morton in a meek voice, as he rather ruefully watched his peppery friend wiping his moustache.

"Recommend!" exclaimed the small man. "I have only two words to say to you: diet — ipecacuanha." As he pronounced each of these names he gave the table a vigorous slap that nearly capsized the remaining tumbler; observing which he hastily caught it up and emptied its contents down his throat with a wrathful gurgle.

"Ipecacuanha!" murmured Morton. "They gave me that when I had dysentery at Bangalore. It makes you most awfully sick."

"Of course it does if you fool enough to take an emetic dose of it. Now you just listen and I'll tell you how *I* take it. I got the tip from old McSwiney when he was in charge of the hospital at Hyderabad.

"You get some ipecacuanha wine — I buy a pint at a time myself — and a bottle of good old dry sherry. You put about half a small wine-glassful of the ipecacuanha wine into the bottle of sherry and then you take for a dose half a wine-glassful, or say two tablespoonfuls, of the sherry an hour before each meal. If you do that, and exercise some self-control, mind you, about your diet, you'll feel no more of your liver."

"It seems a simple and agreeable remedy," remarked Morton, dejectedly.

"It has made a new man of me," rejoined the other. "I wouldn't be without it for the world. I never go anywhere without it. In hotels I keep it in my bedroom; on board ship I keep it in my berth; it's my only medicine. It's a — by Jove! there's my steamer dropping her anchor opposite. Hi! you! is that your boat?"

This question was addressed to a seedy-looking man who stood on the steps, dreamily regarding a wherry that was made fast to the Clarendon's landing-stage.

"Why, yer know, mister," was the drowsy reply, "I wouldn't go so fur as to say as how that there boat belonged to me, but –"

"Well, then, whose is it? His?" and the little man pointed to an elderly waterman who was seated on a spar hard by and thoughtfully stopping his pipe with a grimy forefinger.

"Yes," responded the dreamer, "it's 'is boat. 'Ere, Bill Jakins!"

"Hallo, there!" shouted the small gentleman. "Come, wake up, you beef-faced old rascal."

Jakins rose slowly and regarded the speaker with silent amazement. Then recovering the power of speech he inquired: "Was you addressin' me, mister?"

"Was I addressing you! Was I bellowing myself black in the face, you infernal, blear-eyed, old sleep walker! Can't you see I'm waiting for a boat?"

"*Hall* right!" protest Jakins, "I ain't deaf, and there ain't no call for you to go on a-cursin' and a-swearin' like that there. Wot ship?"

"Go into the hotel and fetch my luggage," commanded the small gentleman.

"Your wot?"

"Luggage!" roared the little man.

"I say, guv'nor," said Jakins reproachfully, "do you take me for a porter?"

"A porter!" yelled the other. "I take you for a confounded, long-winded, chattering magpie; a lazy, drunken, profligate, skulking, idle, scrimshanking old shell-back. That's what I take you for. Go and fetch my luggage!"

"'Ere, come on, Bob," said Jakins, beckoning to the other waterman, as he slunk off towards the hotel.

"Room 24, name of Currie," shouted the little man, as the two discomfited amphibians retreated towards the door.

"Well, I'm jiggered!" reflected Jakins as he disconsolately trudged up the stairs. "Of all the blooming foul-mouthed, abusive, insulting little beasts — just look at 'im, Bob, the yaller-chivvied little swab. My eye! but I'd put a few spots of colour on that wash-leather mug of 'is, if I 'ad my way."

The two watermen paused at the landing window and gazed malevolently at their employer, as Mr. Jakins thus unfolded his views.

"Now, then! what the deuce are you staring at?" shouted Mr. Currie, suddenly becoming aware of their presence at the window; and at the sound of his strident voice the pair hastily drew back into the obscurity and stumbled up towards the bedroom.

"Obnoxious little varmint!" muttered Jakins. "I wonder 'oo 'e is. Looks to me like a lobster."

"Not 'e," said Hunkers. "'E ain't no lobster."

"Well, I say 'e is." persisted Jakins. "Some bloomin', gravel-grinding hadjutant; that's about wot 'e is."

"I tell yer 'e ain't," returned Hunkers, "'e's a bank bloke. I know 'oos the boots 'ere is a friend of mine, and e 'told me about 'im."

"Holy fly!" exclaimed Jakins, "d'ye mean to tell me that cove keeps a bank?" He stole back a step or two to peer out at the irascible little gentleman with renewed and heightened interest.

"'E does so," replied Hunkers triumphantly, "and wot's more, 'e's a-going out now to a forrin branch and takin' a cargo of the rhino with 'im."

"Jee-roosalem!" ejaculated Jakins, "let's go and 'ave a look at 'is luggage," and the pair of rascals bundled into the open door of No. 24 with a haste that was in striking contrast to their previous tortoise-like sluggishness.

The luggage consisted merely of two small iron cabin trunks, and upon these Jakins pounced voraciously, hoisting and poising them critically in his arms.

"If the oof is stowed in these here boxes," he decided, "it can't be brass: they ain't heavy enough. Why, bless yer, a good 'atful of jimmies would weigh as much as this trunk."

"P'raps it's all in paper," suggested Hunkers.

Jakins licked his lips. "Lor," he commented, "to think that these here tin boxes may be stuffed full of fi-pun-notes, for all we know! It's enough to turn a man's 'air grey to think of it. But yet, yer know," he added after a pause, "if they was, 'e'd 'ardly leave 'em kickin' about like this."

"No, Bill," agreed Hunkers. "I 'adn't thought of that. Well, if the stuff is all in notes 'e might 'ave it all packed in 'is 'and-bag."

"Wot 'and-bag?" asked Jakins eagerly, peering round the room.

"Didn't yer see 'e 'ad a 'and-bag on the chair by 'is side?"

"No, by gosh! 'as 'e?" and Jakins stole off on tiptoe to again inspect his prey; but his purple countenance no sooner appeared at the window than it was greeted with a yell of execration that sent him flying up the stairs like a startled rabbit.

"Bob," he whispered when he returned, "it's there! 'E's got it on a chair by 'im. I say, mate, we must get 'old of that bag."

"That's all very fine," was the disconsolate reply, "but I'd like to see yer at it with that there darned little red-'ot scorpion of a nigger-driver a-'anging on to it."

"Scorpion or no scorpion," returned Jakins resolutely, "wot I say is, we've got to get 'old of that bag," and having reached this conclusion he shouldered the smaller of the two trunks and lumbered down the stairs, followed by his confederate.

The two trunks were neatly stowed in the stern-sheets of the wherry when Jakins essayed the first move towards the appropriation of the hand-bag. It was simple and masterly — but not successful. Carelessly approaching the table at which the little man was seated he made a feint of removing the bag to the boat; but his hand barely touched the handle when its owner discharged such an avalanche of expletives that the waterman shrunk back appalled.

"I thought yer wanted me to put yer things in the boat," he explained, as he recoiled down the path.

"You leave that bag alone," responded the little gentleman tartly, "I can carry it myself, thank you."

"Are yer goin' to stay 'ere all day?" grumbled Jakins.

"I'm going to stay as long as I please," was the conciliatory reply. "You go and wait in the boat and don't chatter."

Thus dismissed, the conspirator dejectedly returned to his wherry, where he seated himself upon a thwart and glared viciously at his confederate.

"It's no go, I tell yer, Bill," observed the latter, after enduring his companion's scowl for a minute or two in silence; "yer'd better chuck it afore yer makes trouble. That cove's too much for yer, he is; 'e's as sharp as a heagle and as bloomin' unpleasant as a dog-fish."

"You dry up, Bob Hunkers," was the irritable reply. "I'm a-thinkin', that's wot I'm a-doin'. And, by the livin' Jingo!" he added suddenly, "I've got an idea. I have, swelp me!"

"'YOU LEAVE THAT BAG ALONE.'"

"Wot is it?" asked Hunkers, infected by his friend's excitement.

"Ain't there a length of cod-line in that stern locker?"

"I believe there is."

"Well, then, cut me off a fathom and a 'arf, and I'll show yer somethink."

Hunkers rummaged in the stern locker, and presently produced a hank of the thin tough line, from which he cut off the required length and handed it to his companion, who, drawing up his sleeves, and taking a hasty look at the two gentlemen who still sat earnestly conversing by the table, leaned over the stern and plunged his arms up to the elbows into the water.

"Wot are yer hup to, Bill?" inquired the astonished Hunkers.

"Can't yer see?" was the response, in a muffled growl.

Hunkers peered cautiously over the boat's quarter, and then perceived that his wily confederate was making fast one end of the cod line to the lower gudgeon on which the rudder swung, some six inches under water.

"Wot's that for, Bill?" he asked, as Jakins arose purple-faced and puffing from his inverted position.

"I'll igsplain it to yer," said the latter, wiping his brow and leering towards the hotel garden. "Yer see that there cod-line. One end's fast to the rudder 'arf a foot under water. The other end's a-layin' loose in the starn sheets. Now we got to wait for a oppertoonity, and whichever of us gets the chance 'as got to take it — it may be me or it may be you. 'Spose the slant comes to you. Them two blokes 'as got to be bustled on to the ladder so as they can't take the bag with 'em. Then d'reckly their backs is turned you nips in and bends that cod-line on to the 'andle of the bag with a couple o' 'arf-'itches, and then w'en that yeller-faced little cove begins to 'oller out for 'is bag, yer just drops it overboard, and then you and me's got to yell like blue blazes so as to prevent 'em a-suspectin' ennythink. D'yer twig?"

"Bill Jakins," exclaimed the awestruck Hunkers in a solemn whisper, "you're a masterpiece, that's wot you are. A blimy masterpiece."

At the moment there sounded across the anchorage a prolonged and dismal toot, and attention being thus directed to the steamer it was seen that her cable was being hove short, while the Blue Peter fluttered down from the foremast head and disappeared. Simultaneously the little gentleman came skipping down the path, bag in hand, in a state of suddenly developed agitation.

"Now, then, you," he shouted, "don't you see that the steamer has lowered her Peter. If you don't stir yourselves, I shall lose my passage."

"All right, mister," replied Jakins in an aggrieved tone. "Ain't we been waitin' for yer this quarter of a hour?"

"No chatter now, no chatter," said Mr. Currie shortly. "Cast off your painter and pull out. Well, good-bye, Morton, don't forget what I've told you, and mind you let me know how the remedy works. Now, pull away!"

A few minutes' steady rowing brought the boat close alongside the steamer; and none too soon, for already the clatter of the steam windlass was audible, winding in the chain cable.

"Other side, other side," exclaimed Mr. Currie impatiently; "can't you see there's no ladder on this side? Why, confound them," he added, as the boat passed under the vessel's stern, "there's no ladder this side either. Hi! *Blackbird*, ahoy! where's your accommodation ladder?"

A head appeared over the quarter-rail, and a voice proceeding from it inquired, "What do you want?"

"Passenger coming aboard!" shouted the small gentleman; "where's your accommodation ladder?"

"It's being repaired," replied the officer. "I suppose you can get up a Jacob's ladder, can't you?" and without waiting for a reply, he tumbled the wooden-runged rope ladder over the gangway.

"Hup with yer," said Jakins gleefully; "I'll bring yer bag after yer."

"No, you won't," replied the passenger. "You keep your hands off that bag. I can take it myself."

The waterman's countenance clouded somewhat at this, but he glanced at the ladder swinging some two feet away from the vessel's side — for she had a slight list to port — and hope revived within his heavy breast.

The little gentleman seized the bag with one hand and with the other made a grab at the swinging ladder, on to which he hoisted himself; but after dangling helplessly for some moments, twisting round and kicking his legs frantically in the air like a gigantic spider suspended on a single thread, he dropped back into the boat and enveloped himself in a lurid atmosphere of imprecation.

"Hurry up, please," said a voice from above, "the anchor's broken out and we want to get off."

Mr. Currie banged the bag down on a thwart, and turning to Jakins exclaimed hoarsely:

"Here, you stand by to pass that bag up to me as soon as I get on deck and mind you handle it carefully, d'ye hear?"

"I hears," replied Jakins, repressing with difficulty a grin of delight (for he felt his heart as light as a bag of feathers). "I hears and I understands. Now, hup with yer."

Once more did the irritable little gentleman commit himself to the swaying ladder, up which he slowly crept hand over hand, swearing to himself as he went, in a hoarse undertone. He had not, however, ascended more than halfway when his ears were saluted by a loud splash and a simultaneous howl of dismay from the two watermen.

"What's that?" he asked, as he paused, dangling in mid air.

"Bags gone overboard," said Jakins, in a tone of alarm which was only half feigned.

"*What?*"

"Overboard it is, guv'nor," corroborated Hunkers, "and went down like a bloomin' stone."

For a few moments the neighbourhood of the boat was pervaded by a frightful calm such as broods over the sea before the bursting of a hurricane. Then the hurricane burst, and the air was literally darkened by a torrent of imprecations that fairly swept the watermen into the sternsheets of the wherry, speechless and appalled.

"Hurry up, please," said the voice from above once more "and you watermen pass up those trunks, and look lively, will you?"

"'BAG'S GONE OVERBOARD,' SAID JAKINS."

The stream of denunciation rumbled on like distant thunder as the passenger slowly dragged himself over the rail and the two conspirators proceeded to hand up the trunks with such alacrity as their shattered nerves would permit.

Then the question of the fare arose, but at the first tentative mention of the subject there was such a terrifying recrudescence of the hurricane that the two watermen hastened to unhitch their painter and push off fareless.

"Well, I'm blarmed!" muttered Jakins, mopping his purple forehead with the remnant of a blue-spotted handkerchief, as he watched the gush of water churning from the steamer's screw-port. "If this 'ere kind of sport ain't enough to make a man old before 'is time. Did jever see sech a venomous little viper! Sech langwidge, too. Why, it was purfectly shockin'."

"Is the bag all safe?" Hunkers inquired anxiously.

"Bob Hunkers," said the other solemnly, "do you take me for a blooming mug or do you not?"

"I do *not*," replied Hunkers emphatically.

"Then pull in shore there below the Lobster," and Jakins lolled back in the stern sheets and again had recourse to the blue handkerchief.

In and out among anchored barges and bawleys the boat threaded its way, until it arrived opposite the lonely, marshy stretch of shore just below the "Ship and Lobster." Here Jakins arose from his seat, and leaning out over the stern plunged one arm nearly up to the shoulder into the water.

"Have yer got it?" asked Hunkers eagerly.

By way of reply Jakins held up his dripping arm, displaying the cod-line hanging down taut into the water; and this being smartly hauled in, up came the bag with a squelch and a gurgle.

"The question is," observed Jakins, as he and his rascally companion sat gloating over their treasure, which stood in a little pool of water on the bottom boards of the boat, "the question is, is it notes or is it brass? It's 'eavy enough for brass."

"We'll soon see w'en we bursts the bag open," said Hunkers.

"I wonder if the fastenin's is strong," mused the other. "I should reckon a bank bloke 'ud keep 'is tin locker pretty secure, wouldn't you?" He reached out his hand as he spoke and began to finger the press-button on the clasp. Suddenly, to the men's astonishment, the bag flew open, and the two scoundrels craning forward simultaneously to discover its contents, their heads came together with a sounding crack.

At other times and under other circumstances mutual recriminations of a highly pungent quality would have resulted, but the moment was too tremendous for thoughts of personal injury. As the two pairs of eyes commanded the gaping mouth of the bag their owners recoiled and gazed upon each other with such an expression of stony horror and dismay as might have been called up by the face of the fabled Gorgon.

Yet the contents of the bag were not in themselves of a specially terrifying nature, consisting, in fact, of nothing more nor less than a black wine bottle.

"Well, this beats heverythink, this do," gasped Jakins, after an interval of awful silence.

"Wot's in the bottle?" groaned Hunkers.

Jakins picked it gingerly out of the bag and wrenching out the cork — which was already drawn — took several deep sniffs.

"Sherry wine, it smells like," he pronounced in funereal tones.

"Them let's jolly well drink it," exclaimed Hunkers.

"I 'spose we may as well," sighed Jakins ruefully. "My Mary Hann, wot a orful suck in! I tell yer wot, Bob," he added, "we'll 'ave as comfortable a day out of it as we can. You just step ashore and cut along up to the Lobster, and give Miss Merkin my compliments and hask 'er to lend us a couple of tumblers. It's a pity to waste good sherry wine by suckin' it out of a bottle."

"Right y'are," replied Hunkers, and stepping on to the little causeway he shambled off to the inn.

"Got em?" sung out Jakins, as his partner returned down the causeway, and on Hunkers hauling the tumblers out of his coat pockets with a flourish of triumph, he continued:

"Jump aboard, and we'll just paddle down to the grass flat and 'ave our drink all quiet and rural-like."

With slow and deliberate strokes they pulled down to the pastoral spot that Jakins' poetic fancy had selected, and here they ran the boat's head aground, and having hitched the painter round a block of stone strolled across the sodden green to the river wall, Jakins carrying the precious bottle tucked under his arm, and Hunkers following as cup-bearer with a tumbler in either hand.

Arrived at the river wall the convivial pair seated themselves among the coarse, tussocky grass on the bank that forms its northern face, and Jakins having solemnly removed the cork and dusted the mouth of the bottle with the blue handkerchief, proceeded to dole out the liquor.

"Well, mate," said Jakins, holding the tumbler of golden liquid up to the light, and licking his lips at the anticipated treat, "'ere's better luck next time." Having proposed this toast — with grunted applause from his partner — he tipped up the tumbler and swallowed half its contents at a draught.

"My eye!" he exclaimed, smacking his lips with intense appreciation, "but these 'ere toffs knows a good drop of liquor. That stuff's better than four 'arf — ah! It's better 'n Jamaica rum, that it is."

"Chunks better," assented Hunkers, who was at that moment viewing the anchorage through the bottom of his tumbler.

"If we'd only got five bob out of 'im." said Jakins, as he put down his empty glass on a level patch of earth, "this 'ere sherry wine 'ud have been worth all the trouble we took; as things is, it's come a bit dear." He lifted the bottle by the neck and held it up to the light.

"There'll be another 'arf tumbler apiece," he remarked.

"There ain't no hurry to finish it," said Hunkers.

"No," agreed Jakins, "it 'ud be a pity to mop it all up at once as if it was beer."

So the two men sat, their countenances beaming with contentment, and gloated in silence over the bottle which stood on a flat stone at their feet.

Presently their faces began to undergo a curious change. In the first place their ruddy complexions faded by degrees to a dirty grey, while the expression of joyous contentment gradually gave place to one of anxiety and watchfulness. Each furtively observed the other out of the corners of his eyes, and each commenced to display an increasing anxiety and depressing mood.

"Did I 'ear the sound of firin'?" said Jakins suddenly — looking round with staring eyeballs and a drooping under-lip. "I believe I 'ears 'em a-shootin' at the butts: I'll just run up and have a look." He rose wearily and began to slowly crawl up the bank: half-way up, however, his pace, of a sudden, became greatly accelerated, and he shot over the wall with the agility of a kangaroo, and vanished towards the ditch.

Scarcely had he disappeared when Hunkers leaped to his feet and madly scrambled up the bank a few yards farther down, vanishing with even greater precipitancy than his partner.

Some five minutes later two pale and careworn watermen appeared over the river wall (from slightly different directions). each wiping his eyes assiduously and each ostentatiously unaware of the proximity of the other. They resumed their seats by the half-empty bottle, at which they glowered for a while in gloomy silence.

Presently Jakins spoke in quavering tones, and with an air of sorrow. "This 'ere liquor," he remarked, "ain't the sort of stuff that a cove cares to go on a-drinkin'. It's a bit too rich-like, and it kind o' sticks on the palate."

"'Ere, you stow it, Bill," exclaimed Hunkers huskily.

"D'ye care for another drink, Bob?" asked Jakins suavely.

Hunkers did not reply. Some sounds from the other side of the river wall had apparently attracted his attention, and with characteristic impetuosity he had hastened to investigate.

When he returned Jakins was still pensively regarding the bottle.

"Bob," he murmured as his partner approached, "wot are we going to do with it?"

"Let's heave it overboard," returned Hunkers promptly, and the proposition meeting with Jakins' approval, he picked up the bottle, and the two men advanced in procession to the water's edge and solemnly committed it to the deep.

A Bird of Passage

A SOFT south-westerly wind had stolen up in the night upon the frost-bound town of Gravesend, and covered it with a fleecy mantle of fog.

The pavements glistened with the wet, the bare trees burst into tears of joy, which they shed upon the hats of passers-by and the streets were dim vistas of vaporous light, peopled with moving shadows.

Down by the river nothing was visible but a blank and formless expanse of white, save when, as the fog thinned for a moment, the form of an anchored collier loomed up, shadowy and unreal, disclosing a ghostly cook cleaning a spectral saucepan outside the galley, and then slowly faded away like some marine Cheshire cat, leaving her stumpy jibboom sticking out of the void some seconds after she had vanished.

A unnatural silence had fallen upon the river. The usual chorus of hoots and growls was hushed, but there came out of the woolly void a new and unwonted sound. "Ding, ding, ding, ding, ding! Dong, dong, dong, dong, dong!" It seemed as if out in the fog there was moored some floating asylum for insane stewards, whose delusions kept them perpetually ringing up an endless succession of imaginary dinners.

Mingled with this chiming and tolling there came a flatter sound which an expert ear could resolve into the warning note from some belated craft, whose skipper, in the absence of a fog-bell. battered the bottom of a saucepan with the butt-end of a marlin-spike.

The muffled chime of a church clock had just announced the hour of eleven when the white space framed by the railway arch was sullied by an elongated smear, which presently took shape and assumed the visible characters of an elderly lady of a gracious and benevolent aspect, and apparently in comfortable circumstances. She wore an ample sealskin cloak and carried on her arm a travelling rug, from which. as well as from her overshoes and a capacious bag. it would have been reasonable to infer that she had just come from the adjacent station.

She stepped briskly out to the edge of the quay opposite the yacht club, and hailed with her umbrella a Customs gig that at that moment emerged from the fog.

"See that old jude, Bill," exclaimed the man in the stern. "a-wavin' 'er umbrella at yer. She's got 'er eye on yer. Bill. There's a old puss for yer!" The three men broke out into simultaneous grins and vanished, grinning.

A few seconds later a boat containing two men appeared, crawling westward, and at these the old lady held up her umbrella, as though hailing a cab.

"Was you a-wantin' a boat, mum?" one of them asked, standing up and staring at the apparition on the quay.

"Yes, certainly: boat ahoy!" And the lady waved her umbrella with a gesture of impatience.

The two men brought the boat alongside the causeway, and with great deliberation hitched the painter to a ringbolt. Then they slowly made their way up the sloping pavement, accompanied by two elfish inverted reflections.

"Did I understand as you was wantin' a boat?" the elder of the two inquired, turning a dim and filmy eye somewhat doubtfully on the lady.

"I don't know what you understood." replied the lady, "but in point of fact I do want a boat."

A tart rejoinder was on the waterman's lips, but he noted the sealskin cloak, which seemed to hint of affluence, and he determined to hold his vocabulary in reserve until the fare had been paid.

"Wot ship?" he inquired shortly.

"*Cornwall*," replied the lady.

"*Cornwall*, did you say, missus?" exclaimed the second man in a tone of dismay. "Why, d'yer know — "

"Now you bloomin' well dry up, Bob Hunkers," interrupted the elder waterman wrathfully. "Always a-shovin' in your oar where it ain't wanted, you are. It'll be wanted bad enough presently, so you can save yerself up. See?"

Mr. Hunkers grunted, and, turning away, began to whistle.

"I think you said the *Cornwall*, mum," said the elder waterman, turning to the lady with greasy suavity.

"Yes, the *Cornwall* training ship. You know her, I suppose?" she added, a little impatiently.

"Know her?" exclaimed the waterman. "I should bloomin' well think I do. Every timber and every trunnle of 'er is as formiliar to me as — as — ennythink. 'Owsoever, I'll jest 'ave a few words with my mate if yer don't mind, mum."

"Let them be as few as possible then," replied the lady, drawing out a tiny gold watch and regarding it significantly.

The two watermen drew apart a few paces, and Mr. Hunkers proceeded to unburden his mind in a hoarse whisper.

"Are you clean off that fat 'ed o' yourn, Bill Jakins?" he inquired with suppressed fury. "Ain't the *Cornwall* off Purfleet?"

"Used to be," responded Jakins.

"Well, how the blazes are we going to get to Purfleet in this here fog, with a strong ebb tide a-runnin', too?"

"P'raps we shan't get there," answered Jakins serenely. "But we can start, can't we?"

"Wodyer mean?"

"Old wimming," said Jakins oracularly, "is nervous creechurs. She's got a gold watch — I see it jest now."

The two men regarded one another silently for a moment. Then Hunkers murmured. "Right y'are, Bill, lead the way," and they turned towards their victim.

The latter had, in the meantime, been somewhat curiously employed. As the watermen retired to confer she stepped a few paces apart, and, turning her back to them, plunged her hand into the recesses of her cloak and drew forth the end of a small india-rubber tube, which was capped by a brass valve. This valve she quickly unscrewed, and, lifting her veil, applied it to her lips and commenced to blow into it with surprising vigour. And as her breath hissed into the tube, a muffled crackling was audible in the depths of her clothing, while at each blast there was a visible increase in the girth of her chest. She had just screwed down the valve and replaced the tube under her cloak when the waterman finished their colloquy and approached.

"We're ready, mum, when you are," said Jakins.

"Then let us start," she replied.

"You'd better let us help you, mum," said Hunkers gallantly. "The steps is wet and them rubber shoes o' yourn is precious slippery."

Each of the watermen then took one of the lady's arms, and the little procession moved cautiously down the shining causeway towards the boat.

"You set yerself there in the sternsheets and wrop yer rug round yer. This 'ere fog's cold on the water." Thus the paternal Jakins as he took his seat on the thwart and moistened his palms for the prospective labour. And his fare, tucking the rug around her, settled herself cosily for the long journey with an air of placid preparation; but a close observer might have noted under the enshrouding veil a pair of glittering eyes, that wandered anon restlessly towards the quay while the slothful Hunkers, with great deliberation. disengaged the sodden painter from the ring-bolt.

At length the boat was free. The watermen seized their oars, and with a sturdy shove sent the craft clear of the causeway. Then the blades dipped with a soft splash, the tholes creaked, the water gurgled under the stern, and the boat, with its occupants, faded away into the fog.

The plash of their oars had hardly ceased when the silence of the quay was broken by the sound of heavy and rapid footfalls, and there came forth from the void under the railway arch two men, who strode forward as though in haste. They were tall men and powerful, of a semi-military cut, and they wore boots of the pattern patronised by the Metropolitan Police. As they came opposite the causeway they paused, and peered into the fog on all sides.

"What infernally bad luck!" one of them exclaimed, as he gazed with screwed-up eyes into the woolly blank. "Who would have thought of the door being locked?"

"We ought to have tried it, having got in from the off side," said the other.

"Yes," growled the first man dejectedly, "and one of us ought to have had the gumption to carry a railway key."

"I generally do," returned the other, "but this company has a special lock. However, we ought to bring it off yet. He certainly came down this way, for there were only two, and the one we followed was the wrong one. I vote we separate. You go along here and I'll go towards the town. If you don't see him you can run back and overtake me."

"I suppose it's all right to separate?" said the first man doubtfully.

"Oh, yes," replied the other. "He's not a big chap, and we've got our whistles."

"Very well, then," rejoined his companion. "You'll go straight on to the pier?"

"Yes. So long."

"So long."

And they turned respectively east and west, and were speedily swallowed up in the fog.

Out on the dim and ghostly river the little craft with its three occupants seemed environed in a vast solitude, for though the clang of multitudinous fog-bells vibrated in the thick air, and seemed, indeed, to grow ever nearer, yet the voyagers carried with them their own circumscribed horizon, and the visible universe for them was comprised in the circle of yellow water that surrounded the boat. Now and again, indeed, some thin and vaporous shadow appeared on the white wall that closed in their moving solitude, but the wary watermen at once altered the boat's course so that the shape vanished before it had come within the field of vision of the passenger in the stern. For these shadowy forms had in common one peculiarity, and a very remarkable one it was when duly considered. They all emerged from that part of the fog that lay astern of the boat, and slowly overtook her at a singularly uniform pace, whence, as we have said, they were first perceived by the rowers who faced aft, and who speedily turned the boat away from the neighbourhood of these strange apparitions.

They had rowed on in unbroken silence for nearly half an hour when a tall barque thrust her jibboom through a specially dense bank of vapour, and, before the boat could be sheered off sufficiently, slid majestically across the verge of their little horizon. At the lofty fabric thus brought within view the old lady gazed with uncommon interest and some little surprise, and as it faded away she turned her eyes inquiringly on Jakins.

"Some large steamer, I suppose, going up to London?" she remarked.

Jakins coughed behind his hand with an air of embarrassment, but the less diplomatic Hunkers burst into undisguised guffaws.

"Haw, haw! Steamer, eh? Oh, Lord! Why, that ain't a steamer. That's a sailing vessel — what we calls a barque. that is."

"But," objected the lady, "I saw no sails set."

"Lor, bless yer, mum," chuckled Hunkers, "yer don't suppose a sailing vessel always keeps 'er sails set, do yer?"

"Certainly not," replied the lady sharply; "but what I mean is, as she has no sails set, how was it that she was moving along so rapidly?"

"Well I'm blowed!" Hunkers began with renewed merriment, but his speech was cut short by an interruption from the astute Jakins.

"Why, you bloomin' juggins, Bob Hunkers," exclaimed that ancient mariner, "do yer call yerself a seaman born and bred, and not know a steam vessel from a bally wind-jammer? Couldn't you see as that barque was a-bowlin' along under horgzilliary steam?"

As he turned to put this question he scowled at his partner in such a peculiarly horrifying manner that the appalled Hunkers relapsed into speechless bewilderment.

The ice of silence being thus broken, the tedium of the journey began to be relieved by snatches of conversation.

"Is the *Cornwall* anchored far from Gravesend?" the lady asked.

"Oh, she ain't nowheres near Gravesend," replied Jakins. "She's off Purfleet, she is, and that's getting on for half way to London."

"You don't say so," exclaimed the passenger. "Then I need not have come to Gravesend at all. How foolish of me! But I suppose you won't be so very long getting there with the tide in your favour."

"Ah! but it ain't in our faviour, yer see. It's a-runnin' down 'ard and strong." Here Jakins paused to mop his face with a red handkerchief.

"Then I suppose we're not more than half way there yet," said the lady in a tone of disappointment.

"'Arf way!' exclaimed Jakins. "Why, we've on'y jest started. I tell yer we're a-creepin' up agin a strong ebb tide."

"Dear, dear, how unfortunate! And to think how easily that steamer seemed to glide through the water, quite regardless of the tide."

"Yer right there, mum," said Jakins sadly. "The days of sails and oars is gone by. Steamers is the things nowadays — there's another of 'em," he added hastily, as a collier brig hove suddenly out of the fog astern and slid slowly past the boat.

The lady gazed at the vanishing stern of the collier and sighed.

"How swiftly, how easily she moves," she remarked, "propelled by the invisible but giant power of steam! There seemed to be something like a buoy attached to her bows by a rope. Now what would that be?"

"Trinity vessel, most likely." replied Jakins promptly. "She'll be takin' the buoy up to London to be repaired. And talking of buoys," he added, as if anxious to change the subject, "was you ever aboard the *Cornwall* afore?"

"Never."

"Goin' to have a look at the reformatory boys, I s'pose?" suggested Jakins.

"Well, yes — that is to say. I am going to see one of them."

"No relative, I 'opes," said Jakins anxiously.

"Oh, no. A former servant of mine — a page boy, you know."

"Ho! And wot might 'e a-been a-gettin' up to?"

"Well, it's a sad story, and I've always thought my husband was a little severe with him. He was a good boy, a dear affectionate lad, but he had one fatal weakness — it was spoons."

"Ah! 'e wos too bloomin' affectionate, 'e wos," observed Jakins.

"Yes," continued the lady, "that was his ruin, the naughty dear. He couldn't resist a spoon."

"The young varmint!" murmured Jakins. "'Ow old might 'e 'ave been, mum?"

"He was just thirteen when he left us," replied the lady.

"Scissors!" exclaimed the waterman. "D'ye 'ear that, Bob? Only thirteen! There's a young rip for yer!"

"Yes, he was but a lad," the lady sighed regretfully, "and, for my part, I should have let the matter pass, but the other servants wouldn't have it."

"I should think not!" declared Jakins virtuously. "From a kid in buttons, too. Quite right of 'em."

"I don't think you quite understand me," said the passenger. looking a little puzzled. "What I mean is that when he was washing the spoons he had a silly way of slipping one into his pocket now and then; and when his box was searched, we found six dessert spoons, all Potosi metal. The poor lad had mistaken them for real silver."

"Wot a do!" grunted Jakins sympathetically. "That comes o' bein' a 'ammer-chewer. 'E orter a-got skilled advice."

There was a silence that lasted some minutes. Suddenly, there hove up out of the fog right astern of the boat a strange, tall shape. that slowly swept alongside and passed away into the mist ahead. It floated upon a circular base, and was surmounted by a conical iron cage, upon the summit of which was a small lantern that winked periodically with solemn irony, and on the side of the cage the word "Ovens" was painted in large, white letters.

"Now, what on earth can that thing be?" exclaimed the lady, gazing in the utmost astonishment at the tall structure as it bobbed and curtsied on the swell.

"That, mum," said Jakins, off his guard for the moment. "is wot we calls a gas buoy. It is planted 'ere for to warn mariners of a dangerous quicksand wot'll swoller 'em up if they don't mind their eyes."

"Indeed! How very interesting! And what is the meaning of the word 'Ovens' which was painted on the buoy?"

"That's the name of the quicksand, mum, that is. So called becos the ships wot run-on it gets done so jolly brown."

"Really. But I thought that buoys were always fixed — tied up to something, you know."

"So they are, of course," said Jakins; "else wot 'ud be the good of 'em?"

"Well, but this one was moving along." objected the lady.

"Lor' bless yer, mum!" broke in Hunkers, "that wasn't the buoy what was moving. It was *hus* a-passin' 'er."

"But how could that be?" the lady persisted. "It was going the same way as we are — only faster."

"By gosh, but the lady's right!" exclaimed Jakins, with sudden enlightenment. "The Ovens buoy's adrift, Bob!"

"Get out, Bill," protested the obtuse Hunkers.

"I tell yer it is, straight," vociferated Jakins, turning to his partner with the most frightful facial contortions. "And wot are we goin' to do now?"

"Blowed if I know!" replied Hunkers, speaking the literal truth for once.

"'Ere's a pretty go," groaned Jakins. "Oven's adrift and us right a-top of that orful quicksand, for all we knows!"

At this moment a dismal hoot from some outward-bound steamer came faintly through the fog.

"Some pore fellers in distress," muttered Jakins sorrowfully.

"You don't say so!" exclaimed the lady.

"I do, indeed, mum, Ah, a perilous place is the London river, specially in a fog. Wot with the rocks and shoals and the quicksands and the silent deaths a-creepin' down on yer, it's a bad place for a big ship, but it's wuss for a little open boat."

"You don't anticipate any danger, I hope?" said the lady, with an air of alarm.

"Well, mum," replied Jakins, "as to danger, yer see, accidents will 'appen. They do every day — specially in fogs — lots of 'em. Why, I've been capsized myself some forty or fifty times, and always in a fog; and as to my mate here, 'e's a regular hamphibian. In fact, mum, when there's a fog on the river we generally likes to be paid our fare as soon after starting as possible."

"Indeed. Why?"

"Well, mum, d'ye see, it's like this. Sipposin' ennythink 'appens, sech as gettin' run down by a steamer or the likes o' that. Then wen our bodies comes to be picked up or floats ashore, if we ain't been paid, the money's in your pocket instead of our'n, and our widders and horphans is left without so much as a bloomin' stiver for to pay for a kick-up at the funeral. Which ain't right, mum."

"No, certainly not," replied the lady in a somewhat agitated voice. "Then I suppose you would like me to pay you now?"

"If it's all the same to you, mum, we should," replied Jakins.

"And what will the fare be?" the passenger asked, as she unclasped a dainty Russia-leather purse.

"Wot d'yer say, Bob?" inquired Jakins, addressing his partner over his shoulder. "Can we do it for two quid?"

"'Tain't much," grumbled Hunkers. "Still times is 'ard, so we must be content, I s'pose."

"Then shall we say two pun, mum?" suggested Jakins.

"It seems a great deal," objected the passenger. "However, you know best what is the proper fare. Two pounds," and she handed two sovereigns to the waterman, who, having examined the coins narrowly, tied them in a corner of his handkerchief and stuffed the latter into his breeches pocket.

"Now we're all right, wotever 'appens." he said cheerfully. adding, as he noted the expression of alarm on his passenger's face, "not as there's any occasion for you to be decomposed, mum. We *may* bring it orf all right yet."

Nevertheless, from the moment that he pocketed his fare, Jakins' nervousness increased in the most surprising manner. Every few strokes he paused to listen and peer into the fog, and every few minutes he discovered and eluded some unseen peril.

"Look out, Bob!" he yelled, and as the bewildered Hunkers stared about on all sides without perceiving anything, he wrenched at his oar furiously and then paused to mop his face.

"By gum, that was a narrow shave!" he exclaimed solemnly.

"Wot was?" inquired his partner. "I didn't see nothink."

"Didn't yer 'ear that silent death?" demanded Jakins paradoxically, turning to his mate and winking like a paralytic owl.

"I did think I 'eard somethink," conceded the mystified Hunkers, "but I didn't see nothink."

Disconcerting episodes of this kind occurred on an average about every three or four minutes, and as the dangers increased, so did the passenger's alarm, which was perhaps intensified by the invisible nature of the perils that hemmed them in.

"Do you think." she presently suggested, "that it might be advisable to abandon the journey and put me on shore somewhere?"

"Well, mum, that might be considered," replied Jakins. "Of course, it would be a extra."

"How an extra?"

"Our agreement wos to take yer to Purfleet. If we puts yer ashore ennywheres else it's a extra. One pound we should charge yer."

"That doesn't seem fair at all."

"P'raps it don't," rejoined Jakins, "and p'raps it do. Look out, Bob!"

But Hunkers had become callous to these alarms, and merely backed his oar indolently.

"Look out!" shouted Jakins again. "Don't yer see?"

A hoarse hoot from ahead drew the attention of the less vigilant Hunkers to a tall shadow that was stealing out of the fog, and bearing down right on to the boat, and he pulled with a will. But it was none too soon, for the sharp bow of a Grimsby fish carrier passed within a dozen feet of the boat's stern.

"Look out for 'er wash now," said Jakins, turning the boat's head round to meet the onrushing swell; "and you please to sit quite still, mum, or you'll 'ave us a-capsizin'."

But even as he spoke a deeper, hoarser roar boomed out, and the two startled watermen, turning simultaneously beheld the shape of a large steamer looming up end on.

"Round with 'er, Bob!" bawled Jakins. "Never mind the wash. Sit still, mum, if you please. D'ye 'ear? Sit down, will yer, yer chuckle-'eaded old catamaran–"

But it was too late. As the boat came broadside on to the heavy wash of the fish carrier, the affrighted passenger gave a loud shriek and sprang to her feet. With a hollow gulch the water poured in over the gunwale, and the boat quietly settled, and turned bottom upwards.

As the knot of deck hands, who had rushed to the steamer's gangway in response to the look-out man's alarm, peered over the side, they saw approaching them an overturned boat, two very wet watermen clinging to floating oars, and an elderly lady, who bobbed about on the swell with the buoyancy of an empty bottle.

"Chuck the line to the old woman — she's the nearest," shouted the mate to a seaman who was hastily gathering up the fakes of a coil of light rope. "Now!" And as he spoke the skilfully flung line darted straight towards the old lady, who grabbed it eagerly, and instantly came splashing and wallowing alongside like a well-hooked pollock.

"Hoist her up there!" shouted the mate but there was no need, for the dame came shinning up the side with an agility as remarkable as had been her previous floating capacity.

"Stand by to lower a boat called the captain from the bridge; but the boat was never lowered, for even as the watermen floated away astern, a tug was seen to emerge from the fog and make straight for the capsized boat.

"Now, ma'am," said the captain regarding the rescued fair one somewhat sourly, "what's to be done with you? We can't be hanging about here in this fog, you know."

"What is your first port of call?" asked the lady with chattering teeth.

"Lisbon," replied the captain.

"Very well, I'll take a passage," rejoined the lady.

"Lady's coming on with us!" shouted the captain to the pilot, who stood with his hand on the telegraph.

The pilot breathed a sigh of relief. The engine-room bell clanged, the propeller throbbed. and the steamer slowly forged ahead down the Lower Hope.

On a certain evening, about a fortnight later, Mr. Jakins sat at his ease in the riverside parlour of the "Old Amsterdam." On the opposite bench sat his faithful ally, Bob Hunkers; on the table by his side was a tumbler of gin and water (hot with); in his hand was a copy of the *Gravesend Standard*.

Suddenly he laid the paper on his knee, and gazing at his partner, exclaimed in a tone of deep conviction —

"Well, I'm jiggered!"

"What's up?" inquired Hunkers.

"Wot's up? Why, jest you read this 'ere, and then you'll know wot's up." And he passed the newspaper to his partner, indicating a paragraph with a neutral-tinted forefinger.

Hunkers took the paper, and somewhat haltingly read aloud the following notice: –

"The Great Banknote Forgery. The man Jackson still eludes the vigilance of the police. It now transpires that about a fortnight ago he was tracked to Gravesend by two detectives from Scotland Yard. but as he was cleverly disguised as an elderly lady wearing a handsome sealskin cloak, they had some doubts as to his identity. Unfortunately, the door of the compartment in which the detectives travelled was locked, and before they could liberate themselves, the fugitive escaped from the station, and, a dense fog prevailing at the time, he disappeared, and has not since been seen of or heard of. A careful watch has been kept at all ports of embarkation on foreign-going vessels, so that it seems pretty certain that he has not left the country.

"Did jever 'ear of sech a do, Bob?" groaned Jakins. "A reg'lar plant it was from beginning to end. 'E come aboard a puppos to capsize us and git picked up by a ship wot 'ad passed the Customs. Why, we orter a' bled 'im for a 'undred quid at least!"

The Sleuth-hounds

A select party of three lighter-men, who occupied a bench outside the "Ship and Lobster" on a warm spring afternoon, suspended their earnest conversation as a seedy-looking boat. propelled by a seedy-looking waterman, approached the landing-stage.

"Here comes Bill Jakins," said one of them, with gloomy disapproval. "I suppose he'll be pokin' his nose into it. Always on the make, is Bill."

"He won't see it, bless yer," said another. "He'd make straight for the bar like a tin-tack to a magnet. You see if he don't."

Apparently the last speaker was right, for the new-comer, having secured his boat, came up the steps with a thirsty eye fixed on the tavern door. His hand was extended to push it open, when it was drawn inwards and a man emerged, wiping his mouth.

"Wot-O, Bill!" exclaimed the emergent one.

"Wot-O, Bob!" was the answering greeting.

"Have yer seen the notice?" asked Bob.

("There, what did I tell yer?" growled the first lighterman.)

"Wot notice?" demanded Jakins.

"Come and have a look at it," said Bob.

Jakins gazed wistfully into the bar, but, after a moment's hesitation, turned and followed his companion.

The notice, which was affixed to the front of the tavern, set forth that Whereas it had come to the knowledge of the Comptroller of His Majesty's Customs that certain persons had from time to time unlawfully imported quantities of tobacco from craft anchored in the river, and were believed to have transported the same across the Kent and Essex Marshes: Now the said Comptroller of His Majesty's Customs was willing to pay the sum of twenty pounds to any one who should give to the Chief Preventive Officer at Gravesend such information as should lead to the arrest of the said persons; who were believed to be two in number, and of one of whom the following description was given: Age, from twenty-five to forty, of medium height, fair (or medium) hair and moustache, grey eyes, nose slightly twisted to the left (or right). When last seen was wearing a blue cloth jacket and trousers, a check shirt, and a red neckerchief.

"Twenty pund!" murmured Jakins. "That's a tidy sum to go a-beggin'." He leered round cautiously at the three lightermen, who had risen to look over his shoulder.

"Yes," said Bob, "it is that. And you could spot one of 'em, anyhow: you'd know him by his nose. What does it say?" He drew his finger down the bill and read out: "'Nose slightly twisted to the left (or right).'"

"If it's twisted at all," said the first lighterman, "it's got to be twisted to the left or right, unless it's upside down — which ain't likely."

"Oh, you're bloomin' smart, you are, Sam Gollidge," said Jakins, sourly; and he was about to pursue the subject, when a collier's boat was seen approaching the inn; whereupon the party broke up in an instant and the several members disposed themselves in postures of easy negligence at the railing overlooking the landing-stage.

A man stepped out of the boat, leaving a boy in charge, and strode up the stage swinging a large market basket, blissfully unconscious of the silent notes that were being taken of his blue jacket and trousers, his check shirt, red neckerchief, fair hair, and grey eyes. Half-way up the steps, however, he halted suddenly and addressed Jakins:

"What the blazes are you staring at me for, you monkey-faced old scarecrow?"

"I thought I know'd yer," replied the abashed waterman.

"Well, you'll know me next time, I reckon," retorted the mariner.

"He was a-lookin' to see if your nose was twisted, mate," said Sam Gollidge, slyly.

He'll be lookin' to see if his own nose is twisted, if he ain't careful," was the wrathful rejoinder, and the speaker stalked up the steps and dived into the inn.

Jakins bestowed a baleful glance on the grinning lightermen, and, touching his friend Bob on the arm, followed the sailor into the bar.

Two "goes" of cold Scotch had been consumed in meditative silence, and the third had just been tipped into the glass from the little pewter measure, when the door opened once more and two strangers entered. Jakins turned in the act of raising the water-bottle, and, as his filmy eye lighted on the new-comers, his arm became arrested as though he had encountered the petrifying glance of the snaky-haired Medusa. It was certainly an astonishing coin-cidence. Each of the strangers bore with callous unconcern, in the full glare of daylight, the incriminating stigmata of the printed description. Not only did each present, naked and unashamed, the grey eye, the fair hair and the moustache *en suite*; not only did each man flaunt the damnifying insignia of the blue suit, the check shirt, and the red neckerchief; but, to clench the matter beyond all dispute, the nose of each exhibited a noticeable lateral deflection, the one to the right and the other to the left.

And therein lay the abstruseness of the problem that engaged the mighty intellect of William Jakins. Which of the two was the genuine Simon Pure? Was it Tweedledum with the nasal inclination to starboard, or Tweedledee with the list to port? Each answered fully to the description on the bill, which nevertheless specified only one man. It was a mystery; in fact, it was a corker. In a word, it was a fair knock-out.

Jakin's meditations had reached this point when he caught the eye of the collier, who had just stuffed two half-quartern loaves into his basket. The collier glanced meaningly at the newcomers; then he looked at Jakins and winked solemnly, after which, with a sphinx-like grin, he opened the door and vanished. Rousing himself from his reverie, Jakins approached one of the strangers (Tweedledum), and asked in insinuating tones, as he displayed an empty pipe:

"Yer don't happen to 'ave a scrape of baccy about yer, I suppose, mate?"

"Baccy?" exclaimed the other, jovially. "Lashin's of it, mate." He hoisted out of his pocket a colossal slab of "hard," and, sawing off a hunk with a jack-knife, handed it to the waterman. Jakins accepted it with effusive thanks, and, having shredded a pipeful, swallowed his whisky, beckoned myster-iously to his friend, and went out.

"Did yet see 'is nose, Bob?" he asked, in a hoarse whisper, as soon as they were outside.

"Where?" demanded Bob, looking eagerly about the gravel path.

"That cove inside," said Jakins, impatiently. "That's him right enough."

"That's 'oo?" inquired the bewildered Bob.

"Don't holler so loud, Bob," admonished Jakins. "Can't yer see they're alistenin'?"

The three lightermen had resumed their seats on the bench, and were, in fact, bestowing the most flattering attention on the two friends. One of them had produced a telescope, and he now playfully levelled the instrument at Jakins.

"Don't go a-lookin' at 'is ugly mug, Ted," protested Sam Gollidge. "You'll break the telescope."

Jakins glared malevolently at the speaker, and beckoning to his friend, sauntered off along the river-wall. "Now, you listen to me, Bob Hunkers," he said, impressively, when they were out of earshot. "That cove in there is the man wot's wanted for this 'ere smugglin' job, and the other one's 'is pardner. Now, we're a-goin' to see where they goes to. We ain't got no telescope like Ted Hotten — mine is at this moment in a shop winder in Windmill Street, labelled 'Unredeemed pledge, five-and-six,' — but we've got eyes. We'll see what craft they goes to, and we'll keep an eye on that craft. Twenty pund is twenty pund."

"So it is, Bill," agreed Hunkers. "It's ten pound apiece."

Jakins coughed, and, seating himself on a promontory of the sea-wall, directed a fishy eye towards the landing stage of the "Ship and Lobster." Presently two figures were seen to walk down the wooden causeway and step into a boat. A moment later they were seen shoving off, and then, turning the boat's nose down-stream, they came paddling quietly in the slack water.

"They're a-comin' along in-shore, Bob," said Jakins, rising from his seat. "Better not let 'em see us a-watchin' of 'em." He crept down the landward side of the sea-wall and sauntered along the path by the side of the ditch, followed by Bob Hunkers. From time to time he crawled up the wall to peer cautiously at the boat, and, as it drew nearer, he quickened his pace.

"There's a billy-boy brought up in the bight down below Shorne Mead," he reported, after one of these excursions. "I expect they belongs to 'er. Rare beggars is the Goole men for pickin' up stuff off the Dutchmen in the North Sea."

His surmise turned out to be correct, for as the two spies sneaked past the battery at Shorne Mead and concealed themselves in a ruined boat that lay rotting on the shore, they saw the two seamen pull alongside the anchored billy-boy, hand up their bundles of provisions, and climb on board.

"Now we knows where they belongs to," said Jakins, complacently shredding a pipeful of tobacco from the slab of "hard" that he had received from his prospective victim, "and I reckon we've got 'em — without the meddlesome swab Sam Gollidge and 'is lot goes stickin' their dirty fingers into the pie. I expect they're a-watchin' now through Ted Hotten's telescope, the inquisitive swines! Wot does lightermen want with telescopes, I should like to know?"

"Of course they don't," said Hunkers. "Eyes is good enough for the likes of them. How do you find that terbaccer, Bill? Smells rather good."

"Middlin'," replied Jakins, dropping the slab carelessly into his pocket. He puffed at his pipe thoughtfully for a minute or so, and then turned to his companion.

"The way," said he, "as they works the trick is this. They waits until the patrol boat 'as gone by, and then they pulls ashore to the saltings somewheres hereabouts. They lands and comes up the path to Shorne Mead, and then they takes the cart-track across the marshes to Higham Lane. Then they legs it along the Rochester Road through Chalk into Gravesend. See?"

"I see," replied the admiring Hunkers. "Lord, Bill, you 'ave worked it out pat, to be sure."

"Yus," said Jakins, "I reckon as I knows 'ow many beans makes five. Well, now, this is wot we're a-goin' to do. We comes down 'ere to-night — it'll be dark, d'ye see, 'cause there ain't no moon — and we brings that young limb of a brother o' yourn with us. We plants ourselves be'ind this 'ere boat and we lies dormant, so to speak. If they don't land, we must, come ag'in the next night; but if they do land, we watches which way they goes and we follers 'em, and your young brother, he nips off along the wall into Gravesend and gives 'em the word of the Custom 'Ouse which way we've gone. They sends out a party to meet us, and when we do meet we gives the smugglers into custody, and there y'are. Twenty pund."

Hunkers regarded his chief for a while in silent admiration. Then suddenly his face clouded.

"But suppose, Bill," said he, "suppose they didn't have no baccy on 'em, arter all?"

Jakins bent a look of stern reproach on his companion. "Bob Hunkers," he exclaimed, impressively, "did you suppose as I was sech a blitherin' fat'ead as to start on a jaunt of this sort without pervidin' for all emergencies?"

"Why, what do you mean to do?" asked Hunkers.

"I'll tell yer," replied Jakins. "I 'appen to 'ave a couple o' pound o' Dutch terbaccer at 'ome. I shall make that terbaccer into two packets and bring it with me to-night. Then when we sees the Customs blokes approachin', I drops the terbaccer into the road and we hollers out and makes a run at the smugglers. They naturally resists. Up comes the Perventives, and we gives the smugglers into custody. They searches the road and finds the terbaccer, and there y'are. Twenty pund. See?"

Hunkers gazed at his chief with undissembled reverence. "Bill Jakins," he exclaimed, struggling with his emotion, "you're a reg'ler Solomon, that's what you are. S'welp me! a bloomin' Solomon!"

The night was, as Jakins had anticipated, thick and murky as the two self-appointed guardians of His Majesty's revenues stumbled along the rough summit of the sea-wall, accompanied by a dark lantern and a lanky boy. As they came out on the flat by Shorne Mead they stooped and made their way through the long grass on hands and knees, Jakins hampered not a little in this mode of progression by the lantern.

"Not a word, you two," he hissed into his companions' ears, as he crawled forward, pushing the lantern in front; "not a sound, d'ye hear?"

At this moment he tripped over a hummock and sprawled forward, sweeping his nose tightly over the heated top of the lantern.

"'Ere! not so loud, Bill," protested Hunkers; and Jakins, thus admonished, continued his soliloquy in a lurid whisper.

They advanced thus quadrupedally until they reached the shelter of the boat, from whence the anchored billy-boy could be seen at intervals, when the murky sky lightened, as a dim blob of darkness. Here they waited, crouching in the long grass and peering from time to time round the bow of the decaying boat at the anchored craft, whose riding light twinkled cheerfully through the gloom, casting a trickling golden thread of reflection down into the quiet water. Bereft of the joys of conversation, and deprived of the consolation of a pipe, the watchers found the time pass heavily, and longed for some diversion to break the monotony. Hunkers sought to pass the time by gnawing the corner of a cake of negro-head; the boy refreshed himself by masticating stalks of grass; while Jakins lightened his vigil by addressing whispered maledictions to the lantern.

Suddenly Hunkers stopped champing and raised his hand to his ear. "Did you hear anything, Bill?" he asked, in a muffled voice. "I thought I heard someone a-talkin'."

Jakins paused in an abortive effort to lick the end of his nose, and listened. And then the boy, having got a long stalk of grass into his throat, became involved in respiratory difficulties.

"Oh, you infernal, fat-headed, misbegotten young blighter!" exclaimed Jakins, in a hoarse and threatening whisper. "If you don't stop that 'awkin' and splutterin' I'll skin you alive, I will. You'll go and give the whole show away."

Here Hunkers nudged his leader vigorously. "Listen, Bill," said he. "There, don't you hear nothing now?"

Jakins ceased his objurgations and listened. There were unquestionable sounds now, not of voices, however, but of oars, and the stealthy dip and muffled jar upon the tholes hinted broadly of some secret mission. Soon, out of the dimness on the river, the dark shape of a boat stole almost noiselessly shorewards, and, taking the ground at the edge of the saltings, emitted three silent and spectral figures.

"There's three on 'em, Bob," whispered Jakins. "We must get nearer, else we shall lose sight of 'em. 'Ere, you take this blighted lantern and I'll lead the way." He passed the lantern to Hunkers and started off through the long grass on all fours, looking in the dim light uncommonly like a not particularly anthropoid ape. He had proceeded some distance at as rapid a pace as this unusual mode of progression would permit, when his advance was suddenly checked by his head coming into violent collision with some hard object — which object turned out, on inspection, to be the head of another person proceeding in the same manner, but in the opposite direction. The exchange of mutual compliments was speedily followed by mutual recognition.

"Bill Jakins, by Gosh!" exclaimed the stranger.

"Sam Gollidge!" ejaculated Jakins. The two men glared at one another for a stupefied instant; then they grappled and rolled over on the grass with warlike bellowings.

Hunkers started to his feet, as did also the boy. Simultaneously two other figures arose as if out of the ground. The boy, with singular presence of mind, made off at a brisk trot towards Gravesend, and the two strangers bore down upon Hunkers, who greeted them warmly — one in the eye and the other in the stomach. Undismayed by this reception, they grabbed him with a tenacious grasp, and the three men, closely embracing, swayed to and fro and revolved around one another until, invidious Fate leading their footsteps to the vicinity of the prostrate warriors, they tripped up and fell in a squirming heap on the other two combatants.

Meanwhile the three spectral figures on the shore, who had at first moved forward with stealthy but uncertain steps, now, attracted no doubt by the noise of battle, advanced across the saltings at a swift run. Simultaneously three other figures came out from behind the shed by the ruined boat, and the two groups converged upon the struggling heap. One of the newcomers carried a lantern wrapped in a cloak, which, being duly unveiled, shed its light upon the prostrate men, who thus became aware of the new arrivals; and though their eyes were dazzled by the glare, they were not so much dazzled as to be unable to recognize the uniform of His Majesty's Customs.

Five pairs of eyes looked up and five voices announced in husky triumph: "We've got 'em!"

"So it seems," said the man with the lantern, apparently the chief officer of the party. "And now you can hand them over to us." At a sign from their leader each of his subordinates grabbed one of the men and hauled him to his feet. Then the chief flashed his lantern on to the faces of the captives.

"Just what I thought," said he. "All Gravesend men."

"It was us wot caught 'em," said Jakins, in a breathless voice; "Bob Hunkers and me. And we hereby gives 'em into custody."

"Why, you lyin' old reprobate!" snarled Sam Gollidge, "it was *us* caught *you*, and *we* gives *you* into custody."

The officer grinned genially. "It's a quaint position," he remarked. "Each of you caught the others, and you all give each other into custody. Well, I give it up; you'll have to settle it before the magistrates. Hallo! what's this?" Drawing his hand down Jakins's coat, he detected on either side a bulging mass, and with an adroitness born of long practice he extracted from the respective pockets two angular parcels.

"That there seems to be terbaccer," Jakins explained rapidly. "I just took it away from Sam Gollidge."

"Why, you old perjurer," bawled Sam, "haven't I just took a full two-pound of baccy away from you and got it in my pocket at this very instant?"

"Pass it out, then, and let us have a look at it," said the officer.

Sam Gollidge handed out his two parcels, and the officer, having unfastened all four packages, examined their contents by the light of the lantern. And as he did so his mouth widened into a grin.

"You say, Jakins, that you took this tobacco from Gollidge?"

"I do," replied Jakins, doggedly.

"And you, Gollidge, say that you took your lot from Jakins?"

"That is so, sir, s'welp me –"

"Don't trouble to s'welp you," said the officer; "but what you'll have to explain to the magistrates is this: that whereas Jakins's parcel contains Dutch East Indian stuff, yours, Gollidge, contains American plug. Now then, no more jaw. Get along down to the boats."

The Free Trip

THE SUN had already sunk into a bank of cloud behind the tall chimneys of Northfleet when a down-train rumbled into Tilbury Station. Its advent was duly noted by the officials of the ferry steamer that lay alongside the pier. Deck hands secured the gang-planks, firemen withdrew into the stoke-hold, and the captain mounted to the bridge.

But there was another observer by whom the train's arrival had not passed unheeded. Swinging from the iron steps to the scope of a couple of fathoms of a frayed rope was a shabby waterman's boat, toned by age and weather to that indefinite grey beloved by artists and despised by mariners; and seated in the stern was a waterman who matched his boat so admirably that, like her, he seemed to cry aloud for a coat of paint.

The passengers poured out, with hurried tramplings, from the tunnel-like bridge that leads from the station to the pier, and, at the sound, the waterman crept up the steps and cast a pale, inquisitive eye along the pontoon. Particularly was his attention attracted by a young woman, who separated herself from the other passengers, and was apparently not going by the ferry-steamer. She was accompanied by a porter wheeling a trolley-load of luggage, and, as she talked to him volubly and with evident excitement, she looked rather wildly up and down the pier.

"Here's one," said the porter, as his eye lighted on the waterman.

"You stay here a minute, ma'am."

He up-ended the trolley and bore down upon the waterman.

"'Ere, Jakins," said he; "I've got a job for you."

"Ho? 'Ave yer?" The waterman ascended another step, and regarded the trolley with haughty indifference.

"Yes," pursued the porter. "This lady wants to be put aboard of a steamer what's coming down presently. Now, if I recommend her to employ you, you've got to treat her fair, d'ye hear?"

"Oh, 'ave I? And don't I treat everyone fair?"

"No, you don't," replied the porter with emphasis.

"The charges what I've known you to make for allowin' people to risk their lives in that crazy old basket of yours, what hasn't had a coat of paint in the memory of man, and is fair fallin' to pieces with natural decay –"

"Wot d'ye mean by this here langwidge," demanded Jakins, "and by a-runnin' down my boat, wot's as good as noo and as tight as a whisky barrel—"

"Git out!" said the porter. "You're confusin' the boat with the boatman. Tight indeed!" And having delivered this shaft of wit, he retired grinning to fetch the trolley.

Two substantial sea-chests and a large canvas bag having, by the united efforts of Jakins and the porter, been deposited on the boat's half-deck, the waterman cast off the rope, and, bestowing a malignant scowl on the porter, seated himself, and began to pull out into the fairway.

"Wot ship was it as you was a-wantin' to board, mum?" asked Jakins, regarding the homely luggage with considerable disfavour.

"The *Avonmore*," was the reply, and the passenger continued rapidly: "She is a small steamer painted grey with a yellow funnel. I should know her at once. She was lying at Purfleet, and I ought to have gone on board there, but I fell asleep in the train and missed the station. I am going to Hamburg in her to meet my husband, who is the captain of a barque, and, as he expects to sail from Hamburg early the day after tomorrow, it won't do for me to miss him."

"No, you'd be reglar up a tree," agreed Jakins.

"It was unlucky for me that I dropped off to sleep in the train," pursued the passenger, "but it's an ill wind that blows nobody good. It has made a job for you."

"It have," said Jakins. "Wot's one man's meat is another man's poison." He was not exerting himself violently. The ebb tide had only just commenced to run down, and by pulling gently up stream, slightly athwart the current, the boat was carried towards the slack water by the Gravesend shore. Already the twilight was fading, and the night was coming on apace. The twinkling light on Tilbury-ness popped in and out with a brightening lighthouse, and the anchorage glimmered like a constellation of glow-worms.

"How much is that doze in the train going to cost me?" the passenger asked with a sly smile, as she peered into the gloom up Northfleet Hope.

Jakins had already considered the case in all its bearings, and now replied deliberately:

"Untimely slumbers is apt for to be expensive. The cost of this here jaunt will be two pounds."

"Two pounds!" repeated the passenger in incredulous dismay. "You don't mean that I've got to pay you two pounds just for rowing out to this steamer?"

"That is igzactly wot I do mean," replied Jakins, "and forty shillin' is the exact amount."

"Oh! but I can't afford all that; I can't really. I'm only a ship-master's wife, you know."

"I wish you'd mentioned that sooner," said Jakins reproachfully, "cos then I needn't 'ave 'ad the trouble of pullin' yer all the way back to the pier."

"But I can't go back now; I should miss the boat. Couldn't you make it a little more reasonable?" she added, coaxingly.

But the waterman was obdurate.

"Forty shillin' is the sum," said he. "If you likes to pay it, we goes on. If you don't, we go back. It's for you to choose."

The woman reflected, and tears of vexation gathered in her eyes. But as she looked once more into the darkness of Northfleet Hope, a triangle of lights — red, white and green — stole out of the gloom, and the dim shape of a steamer appeared in their midst.

"I've no choice," she said bitterly, "and you know it. I call it downright robbery." She drew out a shabby purse and with trembling fingers extracted two sovereigns.

"There you are," she said, choking down a sob as she handed the coins to the impassive waterman. "I don't know what my husband will say."

"I think I do," said Jakins; but he did not mention the nature of his surmise, and if he had it would probably have been unsuitable for verbatim reproduction in these blameless pages.

Meanwhile the steamer loomed up larger and more distinct against the dim sky, and details of funnel and mast and derrick cam into view.

"This looks like the *Avonmore*," said the passenger, watching the approaching vessel closely. "You'd better get ready to pull alongside and hail her. Yes," she added after a pause, "it is her, I am sure."

"*Avonmore* ahoy!" roared Jakins, manoeuvring to run alongside.

"Say it's Mrs. Parkins," requested the passenger, as an interrogative bellow proceeded from the steamer's bridge.

Jakins did so, in a voice like that of an asthmatic buffalo, and added a demand for a rope's end. Instantly the steamer's engines stopped and then slowly reversed. The boat swept alongside, a coil of rope dropped into her from the forecastle, and a rope ladder tumbled down from the gangway.

"Thought you'd missed your passage, Liz," said a cheerful voice from the bridge, as Jakins scrambled after the escaping rope — which he only caught by the extreme end. "Here, Simmons, help Mrs. Parkins up the ladder and get a rope over to hoist up the luggage."

The lady ascended the ladder with the agility of one used to the ways of ships, the chests and the canvas bag were hauled up after her, and Jakins was about to cast off the rope when the voice from above hailed him.

"Hi, waterman! Just hold on a minute. I want you to post a letter for me."

"Right O!" said Jakins; "let's 'ave it then."

"I've got to write it first. If you like to come up, you can have a glass of grog while I'm writing it. Your boat'll be all right; we're going dead slow."

Jakins mounted the ladder, moistening his lips, and followed the captain into the little saloon.

"There now," said the skipper genially, putting a bottle of whisky on the table, "you mix yourself a glass while I write this letter." He supplied himself with paper from a stationary rack and sat down at the table, while Jakins surreptitiously poured out two-thirds of a tumblerful of whisky. The letter was not more than half written when five hurried blasts of the whistle were followed by that particular kind of tremor of cabin floor and furniture that means full-speed astern.

"What the deuce is that?" exclaimed the skipper, justifying the colloquial epithet by the manner in which he rose from his chair and left the saloon. He was absent nearly five minutes, and he returned wiping his brow and muttering.

"These confounded barges," he growled, "are the plague of this London river — all over the channel like a lot of sheep on a turnpike road."

"Ah," said Jakins, "'specially when the wind's agin the tide, same as it is now."

The skipper nodded as he noted with surprise that the waterman's glass was fuller than when he went out.

The letter finished, the skipper enclosed it in an envelope, affixed a stamp, and laid it on the table, together with a half-crown.

"Ther you are," said he. "Now get into your boat sharp and post that as soon as you get ashore."

Jakins regarded the letter and the coin gloomily, and remarked: "It's usual for to make it five bob."

"What! Five shillings for posting a letter?" demanded the captain, growing suddenly red and wrathful. He snatched both objects from the table, and, dropping them into his pocket, pointed to the door.

"Clear out!" he commanded.

"Give 'em to me," said Jakins: "I'll take 'em."

"No, you won't," said the captain, "you'll just get overboard and be quick about it. Of all the greedy money-grubbing old rascals," he continued, as he hustled the discomfited waterman out on to the deck, where Mrs. Parkins was standing, watching the lights of Gravesend slip past. "I hope he didn't make you pay on the same scale, Liz. Eh? What did he charge you for putting you on board?"

As the captain approached this delicate topic Jakins accelerated his movements, and, at the final question, he went over the bulwark and down the ladder with an agility surprising in a man of his years. Mrs. Parkins briefly stated the amount of the fee.

"What!" bawled the skipper, with an incredulous scowl: "two pounds? ... Two ... pounds! The infernal, outrageous, grasping, swindling, unconscionable, shameless, bear-faced, extortionate old THIEF!"

As the skipper poured forth this cumulative string of adjectives, he backed towards the side, and, to give better effect to the final epithet, was about to thrust his head over the bulwark. But at that moment the waterman's face rose, like the harvest moon, above the rail, within a couple of inches of his own, so that the denunciation was discharged at point-blank range, and with a violence that nearly blew the denounced one over-board.

Jakins paused in his ascent and gazed blankly into the furious face that confronted him. The skipper paused from sheer lack of an adequate vocabulary, and the two men stared at one another like a pair of rival hypnotists. At length the skipper partially recovered the power of articulate speech.

"Geg-get-get down into your rotten boat, you — you — you old body snatcher!" he spluttered, raising a threatening fist.

"There ain't no boat there," groaned Jakins.

"What?" bawled the skipper.

"The boat's broke adrift," whined Jakins. "The rope's parted."

The skipper drew a deep breath.

"Pass me up the end of that rope," he shouted to the deck hands.

The dripping line was hauled in, and, as one of the men brought it aft, the skipper ran it through his hands.

"Look at that, you superannuated Ananias," he exclaimed wrathfully, holding out the whipped end of the rope. "What do you mean by saying my rope's parted? Do you think I should let my hands throw you a rotten line? It's your own incompetence; you must have made fast with a granny or a tom-fool's know, perhaps — sort o' thing you would do, you darned old shore-rat. Come off that ladder and let 'em haul it in. Ring on full speed, Mr. Jones," he added, looking up at the bridge.

"But wot am I goin' to do?" moaned Jakins, crawling over the bulwark.

"You're going to pay your passage to Hamburg or else jolly well starve," was the cheerful reply. The skipper's spirits seemed to be rising quite suddenly.

"But wot about my boat?" persisted Jakins. "She's a-driftin' about in the river."

"I suppose she is," said the skipper. "You'll have to pick her up on the way back — that is, if you've got enough money to pay your passage from Hamburg."

"I 'aven't," said Jakins. "I shall 'ave to come back as I goes — as a distressed mariner."

"A distressed what?" roared the captain.

"Mariner," repeated Jakins.

"You'd better not let any of the hands hear you call yourself a mariner," said the captain, "or I won't be responsible for the consequences."

Jakins was silent for a while, and the skipper, affecting to ignore him, watched him out of the corner of his eye. Presently the waterman approached him with an air of deep humility.

"Look 'ere, captain," he said in a wheedling tone, "I'm a pore man, I am, and my boat is all wot stands betwixt me and the work-'us. Now if you was to 'ave the goodness and the charity for to bring up alongside one of the coal hulks, it wouldn't take you not five minutes, and I might save my boat, which is all wot stand betwixt –"

"Can't be done," said the captain, brusquely. "I can't waste my owner's time on a parcel of longshore pick-pockets. You'll have to go on to Hamburg."

Jakins snatched off his cap, apparently with the intention of tearing his hair, but Providence having fore-stalled him, he scratched his polished scalp instead and groaned aloud.

The coal hulks slipped by, one by one; the light on the Ovens buoy loomed up ahead, winking frantically, and the crimson eye of the Mucking lighthouse glared fiercely across the Essex marshes; and, at the sight of these familiar landmarks, soon to be exchanged for the monotonous and unfamiliar ocean, the waterman shook his head and sighed gustily.

"Don't make that noise," said the captain. "We shall have the harbour master complaining."

Jakins turned upon him with a look of reproach.

"Captain," he said, in a funereal voice, "my 'eart is a-bustin'."

"Oh!" was the callous rejoinder.

"Well, stand a bit further away from the door of the saloon."

"Mrs. Parkins, mum," whined Jakins, casting an imploring eye on his late passenger, "couldn't you try and persuade the captain?"

"No, I couldn't," she replied tartly. "Captains usually know their own minds." ("Husband wallops her," Jakins decided, and he derived secret comfort from the thought, though his woeful countenance in nowise relaxed.)

The steamer rounded the Ovens Spit and turned into the Lower Hope. The captain lit a cigar and resumed his pendulum walk up and down the deck. Presently he halted opposite the waterman and surveyed him with a benevolent smile.

"I tell you what I'll do, my man," he said. "I'll try to accommodate you. You don't want to go to Hamburg, and you do want to look after your boat. very well; I'll put you ashore at Thameshaven; only, of course, you'll have to pay for the loss of time and extra consumption of coal, and that sort of thing."

Jakins regarded him suspiciously. "How much?" he asked.

"Two pounds," replied the skipper.

"Wot?" gasped the waterman; "you don't mean two pounds for jest puttin' me ashore?"

"That's it," said the skipper; "just the ordinary waterman's fare for putting you ashore, and that's making no charge for the voyage to Thameshaven, or the wear and tear on the rope ladder, or the depreciation of the deck from your standing on it, or anything. Just the simple waterman's fare."

Jakin's heart was too full for speech — or, at least, for such speech as he would be allowed to use on the steamer's deck — and he fairly sweated with rage as he realised that he was being hoist with his own petard.

"Couldn't you redooce the passage money?" he pleaded. "I'm a pore man–"

"But I'm not charging you any passage money," the skipper pointed out. "You're having the voyage for nothing and just paying the bare waterman's fare for being put ashore."

"I can't afford it," groaned Jakins.

"That's your affair," said the captain. "It'll cost you all that to get back from Hamburg, and you'll stand to lose your boat into the bargain."

He resumed his walk and no other word was spoken until the steamer rounded Lower Hope Point. Then he halted once more and delivered his ultimatum.

"Now, make up your mind. Thameshaven's close aboard, and it's your last chance. Take it or leave it."

Jakins gazed into the inexorable face. Then he thrust his hand into his pocket and, drawing out two sovereigns, handed them silently to the skipper.

"Here you are, Liz," said the latter; "here's your two quid back."

He dropped the two coins into the woman's hand and stepped briskly up to the bridge. Immediately after the telegraph rang, the whistle emitted a long blast, and then a blue light flared up in the captain's hand.

The response to these signals was quite extraordinarily prompt, for the blue light had not completely burnt out when a voice hailed from the darkness on the steamer's bow, and a boat swept into the circle of lurid greenish light. A rope was flung and caught, and, a moment later, a man scrambled up on deck.

"Come aboard, sir," he announced cheerily.

"Very well, Mr. Shand," the captain called down from the bridge.

"There's a man here wants to go ashore. Now, you old rascal, over you go."

Jakins lost no time in getting down to the boat, but, arrived there, he stood up and shook his fist at the bridge.

"This here," he shouted, "is a conspiracy. You was a-slowin' down 'ere anyhow, and you know'd this boat was a-comin' alongside to bring your mate aboard. You've swindled me out o' two pounds, and, I'll have the lore on yer when you comes back."

The captain chuckled softly, and, waving his hand towards the boat, rang on full speed ahead.

The Comedy of the Artemis

"A NICE, fresh, pleasant morning, this."

The speaker, a sun-browned, middle-aged man of gentlemanly aspect, glanced down the anchorage with its clustered groups of waiting craft, its water of lively blue, and background of warm sky made gay with flying clouds. The remark was addressed to an amphibious-looking person who was seated on a bench outside the "Ship and Lobster," thoughtfully shredding a cake of tobacco into the palm of his hand.

"Yus," replied the amphibian, without looking up, "it's a pleasant mornin', as you say." He paused to stuff the shredded tobacco into the bowl of his pipe, and then added, "It's the sort o' mornin' as makes a man enjoy a glass o' liquor."

The stranger displayed a disappointing lack of intelligent interest in this curious fact. He looked up at the sky, and down at the sharp horizon, and observed: "Looks like settled weather, too. Have you noticed the glass this morning?"

"Haven't had no opportunity," said the amphibian, "not 'avin' any small change about me."

"Ah," said the other indifferently — ("a thick-skinned blighter, and stingy, too," his companion decided, "not to understand a delicate hint like that there") — "you look like a waterman."

"There's nothin' singler in that," was the sulky reply, "'cos I am a waterman. A free waterman of the City of London, and Jakins is my name." The last item was announced with a sort of scriptural twang, accompanied by a look of awakening interest.

"I am looking," said the stranger, "for a respectable man to act as caretaker of my yacht. Perhaps you can help me, as I know nobody down here. Perhaps you can tell me of some suitable man who would take on the job on reasonable terms?"

Jakins reflected awhile. "You would want an honest man, a man of unreproachable character? he suggested.

Undoubtedly."

"And would be willin' for to pay accordin' to that man's unusual merits?"

"I will pay anything that is fair."

"Then," said Jakins impressively, "Providence have guided your footsteps, for that man is a-standin', or leastways, a-sittin' before you at this very instant. Was you a-goin' to lay 'er up?"

"No, she is to be sold. I expect a gentleman down to look over her next Friday, and as I can't be here myself to manage the business. I want a responsible man to look after my interests. I suppose you know something about yachts?"

Jakins regarded his questioner with pained surprise.

"Man and boy," said he, "for nigh upon sixty year come next February twelvemonth, have I used this here river, and never before have I been asked if I knoo my bizness."

"Then I understand that you are prepared to take the job?"

"Yus. On sootable terms."

"Very well: then the first thing is to get the yacht hauled into the basin. Can you get a boat?"

"I can," said Jakins, casting a pale and rheumy blue eye on to the anchorage. "My own boat is at this moment approachin' the stairs in charge of my mate, Robert Hunkers, a worthy and respectable man, though thick-'eaded."

Thus announced, Bob Hunkers stepped on to the causeway, and, having made fast his painter to a ring, came up the stairs gazing sheepishly from his partner to the stranger.

"Wot O! Bill," said Hunkers, using the invariable and comprehensible formula.

Jakins growled and rose stiffly from the bench. "Is the lock gates yet?" he inquired.

"Will be by now, I should think," replied Hunkers.

"Then," said Jakins, "we'll get down to the boat. This gentleman wants me to take charge of his yacht, and we're a-goin' for to haul her into the basin."

He slouched off towards the stairs in company with his new employer; and Hunkers, when he had slightly recovered from his astonishment, followed, scratching his head.

During the operations of getting up the yacht's anchor and playing out the tow-line, Hunkers behaved like one in a dream, glancing from time to time at his partner with incredulous admiration. At length the yacht was aweigh, the owner took his place at the tiller, and the two watermen pulled away with the long tow-line fast to their boat.

Then it was that Hunkers unburdened his soul.

"Do you mean to tell me, Bill, as that cove has made you skipper of his yacht?"

"No, you silly juggins," replied Jakins, "he's a-goin' to sell 'er, and he's appointed me to act as his agent."

"My eye!" exclaimed Hunkers, dazzled by the possibilities of this arrangement, "wot a bloomin' beano!"

"Rather!" assented Jakins. "There's goin' to be pickin's out of this job, let me tell you, so you must listen to me. The bloke wot's a-goin' to buy her is a-comin' down on Friday. Now I'm a-goin' to start this afternoon to 'elp old Sam Waters sail 'is barge up to Maidstone — 'is mate 'as got the yeller janders and can't go. Now, while I'm away, you just keep an eye on that yacht, and don't you let on as I'm not in Gravesend. D'ye see?"

"I twig, Bill. But I suppose you'll be back on Friday all right?"

"That was wot I was a-goin' to explain," said Jakins, "supposin' the weather goes crooked, and we missed a tide at Chatham so as I can't get back 'ere in time, why then you got to meet the chap and show 'im over the yacht."

"I see. And I jest tells 'im that you're called away on important business?"

"Do yer?" exclaimed Jakins, indignantly. "Why, you chuckle-headed blitherer, you'd bust up the whole bloomin' show! No, you meets the chap, and you sez 'I am William Jakins, I am,' you sez; and then you takes 'im aboard the yacht and shows 'im round; and you makes 'im buy 'er, mind you, whether 'e wants 'er or not. And then you takes a trifle — say ten or twenty pun' — on account, and you gives 'im a receipt for it signed 'W. Jakins.' D'ye understand now?"

"Yes, Bill." said Hunkers. "But would that receipt hold good?"

"Good enough for 'im," replied Jakins. But the question opened up further possibilities which he determined to consider at his leisure.

The lock gates were just opening as the yacht came abreast of the entrance to the basin. The bridge swung clear, and the two men pulled into the narrow lock, towing the yacht astern.

"You'd better bring her alongside the quay for the present," said the lock-keeper. "I'll find her another berth in a day or two, but we're pretty full up just now." He nodded to a dense crowd of yachts, with a sprinkling of bawleys, that filled up the middle of the basin, and, taking an extra tow-line, hauled the yacht through the entrance to the berth he had indicated.

"She'll be all right there," he assured the owner, when the latter had stepped up on to the quay and briefly explained the position. "I keep an eye on all the craft in here, and then, of course, there's your caretaker."

"Yes; by the way, do you happen to know anything of him?"

"Jakins?" said the lock-keeper. "Oh, yes. I know him." The latter statement was made in a tone so enigmatical that the owner would fain have pursued the subject; but the lock-keeper had turned away, and the caretaker approached.

"If you will step on board with me, Jakins," said the owner, "I will give you your instructions, and then I must be off to catch my train." He jumped down on to the yacht's deck, followed by the waterman, and the two men entered the cabin.

"Now," he said, seating himself on a locker, "there are two gentlemen in correspondence with me about this yacht: Mr. Matley and Mr. Hartzhorne. Mr. Matley is coming down on Friday, probably in the evening; he knows the yacht, and merely wants to look at the cabin fittings. Mr. Hartzhorne may come on the same day, or he may not; but whichever comes first will have the right to complete the purchase. I am going abroad immediately, and I want the matter settled."

"Supposin' they both comes together?" suggested Jakins.

"Then you will let them both see the yacht, and they will have to settle between themselves which is the buyer. And now I'll hand you over the keys and give you an authority to conclude the sale on my behalf."

He laid a small bunch of keys on the table, and taking a sheet of paper from his pocket-book, wrote out and signed a document authorising William Jakins to sell, on behalf of the owner, Stephen Halket, the twenty-ton cutter yacht *Artemis*, at present lying in the canal basin at Gravesend.

"There," he said, handing the paper to Jakins, "now you have full authority. Just give me your address and I will tell each of these two gentlemen to send you a card to say what time he is coming. You had better meet them on the bridge over the entrance, as that is easy to find and is close to the yacht's berth."

"Right you are, sir," said Jakins.

He followed his employer out into the cockpit, locked up the cabin, and climbed up on to the quay.

"All's a-goin' well, Bob," said he, as he watched his employer stepping out briskly across the bridge. "It'll be as easy as drinkin' swipes. You jest looks in at my lodgin's every mornin' whilst I'm away, to see if there's any post cards. If there is one namin' a time, then at that time mentioned you wait on the bridge until the cove — Matley or Hartzhorne — turns up. Then, when he comes on to the bridge, 'Mr. Matley,' sez you — or 'Mr. Hartzhorne,' as the case may be. 'Yes,' sez he. 'I'm William Jakins,' sez you. Then you takes 'im aboard, and mind you, you're got to sell 'im that yacht, whether 'e likes 'er or whether 'e don't; and you're got to get somethin' on account, and the more the better. 'Ere's the keys. Now you remember wot I've told yer, and don't go a-makin' any stoopid mistakes, like wot you generally does. I must be off now, else old Sam Waters'll think I ain't a-comin' after all."

Friday evening closed in murky and thick, with never a hint of moon or stars. At seven o'clock the lock-keeper lit the leading light at the entrance, and by half-past the basin was shrouded in darkness, through which the huddled craft loomed in vague shapes of deeper black. It wanted some five minutes to the half-hour when a shadowy figure halted at the middle of the bridge and leaned upon the railing, looking back along the road.

"Durned funny thing, this," muttered the voice of William Jakins. "'arf-past seven, the card said, and 'ere it is close on the time, and that silly chuckle-head, Bob Hunkers, not turned up yet. And 'im with them bloomin' keys in 'is pocket. Nice state o' things if 'he forgets to come. But p'raps he's gone on board a'-ready."

With this ray of hope before him, Jakins crossed the bridge quickly and made for the quay. There was the yacht, still lying in her original berth; but she was wrapped in silence and darkness, and he hastened back disconsolately to his post on the bridge. Three bells struck on an invisible liner out on the river and, immediately after, the bell of the *Jubilee* clock chimed the half-hour.

"'ere comes someone," said Jakins, as a quick footstep became audible.

A figure appeared out of the gloom, and took on the form of a short, middle-aged man.

"Mr. Matley?" queried Jakins, as the new-comer halted.

"Mr. Matley it is," was the reply. "You're Jakins, I suppose?"

"I am," said Jakins, staring anxiously down the dark road.

"Then," rejoined Mr. Matley, "we'll go on board at once, please."

His manner was imperative though pleasant enough, and Jakins had no pretext for delay. With a wild, despairing glance into the encompassing darkness, he led the way to the quay.

"Look sharp, man," said Mr. Matley, impatiently, as Jakins stood in the cockpit rummaging his pockets frantically.

"Well I'm blowed!" exclaimed Jakins. "'Ere's a pretty go! I've forgot to bring the keys."

"The devil you have! And how far off is your house?"

"'Tween three and four mile," replied Jakins.

Mr. Matley stared incredulously.

"Three or four miles from here to West Street, Gravesend? Here, come out of the way!" A bunch of keys jingled in his hand as he stooped at the cabin door; there was a rattling and a fumbling at the keyhole, the lock clicked, and Mr. Matley, pocketing his keys, the door open.

"A nice gim-crack sort of lock!" he growled. "I must see to that. Now, in you go." As he entered the cabin he struck a wax match and held it aloft. A lamp swung in gimballs from a bracket fixed to the mast, and when this had been lit the two men glanced round the cabin; and on the face of each was an expression of faint surprise.

"He's been making a good many alterations, I see," said Mr. Matley. "Have you got a copy of the inventory?"

"No, I haven't," said Jakins, "but I can give yer perticklers. This 'ere commodious yacht," he continued in his best auctioneering manner, "built of English 'eart of oak, and coppered with the finest copper –"

"Here, you can stow that rigmarole," said Matley, with a broad grin, "I know the yacht of old. She happens to be built of teak and sheathed with yellow metal."

Ignoring the discomfited waterman, he dived under the swing table to test the counterpoise, punched the locker cushions, rapped his knuckles on the maple panelling, peeped into the forecastle, and rummaged in the sail-room.

"What is the condition of the ballast?" he demanded.

"The ballast," said Jakins, "is the very finest lead-pig –"

"Oh, dry up!" snorted Matley. Turning back the carpet, he lifted a trap in the floor-boards, and, reaching down into the hold, hoisted out a rusty iron half-hundredweight.

"H'm," he grunted, as he replaced it, "they'll want scraping and painting. However, everything seems to be in order, so if you'll show me your authority, I'll write out a memorandum of transfer and you can sign it. H'm?"

"I shall want twenty pounds on account," said Jakins.

"Well, you won't get it," replied Matley, sitting down at the table and producing a sheet of paper and a fountain pen. "I'll give you a fiver to clench the transfer, but that's all I have about me. Will that do?"

Jakins groaned, but bowed to the inevitable. The assignment was duly written out, and a receipt for five pounds being attached, the autograph of W. Jakins was appended to both. The ceremony was just concluded, and the five sovereigns were jingling into the waterman's pocket, when a duplicate thump was heard on the deck above, and a couple of young men dropped into the cockpit. They scrambled boisterously into the cabin, and then halted suddenly.

"Morton not turned up yet?" one of them asked, looking equally astonished.

"And if I might harsk," said Jakins, "wot you mean by a-intrudin' –"

"Shut up, Jakins," growled Matley. "This is my yacht now remember."

"Your yacht!" exclaimed both the new-comers in unison; and one of them added: "Why, we come down to look over her."

"Then you've come too late," said Matley.

Jakins regarded the stranger who had spoken last with a bland and hopeful smile.

"Name of Hartzhorne?" he inquired.

"Name of fiddlesticks!" replied the other impatiently; "but I'm hanged if I understand –" Here a heavy thump on the deck was followed by the abrupt entrance of a large, red-faced man in a yachting suit. He halted near the door, and staring hard, first at Matley and then at Jakins, finally addressed the latter.

"Who the devil are you?"

Jakins fairly gasped with wrath and amazement.

"Well!" he spluttered, "of all the bloomin' bare-faced impidence–"

"Oh, shut your head and clear out," commanded the red-faced man. "D'ye hear? Get off my yacht, you beef-faced old horse-marine."

"Your yacht!" exclaimed Jakins and Matley with one accord. "Pardon me, sir," continued the latter, "but this is my yacht."

It was now the red-faced man's turn to gasp, and gasp he accordingly did.

"May I ask," he inquired, when he had somewhat recovered, "how she came to be your yacht?"

"Bought her," replied Matley. "How did you think?"

"And from whom did you buy her?" demanded the red-faced man. "Not from me, I'll swear."

"Naturally," said Matley, "I bought her from her late owner, Mr. Halket."

"Look here, Morton," interposed one of the strangers, "there is evidently some mistake. Some of us are on the wrong yacht."

"Obviously," agreed Morton. Then turning to Matley he demanded: "What yacht do you suppose this to be?"

"This 'ere," said Jakins, "is the commodious twenty-ton cutter *Arty Miss*, wot –"

"Nothing of the kind," said Morton. "This is the *Dolphin*. If you don't believe me, go and read the name on the counter."

A general adjournment and the expenditure of a wax match proved Morton's statement to be correct; and the company (with the exception of Jakins and the crest-fallen Matley) dissolved into broad grins.

"The *Artemis*," said Morton, "is lying over by the Canal Tavern. I'll put you across in the dingey if you like."

"Very good of you," said Matley, "and I hope you'll excuse–"

"Oh, that's all right," laughed Morton. "Are we taking the old gentleman with the complexion?"

"Look 'ere," said Jakins, "I'll harsk you to be more respeckful in your –"

"Are you ready?" asked Morton, casting off the painter.

Jakins scrambled into the boat, and Morton, dropping down after him, pushed off and began to ply the paddles. They had not pulled a dozen yards when another dingey passed them swiftly, and its single occupant was seen to mount the landing-stage and make off at a run.

"Seems in a deuce of a hurry, that chap," remarked Morton, driving the little tub forward with powerful strokes. "Ah, here's the *Artemis*," he added, as a cutter emerged from the gloom: "they moved her over yesterday to this berth."

He brought the dingey alongside, and hitching the painter to a shroud, stepped on deck, followed by his two passengers. The three men dropped down into the cockpit and looked curiously through the open door into the lighted cabin, in which a man could be seen industriously turning out a locker. He looked up at the sound of entry and demanded sharply:

"Well, what do you want?"

"The question is," said Jakins, "wot do you want?"

The man stood up and stared angrily at the intruders.

"I want you to clear out of my yacht, that's all."

"Your yacht!" exclaimed Jakins and Matley in a breath.

"Yes, my yacht," replied the stranger; whereupon Morton sat down on the floor of the cockpit and buried his face in his handkerchief.

"Good Lord," he murmured. "Is this the 'Arabian Nights,' or is it all a dream?"

"May I ask," said Matley, "how you came by this yacht?"

"Bought her, of course," replied the stranger. "How did you think?"

"Pardon me," said Matley, "but would you mind telling me when and from whom you bought her?"

"I don't see what business it is of yours," replied the stranger, "but, if you must know, I bought her about ten minutes ago from Mr. Stephen Halket, her late owner."

"I didn't know Mr. Halket was down here," said Matley.

"He wasn't," answered the stranger. "I bought her, actually, from his authorised agent, William Jakins. I'll show you the memorandum of transfer, if you'd like to see it."

"I should," said Matley, "because I, also, have just bought this yacht from Mr. Halket through his authorised agent, William Jakins, and can produce the memorandum of transfer."

The two purchasers stared blankly at one another, and each laid his memorandum on the table for the other's inspection.

"I should like to get hold of that man Jakins," the stranger remarked gloomily.

"There is no difficulty about that," said Matley, "because here he is."

"This!" exclaimed the stranger, glaring at Jakins. "But this isn't the man."

"I am William Jakins," affirmed that ancient mariner, "and here is my authority, signed by Mr. Halket. The other person was an imposter. I hopes you didn't pay 'im nothing on account, Mr. 'Artzhorne — for such I takes you to be."

"By Jove! I did, though. I paid the beggar ten pounds. I tell you what it is," he added, "there's more in this than meets the eye."

"There is, indeed," said Morton, with a broad grin. "There's the other man with your ten pounds. And to judge by the speed of his movements — if that was he who passed us just now — he hasn't any intention of meeting the eye."

"You see," said Matley, "my Jakins has the written authority, so we must assume that he's the right man."

"Yes," replied Hartzhorne, "but my Jakins had the keys of the yacht, so we must assume that he was the right man. I don't see what we are to do. It's a regular deadlock."

"I'll tell you what," interposed Morton. "Split the deal and go shares in her."

The two buyers looked at one another. "Not a bad idea," said Matley.

"Not at all," agreed Hartzhorne. "One man can't sail a twenty-tonner alone. I'm on if you are."

"Done," replied Matley. "We'll make it half shares."

"Then in that case," said Jakins, "you won't want me no more." He backed out into the cockpit and faded away into the upper darkness.

"By the way," said Matley, "what's to be done about that ten pounds of yours?"

"Oh, that's all right," replied Hartzhorne. "It was a crossed cheque payable to Stephen Halket, but I'd better drop a line to the bank."

"Well, gentlemen," said Morton, "I wish you joy of your bargain, and now I'll put that old rascal ashore, and look after my own little deal. Good-night."

He went off to the dingey, in which Jakins was already seated, and having delivered that ancient mariner at the landing-stage, pulled back to his yacht in high spirits.

And, meanwhile, Jakins strode off joyously towards the "Fountain Inn" to seek his partner, and to meet the greatest disappointment of his life.

Other Sea Stories

The Resurrection of
Matthew Jephson

ABOUT eleven o'clock, on a sultry autumn morning, a small fore and aft schooner, which had been lying by the quay in the harbour of Las Palmas, Gran Canaria, having set her various sails with much squeaking on the part of the blocks and much shouting on the part of the crew, slipped her mooring rope and slowly got under way. The light airs hardly stirred the sails, and when the sweeps, with which she had been worked out of the harbour, were taken in she crept out to seaward with a motion that was barely perceptible. On board the vessel the somnolent influence of the calm was evident; the master yawned by the tiller, the crew sat on the deck with their backs against the low bulwark, conversing sleepily and blowing clouds of smoke into the still air, while on that which would have been the weather side of the deck had there been any perceptible breeze, a solitary passenger walked meditatively to and fro. The short briar pipe that he held in his mouth and the cut of his clothing, no less than the truculent blue eye that he turned contemptuously now and again on the lounging Spaniards, proclaimed him beyond doubt an Englishman.

Matthew Jephson — such was the passenger's name — had been brought up to follow the sea as a profession, and he had, in fact, taken his master's certificate; but, after serving for three years as mate of a large Australian sailing ship, he had accepted the offer of an agency at Las Palmas and had settled down ashore. A couple of days before the commencement of this story he had, while sauntering down the mole, noticed a small schooner loading by the quay. During a talk with the men he learned that she was owned by his old friend, Señor Aldecoa, and was bound for Valverde on the outlying island of Hierro (or Ferro), and that she would probably be back in Las Palmas in the course of a week. Now Jephson had visited most of the Canary Islands and had frequently wished to see Hierro, but had not hitherto had an opportunity. He resolved, however, not to allow the present chance to slip, and so we find him a passenger on the *Manoel*, bound for that somewhat remote and out-of-the-world region.

He was not the only passenger. Half a dozen peasants were returning to their homes in Hierro, and two petty traders were bound for Valverde on business. These all squatted on the deck forward, chattering to one another and taking little notice of Jephson or of the crew.

About noon the breeze freshened somewhat, and the little schooner, with her sails now well filled, slipped along at quite a brisk pace, so that by the time evening began to close in, the Punta de Las Palomas, the most southerly point of Grand Canary, was passed and the vessel's head pointed west by north, straight on to Hierro.

Shortly after taking his frugal supper on deck (from a canvas bag which he had wisely stocked with provisions and brought with him), Jephson tumbled down the rude companion-hatch with the idea of turning in, but, he returned to the deck with much greater precipitancy, for the combined aroma of cheese, garlic, and humanity with which the tiny cabin was filled would, as he afterwards declared, have suffocated a polecat. He looked about the deck for a convenient spot on which to rest for the night, and finally made his bed on some spare sails in the bottom of the jolly-boat, which was supported on chocks on the main hatch. Here he lay smoking and dreamily watching the stars pass to and fro over the swaying mastheads. Presently his pipe went out, and he began to doze, and was just dropping off to sleep when he was roused with a start by a heavy thump on the vessel's bows.

In a moment he was out of the boat, and, running along the deck, he peered into the darkness on either side of the bows. For a little while he could see nothing beyond the dark water; but the steersman, who had left the tiller and rushed forward, suddenly pointed with an exclamation to the sea on the schooner's quarter, and Jephson could then distinguish faintly a long dark body, which almost immediately passed astern and vanished. It was evidently the mast of some wrecked vessel, and had been floating end on to the schooner when her bow struck it; hence the force of the impact. Having ascertained this reassuring fact, Jephson went back to his bed in the boat, and the steersman returned to his post.

Jephson's rest was not, however, very prolonged, for the dawn had scarcely broken when he was awakened by somebody dragging at his arm.

"What the deuce is the matter now?" he angrily demanded, as he stood up in the boat and bumped his head against the overhanging boom. By way of reply, the skipper — for it was he who had disturbed the Englishman's slumber — pointed to the large, one-handled pump, which was now manned by two of the passengers, who were working frantically while the sweat trickled down their fear-stricken faces.

"The hold is full of water," he remarked. "Last night we struck some wreckage and must have opened a seam, for just before daybreak the water began to come up through the cabin floor, and we started to pump out at once. It will be your turn after these two men."

"Do you know if the leak is a large one?" inquired Jephson.

"I can't tell at all," replied the skipper; "but I know that if I had not been sleeping on the cabin floor, we should have had a good chance of going to the bottom before anything was noticed."

At this moment the two men finished their spell and retired puffing and perspiring, in search of a dry spot in which to lie down. Jephson slipped off his coat and waistcoat and set to work with a will, sending a stream of water down the deck into the scuppers.

He had hardly been pumping ten minutes when the water that issued from the pump, from being clear and sweet, became suddenly dark and foul-smelling.

"Bilge-water," he exclaimed to the group of passengers and sailors that stood round encouraging him and waiting their turn, "we shall soon have it all out now."

This prediction was soon after confirmed when the pump sucked, showing that the hold was clear of water, and the alarm of the passengers and crew, to a great extent, subsided.

At this time the island of Grand Canary was visible on the horizon some thirty miles to the north-east. When the leak was first discovered the schooner was put about with the idea of making one of the ports in the south of the island without delay, but now that there seemed no immediate danger she was turned back on her original course, for the captain declared — as was indeed evident — that the leak could be easily kept under, and that in twenty-four hours they would be in Valverde.

The vessel sailed on all day before a steady breeze from the north-east. The island that they had left sank and vanished below the horizon about seven o'clock in the morning, and by five in the evening they were within forty miles of their destination. The passengers and crew took their turns regularly and cheerfully at the pump, and the stream of water from the scupper-holes flowed almost continuously, excepting for the hour's rest that was taken each time that the pump sucked.

It was about sunset that Jephson noticed, as he thought, an increase in the time taken to pump the vessel out completely. The two following spells of pumping he carefully timed with his watch without attracting notice, with the result that the second spell was clearly two minutes longer than the first. In the next interval he took the captain aside and mentioned the fact to him; but that officer had evidently observed the increase in the leak himself, for he said rather gruffly:

"The best thing for you is to do your work and make no remarks. If you frighten the men they will not pump at all, and then we shall lose the vessel."

There was little rest for anyone on board the *Manoel* that night, for before a man had time to settle himself comfortably for a doze his turn came round to work the pump.

Jephson took short rests in his old berth in the boat, and as he lay he could hear the water washing heavily from side to side in the hold.

At the first glimmer of dawn the passengers and crew crowded into the bows and strained their eyes into the west. A rosy haze at first obscured the horizon, but presently, as the light increased, there appeared in the west a faint blue shadow. It was Hierro.

A murmur of satisfaction arose as this was made out, and those who were not engaged in pumping sat down on the deck and consumed their simple breakfasts.

But as the day went on this satisfaction gave place to impatience and then to anxiety, for the faint breeze of the early, morning soon died away, leaving the schooner helplessly becalmed within twenty miles of the island. To make matters worse, the current, which here sets strongly to the south-west, carried her rapidly away from her destination and moreover to leeward of it, so that for every mile that she drifted she would have to sail six as she tacked back. As the morning passed the intervals of rest between the spells of pumping had to be reduced, and both passengers and sailors noticed the increasing length of the spells of work with undisguised anxiety.

"This leak is getting much larger, captain," said one of them as he finished his spell. "If a breeze does not spring up soon, we shall have to put off in the boat."

"Why not put out the boat now?" suggested another. "We shall never be able to keep the vessel afloat to get her into port; let us get the boat out before the schooner goes down under us."

The refrain was taken up by several more, and these were with difficulty appeased by the captain. It was evident that a panic was imminent among the passengers and crew; the leak was clearly increasing while their strength was as surely failing and with it their courage and self-control.

By four o'clock the vessel had drifted so far that the land was no longer visible. As this fact was observed the perturbation of the passengers and crew increased. They gathered in a knot by the windlass and talked excitedly for a few minutes; then they came aft in a body, and one of the passengers, acting as spokesman, addressed the captain.

"Captain, we want the boat launched. If you do not consent, we shall do it without your leave."

The captain, who was now seriously alarmed himself at the aspect of things, was not sorry to find himself thus relieved of responsibility if the vessel must be abandoned.

"Well," he answered, "there is no harm in having the boat alongside; in fact, it is better not to wait until the last moment if we should want her."

"That is all very true," interposed Jephson, "but you know perfectly well that as soon as the boat is in the water these fellows will stop pumping and crowd into her. If you want to keep your vessel afloat, you had better keep your boat on the chocks."

"If you take my advice, my, friend," said the passenger to Jephson, "you will not meddle with matters that do not concern you. You understand," he continued, addressing the captain, "that we are all agreed that the boat shall be launched, with your permission or without."

"You hear what they say," said the captain sulkily in reply to Jephson's look of inquiry. "There are twelve of them, and they mean to do as they please."

"If you intend to behave like a man you may count on my support at any rate," responded Jephson.

"Why, what will you do?" inquired the captain and the passenger together.

"I'll knock down the first man that attempts to touch the boat," replied the Englishman hotly, and by way of illustrating his intentions he picked up a marlin-spike that lay in a coil of rope.

"Come now, put that thing down and don't be a fool," urged the captain angrily. "You can't hold out against twelve men as good as yourself; besides, the boat ought to be got out in readiness in case she is wanted."

"That means that you agree to abandon the vessel?"

"It means, sir, that you had better mind your own business," retorted the captain as he turned his back on Jephson and walked away.

Jephson pursued him to the waist, where the men, who had already opened the gangway, were preparing to raise the boat from the chocks.

"It seems to me, my good sir," he said contemptuously, "that you would have done better to stay at home and attend to the house work and send *men* to sea. When I see my friend, Señor Aldecoa, I shall –"

With a curse like the growl of a wild animal, the man, infuriated by these taunts, rushed, knife in hand, at his tormentor. There was a momentary scuffle as Jephson dodged out of the way of the knife; then the Englishman's fist shot out and met his assailant's cheek with a resounding smack, and the Spaniard staggered backward through the open gangway plump into the blue water.

There was a general shout as all the men on the vessel ran simultaneously to the side, and in a few moments the captain was hauled in and stood dripping on the deck, scowling malevolently at Jephson but not attempting to renew the attack.

The boat was now dragged across the deck and launched through the gangway, and as soon as it floated alongside the passengers and crew began, as Jephson had predicted, to swarm into it with their goods and their bags of provisions. A reserve of food was brought from below by the sailors and a large beaker of water, and when these stores had been stowed in the stern sheets the sailors jumped in, and the captain advanced to the cleat to which the boat's "painter" was made fast, and, taking the rope in his hand, was about to cast it off.

"So you are going to desert your vessel?" said Jephson.

The captain made no answer, but commenced to cast off. Jephson took him by the shoulder, and roughly pushed him away from the cleat.

"What are you going to say to Señor Aldecoa when he asks how his vessel was lost? Will you tell him you ran away because you hadn't the pluck to stay and do your duty?"

"Knock him down! Stick your knife between his ribs!" shouted the men in the boat, who were rapidly becoming mad with fright lest the schooner should sink and draw them down with her. But Jephson still held the marlin-spike in his hand, and his appearance was not inviting.

"Are you going to cast off that rope?" asked the captain, white with rage.

"Are you not going to make some effort to save your vessel?" inquired Jephson by way of giving a Scotch answer.

For reply the captain sprang into the boat, and, whipping out his knife, cut the rope, while a sailor pushed off with the butt of an oar.

Jephson waited for a few seconds, expecting the men to pull alongside for him to get in; but when they had settled the oars in the rowlocks they began to pull steadily, and the boat rapidly receded from the schooner. Jephson shouted until he was hoarse, but neither the captain nor the men took any notice, and in ten minutes the boat was fully half a mile away.

He was abandoned with the sinking vessel.

II.

For the first few moments after he realised his position Matthew Jephson stood gazing after the fast-receding boat in a state of complete bewilderment.

The treachery and vindictiveness of the Spaniards appeared incredible, and he could not at first help cherishing a hope that they would presently relent and return for him. But as minute after minute passed and the boat kept steadily on her way, it became evident that if he did not wish to go down with the vessel he must take some measures to save himself, since the water had now been pouring in unchecked by the pump for half an hour.

Jephson looked round the deck in search of the materials for the construction of a raft, if there should be time to make one. At first sight there seemed little enough. There were no spare spars excepting a couple of long ash sweeps and a pair of small yards for rigging a square topsail — quite insufficient to form even the frame of a raft. Suddenly his eye fell upon a row of cases ranged along under the bulwarks on each quarter. The stencilled inscriptions on them stated that they were wax candles, and they were consigned to the priest at Valverde. They were evidently the long church candles, and these Jephson knew were commonly sent out soldered up in airtight tin cases. Here, then, was the material that he wanted, and without further delay he set about making such a raft as could be put together in the short time that was left to him.

First the four spars were loosely lashed together with pieces of lead-line into a square frame just large enough to hold comfortably nine of the cases. This frame being launched through the gangway and moored alongside, the cases were, one by one, worked down the deck and tumbled overboard into it until nine of them floated inside it.

The spars were now brought nearer together, so as to embrace closely the floating cases, and firmly lashed. A stout rope was also carried round each row of cases, passing underneath and over outside the frame. By this means a raft, some nine feet square, of fair floating capacity was produced — a ramshackle contrivance, indeed, that a heavy sea would have broken up in five minutes, but still an immediate refuge from drowning.

By way of making it more comfortable, Jephson thought he would fix a few floor boards across the raft, and he ran down the companion stairs with the idea of tearing up a few boards from the cabin floor. But there were already eighteen inches of water washing about in the cabin, and Jephson determined that he had better be off without further delay. He therefore gathered up hastily a portion of the provisions that were left in the lockers, and deposited them on the raft, together with a large stone bottle, which he filled with water from the butt near the companion hatch. At the last moment he discovered a spare oar lying by the windlass, and with this and a coil of rope he stepped on to the raft, cast off the line, and pushed away from the schooner.

Not a moment too soon, he thought, for even as he left the vessel the water was lapping up on to the deck through the open gangway, and bubbling up into the scuppers. He worked the raft away about twenty yards, and then stood by to see the *Manoel* go down.

Ten minutes passed.

Every moment the vessel seemed on the point of foundering, yet she kept afloat. She wallowed heavily but slowly, for the sea was still smooth and the calm continued. As she rolled towards the raft, Jephson could see that her boom nearly dipped into the sea, and the deck was wet for a foot from the gangway. But still she did not go down.

Half an hour passed.

The sun, which had been hovering a few degrees above the horizon, dived into a bank of slaty-blue cloud, leaving the sky all crimson and gold, and the sea like burnished copper. The form of the schooner, now a couple of hundred yards distant, stood black against the rosy glow of the sky as she slowly heaved from side to side, and the thump of the sheet-blocks as the booms swung over came across the water at regular intervals, like the throb of a large engine.

Why did she not go down? This question puzzled Jephson more and more as the time sped on. The light waned, and still the schooner floated.

Suddenly a light broke in upon his mind, and with it there came a ray of joyful hope. He remembered that while he was standing on the quay, watching the *Manoel* loading, he had seen a large number of casks — big wine casks — put on board. He had noticed that they were empty, and also that they formed the upper tier of the cargo, being stowed immediately under the deck. Clearly, then, the *Manoel* had settled as far as she was going to. Her cargo consisted mostly of light goods, and so, in spite of the leak, she was kept afloat by the tier of casks.

When he had finally come to this conclusion, Jephson put out his one oar and began to paddle the raft in the direction of the schooner, the form of which was rapidly fading in the gathering gloom. He was now as anxious to get back as he had been to escape a short time before, and he was fearful lest he should lose sight of the vessel; but a quarter of an hour's work brought him close alongside, and he commenced to cautiously reconnoitre.

As far as he could see, the vessel's condition was unchanged. The streak of wet upon the deck extended only a foot or so from the edge at the gangway, and when she was upright she still had a freeboard of fully six inches. Having noted these facts, Jephson stepped on to the deck and made a line from the raft fast to a shroud. He then ran to the companion hatch and looked down into the cabin. Here the condition of things was unchanged. About eighteen inches of water still washed about over the floor, and it was evident that no more had come in since he left. Jephson realised with a sigh of relief that, at any rate as long as the weather was moderate, the schooner was as safe as ever.

For some time past he had been filled with an overpowering desire for sleep, and it was by an almost superhuman effort of will that he set himself to do what was absolutely necessary.

The first thing was to transfer the provisions from the raft to the schooner;

and when this was done, the vessel had to be eased of some of the weight aloft. During the calm every inch of canvas that she could carry had been crowded on, and a considerable part of this would have to be taken in; so Jephson rubbed his eyes and set manfully to work. The schooner carried two large gaff topsails, as well as a jib topsail, and when these three sails had been taken in and both topmasts lowered on to the deck, the vessel was greatly eased, and no longer rolled so heavily.

She would undoubtedly have been more snug with most of the remaining sails lowered, and Jephson was considering the advisability of stowing them as he sat for a rest on the main topsail, which lay, on the deck, when his head dropped on to the heap of canvas, and into a deep sleep.

When he awoke the sun was near the zenith; and on looking at his watch, he found that he had slept nearly twelve hours, which, indeed, was not surprising, considering the fatigue and loss of rest that he had suffered.

The north-east trade wind had awakened too, and was blowing quite freshly, and the schooner lay head to wind with her canvas shivering; but when Jephson took the helm and put the foresail aback she paid off, and he then found that she carried her canvas fairly well in spite of her partially waterlogged condition, and travelled through the water at a good four knots. The compass had been taken from the binnacle by the skipper when the boat put off, but Jephson had a small charm compass on his watch-chain, and with this, as well as he could, he put the schooner's head on a course northwest-by-north.

III.

The boat which put off from the *Manoel* was launched at about five in the afternoon, and for fully an hour she was rowed briskly in a north-easterly direction.

In the hurry and scuffle that attended their departure the crew had neglected to bring a sail, so that every mile would have to be covered by sheer muscular effort. To make things worse, one of the four oars with which the boat was provided had been left on the deserted schooner, and although it was, of course, missed at once, no one cared to go back for it and face the infuriated Englishman. So the boat had to be worked with three oars, and with these she went slowly and heavily, but still for the first hour the men pulled briskly enough in their excitement. Then the fatigue, anxiety, and broken rest to which they had been subjected began to tell on them; several fell asleep as they sat, and as night approached it became necessary to divide the boat's crew into definite watches.

The first watch, consisting of the skipper and two seamen, was set about half-past seven. The remaining occupants of the boat lay down at the bottom, and, covering themselves with their wraps, fell into a dead sleep, while the two seamen pulled drowsily at their oars and the skipper held the tiller. Presently the skipper began to nod, then his head dropped forward on his chest, and he slept the sleep of utter weariness. The two seamen rowed on for a while, and then they, too, began to nod over their oars, and at length their hands fell motionless on their knees; they leaned forward, dropped from the seat into the bottom of the boat, and lay there wrapped in profound slumber. Meanwhile the oars, released from the sailors' grasp slipped up and down between the thole-pins as the boat rolled, and at each roll they fell a little lower. At length one of them went, with a quiet splash, into the water, and shortly after was followed by the other. For a few minutes they both lay alongside, now and again tapping against the boat's side as if asking for readmittance; then the light breeze that had just sprung up carried the boat slowly to leeward, and soon there was half a mile of heaving water between them.

IV.

There was no little excitement among the quay loafers of Santa Cruz de Teneriffe when it became known that the large steamer, which had just dropped anchor outside, had brought in a shipwrecked crew. Particularly interested was Señor Aldecoa, merchant and shipowner, of Las Palmas, Gran Canaria, who had come over to Santa Cruz on business only the night before, for he had just learned from the skipper of a coaster from Valverde that his schooner, the *Manoel*, was not only ten days overdue at that port — a thing in itself unheard of — but had not been seen or heard of since she left Las Palmas.

When the shore boat, therefore, was seen returning from the steamer, he was not surprised to distinguish, among the passengers with which it was crowded, the rather ill-favoured countenance of Juan Gomez, the skipper of the *Manoel*. Gomez, however, was not quite so prepared to meet his owner, and when, on reaching the top of the steps, he suddenly encountered Señor Aldecoa, he turned as pale as a ghost and staggered against a post. But that his nerves should be somewhat shaken was only natural, and Aldecoa, quite affected by the man's apparent grief, laid his hand kindly on his shoulder and bade him tell the story of his misfortunes. "So our poor little ship has gone to the bottom, has she?" he asked.

"Yes," Gomez exclaimed, in a tone of the deepest distress, "the beautiful little schooner is gone! The little *Manoel*, the pride and pleasure of my life — she is at the bottom of the sea. I shall never see her again! Ah!" and the man snatched off his cap and flung it on the ground, and, clutching his greasy hair with both hands, he burst into fresh tears.

A sympathetic bystander picked up the cap and replaced it on the head of the weeping mariner, remarking:

"Well! if she is at the bottom of the sea we may hope that you never will see her again."

"Yes, indeed," assented Aldecoa; "but tell us how it happened. Did she capsize?"

"No, no," replied Gomez. "She foundered. The very first night out we struck some sunken wreckage, and she sprang a leak and the water came in and filled the hold and filled the cabin, and although we pumped and pumped until we nearly dropped, still it kept rising till at last we were obliged to take to the boat; and before we were a dozen lengths away, the poor little schooner settled and went down like a stone." Here the skipper was again overcome.

"Then," he presently, resumed, "we drifted about in the boat for over seven days –"

"Why, how in the name of all the saints was that?" asked Aldecoa in astonishment. "You could not have been more than a few miles off the land when the schooner went down. Why were you not able to row ashore? — and where is the English gentleman? Where is Mr. Jephson?" he added quickly, looking round anxiously.

The skipper's already pale countenance became ghastly. He picked uneasily at his clothing, and his eyes wandered restlessly about on the ground.

"Ah, the poor English gentleman!" he exclaimed, glancing askance at his companions. "He, too, is lost; he also is at the bottom of the sea."

"What?" screamed Aldecoa. "Do you tell me that my poor friend is lost too? That is bad news indeed. The vessel was loss enough and all her cargo too; these could be replaced in time, but a human life and that of my dear friend –" Here the kind-hearted merchant, who was really attached to Jephson, drew out a large black handkerchief and wiped his eyes.

"Yes," continued the skipper, now speaking rapidly and keeping an eye on his companions; "it was in the first night after we left the *Manoel*. Mr. Jephson was rowing when he fell asleep for a moment and his oar slipped from his hand into the water. That woke him, and he jumped up and leaned over the boat's side to pick up the oar when he fell right over into the sea; he vanished completely in the darkness, and we never saw either him or the oar again. Do I not speak truly, my friends?" he added, addressing the crew and passengers, who stood around.

These miscreants corroborated the skipper's story in every detail with complete accuracy and consistency (which was not surprising seeing that the whole account had been rehearsed several times a day for over a week). They even enlarged on it. One of them pointed out that all their subsequent sufferings were due to this accident, "for, you see, we had to leave the schooner so hurriedly that we only brought two oars, and after this disaster we were left with one, and so could not bring the boat to land, but drifted right out to sea."

These explanations were for the present interrupted by the arrival of the Liverpool steamer *Secondee*, on which they would have to travel back to Las Palmas; and as she was blowing her whistle lustily, as an intimation that she did not intend to make a long stay, they all proceeded on board without delay.

It was late in the afternoon of the same day when the *Secondee* rounded La Isleta at the northern extremity of Grand Canary. Our voyagers, including Señor Aldecoa, were grouped together on the foredeck, leaning on the starboard bulwark and telling over again and again the story of the wreck. As they rounded the point and opened out Las Palmas a schooner was seen making for the harbour.

"Now just look at that," exclaimed Aldecoa, indignantly pointing out the little vessel to the skipper of the *Manoel*. "Do you see? She is loaded to the very water's edge. Why, a single heavy sea would send her to the bottom." As he spoke the schooner, the hull of which was barely visible above the water, slipped into the harbour, and vanished behind a large steamer that lay at anchor.

The sight of the harbour and the shipping awakened painful reflections in Aldecoa's mind. "Poor Mr. Jephson!" he murmured. "We shall never see him about the harbour again in his trim smart boat. Gladly would I give the value of the *Manoel* over again to have him back, but it can never be."

Juan Gomez and his comrades listened with secret uneasiness to Aldecoa's lamentations. They, too, had often wished that Jephson were with them, for they were haunted not only by remorse but also, and especially, by a sense of the insecurity of a secret that was shared by thirteen persons.

Gomez strove to conceal his dislike of the subject under an appearance of grief. "I, too, señor," he exclaimed with exaggerated fervour, "would give all that I possess — which is little enough, it is true — but I would give it all cheerfully if I could only once more see that brave gentleman. Yes, indeed, I would even –"

He paused suddenly, and his companions, looking up at his face, saw that he was staring before him with gaping mouth and distended eyeballs as one who sees an apparition.

Following the direction of his gaze, their eyes fell on the schooner which had just entered the harbour, and which they were now close alongside, and a simultaneous exclamation of amazement burst from them all; for her half-submerged counter bore the inscription, in white letters, "'Manoel' — Las Palmas," and there, leaning over the taff-rail, was none other than Matthew Jephson.

A Signal Success

The men have come aft, sir, and they say they want to speak to you."
"They want to speak to me, Mr. Jopling, do they?" said Captain Merriman in a tone of surprise. "Do you know what about?"

"I don't, sir," replied the first mate, "but by the look of them I should say there's something brewing."

Captain Merriman dropped the compasses on to the chart on which he had been working out his position and strode out of his cabin and up the companion way, followed closely by the mate.

The men were gathered in a knot just by the break of the poop, and a glance at their faces and attitudes told the Captain that there was something amiss.

"Well, my lads," he called out in a cheery, good-humoured voice, "what is it that you have to say to me?"

The men were silent for a few seconds and fidgeted about with an air of embarrassment. At length, one Joe Salter, the boatswain, stepped forward a pace and cleared his throat.

"Why d'ye see, Captain Merriman," he said, "the thing's like this here. We've been hearing a lot about Klondike and the fortunes that's been made there by able-bodied workin' men like us, and we've been a-thinkin' — in fact, the long and short of it is, we're going to Klondike ourselves."

"Very well, men," said the Captain, "but it's early days to talk of that matter, seeing that we are only four days out from Sydney; moreover, it is no business of mine where you go after you're paid off, so long as you do your duty while you're aboard."

"But we ain't agoing to wait till we're paid off — we're a-going now, on this here ship."

"The deuce you are," exclaimed the Captain angrily, "I can tell you, my men, you'll have to settle with me first."

"We're quite ready to settle with you, if you want us to," replied Salter with a grin. "Here, boys, show him your teeth," and, to the skipper's amazement, every man, including the boatswain, whipped out a regulation navy revolver.

189

"You see," said Salter, "we're ready for anything that may turn up, and I may tell you that we've got all your firearms as well. And look you here, Captain Merriman," he added, "you'd best keep a civil tongue. We're masters of this here vessel and you've got to obey our orders. We made all our arrangements before we left the London Docks, and the whole thing's settled; and if you do what you're told, and don't give us none o' your lip, you'll find we're uncommon pleasant bosses to work under."

The skipper bit his lip and reflected.

"You'd better think again, men," he said presently, regarding the men without a sign of irritation — "mutiny is a serious thing, and you have no excuse that I know of; you have good food and comfortable berths, haven't you?"

"Now you needn't try to come round us, you know," said Joe Salter, "with yer argiments. If the grub hadn't been all right you'd ha' heard from us before this. No, we ain't a-makin' no complaints, but wot we says and wot we sticks to is that we're going to take charge of this here ship and we're goin' to employ you to navigate her for us."

"And supposing I refuse?" asked the Captain.

"Why then overboard you goes, and we'll employ Mr. Jopling instead; and if he refuses, overboard *he* goes and we tries Mr. Saunders, and if none of the mates won't do as they are asked, we chucks 'em all overboard and works the bloomin' ship ourselves."

"I should like to talk this matter over with my officers," said the Captain.

"I daresay yer would, but yer won't. We ain't a-goin' to have you a colloguin' and a-plottin' against us. We're goin' to give them there mates nice compact quarters in the forecastle, but you'll be allowed to keep your cabin, and I shall take Mr. Jopling's so as I shall be near to you if you should want my advice in navigatin' the ship."

These last remarks of the boatswain's were received by the crew with sniggers of enjoyment, and Salter, thus encouraged, proceeded:

"And now if them three mates will do us the honour to step forrard they will be shown to their apartments."

"What do you wish us to do, sir?" asked the first mate with a face like thunder.

"Well, Mr. Jopling," replied the Captain, "here are thirty men armed, and here are we four men unarmed. That is the situation, and I am afraid there is nothing for us but to accept it."

"Spoken like a sensible man," commented Salter jeeringly, and without another word the three mates descended on to the main deck and marched forward with the crew.

"What port is it you want to make for?" asked the Captain of Salter, who had now stepped up on to the poop.

"The nearest port to Klondike," answered the boatswain.

"That would be somewhere about Cross Sound, I suppose."

"Very well, that will do; you can show it me on the chart presently. You will make direct for Cross Sound, and, when we're a day's easy sail off the land, let me know and I'll tell you what to do next. And see here; if I catch you at any tricks, takin' the ship into any other port or trying to make signals to any other vessel, you're a dead man that very instant."

Captain Merriman nodded and passed down the companion way.

That night Captain Merriman retired to his cabin at about half-past nine. Having lit a pipe, he reached down from his small bookshelf a leather-bound volume marked "International Code Signals," and studied it attentively, making a few brief notes on a sheet of paper until, hearing a footstep on the companion stair, he hurriedly replaced the book, turned the paper over and fixed a meditative gaze upon the tell-tale compass just over his head.

"Havin' a quiet pipe, are yer?" observed Joe Salter, thrusting his head in at the cabin door and peering round suspiciously.

"Yes, I'm having a pipe," returned the Captain without removing his gaze from the compass.

"Well, I'm going to have a weed myself. Keep yer pecker up, Cap'n. So long," and he vanished into his — or, rather, into Mr. Jopling's — cabin whence presently issued the aroma of one of Mr. Jopling's special Havanas accompanied by the sound of frequent expectoration.

Now, if Mr. Joseph Salter had possessed an abnormally acute sense of hearing he might have detected certain faint but curious sounds in the direction of the adjoining cabin. He might, for instance, have heard a key turned very softly in a lock, and then the scarcely distinguishable creak of a pair of hinges, followed by a prolonged soft rustling. He might then have been aware of a second faint creak and another soft revolution of a key. But Mr. Salter's senses were not abnormally acute, and there are many noises in the cabin of a wooden sailing ship under way.

II.

"Put up the helm there and keep her away a point or two. Ease off the lee braces and let her go free."

It was Joe Salter who issued the above orders, notwithstanding that the Captain was on deck and was nominally in command of the ship.

The latter's face flushed angrily for a moment, but he controlled himself by an effort and said coldly to the boatswain:

"You perceive that you are putting the ship off her course."

By way of reply the boatswain expectorated on the deck and strolled forward to the break of the poop to watch the hands manning the braces.

Captain Merriman walked to the taffrail and gazed intently at the horizon astern, but could distinguish nothing; as he turned, however, he perceived for the first time a man perched on the main yard looking in the same direction, and presently Salter came aft, and, taking the telescope from the companion hatch, ascended into the mizzen top, where he stood observing some object on the weather quarter.

"Set the foretopmast stun' sails," roared the boatswain.

The Captain again gazed in the direction in which the boatswain's glass pointed, and presently his practised eye detected a minute grey speck.

He rapidly descended to his cabin, and in a few moments returned with his own glass, through which he examined the object on the horizon.

Seen in the field of the telescope the grey speck resolved itself into a buff-painted funnel, from which no smoke issued, and the three masts of a barque with single topsailyards and no sail set.

The Captain drew a deep breath.

"Well, what do you make of her?" asked Salter sulkily.

"A cruiser under steam, I fancy," replied the skipper.

"Englishman or foreigner?"

"English, I think."

"So do I," replied the boatswain; "and look here," he continued, coming close to the Captain, his revolver in his hand, "if she comes within speaking distance, you mind what I said. No tricks, or –" And he scowled significantly, and rolled away forward.

The Captain looked at the retreating figure of the boatswain, and a faint, quizzical smile spread over his face for an instant.

"Luff her up again," bawled Salter some ten minutes later, "slack off the weather braces and look smart, my lads. That cruiser is end on again. And get in them stun' sails as quick as you can."

Once more the braces were manned and the yards swung round as the ship luffed up until the wind was right abeam.

The Captain took another peep at the approaching stranger, the white hull of which was now well above the horizon. As the ship luffed and presented her broadside to the cruiser, the latter also changed her course and made for a point well ahead of the *Patagonia*. This manoeuvre was quickly observed by the knot of men who had gathered on the poop to watch the man o' war.

"She's a-headin' us off, Joe, she'll be right aboard us presently," said one of the hands to Salter, "what are you goin' to do next?"

"Do?" repeated the boatswain irritably. "What can you do? If she wants to speak us she'll have to, seeing that she's doing sixteen knots to our eight."

"No, that won't do, Joe Salter," retorted the other. "If any of her people board this here ship it means chokee for us, that's wot it means. Ain't that so, mates?" he continued, turning to the rest of the crew.

"Ay, that's so," was the rejoinder in a growling chorus.

"Well, what would *you* do, Bill Hurst?" asked the boatswain turning to the first speaker defiantly.

"Why I'd wear ship and show her our heels," replied Hurst.

"And let her see as we're a-running away from her," sneered Salter.

"Bill Hurst's right," said another of the men. "We'd best wear right away," and this statement was met by a chorus of approval.

"All right then, wear ship and be hanged to you," exclaimed Salter turning his back to his comrades.

Once more the helm was put up, the brace-blocks "cheeped," the big yards swung round, and the *Patagonia*, having fallen off, came up on the opposite tack on a course at more than a right angle to her previous one.

As soon as this manoeuvre was executed, all hands came aft and mounted the poop to watch the cruiser, Salter and the captain keeping her covered by their glasses.

"Hang me if she ain't a-follerin' us," exclaimed the boatswain suddenly, and sure enough the cruiser's white hull rapidly shortened as she turned right into the *Patagonia's* wake.

An expression of alarm soon made its appearances on the faces of the men, and their anxiety continued to increase in spite of the boatswain's efforts to reassure them.

In half an hour the cruiser had reached a position about one mile away on the *Patagonia's* starboard beam. The crew, ranged along the weather bulwark, watched the stranger for a time in silence, while Salter followed her movements closely with his glass, which he had steadied against one of the mizzen shrouds.

"There she goes!" suddenly exclaimed Bill Hurst as two tiny coloured specks mounted to the cruiser's peak.

"B.D.,"[1] commented the Captain, putting down his telescope.

"All right," exclaimed Salter turning insolently towards him, "nobody asked you to speak. I reckon every seaman knows what the red burgee and the blue pennant means seein' as they are always a flyin' from Lloyd's stations all over the world. Now then, boys, where's the flag chest?"

"Why, it's kep' in the Cap'n's cabin," said Fox, the steward.

"Well, then, get it up here, two of you, and look lively, or we'll have them sending a boat," shouted the boatswain.

Several men scrambled in a great hurry down the companion, and in a very few seconds the chest was planted on the deck close to the wheel.

"What's our number, you?" asked Salter of the Captain.

"There's the code-book in the chest," replied the latter. "You can see for yourself."

"Well, show us where it is," said Salter, handling the book rather foolishly.

The Captain opened the book at the list of ships' names and gave it back to the boatswain. "There is the list," he said, "you will find our name among the 'p's.'"

Salter drew a stumpy forefinger down the column of names commencing with "p." "Ah! here we are," he said at length, as his finger became stationary, "*Patagonia*, of London, 1,200 tons, official number 388641. M.P.W.G.' Now, Hurst, you toggle the flags on to the halyards as I pass 'em to you. Here's M," and he fished the ball of bunting out of the compartment labelled "M" and passed it to Hurst — "here's P, this here's W, and there's G. Up with 'em smartly."

---

[1]   "What ship is that?"

Hurst made fast the toggles, and then hauled briskly on the halyards, and the four balls of bunting mounted rapidly to the peak. A smart jerk on the halyards unrolled the four balls simultaneously, and the four brightly-coloured flags fluttered gaily against the blue sky. The cruiser's signal was instantly lowered, and shortly afterwards a single coloured speck was seen to rise to the mast-head.

"There goes the answering pennant," observed Salter with his eye to the glass. "Now they've got their answer they can hook it as soon as they like. Down with them signals and let's stow 'em away."

The Captain, standing by the binnacle, watched furtively as Salter detached the flags and stuffed them untidily into their compartments. Then, as the boatswain slammed down the lid of the chest and turned the key, he heaved a sigh of relief and turned to take another look at the cruiser.

"I say, Joe," shouted Hurst excitedly, as he gazed intently at the man-o'-war, "she's a-roundin' to. S'help me if she ain't a-headin' straight for us." He picked up the telescope and pointed it at the cruiser.

"Why, dash my eyes, if they ain't a-gettin' ready to lower a boat," he exclaimed, turning to Salter.

The boatswain snatched the Captain's telescope from his hand and took a long look at the approaching vessel.

"Let's have a squint, Bill," said one of the men, taking the glass from Hurst and levelling it at the cruiser.

"Yes," he exclaimed after a moment's inspection, "there's the boat right enough a-swingin' from the davits. Why," he roared, after a pause, "there's a whole crowd of guffies a-gettin' into her."

Salter, who had observed the knot of red-coated marines climbing into the boat, laid down his glass and, discharging a volley of oaths and imprecations, strode up to the Captain and shook a large and dirty fist in his face.

"You hound," he screamed, huskily, "I'll learn yer, I will."

The precise character of the instruction he proposed to offer his commander did not appear, but the latter having regarded him for a moment with a bland smile, turned to the crew who were standing looking blank enough by the rail.

"Now listen to me, my lads," he said, "and don't be fooled any longer by that mutinous scoundrel –"

His speech was brought to an abrupt end by a sounding smack on the face delivered by the infuriated boatswain; but before anyone had time to realise what had happened, the skipper had adroitly executed what is known to pugilists as a postman's knock on the unlovely countenance of Mr. Salter, who staggered backwards across the deck until he brought up heavily against the binnacle, thereby knocking the breath out of his own body, and driving his elbow through the plate glass front of the instrument.

Captain Merriman was about to follow up the attack when a rush was made at him, and his arms were pinioned by several of the men. The boatswain picked himself up, and, drawing his revolver from his pocket, roared out in a voice made husky with fury:

"Stand clear there while I blow his brains out!"

"Here, none o' that, Joe Salter," exclaimed Hurst sternly. "The stone jug's enough for us; we don't want no running bowlines round our scrags, so you just stow it."

"All right, Bill," replied Salter conciliatingly, returning his pistol to his pocket; "I allow I'm a bit hasty, but *I* don't want no bloodshed if I don't get too much aggravation. But see here, mates; that boat will be alongside in a few minutes: so if we're going to do anything we'd best set about it quick."

"But what *are* we going to do?" queried Hurst.

"Why, this is what I'd do," answered the boatswain. "I'd first lock that swab," pointing to the Captain, "up in the forecastle along o' the others."

"But," interrupted Hurst, "they'll want to see the Captain."

"O' course they will," rejoined Salter, "and they *will* see him. *I'm* the captain of this blessed ship, and so you'll know what to say."

"My eye!" murmured one of the men, glancing round at his grinning messmates, "that cat won't jump, I reckon."

"Well, are you going to be taken like a pack of fools, or are you going to have a try for Klondike?" asked Salter glaring contemptuously at the men.

"We'll have a try," answered the men, without very much enthusiasm however.

"Very well," said Salter, "that's settled. Now get the skipper stowed away forward as quick as you can, and leave the rest to me."

The Captain was thereupon bundled forward and locked up in the forecastle, while the boatswain hurried down into the cabin.

In a few minutes the man-o'-war's boat — a large launch — came alongside, and as the three officers who had come with her stepped on deck, the boatswain, rigged out in a coat and cap belonging to the Captain, appeared at the break of the poop and descended to meet them.

Salter's appearance was the signal for the outbreak of an epidemic of grins from the crew of the *Patagonia*, which his admonitory scowls and grimaces only served to increase.

"Could we see the Captain?" asked the senior officer, a dry, brown-faced, little lieutenant, addressing Salter.

"Yer could," replied the latter, "if yer was to cast yer eyes on me."

"Oh!" responded the lieutenant, regarding Salter in undisguised astonishment, especially as to his shirt collar and his immense grubby paws.

"Why 'Ho?' " enquired Salter tartly, upon which the youngest officer — a lanky midshipman — retired to the bulwark and apparently suppressed a sneeze.

"For what purpose might you have boarded my vessel?" persisted the boatswain.

The lieutenant glanced at his companions with a puzzled expression, and after a short pause, said: —

"Our Captain thought that perhaps you would be kind enough to allow us to compare our chronometers with yours."

"Why cert'nly," replied Salter, "with pleasure. Where are they?"

"Where are what?" asked the astonished officer.

"Your chronometers. Have you got 'em with you?"

"Good Heavens! No!" replied the lieutenant, in a tone of amazement. "I've brought a hack watch, of course."

"Oh! ah!" responded Salter, in no little confusion. "Well, come along below," and he scuttled down the companion way cursing softly under his breath.

"Stay on deck, Woodburn," said the lieutenant in an undertone to his junior, "and keep your weather eye lifting."

"Rather," responded the sub significantly, as the lieutenant and the midshipman followed Salter below.

"Now as to these here chronometers," said the latter, slapping the instruments with his great paw, "which one will you see first?"

"Whichever you please," replied the lieutenant.

"Well, we'll try this one, then," said the boatswain, unfastening the hooks and endeavouring vainly to raise the lid of the case.

"The thing's locked," he muttered, turning crimson. "Here you, Fox."

"Yes, sir," said the steward, thrusting a scared face in at the cabin door with rather suspicious promptitude.

"Go and fetch the key of the chronometers."

"Beg pardon, sir, but the keys is kept inside the cases," said the steward hastily.

"But the cases are locked, you idiot. Go and fetch the keys, and look sharp." Here the boatswain shook his fist and scowled frightfully, and the steward, suddenly comprehending, hurried away

During this dialogue the two officers exchanged brief but significant glances.

Barely two minutes had passed before the silence was broken by a confused noise from the deck, followed by the scuffling of feet on the companion stairs. As the footsteps reached the cabin door Salter leaped from his chair with a loud curse, and the officers turning round beheld Captain Merriman and the sub-lieutenant, closely attended by a sergeant of marines, who carried and ostentatiously clinked a pair of handcuffs.

"How the deuce did you manage it?" asked the lieutenant of Captain Merriman when the officers had the cabin to themselves.

"Manage what?" queried the Captain.

"How did you get them to run up that signal of all others?"

"Well, I'll explain," said Captain Merriman cutting the end off a cigar and regarding the lieutenant with a twinkling eye. "The flag chest, which you may have noticed on deck, was always kept down here. Now, on the night when the mutiny broke out, after the lights were extinguished I had a brief interview with that flag chest, and ventured to make a few trifling alterations in its arrangement. Our number is M.P.M.G., and as it was almost certain that that signal would be made before any other I changed those particular flags. I took *M* out of its compartment and stuffed *D* in its place, *P* changed places with *K*, *W* with *P*, and *G* with *R*. Now when Salter got the flag chest on deck and asked me what signal to make and how to make it, I referred him to the code book where he found our number without any difficulty. I was afraid he would notice the change in the flags, but he never unrolled them, and they remained in a ball until the halyards were jerked.

"Now Salter got the flags out of their compartments quite correctly, but of course when they went up instead of making M.P.W.G., '*Patagonia*, of London, 1,200 tons, official number 388641,' they made, 'D.K.P.R., mutinied.'"

The midshipman fell back in his chair with a bellow of enjoyment as the skipper concluded his recital, while the grinning lieutenant remarked. "Well, Captain, I must say that you've salted their tails very nicely."

The Ebb Tide

IT WAS getting late in the season for excursion traffic on the river, and the weather recently had been far from favourable, even for the time of year, so that it was no matter for surprise that when the *Benfleet Belle* drew up alongside Southend Pier on her homeward voyage the party of passengers that dribbled down the gangway was a small one, while the saloon deck, of which the newcomers took possession, was practically deserted. But if the party of fresh passengers was small it was not entirely undistinguished for it included no less a person than Mr. Jonathan Lurcher, a gentleman of antecedents so remarkable that a grateful and appreciative country had for some time past taken upon itself the entire cost of his maintenance, and had even furnished him with the means of enjoying the fascinating pastime of oakum picking. It was perhaps in consequence of a too diligent application to this contemplative but sedentary recreation that Mr. Lurcher had found it desirable, when the time arrived for him to quit the nation's hospitable roof, to seek the ozonic breezes of Southend. At any rate, here he had been in residence for the last fortnight: and there being, unfortunately, no available oakum to pick, he had been compelled reluctantly to substitute for that commodity the pockets of his fellow trippers. Now, this variety of sport suffers from one serious drawback — it cannot be carried on for an indefinite time in one place. Not only is there a tendency for the material to become exhausted, but the subjects of the picking operations develop an unreasonable prejudice which is apt to result in meddlesome and highly objectionable attentions on the part of the civil authorities. To this fact Mr. Lurcher's attention had during the last few days been unpleasantly drawn, and as he arrived, bag in hand, on the steamer's deck, he scrutinised his fellow-passengers with a keenness bordering on anxiety.

The result of the scrutiny was, on the whole, satisfactory, for none of the Southend passengers presented a definitely constabulary aspect, although one of them, a tall heavily bearded man, seemed to regard Mr. Lurcher with more interest than that gentleman considered strictly decorous in a perfect stranger.

On this person, therefore, Mr. Lurcher bestowed a certain amount of furtive regard; but his attention was more particularly attracted by another passenger, of the feminine gender, whom he had watched with no little interest as she stood on the pier waiting for the boat. It was not her beauty that attracted him, for she had none; nor her brilliant golden hair, of which she had a good deal: for Mr. Lurcher was not highly susceptible.

He had, however, noted a certain staginess of style and a flashy extravagance of dress; he had observed her consult a handsome gold watch attached to a massive gold chain, and he had especially taken note of certain significant bulgings upon her gloved fingers, and certain still more significant bulgings upon her gloved wrist.

Following s simple process of inductive reasoning, Mr. Lurcher reached the conclusion. "Successful actress on tour — handsome and costly jewels which she carries on her person for safety, not caring to trust them in the trunk that the porter has just dumped down on the deck."

The sight of that gold watch and these bulgings on the gloved hand sent strange thoughts surging through Mr. Lurcher's speculative mind; and seating himself on a bench at the after end of the saloon deck, he fell into a brown study. To his intense annoyance he was presently aroused from his meditations by a red-faced, amphibious-looking man, who came and sat by his side, and, having expectorated on to the deck by way of introducing himself, remarked:

"By gum, but the tide do run down just 'ere."

"Ah!" said Mr. Lurcher, a trifle ambiguously.

"Yus: and it'll run down more yet. The ebb ain't only just begun."

"Ho?" said Lurcher interrogatively, but with faint interest.

"Yus," continued the amphibian; "that's so." He expectorated again — on Mr. Lurcher's boot this time — and rubbed his hands.

"Lor," he continued, "wot a thing the tide is! I've sailed a barge on this 'ere London river this twenty year agone, so I ought to know. And when yer sails a barge, d'ye see, yer got to know yer tide. 'Tain't the wind as yer got to think about with a barge, 'specially if she's bluff built and got a lot o' 'eavy stuff inside 'er — it's the tide. Now you landsmen thinks the tide runs the same all over the river; but that's where you're jolly well mistook. It *don't*."

He paused and stared argumentatively at Mr. Lurcher, who remarked gruffly that he "never said it did."

"No, yer didn't," agreed the bargee, briskly taking up the thread of the argument; "and if yer did yer'd tell a bloomin' lie. Why, bless yer, there ain't two places in the river where the tide runs the same. When it's a-runnin' down these here deep channels like a mill-race there's places under the land and in shoal water where it's as quiet as a pond. Now, you look there" — he pointed to some brown cliffs on the south shore — "that's Warden Point, that is, on the Isle of Sheppey. Now, the main tide stream runs down outside the island, and the tide stream from the Medway runs down inside, through the Swale, d'ye see, and them two streams meet at Warden Point, and they forms wot we calls a heddy; and the remarkable thing about a heddy is that it collects all the loose stuff wot's a-floatin' about, and when the tide goes out it leaves it all 'igh and dry on the shore."

"Does it, though," said Mr. Lurcher with a yawn. In the extremity if his boredom he leaned back over the rail and looked down upon the little after deck below. It was quite unoccupied, excepting that on a campstool immediately beneath him was seated the golden-haired lady with whom his thoughts had been so much occupied. In an instant Mr. Lurcher's *ennui* vanished as if by magic, and he was thrilled by an excitement so keen as to be almost painful; for the lady, taking advantage of the solitude, was carefully trimming her finger-nails with a pair of pocket-scissors, and as this process had necessitated the removal of her gloves the cause of those mysterious bulgings was now laid bare to Mr. Lurcher's dazzled vision in the form of seven or eight massive diamond rings and a bracelet set with brilliants of quite unusual size and lustre.

Having made these observations, Lurcher withdrew his head without being noticed by the unconscious fair, and turned with renewed and increased distaste to this companion, who placidly continued his remarks on the phenomena of the tides.

"Yus; it's wonderful wot a lot o' stuff will get cast up on the shore where there's a heddy. There was a friend of mine wot was in the Coastguard, and 'e was stationed for a time at Leysdown, which is just round Warden Point — leastways, a mile or so; and that cove 'e told me that 'e used to walk over the flats by Warden at low water and pick up all sorts o' things. *And* the bodies 'e found! Any number of 'em. In fact, 'e declared to me that as sure as ever anyone went overboard in any part of the river from Gravesend to the Nore, so sure would the body, sooner or later, come ashore on the flats at

Warden, if not picked up floating. Many a time, 'e said, they'd come ashore there within a 'our or two of going overboard, especially when they went over in the upper part of Sea Reach."

"LEANED BACK OVER THE RAIL AND LOOKED DOWN UPON
THE LITTLE AFTER DECK BELOW."

The bargee had succeeded at last. Mr. Lurcher, aroused from his reverie, was staring at him with a frown of deep attention.

"Do you mean to tell me," said the latter, "that if I was to tumble overboard here you could make sure of finding my body to-night on the mud at

Warden?"

"I'm only telling you wot was told to me by a party as ought to a-known wot 'e was talkin' about," replied the bargee. "'E said, 'e did, that whenever a cove went overboard on the ebb in Sea Reach, the body was sure to turn up at low water, that the ebb 'ad run out, on the mud near Warden Point. That man may 'ave been tellin' a lie, but anyhow 'is word's good enough for me." He rose, yawned, stretched himself, and rolled away forward, remarking, "Well, so long. I'm going to 'ave forty winks in the saloon."

For some minutes Lurcher sat absorbed in thought with a fixed frown upon his not very spiritual brow. Now and again he peered over at the lady beneath, who had now replaced her gloves; but from these brief inspections he always returned to an attitude of profound cogitation. From this state he was suddenly aroused by the hoarse roar of the steamer's whistle, and looking up he was astonished to perceive that the bridge and funnel were almost hidden, from sight in consequence of the vessel having plunged into a dense bank of fog. Even as he gazed wreaths of the white, chilly vapour streamed round him, and the fore-part of the steamer completely disappeared.

He rose from the bench, and, stepping somewhat stealthily along the empty deck, made his way down the sponson staircase to the main deck. Entering the saloon, he observed the bargee coiled up asleep on a settee, and looking as much at home on the crimson velvet cushions as a blacking-brush in a jewel-case; but the cabin was otherwise occupied. Passing through on tiptoe for fear of disturbing his friend. Lurcher emerged through the farther door on to the after deck. The lady was still in her corner, and was now looking out dreamily at the mass of white vapour that enveloped the vessel.

"Pretty foggy, ain't it?" Lurcher remarked huskily.

"Very," responded the lady shortly, and without looking round.

Lurcher stood silent for a few moments. He peered into the saloon — it was still empty; then up at the promenade deck — there was no one in sight.

"Gracious me," he exclaimed suddenly. "Did you see that? A man overboard! There he goes!"

He rushed along the deck, pointing over the side as he spoke; and the lady, springing from her seat, ran to his side.

"There he is! I see him!" exclaimed Lurcher, quivering with excitement, and he scrambled up to the grating at the stern, and, jumping over the great coils of rope, leaned out over the iron railing and looked down into the water.

"There he is hanging on to the rudder!" he cried in a husky voice to the woman, who had climbed on to the grating after him. "Don't you see him? Down there."

The woman leaned far out over the railing and stared down at the seething water. Lurcher gave one hurried glance behind him at the saloon door and the mist-shrouded deck; then with a sudden movement he seized the woman and tipped her over the rail, and before she had time to utter a cry she had plunged with a splash into the bubbling water.

A few moments later a muffled shriek came out of the fog astern, and then all was still save the wash of the water and the beat of the steamer's paddles.

As Lurcher, white-faced and trembling from the nervous strain of the last few minutes, climbed down from the grating after listening for a few moments for any further sounds, he experienced a terrible shock, for when he raised his eyes to the saloon doorway he perceived a man standing on the threshold — a tall man with a large black beard — the very man, in fact, whom he had regarded with such suspicion on Southend Pier.

The short hair on Mr. Lurcher's head stirred as he beheld this apparition, and he sank on to a bench with chattering teeth and a dreadful sinking at his heart.

"How long had that man been there?" and "How much had he seen?" were the questions the murderer asked himself as he wiped the cold sweat from his forehead with his coat sleeve. If he had actually witnessed the crime, then might Jonathan Lurcher as well jump overboard and follow his victim by water to Warden flats. A mental picture arose before his eyes of his own body and his victim's lying side by side, limp and still upon the lonely shore; and then there came a vision of an alternative scene — a high-walled prison yard, in which a small crowd of men was gathered around a tall wooden frame; and with a muttered curse he leaped to his feet and made for the saloon door.

"Feel bad?" inquired the bearded man, drawing back to let him pass, but looking at him narrowly.

Without answering, Lurcher pushed by, and, shambling along as fast as his trembling knees would let him, ascended the stairs, and made his way to the bar on the upper deck.

"Scotch and soda," he ordered, slapping down a half-crown on the counter, "and put in a double go of Scotch."

"You look pretty white about the gills," the barman remarked, eyeing him curiously. "Precious bad sailor you must be, to get sea-sick here in the river."

"Yes, I am," Lurcher replied. "The water always upsets me, especially when there's fog about."

He gulped down the whisky, and walking out on to the deck took up his old position at the after end. He had not been long seated when, to his dismay, the bearded man sauntered along in his direction, and, leaning over the rail, appeared to be absorbed in contemplation of the masses of fog that rolled by. But, in spite of his meditative attitude and apparent abstraction, it was soon evident that he was furtively watching Mr. Lurcher, for whenever that individual looked up he found the man's eye fixed upon him, although it was instantly averted. For some ten minutes Lurcher endured this silent and secret scrutiny with increasing disturbance and terror. At length, unable to bear it any longer, he rose and walked quickly up the deck and took up a strategic position behind the smokestack. It was not many minutes before the bearded man appeared on the opposite side of the deck, strolling along slowly and apparently looking for somebody; and with the conviction that that somebody was himself. Lurcher adroitly contrived to keep the smokestack between his own person and the mysterious stranger. Presently the latter went below, and Lurcher then breathed more freely again.

The journey to Tilbury seemed interminable, for a heavy tide ran down swiftly the whole time, and moreover, in consequence of the fog, the steamer had continually to steam at half speed, and often to go astern to avoid a collision. And to Lurcher the weary voyage seemed longer even than it really was, for added to his intense anxiety to reach Tilbury and escape from the boat was the state of perpetual terror in which he was kept by the bearded man, who continued without cessation to wander restlessly about the ship, and was for ever cropping up in unexpected places. Nevertheless by dint of skilful evasion and unceasing watchfulness, now lurking behind the deck cabins, now taking refuge behind the smokestack, Lurcher had contrived to elude his pursuer until one of the deck hands, standing on the sponson, shouted aloud the joyful tidings that Tilbury was close at hand.

"Now for Tilbury! All passengers for Tilbury get ready!"

The fateful moment had arrived. Out of the mist the shadowy shape of Tilbury Pier slowly emerged. Ropes were flung, windlasses rattled, and the passengers gathered on the sponson by the open gangway.

Lurcher, noting with relief that the bearded man was not among the group, took up his position close to the gangway, and waited with feverish impatience for the gang-plank to be hauled up.

At this moment he felt a hand laid upon his shoulder, and whisking round was confronted by the bearded stranger.

"Excuse me," said the latter suavely, "but is your name Fox?"

"No, it isn't," replied Lurcher.

"Oh, I beg your pardon; but I met a gentleman in the commercial room of the King's Head at Manchester some time ago who was very like you — surprisingly like. *His* name was Fox." The stranger continued to gaze at Lurcher with extraordinary intentness as he made this statement.

"ONE OF THE POLICEMEN STEPPED UP THE PLANK."

"Well, mine ain't," said Lurcher conclusively, and the gang-plank being at this moment hauled up, he pushed his way on to it and began to descend. But his attention was so much taken up by the bearded stranger, whom he still watched furtively, that he was half way down the plank before he observed a group of figures at the lower end of the pier.

When he did notice them he stopped like a horse that has just been confronted by a traction-engine, for the group consisted of two sturdy policemen and a woman — dishevelled, wet, and bedraggled, but unquestionably the identical woman whom he had but a couple of hours before pushed over the steamer's stern.

He would have retreated up the gang-plank, but this the press of passengers behind prevented; and while he was hesitating one of the policeman stepped up the plank, seized him by the arm, and dragged him down on to the pier.

"Now you'd better come along quietly," said the policeman; and, Mr. Lurcher's previous experience having convinced him of the truth of this proposition, he replied:

"All right; I'm coming."

"You didn't expect to see me," the lady remarked pleasantly, as Lurcher gazed at her in undisguised astonishment.

"No; I didn't," he agreed.

"No; I'll bet you didn't," said the policeman, with a broad grin. "You made a bit of a mistake this time, young man," and here the two constables chuckled aloud.

"You didn't know who I was, I reckon?" continued the lady.

"No, I didn't; and I don't now," replied Lurcher.

"Well, then, I'll tell you," said the fair one with the golden locks. "I'm Madame Clementina Porpers, the champion long-distance swimmer and aquatic athlete."

"You must be a champion, if you swam here from Southend and passed the steamer," remarked Lurcher incredulously.

"But I didn't," replied the fair one. "I just struck out for the shore until I was picked up by a boat that was sailing into Leigh. When I got there I found that the train for Tilbury was just due, so in I popped, all in my wet clothes, and came on here; and here I am."

"Yes, here you are, sure enough," said Lurcher gloomily.

"Yes, here she is," echoed the jocose policeman, with his handkerchief to his mouth, "and here are you, and here are we — quite a pleasant little party; so you may as well oblige, and just come along quietly."

"All right," said Lurcher; "I'm coming." And he went; and to this day, although in his enforced solitude he has given many hours to the consideration of the subject, Mr. Lurcher has never been able to make up his mind whether that coastguard's tale was true or merely a base fabrication intended to delude and bewilder misguided landsmen.

By the Black Deep

"THE BLOCKADE OF BUENOS AYRES.
 "(*Reuter's Special Service.*)
  "Barbados, June 1st.

"The four-masted ship *Jane and Elizabeth*, with linseed from Buenos Ayres, put in here yesterday for stores and water, and sailed to-day for london, all well. She reported having successfully passed through the blockading fleet on the night of May 9th."

Thus the *Daily Telegraph*, and as the sun shone through the high office window, and flashed again from the tiny sample bottles of essential oils, it only heightened the dismal expression upon the face of Jenkinson Brothers. When people spoke of Jenkinson Brothers, the oldest established firm of drug merchants in Mincing Lane, they meant Josiah. Now, Josiah was ambitious, also he was young when he became the sole representative of the firm. The fluctuations of *ipecacs* and *cumquats* soon ceased to interest him; he forsook humdrum lines of business and wandered into crooked paths of speculation, until he now found himself the possessor of a seriously diminished credit and a capital which had almost ceased to exist. He had long meditated a bold stroke which should revive the sensitive plant of his credit and rob settling-day of some of its terrors, when the failure of the linseed crop of 1899 gave him his opportunity. Linseed, as a general rule, is not an article that can be cornered, but on this occasion everything conspired to render him assistance. A parasite, spreading with extraordinary rapidity from the East, had devastated the Russian crops, whilst a succession of typhoons in the Sundas and adjoining islands made short work of the large reserves which had been accumulated there. Men's eyes turned towards the New World. Argentina stepped into the breach, and every ship that had room on her manifest soon overflowed with the now precious seed; but before a single one could clear from Buenos Ayres a revolution broke out. The five-hundred-and-twentieth president took refuge in the city, and was there

209

besieged by the Army, who had turned their general into the five-hundred-and-twenty-first; whilst the Navy, following the lead of the Army, declared for the insurgents and straigtway blockaded the harbour.

It was now that Josiah, in daring mood aspired to control the market. At first he bought cautiously and quietly; then, emboldened by success, with less and less caution, and as the price soared upwards he continued to buy, until at length the magnitude of the deal reached a figure that he trembled to contemplate. It was a small matter to him that the older men in the market looked askance at his operations; he was regarded with admiration by the smaller fry of speculators, and as they deferentially made way for him in the Lane, visions of a yacht, a country estate, and even — why not? — a seat in Parliament, floated before his eyes.

But these golden dreams were short-lived. On this particular morning of June, 1899, the price of linseed had beaten the record within the memory of the oldest broker. Already there were rumours of synthetical substitutes in the market. The crisis called for all Josiah's nerve, and he was about to commence the interesting zoological process known as "squeezing the bears" (in other words, to demand the impossible feat of delivering the seed of which he was the nominal purchaser), when his eye fell on Reuter's message; and as he read, the room swam round him.

"Captain Jenkinson to see you, sir."

At any other time Josiah would have replied with one of the numerous excuses which people find for invisibility to an impecunious relation, but at present he was too confused to do more than gaze stupidly at his visitor, who had followed close on the heels of the clerk, and took a chair without waiting to be invited.

Captain Jenkinson wore a beard trimmed in the naval style known as "Torpedo-fashion," but his dress showed none of a sailor's neatness. On his jacket, some buttons were odd and some were missing, whilst the whole suit gave evidence of having suffered many things from the elements; his eyes were shaded by a cap from which the house badge had disappeared; his linen, what there was to be seen of it, was frayed and grubby; his boots were cracked, also he exhaled an atmosphere of rank cigars. Altogether, Captain Jenkinson presented an out-at-elbow appearance, as he sat regarding the drug merchant with a half-defiant, half-curious air. At length, feeling the silence oppressive —

"Jos," he said emphatically, "I'm stony broke!"

Josiah started with exclaimed irritably: "And a man who gets drunk on duty deserves to be!" — an amiable allusion to the captain's recent piling-up of a coasting tramp, with the consequent loss of his certificate.

"I suppose it's only by his own brother that a man need expect to be hit when he's down," growled the other. "But I say, Jos, I'm absolutely and completely broke."

"So am I!"

"You! Why, the *Financial Blackmailer* calls you a 'Napoleon of finance!' I read it myself just now in the clerk's office."

"Napoleon be hanged!" was the testy reply. "Here, read that!" and Josiah pushed the newspaper across to his brother, pointing to the telegram from Barbadoes.

The captain read and re-read the paragraph, then laying it down: "Well, it reads all straightforward enough. What's the matter with it?"

"Matter enough!" retorted the drug merchant. "Why, this infernal *Jane and Elizabeth* will spoil the game I've been playing for the last three months. The price has dropped a few points already, and the moment she's sighted of the Lizard there'll be a slump in the market. Matter, indeed!" and he snorted contemptuously.

The derelict emitted a long, low whistle.

"Yes!" roared his brother, "you'll whistle for your grub soon, when I'm going through the Court."

The sailor rose and walked slowly up and down the small office. Then having opened the baize door and looked out, he shut it carefully and drew his chair close to the explosive Josiah.

"Jos," impressively, "that ship's got to be stopped!"

"Yes, yes! What's the use if saying that? Who's to do it?"

"Name the figure, and I'm the man."

"You, Sam?"

"Yes, your 'drunk-on-duty' brother." And as Josiah gasped with the effort to realise the situation, Sam continued: "Look here, I know these four masters — two hundred knots the most you'll get out of them. From Barbadoes it's three-and-a-half thousand miles, more of less — that's a good twenty days' sail. When does it say she left? Ah! the first; so she can't pass the Lizard before the twentieth, and it's now the eighteenth. Well, how much shall we say?"

"Five hundred pounds?"

Sam laughed derisively.

"Say a thousand, then," suggested Josiah with a somewhat injured air.

"No! ten thousand, and dirt-cheap, too," was the firm reply; and as Josiah made a gesture of deprecation, Sam led his trump-card: "Did you think I'm going to risk penal servitude for nothing?"

"Penal servitude!" echoed Josiah faintly.

"Yes, Dartmoor bogs and Portland quarries!" And he chuckled, as Josiah visibly shivered. "Of course, if you're afraid, just say so, and there's an end to it; but it seems to me as if things had got pretty near the knuckle for both of us."

It was curious to see how exactly the positions of the two brothers had become reversed within the last few minutes. The "Napoleon of Finance," as the plan was unfolded, had grown palpably limper and flabbier. His brother, on the other hand, no longer diffident with the burden of a favour to be solicited, towered as it were above him. His back stiffened, as with sparkling eye he strode feverishly up and down the little room, the while he poured forth his scheme in a flood of technicalities of which Josiah only half grasped the meaning.

"See, now! This is the river-mouth, with the North Foreland just here"; and with a pencil he rapidly sketched a chart of the Thames estuary on the newspaper. "She'll likely lie-to for her pilot and a tug in the Downs. Then she'll round the Foreland with the flood tide and come up the Edinburgh Channel. Here's the Edinburgh Channel — Edinburgh lightship at one end, Black Deep at the other, between the Shingles and the Long Sand. Proper course, s'far as I remember just now, is head for Black Deep light, leaving the Shingles on the port-hand. There's a beacon on the Shingles during the day, and a gas-buoy at night — gas-buoy flash and dark, what the Trinity House men call 'occulting.' Now, the flood tide on the fifteenth will run strongest about midnight — anyhow, that's near enough. Now, suppose that it should happen (mind, I only say *suppose*) that that gas-buoy had shifted half a mile south of its berth, when that four-master hooker was about? Well, up she'll come on the top of the tide, and rounding the buoy, fetch up hard and fast on the Shingles. If her masts don't go there and then, with the flood tide running strong, and the least little bit of a wind from the north or nor'-east, it'll be as much as they can do to get the crew off before she breaks up, let alone the stuff she's carrying, for all their rockets and lifeboats. Well I know that bank!"

"Was that where you ran ashore before and –?" commenced Josiah innocently.

The other turned on him savagely. His mouth was hard and there was a stiff look about the "torpedo" beard.

"You let that alone, now! maybe I *have* been starving, and maybe you *have* chucked me a few odd sovereigns during the last year, and perhaps you've made me know it, too; but it's my turn now. You can't do without me, so you'd best be civil. If I'm to see this thing through, I've got to be boss, and don't you forget it! What's more, you've got to find some of the ready to go on with."

"How much do you want?" This very timidly.

"A fiver for exes, and another to get myself some decent slops, and three more of them for a boat."

Sam fingered the notes with the daintiness of one long a stranger to their crisp rustle, then cramming them into his breast-pocket, exclaimed —

"As soon as I'm a bit decent, I'm off to Erith to hunt up any ship's lifeboat that's going cheap. I'll send you a wire to meet me at Margate to-morrow or next day; and if I want any more for exes, you've got to stand to it. Now, so long! Show a little pluck, man; and remember," his mouth hardened again, "we've got to sink or swim together — *together*, mind!"

Josiah's mental faculties had lost some of their poise during the march of recent events, but this unwonted phase of his brother's character, the ship-master's resource, its tyranny, its brutality even, did little to restore their balance.

As Sam stood looking at him with a smile which had something of contempt in it, his hand resting on the door-knob, Josiah rose stiffly and tried to speak.

"Very well," was all he could find to say in return, and as the door closed behind the resuscitated man of action, he unlocked a spirit-stand and helped himself with a trembling hand.

Meanwhile the sailor passed through the outer office, his jaunty gait in such marked contrast to the diffident and almost timid order of his arrival as to cause much wonderment among the clerks. As he clattered down the stairs into Mincing Lane, a reminiscence of an old sea-air mingled with the noise of the traffic as it floated up through the half-opened window: —

"As I was going up Paradise Street;
 With a heave-ho! Blow the man down!"

II

The small crowd of idlers who had stood upon the promenade which fronts the pleasant town of Deal, watching the manœuvres of a small lug-rigged boat as it approached the shore, slowly dispersed when the little craft, having dropped the mainsail, grounded on the shingle, and her occupants leaped out and began to scramble up the steep, shelving beach.

The passengers were two in number, both elderly men and both distinguished by the nautical blue cloth caps which are commonly assumed for some unexplained reason by landsmen, even of the most terrestrial type, when they visit the neighbourhood of the sea. One of them carried, suspended from his forefinger, a string of infant whiting, while the other bore under his arm a well-worn naval telescope.

"Well, Jos," remarked he of the telescope, as the pair reached the summit of the beach and turned to gaze out across the Downs, where half-a-dozen coasters rode at anchor, "I'm glad to see that if you are a bit of a funker, you've at least got a sailor's gizzard. If you couldn't stand a bit of a swell, we should be regularly up a tree."

"I don't know what the deuce you mean by a funker," retorted the other sulkily. "Haven't I agreed to do all that you suggest, to risk my life and liberty in this accursed venture, and to pay you a fabulous sum for your part in it? Funker, indeed!" and he scowled malevolently at the dripping trophies of the angle that dangled from his finger.

"That's all right, old cock," responded the first speaker, whom the astute reader has doubtless recognised as our old friend Captain Jenkinson. "Don't you get your back up about nothing, but just you attend to my instructions. Now, you see, when you want to — hallo! What's this rounding the point there?" and the gallant captain, all on the alert in a moment, pointed his telescope at a dark speck enveloped in a cloud of smoke which had just made its appearance round the promontory.

"It's a tug," he remarked after a moment's scrutiny, "and she's got a tow rope astern — and here comes a — yes, by Jingo! It's a four-masted ship — that's her, Jos, that's our friend right enough."

"I suppose," said Josiah doubtfully, "she's not the only four-masted ship in the world, is she?"

"No, I suppose not," growled the captain, "but she's the only one that has passed Dungeness. However, we'll stroll down to the end of the pier, and then we shall be able to see her make her number. Let me see," he meditated, consulting an entry in his pocket-book, "B.T.L.W., I think it is — yes, that's right."

In half an hour the two vessels had reached the anchorage, the tall, stately ship, with her long, grey hull with its white streak and painted ports, her lofty masts, her long yards and intricate web of rigging, creeping along in the wake of the smoky, bumptious little tug; and just as the pair came abreast of Lloyd's station, a string of bright-coloured flags ran up and fluttered gaily from the ship's peak.

"B.T.L.W." muttered the captain, removing his eyes from the telescope and peering triumphantly in his brother's drawn face. "What do you make of her?" he continued, addressing a jersey-clad sea-monster who was examining the vessel through a pocket-telescope. "She's a large vessel, isn't she? Comes from Australia, I suppose?"

The sea-monster closed his telescope deliberately and regarded the two brothers with that air of ineffable and contemptuous condescension which the 'longshoreman assumes when he addresses a denizen of the land.

"No, sir," he replied in a hoarse double-bass. "She ain't no Australian. She's the *Jane and Elizabeth*, four thousand tons register, from Buenos Ayres, with a cargo of linseed. Got enough linseed aboard of her, she has, for to poultice the entire population of Great Britain, sir. She ain't a fast ship, sir, d'ye understand — no, she ain't no clipper; but she's a whopper; she can carry some cargo — Lor'! she *can* take some stuff aboard, to be sure." Here the old man of the sea turned his back upon the two conspirators and resumed his telescopic observations.

"Come along, Jos," said the captain, "let's scoot for the station. There's just time for us to catch the five o'clock to Margate."

III

"Now, I call this very pleasant," said the captain genially, as he lolled on the stern locker of his newly purchased boat and gazed at the receding harbour and the long jetty, whence came faintly the sound of music across the water. "A good dinner inside, a good cigar, a fine, steady breeze and a tight, handy boat, not to speak of the prospect of unlimited dibs in the immediate future — what more could a man wish for, eh, Jos?"

Josiah Jenkinson sat bolt upright on the midship thwart, with an expression of the extremest dejection, grasping convulsively the fall of the mainsheet.

"I suppose this boat can be depended upon, Sam?" he asked wearily.

"Depended on!" explained the captain. "why, she's got a double teak skin, and there's a copper air-case in each of the side lockers. Depended on! I tell you, man, she'll do anything but talk."

"Well, we don't want her to do that," observed Josiah, with a sour grin.

"No, we don't," chuckled Samuel. "By Jingo! what an evening it is! Just look at the sunset, my boy," and here the captain in the exuberance of his joy trolled forth in a sturdy bass voice —

"As I was walking down Paradise Street;
With a heave-ho! Blow the man down!
I met a young frigate so nice and so neat,
With a heave-ho! Blow the man down!

"By the way, Jos, as we have a little time to ourselves, we may as well rehearse the programme. You see, we're heading north-east, but we're actually travelling about north by west on the tide stream; and sailing as we are now, we shall make the buoy in about a couple of hours, by which time it'll be quite dark. Then we'll commence operations."

"Just explain to me again what your plan is," said Josiah.

"Why, you see, the Edinburgh Channel, through which our ship must pass, lies between the Long Sand to the north-east and the Shingle sands to the south-west. At the east end of the channel is the Edinburgh Channel lightship, and about a mile beyond the west end is the Black Deep lightship. The actual end of the channel is marked by the north-east Shingles gas-buoy, and as soon as the ship has fairly passed that she alters her course to the south'ard.

Now, don't you see, if we can move that buoy to the south-east, our precious hooker will alter her course a trifle too soon and run slap on to the north edge of the Shingles, just near the North Beacon; and as she will probably run on just about high water flood tide, she won't be likely to get off in a hurry."

"But we can't move the buoy, can we?" protested Josiah.

"Of course we can't, you chuckle-head!" responded the captain impatiently. "Haven't I said so already? But what we can do is to put out her light and rig up a little light of our own in humble imitation, and this is how we're got to set to work. As soon as we get near the buoy, we take down our mainsail, and you work the boat alongside with the oars, and be mighty careful you don't bump her against the buoy and get stove in. Then I jump on to the buoy and hang on to the cage while I feel about for the gas-pipe, and as soon as I have found it I cut through it with this little brass-worker's saw and pull the ends apart.

"Out goes the light, and I hail you to come alongside again and take me off — and mind, while I am at work on the buoy, you keep at least five or six lengths away until I hail you, or you will certainly get stove in. Then we shall make our first appearance in public in the character of a gas-buoy, and please pay great attention to this, as you will probably have to work the light while I attend to the management of the boat. As we approach the buoy, you must study the character of its light. You will see that it appears to suddenly go out at regular intervals, or 'undergo occultation,' as the Trinity House people say. This is managed by a small metal screen which drops over the light, and is then raised again, by a kind of clockwork. This particular buoy has, I find, an occultation lasting two seconds, and the light is visible for six; that is to say, you can see the light for six second at a time, when it disappears for two seconds, then reappears for another six seconds, and so on. Now, my inventive genius has evolved a very simple arrangement which we may substitute for this complicated clockwork mechanism. In the stern locker you will find a common lantern and a still commoner chimney-pot hat. Before we dowse the glim of the jolly old buoy we shall light our lantern; then, when our friend appears in the offing, while I conduct the boat to a suitable spot (she won't want much management, for with this breeze she will drift just where I want her to go), you will hold the lantern in one hand and the pot-hat in the other. You pop the hat over the lantern and the light will be occulted; then you count two seconds and whisk off the hat, letting the light shine upon the face of the vasty deep. Count six seconds, and then clap on the hat again, and out she goes. Do you understand?"

"I understand," replied Josiah drearily.

"That's right. You clap on the hat, one — two — off. One — two — three — four — five — six — on. One — two — off, and so on. Sure you understand?"

"I understand," reiterated Josiah.

"Very well, then," returned the captain, and he proceeded to light a fresh cigar.

About two hours and a half from the time they left Margate found our two philanthropists but a few cables from the Edinburgh Channel lightship, at the flashing lantern of which Josiah gazed with the bewildered air of a somnambulistic owl, and another twenty minutes' sailing brought the boat alongside the gas-buoy.

At this new apparition Josiah stared with a feeling of stupefaction; and even as he stared, the light vanished as if by magic, but before he had time to wonder at its disappearance, there it was again bobbing and jigging about like some peculiarly agile will-o'-the-wisp.

Josiah gazed at the light like one in a dream, and he found himself following its vanishings and reappearances involuntarily — one — two — off; one — two — three — four — five — six — on — over and over again. Presently he was sharply awakened by the rattle of the falling mainsail, as the captain let go the halyards, and then an oar was thrust into his hand as his brother called out —

"Come, pull yourself together, Jos, and help me to work her alongside the buoy, and don't forget what I told you to do; and while I am at work, you keep a bright look-out for the *Jane and Elizabeth*. Remember, the tug carries two white lights, one over the other, and you'll see both her coloured side-lights at once, and both the side-lights of the ship. Keep a good look-out with your glasses, and keep the boat clear of the buoy until you hear me call. Now, then, here we are."

Josiah had a momentary glimpse of a large dark object surmounted by a gleaming light, swaying about right over the boat. Then there was a grinding noise, and the next moment he saw his brother clinging to the great cage, while his voice came hoarsely out of the gloom.

"Keep the boat clear!"

Josiah backed a few strokes and then sat down on a thwart, and while the boat drifted slowly he watched the light coming and going.

Soon a rasping sound reached his ear, growing gradually fainter as the boat drifted further from the buoy. Still the lights kept vanishing and reappearing in its strange, disquieting fashion, until at length, after an occultation, it failed to appear again, and all around was formless gloom.

The captain's little saw had done its work.

Seized with a sudden terrible loneliness, Josiah plied the oars vigorously. But where was the buoy? In the black darkness nothing was visible but the winking light of the Edinburgh lightship and the more slowly repeated glare of the Black Deep.

The terrified merchant wrenched at the oars, shouting aloud his brother's name, and peering on all sides into the gloom.

Suddenly there was a crash, and Josiah, looking around, saw the great dark shape, no longer crowned with light, swinging about over the tossing boat.

"Sam!" he shouted. "Sam! aren't you ready to come off?"

But there was no reply.

"Sam!" screamed Josiah, trembling and sweating with a horrible dread, "What are you doing, Sam?"

Just then the pale full moon peeped momentarily out of a bank of clouds, revealing the painted checkers and the great cage, the bars of which stood out black against the dim sky.

There was no one on the buoy.

Josiah slipped off the thwart into the bottom of the boat, where, with his fingers twisted in his hair, he lay for a time alternately weeping and cursing. The pitching of the boat — which was kept head to wind and sea by her mizzen — rolled him about on the bottom boards as though he had been a half-filled sack, so that presently for very weariness he was fain to pull himself up on to a thwart, on which he sat staring moodily and dreamily into the darkness.

To do Josiah justice, he was not greatly affected by the sudden death of his brother; indeed, if that ancient mariner could have contrived to effect his decease under somewhat more opportune circumstances, it is even possible that the event might have been hailed by the "Napoleon of Finance" with some degree of relief. But to perish thus ingloriously while the plot was but half carried out —

Arrived at this point in his meditations, Josiah was recalled abruptly to the realities of the situation by a phenomenon the observation of which set his heart bounding and his limbs trembling. Away on the eastern horizon there had appeared two bright lights like fixed stars, one immediately above the other. Just below there was another pair, but side by side, one red and one green, while even as he watched them Josiah saw yet another pair of lights, also red and green, appear quite close to those he had first noticed.

The meaning of these lights could not be mistaken by Josiah after the captain's repeated explanations. Here, then, he thought, after all his trouble and distress, and all the risk he had faced, was this accursed ship freighted with ruin and disgrace for him, calmly heading for her destination while he sat, an idle spectator, to watch her pass. As he continued thus, with his gaze fixed upon the advancing lights, he was suddenly startled by the appearance of a tall, dark object which seemed to start out of the gloom and creep towards the boat. As it approached and slowly passed close by, he perceived that it was a lofty post or column apparently implanted in the water and surmounted by a great St. Andrew's cross. The astonishment with which he had viewed the apparition now gave place to a very different feeling. This strange, uncanny object was evidently the North Beacon of which his brother had spoken, and its presence, and the manner in which it had apparently swept by the boat. showed that the latter was drifting, as the captain had predicted it would, just in the direction in which it was wanted to go, and that it was still possible for Josiah to carry out his diabolical scheme.

As soon as he realised this, he commenced to take the necessary steps. The lantern was still burning in a box in the stern sheets, and beside it lay the hat. Having mixed and consumed a stiff jorum of whisky-and-water to steady his quivering nerves, he took up the lantern in one hand and the hat in the other, and suddenly held the former up towards the advancing vessels.

"One — two — three — four — five — six — on!" and the hat was slipped on over the light.

"One — two — off!" and the light as once more uncovered.

"One — two — three — four — five — six — on!" and the light was again occulted, to reappear after another two seconds had been counted.

In this was half and hour was consumed. Josiah's aching arm becoming more and more automatic in its action, while his senses became gradually dulled by a kind of auto-hypnotism.

By this time the starboard lights of the two vessels had vanished as the broadsides were presented to the boat, and Josiah had been obliged to creep round from the starboard side to the port bow to follow them as they passed westward. But they were very near now.

As the tug rolled, the light from her cabin skylights could be seen at intervals, and the churning of her paddles was distinctly audible to the wrecker in his boat, while from the ship there came down the wind the sound of rollicking chorus mingled with the drone of an accordion. Evidently a forecastle concert was in progress.

Suddenly there was a report like the crack of a rifle, followed immediately by a rumbling crash. The chorus and the sound of the accordion ceased abruptly and were succeeded by a confused uproar of voices, above which could be heard a hollow roar as an officer shouted an order through a speaking trumpet. Josiah crouched, breathless and shaking, in the bow of the boat, staring at the twinkling lights, which had now begun to move about the ship, with a curious mixture of horror and satisfaction. He watched the tug round to and run alongside her consort, and presently he saw her port and masthead lights creeping away towards the Black Deep lightship. A few minutes afterwards the dark sky was rent by a streak of fire as a rocket soared up from the stranded ship. While the dull boom of its explosion was yet in his ears, and the sparks still floated aloft, the author of all the mischief felt his head swimming and his eyes growing dim, and he sank insensible into the bottom of the boat.

"Ahoy, there! — anyone aboard that boat?"

Josiah sat up on the boat's floor, then pulled himself into a kneeling position do that his eyes were just above the gunwale.

A few yards away a small cutter-rigged smack was hove-to while her skipper hailed the boat. The dawn had broken grey and cold: a leaden sky hanging over leaden sea, with a faint line of sombre grey far away in the south, furnished a prospect that was not inspiring.

"Is it far to Margate?" inquired Josiah.

"Good ten moile," was the encouraging answer.

"How long will it take me to get there?"

"How long?" repeated the man, with a faint grin, "why, yer won't never get there. You'll drift out to sea and die of starvation. Now look here! I'll tow yer right into Margate Harbour for foive barb — take it or leave it."

"Very well," said Josiah.

The man clawed at the boat with a long boat-hook and asked —

"Will yer stay in the boat or will yer come aboard us?"

Josiah stood up shivering and looked at the smack. From her grimy chimney a cheerful little cloud of blue smoke issued and wandered away to leeward, and a man whose head and shoulders protruded through the tiny companion-hatch was masticating deliberately, while he grasped in his hand a large blue mug containing something that steamed.

"I'll come aboard of you," said Josiah.

IV

The next morning Josiah's breach of his usual punctuality was the subject of some remark in the office. Indeed, it was nearly one o'clock when, considerably less neat and spruce than usual, he appeared and, passing to his room, rang for the senior clerk. Obeying with the morning's correspondence, he brought in the last yard unrolled from the tape-machine, and on this Josiah pounced with avidity. As the clerk was sorting the papers, an exclamation form the broker made him look up. Josiah was much agitated, and the tape performed strange gyrations in his hand as he held it out.

"Have I read this aright, Mr. Sales? What's the name of the ship?"

"The *Jane and Elizabeth* from Buenos Ayres passed Gravesend this morning," read Sales stolidly.

"Will you send out for an evening paper?"

Sales passed through the baize door and despatched a junior for the paper, which a boy was already crying in the streets. "Bring two while you're about it," he said, in view of Josiah's evident inability to tackle the morning's work at present.

He started to read with a languid interest until on the third page he saw —

"Ship Ashore off Margate.
"A Mysterious Sailor.
"Our Margate correspondent telegraphs: Early this morning, in response to signals from the Black Deep lightship, which is stationed at the head of Edinburgh Channel (the usual route for ingoing vessels), the Margate lifeboat *Quiver* proceeded to the Shingles sand, when it was found that the

American barque *White Cloud*, laden with hides from Rio, was fast ashore on the north edge. The captain and all hands were rescued, but all attempts at salvage have been fruitless.

"(Later.)

"The *White Cloud* was in tow at the time of the disaster, and when the cable parted from the violent shock with which she took the ground, the tug steamed off for assistance. No attempt was made to tow the ship off the bank, as it was evident, from the position in which she lay, that all efforts with that object would be useless, and it is feared that she will soon become a total wreck. It is conjectured that the gas-buoy, which was anchored in the fair-way to the north-east of the Shingles, had in some way become shifted, so leading the barque on to the sands. It is understood that the Trinity House authorities have been communicated with.

"The tug, in returning to the scene of the wreck, picked up a man swimming near the Shingles in a very exhausted condition. He was at first supposed to be one of the crew of the *White Cloud*, who had probably fallen overboard when she grounded with so much force. But on being conveyed to the Margate depôt of the shipwrecked Mariners' Society, he was not recognized by any of the rescued men. His underclothing was marked 'S. Jenkinson,' and from other indications he is believed to follow the sea. In spite of every care and attention, his condition, as a result of the cold and exposure he had evidently endured remained too critical to allow him to afford any explanation of his presence in the water. This must, therefore, remain a mystery for the present."

Lazily Sales began to wonder whether there could be any possible connection between the half-drowned sailor and his employer's brother, when he jumped and dropped the newspaper as a sharp report penetrated the baize door. He ran and knocked, but there was no answer; and when he tried the handle, the bolt was shot. The added weight of his two juniors made the door shiver, and with a more strenuous thrust it gave, and the doorway framed their white faces as they paused for the air to clear. Then as the smoke roled into the outer office, Josiah was seen huddled, an invertebrate mass, across the desk, a revolver just dropping from his hand. A clean-punched hole between the eyes was the source of a little stream, splashed in darker red across the pink sheet of the newspaper.

Josiah had found his pluck at last.

A Question of Salvage

MR. ELLIOTT stepped down from the deck of the yacht *Daffodil* into the dingy that bobbed actively alongside, and looked up uneasily at his daughter as he prepared to cast off the rope.

"I don't like leaving you on board all alone, Kathleen," he said. "Are you sure you don't feel nervous?"

"Of course I don't, you foolish old person," was the laughing reply. "Why should I? There are no bold, bad sea-rovers cruising about off Shellhaven. Besides, you won't be away long, will you?"

"I shall be back in a couple of hours, I hope, with a new anchor and chain. What a fool I was not to overhaul the ground tackle when I took the yacht over! But it can't be helped now. We are going to have some weather before night, and it would never do to risk riding out a gale with that worn-out chain and no second anchor. I'll get back as quickly as I can, and, meanwhile, Kathleen, you had better keep down below out of sight."

With this he cast off the painter, and, taking to the sculls, began to pull away rapidly towards the distant shore, while Kathleen stood on the swaying deck, holding on by a backstay, and watching the little boat as it bounced over the great, grey hillocks that came rolling in from windward.

With a last glance shoreward, where the boat was now nearing the jetty, she dropped down into the cockpit, and, opening the little, watertight door, entered the cabin and shut herself in. The main cabin was virtually her own room — for her father slept in the forepeak — and was littered by her various belongings; but though her books, and even her not very abundant needlework, mutely offered the means of distraction, she was apparently disposed neither for work nor for study, for, flinging herself on the settee, she composed herself, as well as the pitching of the yacht would allow, to quiet reflection. The earnest hazel eyes looked into the distance far beyond the aneroid on which they were fixed — a distance that held a single figure; and the figure was not that of her father.

The minutes sped until nearly an hour had passed, and still Kathleen lay gazing dreamily before her, wrapped in deep meditation. Absently she had noted that the sea appeared to be rising, that the wind ever moaned more loudly through the rigging; and once she had been somewhat startled by a curious, sharp jar. But the stormy present had faded in the vividness of a scene from the forgotten past; a sunny countryside with a figure that vaulted a stile and turned to wave his hand before he moved away into the shadow of the wood. And as her pretty hazel eyes looked on that phantom from the buried years, they grew dim and wistful and sad, and her lips parted with a little sigh.

Suddenly she started to a consciousness of something new in the yacht's behaviour. A violent lurch had nearly flung her from the settee. Stepping up on the locker, she looked forward along the yacht's deck; and at that moment a man's head, encased in a sou'-wester, rose out of the forecastle hatch.

The new-comer and Kathleen stared at one another for some seconds in silent amazement; then the latter demanded.

"How on earth did you get on board, Mr. Davernon?"

Davernon left the question unanswered, but, as he came out on deck, met it with another.

"Is your father on board, Miss Elliott?"

"No. He has gone ashore to get another anchor and chain. I'm all alone."

"Good Lord!" exclaimed Davernon. "Do you mean to say you haven't another anchor?"

"Only the kedge. But what has happened?"

"The yacht has broken adrift, and the tide is racing us down on the Mew Sand. And there's a squall coming, too. Just run down and slip on your oilees, while I get the kedge overboard."

Kathleen darted below, to reappear in a few moments in a long oilskin coat and a sou'-wester, from beneath which wisps of red-gold hair streamed out in the wind. And as she rose from the cockpit, Davernon's prophecy was fulfilled; for the yacht, rounding up for the moment to the pull of the kedge, gave a violent plunge, snapped the hempen line as though it were packthread, and once more wallowed away on the tide.

Davernon seemed to be a cool, resolute young man and a capable seaman. He made no further reference to the deadly shoal that lay to leeward ready to swallow up the frail craft, but fell to work with unhurried calm.

"Will you take the tiller, Miss Elliott, while I set what sail she will stand?

Thank you! There's nothing to get frightened about, you know."

"I'm not frightened; I'm only thinking of poor old dad. He doesn't know you're on board does he?"

His answer was inaudible to her, for a violent squall, sweeping over the darkening roadstead with a howl of malice, filled her ears with tumult and blinded her with driving rain and spray. Davernon first hoisted the mizzen — the *Daffodil* was yawl-rigged — and as the yacht turned head to sea and wind, he busied himself with the mainsail and foresail, both of which he reefed close before hoisting, and having run in the bowsprit, he scrambled back to the cockpit.

"She'll do for the present," he said, as he took the tiller from Kathleen, "and I don't want to reduce canvas further until we have more sea room."

"Shall we be able to get back to the anchorage?" Kathleen asked.

"No," replied Davernon, "and we mustn't try. We've got to clear the end of the Mew Sand before the gale hits us, and get open water under our lee, or it will be all up with us, I'm afraid!"

As he spoke he glanced quickly at a chequered buoy that had just hove in sight, squelching ponderously on the steep seas: and, watching it furtively, he noted that the yacht was still being swept astern by the tide, and this notwithstanding that she was carrying more canvas than she would properly bear. Less than a mile beyond the buoy he knew that the deadly sand lay in wait for them; indeed, he could see, now and again, a great white plume of spray fly upward from the surf that boiled over the hidden shoal. It would be touch and go in any case. The yacht was being borne obliquely down towards the sand, and the only chance was to keep close hauled in the hope that the tide would bear them past the end spit into the open sea.

For some minutes no word was spoken on board. Kathleen had enough experience of yachting to realise the position.

Suddenly she recalled her companion's mysterious and unexpected appearance through the hatchway.

"You never told me how you got on board, Mr. Davernon," she said.

Davernon ducked to avoid a sheet of flying spray, and answered quietly: "I swam on board."

Kathleen looked at him with a puzzled smile. "Are you sure you didn't fly on board?" she asked.

"Quite! I'm not joking, Miss Elliott. I swam alongside, and climbed on board."

Kathleen stared at him incredulously. His oilskins were wet now, but they had been dry when he first rose out of the forepeak. And his clothing was still dry, as she could see when the oilskins blew open.

"Nonsense!" she exclaimed. "You couldn't swim in oilskins, and keep your clothes dry, too."

"They aren't my clothes; they're your father's. I took the liberty of changing. But what is that noise? It isn't a steamer, is it?"

They both turned their heads and listened. Indistinctly, through the moaning of the wind, the wash of water and the growl of the ever-nearing surf to leeward, came a low bellowing like that of a discontented bull.

"It sounds like a steamer blowing short blasts," said Kathleen, "but I don't see her. And it seems to come from the direction of the sand." She screwed up her eyes to peer into the grey dusk, and after a few moments exclaimed: "Oh, I know! It's the whistle-buoy. Yes! There it is. Don't you see?"

She pointed almost directly astern, and Davernon, following the direction, now perceived a globular, striped object dancing furiously on the waves.

"By Jove! Kathleen, you're right!" he exclaimed gleefully. "It's the South Mew Sand buoy. That means that we are clear of the sand end! And none too soon either, for here comes a snorter. Take the tiller a minute, while I get the mizzen stowed."

Kathleen flushed slightly as she grasped the tiller. Davernon's use of her Christian name had not escaped her notice; for, woman-like, she was able, even in moments of extremist peril, to spare a little attention for the softer emotions. He had called her "Miss Elliott" up to now, as she had noted with faint disapproval, though, to be sure, she had given him the lead; and as Davernon busied himself about the deck of the yacht and the great whistle-buoy swept slowly past, curtsying and bellowing its hoarse warning, she speculated on the meaning of the change. Perhaps it was only absence of mind and the effect of old habit. She would see.

When Davernon had hove the yacht to and fixed the sidelights — for it was now growing dark — he scrambled back.

"Look here, Kathleen," said he — so it wasn't mere absence of mind — "you'd better get into the cabin and lie down. It's of no use for you to stay out here getting drenched for nothing."

A cloud of spray that enveloped the yacht and half-filled the cockpit gave point and emphasis to his words. But Kathleen shook her head.

"I'm not going to leave you to work the yacht alone. You might want help at any moment."

Davernon protested very earnestly, but Kathleen was quite immovable, insisting, reasonably enough, that one pair of hands was not sufficient for safety. So they sat together in the little cockpit, buffeted by the wind, and pelted by the salt spray, while the yacht, plunging, straining and creaking, was driven by the gale farther and farther out over the leaping seas into the pitchy blackness of the night. There was little talk between them. Indeed, the shriek of the wind and the thunder of waves and straining gear made conversation difficult enough, and throughout that wild night, Davernon was silent and grim and alert, watching each approaching sea skilfully evading its effect to overwhelm the staunch little craft.

Meanwhile, Kathleen crouched by his side, quite unafraid, and, but for uneasy thoughts of her father's terrible anxiety, rather enjoying the experience. There was the mystery of Jasper Davernon's sudden appearance on the yacht, just in the nick of time too. That was most incomprehensible. Almost before she knew it, her reflections had fitted themselves with words.

"What a queer coincidence it was that you should happen to come on board just then!"

"Why such a coincidence?" Davernon asked, without looking round.

Kathleen reddened in the darkness.

"I mean, that you should come just as the cable was going to break and send me adrift all alone."

"Yes," Davernon rejoined shortly. "I suppose it was a bit queer," and he put the helm down to meet a specially vicious-looking wave that was breaking at the crest.

The hours sped on, and still the little vessel held her own against the bellowing wind and the very threatening seas. Once a lightship arose astern and slowly passed ahead, flashing its warning glare and measuring by its apparent movement the speed of the yacht's drift before the gale. And all the while Davernon sat grim and silent, fighting his battle with the storm and, so far, winning the fight.

Soon after midnight the roar of the wind became somewhat less deafening, and there seemed some chance of the storm abating. Then it was that Davernon broke the long silence.

"I do wish you'd go and turn in, Kathleen. I can do quite well by myself now."

Kathleen was beginning to frame a refusal when he interrupted:

"Now, do as I ask you, like a good girl. Remember, we're being blown a long way off the land, and when the gale breaks we're got to get back. I may want you to stand a watch while I turn in for a snooze myself. Be a good chum, Kathleen, and take your watch below."

Kathleen stood up, clinging to the coaming. "Very well, Jasper," she said; "if you really wish it, I will. But you'll call me out if you want me, won't you?"

"Oh, yes, I'll rouse you out if I want help."

"And you'll let me take a watch while you have a sleep?"

"If necessary, yes. And now, wrap yourself up well and get a good snooze." He held out his disengaged hand, and, as she took it, she looked at him steadily. But the darkness and the brim of her sou'-wester hid that look from him.

Watching her opportunity, she darted in through the cabin door and, holding it ajar for a moment, called out, "Good night, Jasper," and he answered cheerily, "Goodnight, chick."

It was his old pet name for her, and the utterance of it postponed her sleep for several minutes.

When the thoughtful hazel eyes opened again the sunlight was pouring through the cabin skylight, and the little clock on the bulkhead told a tale of horror. Kathleen sprang from the settee with a gasp of remorse and ran out into the cockpit, where Davernon, pale, worn and heavy-eyed, sat like a graven image, doggedly grasping the tiller.

"Oh, Jasper!" she exclaimed, with a mortified glance aloft, "you said you would call me if you wanted help, and you've set all the sails by yourself!"

"I didn't want help. The gale broke quite suddenly, and this quiet breeze set in. It was only a one-man job."

Deeply hurt, Kathleen went back to the cabin to prepare breakfast, and as they took their meal together in the cockpit — for Davernon, though dead tired, refused to leave the helm even for a minute — she glanced with troubled surprise at her shipmate's face. All the geniality and friendliness of the previous night had vanished. Stolid and wooden, he sat grasping the tiller, staring ahead or into the binnacle, and making only the curtest replies to her attempts at conversation. It was very strange. Kathleen sat furtively watching her companion and wondering more and more at the growing hardness of the set face. And then there arose again that vision of the sunny countryside. It was more than two years ago now, and yet she could see it all so clearly. She saw and heard him asking her, confidently and almost as a matter of course, to marry him. And then, whether from shyness or girlish arrogance or sheer perversity, she never knew, she had said "No," and had been ready to bite her tongue out immediately after. And he, stupid fellow, had actually taken her refusal seriously! It was a wretched affair. But last night it had looked as if all might be well. She had turned in quite happy and confident; and now, behold! there he sat, speechless, frigid and stern.

"Hadn't you better go and lie down and get a little sleep?" she asked gently. "I can keep the yacht on her course if you give me directions."

"There's no need," he replied, without looking round. "That land ahead is Shellhaven. We shall be in the anchorage in about an hour."

She made no rejoinder. Her last hope of a reconciliation was gone. Presently they would say "Good-bye," and it would be good-bye for ever.

After a minute or so of silence Davernon spoke again.

"There's something that you'll get to know — unless you've guessed it already — so I may as well tell you. I told you," he continued, "that I swam alongside and climbed on board. You didn't believe me, but it was true. And I'll tell you why I did it. I am a runaway convict."

Kathleen uttered a cry of horror.

"Jasper!" she exclaimed. "It can't be!"

"I'm sorry to say it's a literal fact," he replied dryly.

She gazed at him a while in stupefied amazement. The, grasping his arm, she declared passionately: "But it must be a mistake! You haven't — you can't have — have done anything wicked, Jasper. You haven't, have you?"

Davernon's face hardened. "The fact is," said he, "I'm getting a little shy of that question. I answered it once to the magistrate, and he smiled and begged me to remember that I was speaking to a man of the world. I answered it again at my trial, and the judge smiled and reminded the jury that they were men of the world. So now I am a little fed up with the subject."

"But, Jasper, dear," she said softly, laying her hand on his, "I am not a man of the world, or even a woman of it. And I am your friend always."

Davernon was visibly affected, and he pressed her hand gratefully, though his voice was stern as he told his tale.

"My story amounts to this. I was staying at Bournemouth, and one night I had a fancy for a moonlight walk in the country. I went farther than I intended, and did not enter the town until past one in the morning. Passing an isolated house, I noticed a French window ajar and a light flashing about in the room. Like an officious fool, I climbed over the wall, and, going up to the window, opened it and entered. There was a man in the room who tried to escape when he saw me, but I headed him off. Then he slipped through into another room, and again like an officious fool, I followed. The room was quite dark, for the man had put out his lantern, and I had barely got inside when he dropped something, slipped out of the door, shut it and locked it on the outside. I struck a wax match and found that the burglar had dropped his jemmy, so I picked it up and jammed it into the door-crack by the lock. I soon had the door open, and then out I rushed — into the arms of a couple of policemen. Of course, I tried to explain, but they only grinned. There was I with the jemmy that fitted the marks on the window. The other man had disappeared.

"At my trial I got a good laugh from the jury and three years from the judge. That was two months ago. Last week I was sent down with a gang to work on the new prison that is building outside Shellhaven. Yesterday, taking advantage of an opportunity, I skipped off and made for the sea, and finding a barge's jolly-boat in a quiet place, I got into her and pulled out into the roadstead towards the barge. Then I saw your yacht break adrift, so I tied the boat up to the barge, jumped overboard, and swam to the yacht — which I hoped was deserted — climbed on board, popped down into the forecastle, changed into a suit of your father's, and pitched the prison suit overboard. You know the rest."

"Yes," she answered earnestly. "I do. You saved the yacht and you saved my life. But, Jasper, dear, this dreadful mistake must be set right." She paused, and then said suddenly: "Did anyone see you come on board?"

"Yes," he answered. "There was a fellow doing anchor watch on a schooner. He was deeply interested."

"Then it will be known that you are on the yacht, Jasper! You mustn't go back to Shellhaven! They'll be waiting for you."

"I know. But it can't be helped. Your father will be out of his mind."

She seized his tiller hand impulsively. "You mustn't go back, Jasper! Put the yacht about and escape!"

But Davernon only answered with a dogged shake of the head. "I'm going to see you safe in your father's hands, Kathleen. That's more important than my trumpery affairs. Besides, it's too late to put about now. D'you see?"

He pointed up to a steam launch that was heading out of the roadstead straight for the yacht.

Kathleen gazed despairingly at it.

"Oh, Jasper! Jasper!" she sobbed, "you have thrown away your liberty for me! Why did you? And they'll make your sentence longer, too! It is dreadful! Dreadful! And to think that it need never have happened at all if I hadn't been such a little fool two years ago!"

She clung to him convulsively until the launch swept alongside, when she wiped her eyes and cast a hostile glance at the two warders and the police inspector who sat in the stern. It was the latter who climbed on board as the launch was made fast alongside, and he addressed himself to Kathleen.

"I have received information, madam, that this man Davernon, an escaped convict, has stolen and made off with your yacht. Is that so?"

"Certainly not!" replied Kathleen. "The yacht was adrift, and he has very nobly salved her and is now bringing her back to her berth."

"I see," said the inspector, with a smile. "Then he is entitled to salvage. Well, that disposes of my little affair, so I'll retire in favour of the chief warder."

He stepped back into the launch, and the chief warder, leaning over towards the cockpit, but not boarding the yacht, addressed Davernon:

"You'll have to come back with me and see the governor, Davernon."

"Naturally," Jasper replied.

"But," continued the officer, "you won't have to stay. The gentleman who did that little job that you were convicted for has been collared, and he fully collaborates your statement. So the Home Secretary has granted you a free pardon, and you leave us without a stain on your character. As a matter of fact, the pardon was in the office when you bolted, so the question of prison-breaking won't be raised. But you'll have to come back with me and get your discharge in regular order. Perhaps we'd better give you a tow in and get the matter settled as soon as possible."

His offer was accepted gladly. A dozen fathoms of tow-line were run out and launch forged ahead with the yacht in tow. For quite a long time the two occupants of the cockpit sat without speaking, Kathleen occasionally mopping her eyes with her handkerchief. It was Davernon who broke the silence.

"So I'm entitled to salvage, am I?"

"Of course you are. A third of the vessel and cargo, I believe, is the usual thing."

"Oh, hang the vessel! It's the cargo I'm thinking of. Do you think your father will pay up?"

Kathleen blushed a rosy red. "I dare say," she answered with a roguish smile, "he'll listen to reason, especially if I tell him he's got to."

Comedy and Romance

Under the Clock

TO MEN AND WOMEN — and particularly men — whose experiences have run upon the usual lines, matter for speculations of the most curious and even puzzling kind is furnished by those periodical publications whose self-imposed function is the promotion of matrimonial engagements. The majority of men, indeed, so far from experiencing any difficulty in attaining to the state of matrimony, have found themselves surrounded by opportunities lavishly in excess of the requirements of any but a dweller in Salt Lake City. To such the perusal of the said publication is a source of wonder, and the occasion of dim surmises that perhaps there exists, unseen and unsuspected, certain human blank cartridges, damp squibs, and unexploded crackers, which, too late, have begun to smoulder and splutter in obscure corners, and yearn for a little belated pyrotechnic display of their own.

To this effect were the meditations of young Dr. Porter, who, with the ink hardly dry upon his diploma, was taking charge of a suburban practice, while its owner snuffed the sea-breezes on the poppy-sprinkled cliffs of Cromer; for he had just entered the trim sitting room of Mr. Adolphus Caddle, and had observed upon the breakfast table a copy of the *Matrimonial Bellringer*.

"Well, and how are we today, Mr. Caddle?" asked the doctor cheerily, and in his most professional manner.

"Picking up a bit, I hope."

"Well, doctor," replied the patient with a complaining wriggle, "I am afraid I can't give a very good account of myself. Ah! my dear sir, we have to pay for our indiscretions."

"We have, indeed," assented the doctor heartily, as he thought of the breach of promise action that loomed faintly but ominously on his own horizon.

"Free living has never agreed with me," pursued Mr. Caddle. "My digestive organs rebel against heavy and luxurious feeding."

Dr. Porter looked at his patient; at his thin pale hair, his faded blue eyes, and his large face, with its complexion as of a boiled custard, on which — as

237

the art-critics would say — a convincing note of colour was struck by a gaily-tinted pimple; and he agreed that the rôle of a riotous liver was unsuitable.

"And," continued Mr. Caddle. "I may as well confess what I have exceeded; that I was yesterday so indiscreet as to indulge in a — er — in fact, in a bun. It was a currant bun with a shiny outside — a most unsafe article of food — and although I carefully scraped off the shiny exterior, and endeavoured to pick out the currants, one of them eluded my vigilance, and I inadvertently swallowed it, and if you will believe me, sir, I can feel that currant at this very moment — here –" and the sufferer laid his hand upon his dicky (from behind which there peeped the corner of a flannel chest-protector).

"Dear, dear! Mr. Caddle," said Dr. Porter, miraculously preserving an unmoved countenance, "we must be more careful. We must not fritter away our health, as so many do, on the pleasures of the table. By the way, how does the new medicine agree with you?"

Mr. Caddle smacked his lips. "I am glad you reminded me of that," he said. "How can I thank you sufficiently for that admirable mixture? There is the advantage of being attended by a young man, fresh from the schools, and primed with all the latest triumphs of medical science. Dear old Dr. Bamber has never prescribed anything that has given me such instant relief. Allow me again to thank you."

"Oh! Not at all, but I am glad it suits you," said Dr. Porter, guiltily conscious that he had filed up the bottle by means of a wooden tap from a huge stone jar in the surgery, labelled *Mistua Sacchari Usti Comp.* Then, by way of changing the subject, he remarked.

"I see, Mr. Caddle, that you have been reading the *Matrimonial Bellringer*. What is your opinion of these matrimonial papers? Do you think that any marriages are really brought about by their agency?"

"There is no doubt of it," replied Mr. Caddle in a tone of conviction. "To my certain knowledge there are hundreds of happy and united couples who owe their present blessedness entirely to this very journal," and he tapped the *Bellringer* solemnly with his pudgy fingers.

"It is not for every one, of course," continued Mr. Caddle, "Who requires such extraneous aids to the attainment of his happiness. Many persons seem to be capable of managing these affairs perfectly well without any assistance whatever."

"Certainly," agreed Dr. Porter, reflecting, as his thoughts reverted to his late landlady's daughter and the impending suit, on the superfluousness of the *Bellringer* in his own case.

"But," pursued Mr. Caddle, "there are others who are not so fortunately constituted; who like — ah, well, like myself, for instance, in the presence of the fair sex, experience a feeling of — er — what shall I say? — of diffidence — shyness — awkwardness, perhaps, and who, therefore, are glad to be able to make the first advances under cover of — er — of entrenchments, as it were."

"Excellent!" commented Dr. Porter. "Excellent! and so I understand that you are really looking out for a matrimonial investment yourself?"

"Well," said Mr. Caddle with a bashful wriggle in his elbow chair, "I don't see why I shouldn't tell you, seeing how friendly we have been together. A man must have someone to whom he can impart a little secret now and again." He rose with a faint blush and, unlocking a small cupboard, drew from it a pile of back numbers of the *Bellringer*.

"Here," he said opening a well-worn copy some three months old, "is the advertisement that first attracted my attention — this one marked with the blue pencil. Perhaps you would like to read it."

Dr. Porter leaned over the paper and read out the marked paragraph:

CHERRY PIE, graceful, plump, petite, with lustrous brown eyes and wavy chestnut hair, would like to meet with an eligible bachelor or widower of independent means (age no object) with a view to matrimony. C.P. is amiable, affectionate, and domesticated, is an expert Berlin wool-worker and plays with great skill and feeling upon the glass harmonica. Address, Cherry Pie, Box No. 220613.

"There," said Mr. Caddle, "I think that sounds rather alluring, doesn't it? The colour, you know, appeals to me, being a fair man. 'Lustrous brown eyes,' eh! 'Brown eye, cherry pie' He! he! What do you think of it doctor?"

"Oh, very nice, indeed," commenced Dr. Porter huskily. "By the way, what a remarkable engraving that is," and darting across the room he flattened his nose against the work of art in question (regardless of good old Sir Joshua's admonition that 'pictures are not intended to be smelled') while his back, presented to Mr. Caddle, heaved tremulously as though he were shaken by some strong emotion.

"Yes," pursued the unconscious Caddle, "I was taken with that description directly I saw it, so I ventured to send a little reply — a very cautious and discreet one, I am sure you will admit. Here it is, if you would just run your eye over it."

Dr. Porter, returning reluctantly from the engraving, took up the paper and read:

> ADOLPHUS, a bachelor of middle age, with an independent income of £500 per annum, fair plump, amiable and domesticated, has seen Cherry Pie's advertisement, and thinking that he might prove suitable to her requirements, would like further details as to her age, etc. — Address Box No. 312403.

"What do you think of that?" inquired Mr. Caddle triumphantly. "Pretty discreet and cautious, I think, don't you?"

"Most diplomatic," responded the doctor.

"Well, since then we've corresponded a good deal — in the same way, of course — no letter — no, no — no letters; but I needn't trouble you with all the details. I'll just come to the matter in hand, on which I should like to have your opinion. You see, I have come to the conclusion that I ought to get a peep at the lady, so that I may know if she is all that my imagination has painted her. So to that end I have devised a little scheme — a very neat little scheme, I think — but you shall judge for yourself. Read that."

Dr. Porter read out another blue-pencilled advertisement:

> CHERRY PIE will be pleased to afford Adolphus an opportunity of seeing her in any public place (as a railway station, for example), the place and time to be fixed by him. In order that he may recognise her without difficulty she will wear a straw hat with two roses in it, one red and one white, a pink blouse with a bunch of lilies of the valley at the throat and a grey skirt. She will carry on her left arm a small basket tied with blue ribbons and in her right hand a copy of the *Gentlewoman* rolled up.

"Now," said Mr. Caddle, taking a sheet of writing-paper from the cupboard, "this is my reply":

ADOLPHUS will be happy to meet C.P. on Saturday, April 1st, at Victoria Station, just under the clock. He will wear a grey felt hat, a green silk necktie, a light covert coat, white spats and patent boots. He will carry in his left hand a roll of white paper, and in his right had a copy of 'Bradshaws Guide,' and will wear in his buttonhole a small bunch of pink geraniums. He will arrive at 7 P.M. precisely.

As Dr. Porter put down the paper Mr. Caddle smiled nervously.

"How do you think it goes?" he asked.

"Merrily as a wedding-bell," replied the doctor, smiling rather more broadly in return. "But, by Jove! Is your clock right? I must be off or I shall never get my round finished to-day," and with a hasty adieu he darted down the stairs and was gone.

As the long hand of the clock in Victoria Station crept on to the third minute before the hour of seven on the evening of Saturday, April 1st, there emerged on to the platform from the main entrance a short, stout gentleman, in whose demeanour there was evident signs of great nervous excitement and trepidation. It was Mr. Caddle; and true to his promise he wore a light covert coat, a grey felt hat, a green silk necktie, white spats and patent boots. In his left hand was a voluminous roll of white paper, while in his right hand was a yellow-covered Bradshaw, and the button-hole of his coat was gay with a bunch of pink geraniums. There was no mistaking Mr. Caddle.

With a quick agitated step he hopped out on to the platform and looked about; then heaved a deep sigh of relief. She had not come yet.

Mr. Caddle walked slowly across the platform and taking up a position directly under the clock began to examine with great show of attention one of the time-tables on the wall, drawing his finger down the column of names and figures, which were as intelligible to him just then as the hieroglyphics on the outside of a tea-chest.

He had stood there about a minute when he gave a sudden start and a thrill of terror ran through his little body, for out of the tail of his eye he had seen a lady emerge from a side entry and stand looking at the platform.

"'Tis she," exclaimed Mr. Caddle — "and yet –" Yes, there was the pink blouse, the straw hat, in which nestled the roses of York and Lancaster, there were the lilies-of-the-valley, and the grey skirt, and the little basket with the blue ribbons, and there was the *Gentlewoman* rolled up in her right hand. Yes! It was she — and yet — "and yet," muttered Mr. Caddle, "she said distinctly 'plump and petite'" whereas the newcomer was undeniably a tall, gaunt woman, and was moreover as dark as a spanish gipsy.

"It's very strange," said Mr. Caddle as he regarded the lady out of the corner of his eye and quaked like an ill-made blanc-mange upon the rickety table. "I really don't quite understand it."

At this moment the apparition suddenly vanished, apparently into the booking-office, leaving Mr. Caddle to his cogitations.

"She certainly said plump and petite," he mused. "Why, she seemed quite tall and — and — Ha!" The charmer had reappeared. Yes! There she was, straw hat, roses, pink blouse, basket, *Gentlewoman* — there could be no mistake — but –

"Astonishing!" exclaimed Mr. Caddle.

"It must have been an optical illusion. I could have sworn she was tall and dark, and thin. But she isn't — that's certain." She certainly was not. Plump and petite, if you like — or short and fat, to be more literal, and with the straw hat perched upon an immense mop of light yellow hair.

"It's hardly what I should call chestnut hair," said Mr. Caddle regarding the mop doubtfully, "yet I am sure she said chestnut — but perhaps she was thinking of the inside of the nut." Even as he gazed at her, this luminary underwent a second eclipse, disappearing again into the booking-office, while Mr. Caddle was left staring uneasily at the time-table, his still-extended finger jigging up and down in his agitation like the indicator of a steam gauge.

"My eyes must have deceived me," he reflected; "clearly they have deceived me. It was the distance, no doubt. I suppose I had better stroll along that way and have a look at her a little nearer."

He stepped back to move away, and as the heel of his patent boot encountered something soft, he became aware that he had set it upon somebody's toe.

The owner of the toe furnished verbal information to the same effect.

"Oh! I beg your pardon," exclaimed Mr. Caddle. "I am so sorry. I hope I haven't — ah! — o — oh!"

As he turned Mr. Caddle found himself comforted by a gentleman — there was nothing surprising in that. But his hat! It was of grey felt! His coat was a light covert coat; he wore a green silk necktie; a bunch of pink geraniums was in his button-hole and he carried in one hand a roll of white paper and in the other a copy of Bradshaw.

"Great Heaven!" ejaculated Mr. Caddle as he turned hastily away, "what a very surprising coincidence! And how very inconvenient!"

He walked quickly across the station towards the side entrance and was just abreast of the booking-office when there stepped briskly out of the doorway a gentleman whose appearance filled the unfortunate Caddle with confusion and dismay; for he was attired in a light covert coat, a grey felt hat, a green necktie, white spats and patent boots; wore a bunch of pink geraniums in his button-hole and carried a roll of white paper and a copy of Bradshaw in his hands.

"Good gracious," exclaimed Mr. Caddle, "I seem to have made a most unfortunate choice in my get-up; why, instead of being unique and remarkable figure, I seem to be dressed exactly like everybody else."

His meditations on this subject were at this point cut short by the sudden emergence from the booking-office of a large, massive, blond lady, followed at a few paces distance by another lady who, on the contrary, was dark, spare, and diminutive. Dissimilar, however, as the two women were in some respects, they both wore straw hats with roses, pink blouses, with lilies-of-the-valley, grey skirts, and they both carried in one hand a copy of the *Gentlewoman*, and on the other arm a basket tied with blue ribbons.

In the bewilderment and dismay which this meeting produced, Mr. Caddle hurried towards the side exit in order that, in its comparative obscurity and seclusion, he might reflect upon these remarkable occurrences. But as he stepped into the entry, among the passengers who were thronging towards the platform he distinguished at least half-a-dozen persons of both sexes whose exterior presented the now too familiar characteristics.

From the shelter of the entry the bewildered Caddle looked out on to the platform at the Adolphuses and Cherry Pies with increasing amazement; for even as he watched they continued to arrive in twos and threes until fully a score of each sex were to be seen, all perambulating the platform sentry-wise, and each anxiously scrutinising the others.

Mr. Caddle strolled out of the station in a brown study, that in the cool outer air he might duly consider this astounding phenomenon. And as he meditated upon it a light suddenly broke upon his mind and illuminated its dense obscurity.

"Of course," he exclaimed, "I see how it is. Our advertisements have been read by others, and envious imposters have come here impersonating me in the hope of snatching the prize from my grasp. Ah! But there are the women! Why, yes! They too have seen the advertisements and have come to try and capture the desirable Adolphus." Here Mr. Caddle smiled complacently and tried to get a view of his reflection in the window of a cab that was drawn up outside the station.

Comforted and encouraged by the conclusion at which he had arrived he resolved to make a final effort to single out the beauteous, the amiable and domesticated Cherry Pie from the crowd of imposters, and to this end retraced his steps and re-entered the station.

During his absence the throng had materially increased and the number of persons parading under the clock in the regulation costume certainly made his task a somewhat difficult one.

"I will be wary," said Mr. Caddle, "wary and watchful."

To give more effect to his wariness he approached the bookstall and began turning over the leaves of some magazines, but he had barely taken up his position when a lanky rawboned woman of fifty, with shoulders like a Burgundy bottle, and attired in the fatal garb edged up alongside, and bestowed upon him a leer that froze the very marrow in his bones. With a grasp of horror he sidled away to the right, but the lady, edging along rapidly, craned her neck towards him and whispered hoarsely in his ear: —

"Be virtuous and you will be happy!"

At this the amazed and appalled Caddle backed away with such ill-considered haste that he came plump into the arms of a female behind him.

"Awfully sorry!" he gurgled, whisking round like a teetotum to find himself confronted by a buxom elderly woman in the everlasting uniform. "Awfully sorry! afraid I — er –"

"Not at all," said the lady, smiling benevolently, "by no means — a — be virtuous and you will be –"

But Mr. Caddle was off like a startled rabbit and plunging into the throng, strode up to the platform.

Suddenly he felt a hand gently laid upon his arm, and turning abruptly beheld a small comely woman with soft wavy hair who was regarding him with a pair of sparkling roguish eyes of the clearest brown that he had ever seen.

"At last," he ejaculated. "This must be really she — ah — did you — er — wish to speak to me?"

"If you please," replied the charmer shyly.

"Shall we walk about as we converse?" suggested Caddle.

"Perhaps it would be better."

They walked on side by side for a few paces, Mr. Caddle stealing now and again a timid but complacent glance at his fair companion.

Presently he remarked, bending his head down towards her — he had not bend far — "You were going to say something to me?"

"Yes, but let me whisper it."

Mr. Caddle inclined his ear towards her and received into it a soft murmur: "Be virtuous, and you will be happy!"

"Good Heavens!" gasped Caddle in a state of positive stupefaction. "Am I going mad or is the place bewitched?"

He broke away from his companion, and betaking himself to the shelter of the main entry, mopped his face with his handkerchief while he endeavoured to frame some rational explanation of these strange portents. His mind, however, was quite incapable of being brought to a focus on the subject, and his attention wandered fitfully from one subject to another until it was presently attracted by a group of three persons who stood not far from him and seemed to be furtively observing him. The group consisted of two elderly ladies and a little bird-like old gentleman, and as Caddle was uneasily preparing to move away, the latter separated himself from his companions and advanced smiling and raising his hat.

"Can you very kindly inform me," he began in bland and persuasive accents, "what is the name of this institution?" He waved his arm around vaguely as he spoke.

"This," replied Caddle, gazing round the crowded interior, "is Victoria Station."

"I know, I know," said the old gentleman, "but I was referring to these ladies and gentleman who are attired in this very becoming uniform."

"I know no more than yourself who they are," returned Caddle huffily, and retired further up the entry.

After a while he cautiously emerged from his retreat and surveyed the scene before him.

To his reeling senses the entire station appeared to be filled with a surging multitude of men and women attired in the uniform of the *Bellringer's* advertisement and all restlessly wandering to and fro and peering into one another's faces. And even in his bewildered state he could not help noticing one very odd feature in their behaviours, which was that now and again one of the ladies would approach one of the gentleman and eagerly whisper something in his ear, upon which the gentleman would hurriedly make off with an appearance of discomfiture and alarm.

Even as he stared blankly, like one newly awakened, at this astonishing spectacle he became aware of a red-faced, dark-haired woman who was bearing down on him with an evident purpose; whereupon, dropping the roll of paper and flinging away the *Bradshaw*, he incontinently fled down the passage and in a few moments was speeding westward in a swift hansom.

Scarcely had Mr. Caddle made his escape from the station when the door of the luggage-office was cautiously opened and a head was thrust forth, to be followed by the remainder of the person to whom it belonged. This person, who was in fact none other than Dr. Porter, stood at the door of the office gazing up the platform with twitching lips, holding one hand to his side as though suffering from some internal pain, while with the other hand he wiped his eyes at intervals.

He had stood thus a minute or more when one of the uniformed ladies sidled up to him with a bashful simper and began to mumble in a low voice. For a few moments he gazed at the woman in silence; then cramming his handkerchief into his mouth, dived down the entry, and vanished into the night.

The events of then evening have always remained to Mr. Caddle a source of unmixed wonder and a matter for such profound cogitation.

Perhaps had he witnessed Dr. Porter's proceedings on that occasion, some glimmer of light might have been shed on the mystery; while a pretty complete understanding of its causes would have been obtained if his attention had happened to be directed to two advertisements which appeared on March 29th in the *Daily Advertiser* and the *London Chronicle* respectively, the substance of which, for the reader's enlightenment we reproduce.

I: A lady who picked up at the corner of Villiers Street a gentleman's gold repeater with gold chain attached on March 24th, is desirous of returning it to its owner. For this purpose she proposes to be at Victoria Station on 1st April at 7 P.M. immediately under the clock. To facilitate mutual recognition she will wear a straw hat with two roses in it, one red and one white, a pink blouse with a bunch of lilies at the throat, and a grey skirt. She will carry on her left arm a small basket tied with blue ribbons and in her right hand a copy of the *Gentlewoman* rolled up. She suggests that the owner might wear a grey felt hat, a green silk necktie, a light covert coat, white spats and patent boots. He might carry in his left hand a roll of white paper and in his right a copy of Bradshaw's Guide and in his button-hole a bunch of pink geraniums. On recognising advertiser he is to approach slowly and exclaim in a low voice "Beware the Ides of March."

II: A gentleman who found on a seat on the Victoria Embankment on March 25th a lady's purse containing six five-pound notes and four pounds in gold, is anxious to restore it to its owner. To this end he will attend Victoria Station on April 1st at 7 P.M. when he will take up his position just under the clock. He may be recognised by the circumstance that he will wear a grey felt hat, a light covert coat, a green necktie, patent boots and white spats. He will carry in his left hand a roll of white paper and in his right a copy of Bradshaw's Guide and will ear in his button-hole a bunch of pink geraniums. He suggests that recognition would be more easy if the owner of the purse would wear a straw hat with two red roses in it, one white and one red, a pink blouse with a bunch of lilies-of-the-valley at the throat, and a grey skirt, and would carry on her left arm a basket tied with blue ribbons and in her right hand a copy of the *Gentlewoman* rolled up. On recognising advertiser she should approach slowly and exclaim in a low voice, Be virtuous and you will be happy!

The Costume Model

ARLY ON an autumn afternoon Cornelius Appleby sat in his studio opposite a large canvas on which was roughly sketched out in charcoal the leading lines of a composition, its foreground being occupied by two figures which loomed out shapeless and spectral, a mass of inarticulate scribble.

While he was yet meditating upon the masterpiece which was to grow out of the void and formless expanse before him, a knock on the outer door of the flat aroused him, and he went forth to admit the visitor.

The opened door revealed a tall, muscular man whose sinister countenance and decayed habiliments conveyed the impression of a housebreaker in unprosperous circumstances. He was, however, a model whom Appleby had picked up somewhat casually and engaged to represent Goliath in his picture.

"Shall I take off my togs here?" inquired the model as he gazed round the narrow, crowded studio.

The suggestion jarred upon the sensibilities of the young artist, whose experience was small, but whose politeness was excessive, and he replied:

"Why, no. I think you had better change in my bedroom," and he forthwith ushered the seedy stranger, with something of a grimace, into the trim little apartment.

In a few minutes the model emerged, a living demonstration of the truth that "the tailor makes the man" — in more senses than one; for, by the simple act of exuviation, the slip-shod, seedy loafer had become transformed into a man — graceful, supple-limbed, well-knit — such a man as might have hurled the disc at the Olympic games or won success on any athletic field.

Pleasing as was his form, however, his face was shifty and sly, a circumstance that rendered him only the more suitable to represent the much maligned Philistine, and as he mounted the throne, Appleby congratulated himself upon his choice of a model.

Rapidly the incoherent mass of scribble gave place to a carefully drawn figure, and on this Appleby was briskly rubbing in the shadows in colour when a neighbouring church clock struck the second hour of their task. The model, stiff with his exertions, stretched himself and shivered.

"Two hours a day, you said," he remarked.

"Yes. Is the time up already?" Appleby put down his palette with a little sigh, and then, with a smile, said:

"Time passes more quickly with me than with you, I expect."

"You're right there, mister," replied the model with unction as he rubbed his stiffened limbs, "this do take it out of yer, a-standin' here with yer arms and legs stuck out like a graven image."

"I dare say it does, and I expect you'll be able to manage a drop of something hot when you get outside."

"Rather!" agreed the model.

"Well, then, here's sixpence for you to get it with, and here's the money for the day's work — two hours. You can find your way to the bedroom, can't you? I am just going to do a bit more to this while the light lasts."

"Right you are, sir. Good-afternoon," and as the door closed behind the model Appleby took up his palette, and was soon absorbed in his work.

The model appeared in a hurry, for he managed to clothe himself in a much shorter time than it had taken him to undress, and in less than five minutes after his exit from the studio Appleby heard him stride quickly from the bedroom to the outer door, and, after this had slammed behind him, his retreating footsteps were audible on the stairs in a hurried diminuendo.

For fully an hour the young artist worked steadily at his embryo masterpiece, trimming up the hasty touches that he had laid on from the model and putting in such fresh detail from memory as he dared, until the fading light warned him to desist from his labours.

Then, like a careful workman, he cleaned his palette and brushes, and finally made for the bedroom to clean himself.

Here a surprise awaited him, for as he entered the room he stumbled over something that lay on the floor. Drawing back the curtains, he stooped to examine it.

"By George!" he exclaimed, "the fellow has gone away without his clothes. Great Scott!" Here there arose before his mental optics a vision of the godlike figure of his model striding down Chancery Lane, and he felt that it could not be.

As a matter of fact, it was not. A very brief survey of the room was sufficient to show that the snowy shirt which had been laid out on his bed, duly fitted with studs and links for the evening's wear, had vanished, while further search revealed the absence of a pair of patent leather boots, a tweed suit, a billy-cock hat, and sundry minor articles of clothing, together with a few unconsidered trifles of a miscellaneous character.

It was only too clear that the model, taking advantage of his similarity on size to the painter, had treated himself to a complete ready-made outfit at the latter's expense.

"Well, I am hanged!" exclaimed Appleby, grinning partly with vexation and partly with amusement. "This is the neatest 'do' I have heard of for some time. But, thank Heaven, he chose that infernal check suit! It is almost worth the other things to get that abomination off my hands."

With this philosophical reflection he picked up the model's rejected garments with the coal tongs and deposited them on the landing outside his chambers, after which he proceeded to make his toilet preparatory to going out.

"I really cannot understand why you should be so extraordinary suspicious of Cornelius. He seems to me the most straight-forward fellow possible."

"I dare say, my dear," said Mrs. Silver with a superior smile. "You are very young."

"But can you tell me what grounds you have for suspecting him of the irregular and dissipated habits that you hint at?"

"My dear child," said Mrs. Silver in a solemn tone, "when a man — a young man, with no parents to guide and watch him — is known to habitually frequent the haunts of vice and wickedness–"

"But, my dear mother," protested Miss Silver, "you know Cornelius visits the poorer parts of the town merely for the purpose of studying humanity under its more simple and picturesque aspects."

"Picturesque fiddlesticks!" snapped the matron. "I tell you, Margaret, that you know nothing of the ways of young men, and it is necessary for me, with my experience of the world, to protect you."

"It seems to me that you are much more likely to make needless trouble between Cornelius and me. I hate all this spying and prying into other people's affairs, especially as I am certain there is nothing to find out."

"We shall see, my dear," replied Mrs. Silver, grimly.

"And you mean to say that you are actually going to follow him — to dog his steps like a spy?"

"I am resolved to find out what he does in those dreadful places that I am convinced he goes to. And now, my dear, you had better run home in case there should be any callers that we might wish to see."

Margaret Silver, with a resigned shake of her head, hailed a passing omnibus that was bound for Kensington, leaving her mother to make her way alone to Staple Inn.

The afternoon was well advanced when Mrs. Silver arrived at Holborn Bars, and, taking up a position just outside Staple Inn, peered inquisitively through the low archway into the little square. She had been standing there for some minutes when her eyes wandered for a moment from the entry of Appleby's chambers, and she became aware of a red-faced man in a gold-laced hat who was watching her from the porter's lodge under the archway with evident disapproval and suspicion. Somewhat confused by this discovery, she backed away up the pavement and began to stare absently into a milliner's shop window, while she debated with some anxiety on the possibility of Appleby leaving the Inn by the little passage that opens into Southampton Buildings and thus eluding her vigilance. She was turning to approach the archway once more when there suddenly emerged from it a tall man dressed in a check suit of a somewhat "loud" pattern, who immediately turned westward and strode off at a rapid pace.

"Aha!" exclaimed Mrs. Silver with a gasp of relief as she caught sight of him. "I think I cannot be mistaken. I could swear to that frightened suit anywhere. How any man — any gentleman at least — can so far forget himself as to go prancing about the streets of London in the costume of a Christy Minstrel is — ha–," here Mrs. Silver's soliloquy ended as her breath gave out; for her victim, who was making for Holborn Circus with swinging strides, had already drawn ahead, and Mrs. Silver now started off in his wake with quick pattering steps like a goose pursuing an ostrich.

Down St. Andrew's Hill went the tall man like a whirlwind, across Ludgate Circus, down New Bridge Street, over Blackfriars Bridge, and down Blackfriars Road; and still his pursuer, growing ever more crimson in the face and puffing like a traction-engine, paddled along some hundred yards behind.

When he reached Great Charlotte Street, the unconscious victim turned sharp to the left, and on reaching Gravel Lane turned to his right. Here Mrs.

Silver finally lost all idea of her whereabouts and plunged, in the ardour of her pursuit, into a labyrinth of alleys so bewildering that her head fairly swam. At length the man in front of her turned suddenly through a narrow archway; the pursuer, panting up to the tunnel-like opening, was just in time to see the check suit vanish into an open doorway on one side of a narrow flagged court of unspeakable squalor. Undaunted by the unsavoury and forbidding aspect of the place, Mrs. Silver made for the open doorway, and, entering the cavern-like interior, essayed to ascend the stairs in quest of the fugitive whose foot-steps were still audible far above.

But the stairs presented unforseen difficulties. In the first place the handrail had disappeared, although this loss was partly made good by a portion of an iron bedstead, which was lashed in its place; then, in several places, a stair or two had fallen out, and Mrs. Silver's attention was first drawn to this fact by finding herself clutching the bedstead-rail and pawing the air with a leg thrust through one of these apertures. Presently, as she became more accustomed to the darkness, she made better progress and at length reached the upper floor of the house, where, selecting a likely door, she boldly entered the room to which it belonged.

"Well, I'm blowed!" said a voice from within, and immediately added, "Shut the door, Ted."

The door slammed to; a dismal squeal came faintly through it; a brief scuffle and then silence.

The tall standard lamp, which should have illuminated Mrs. Silver's drawing-room, performed its office but perfunctorily, for the great red shade with which it was covered so intercepted the light that the room was pervaded by a crimson twilight so faint as to scarcely admit the existence of a shadow. At the more remote end of the room the outline of a settee might have been dimly discerned, and might even have been seen to be occupied by a shadowy and ill-defined shape. The shadowy form was in reality duplicate in its nature, but its constituent moieties were imperfectly differentiated.

The little French clock on the mantelpiece had just struck eight upon a soft-voiced, apologetic little gong, and the under housemaid had just broken a corset bone (in consequence of the absurd position of the drawing-room keyhole) when the shadowy mass on the settee broke into speech.

"I say, Cornelius, won't mother be *awfully* annoyed that she was not in when you came?"

"Won't she, by Jove!" answered a voice which appertained to the masculine element of this compound organism, "by the way, where is she?"

"I don't quite know where she is gone," said Margaret with literal truth, although with a slight mental reservation.

"Well, I wish she would take a little outing rather oftener," said Appleby, "it's so good for her, you know — and for us too. We've had a real good time this afternoon, haven't we, little Madge?"

The response was inarticulate but expressive.

"Do you know, Maggie," Cornelius went on after a pause, "I have a sort of idea that your mother suspects me of something — I don't quite know what, but I think she takes me for a bad sort of some kind — thinks I haunt dens of infamy, or some tommy-rot of that kind."

"Do you think she does?" asked Margaret cautiously.

"I am sure of it, but I can't imagine why; for although I am not exactly what would be called a 'good young man'" ("I should hope not," chimed in Margaret) — "still I've never been at all rackety or dissipated."

"Of course you haven't, you ridiculous old thing," said Margaret, and then another inarticulate interlude occurred.

"I really don't think your mother quite understands young men," pursued Appleby, reflectively. "Fellows of the present day don't as a rule plunge into wild and furious dissipation like the 'bucks' and 'bloods' of the last century; and the Johnnies who do go the pace at all extensively show it pretty plainly in their looks."

"The fact is," said Miss Silver, "that mother does *not* understand young men; she has the funniest ideas possible about their manners and customs — but here she is, I think," and as a cab was heard to draw up outside the house Margaret ran out to the street door.

"My dear mother, what have you been doing with yourself?" she exclaimed as Mrs. Silver appeared on the steps.

"Give me five shillings to pay the cab," said Mrs. Silver shortly.

Margaret extracted and required sum from a dainty purse, and the cabman drove off chuckling and triumphant.

"But, mother dear," exclaimed Margaret as she closed the front door and regarded her parent with amazement, "what *has* happened to you?"

Certainly the elderly lady's appearance was a little unusual. In place of a bonnet she wore a red cotton handkerchief of which the corners were tied under her chin, while the upper part of her person was enveloped in a grey shawl of the most dilapidated description and by no means irreproachable cleanliness.

"Where is your bonnet, mother?" persisted Margaret, "and your sealskin jacket?"

"Ah!" exclaimed Mrs. Silver, tragically, "and where are my diamond brooch and my rings, and my watch and chain?"

With these mystical words she made for the drawing-room, in the door of which stood Cornelius Appleby, not a little astonished by the fragments of conversation he had overheard.

As Mrs. Silver suddenly became aware of his presence she fell back with a little shriek.

"You here!" she exclaimed hoarsely.

"Yes, I'm here," replied the bewildered Appleby; "been waiting for you a long time."

"When did he come?" asked Mrs. Silver, turning sharply to her daughter.

"Oh, he came to tea — rather a late tea, but he was detained–"

"Ha!" ejaculated her mother.

"Yes. He was detained by a most comical accident. A man stole the clothes that he had put out to come in."

"What do you mean?" exclaimed Mrs. Silver. "Explain."

"Yes, that's so, Mrs. Silver," chimed in Cornelius. "A new model of mine — awful bounder — I sent him into my bedroom to dress after the sitting, and hang me if the beggar didn't waltz off in a complete rig-out of mine, and left his own beastly rags in their place. Howling swell he must have looked too," added Appleby laughing, "billycock hat, patent-leather shoes, check suit –"

"Check suit!" interrupted Mrs. Silver.

"Yes, by Jove!" roared Appleby, "check suit — your favourite check suit, ha! ha!"

"Ha! ha!" echoed Mrs. Silver mirthlessly and then, "Cornelius, just run to the dining-room and fetch me a glass of sherry like a good fellow," and as her prospective son-in-law disappeared on his errand she sank down on the now vacant settee in a brown study.

"YE OLDE SPOTTED DOGGE"

O N A MORE than usually bright Whit Monday morning there paced the platform of the little branch station of Horton-Gaby a small thin man in a knickerbocker suit, who carried, slung from his shoulder, a brown canvas satchel of quarto Imperial size, in the flap whereof was strapped a folding sketching stool. From the appearance of this satchel Mr. Sherlock Holmes might have inferred that the bearer was a water-colour painter, while an inspection of the stranger's visiting-card might have enabled the same incomparable observer to deduce the fact that his name was Geoffrey Brandon.

As Mr. Brandon paced the little platform, his manner was indicative of mingled impatience and satisfaction — impatience because the train for which he waited was already ten minutes late, and satisfaction because he anticipated an entire day in the society of the charming Miss Merdle. It was true that Miss Merdle's brother was to accompany her, but he was an enthusiastic photographer, and would doubtless be too preoccupied to be much in the way; besides, one must take the fat with the lean. Not that I wish to imply that Miss Merdle was lean. On the contrary, she was, a lady of those somewhat massive proportions which are so attractive to men of Mr. Brandon's type. But I am digressing from the point, which is that Mr. Brandon had arranged to meet Miss Merdle and her brother, who were to arrive at Horton-Gaby by the 10.13.

The arrangement had been made by the lady herself at the conversazione of one of the London Photographic Exhibitions, where her brother had a pair of masterly "impressions" on the line. It would be so delightful, she said, for an artist of the brush (like Mr. Brandon) to spend a day amidst the beauties of Nature with an artist of the camera (such as her brother). They would learn so much from one another, did he not think?

Most certainly he did, and stated his belief with such emphasis and enthusiasm that the arrangement was concluded out of hand; and so here he was on this fine May morning, pacing the platform and meditating upon the manifold attractions of the beautiful Miss Merdle.

The sudden tinkling of the electric bell in the signal box brought his heart into his mouth, and as the train rounded the curve a few moments later, he rushed to the waiting-room in search of a mirror in which to finally examine his appearance. There was no looking-glass there, but a framed and glazed advertisement of "Dr. Thomas's Black Boluses for Bilious Babies" furnished a substitute, and before this he had just finished smoothing his hair and twisting his moustache as the train rumbled into the station.

A single door opened at the farther end as the train came to a standstill, and from it emerged the rather corpulent form of Mr. Edmonton Merdle, accompanied by what looked like a barrel-organ in a green baize cover, and a heavy folding tripod. Brandon hurried forward with a beatific smile beaming upon his face; but the smile congealed into a stony stare as Merdle, having strapped the green-covered case on to his back, shouldered the tripod and composedly shut the carriage-door.

"How do, Brandon?" he exclaimed, as the latter approached. "Here's a beautiful day, eh?"

"Lovely! lovely!" gasped Brandon. "Where's your sister, Merdle?"

"Oh," said Merdle, "I persuaded her to stay at home. Women are so terribly in the way when one has serious work to do. Don't you think so?"

"No, I don't," replied Brandon decidedly. "Besides, I didn't know we had any serious work to do."

"You may not have, my dear fellow, but I have. The exhibition of the Society of Poet Photographers is approaching, and I have my pictures yet to produce."

"Is that what you are going to produce them with?" grunted Brandon, with a savage glare at the green case.

"I hope so," said Merdle cheerfully. "It is a very complete outfit."

"Looks like it," growled Brandon. And the two men took their way in silence down the lane leading from the station.

"What are you proposing to do?" asked Brandon, as they trudged along the road.

"'I HAVE COME OUT IN SEARCH OF INSPIRATION.'"

"That depends on what turns up," replied Merdle. "I have come out in search of inspiration — and, by Jove! Eh? What do you say to that?"

"To what?" asked Brandon, gazing vaguely around.

"Do you mean to say you don't see anything?" exclaimed Merdle.

"No — unless you mean that sheep."

"That is just what I do mean," replied Merdle enthusiastically. "Look at her! See the motherly concern with which she gazes at that barn, in which, no doubt, her offspring are immured. Out of sight, but not out of mind."

"*She!*" exclaimed Brandon. "Why, it's a ram! Besides, people don't put sheep in barns."

"Well, well," said Merdle: "we mustn't be too literal. The great thing is to avoid vulgar and commonplace realism, and it is a fine subject, you must admit. I shall call it 'Bereavement.' Here goes," and he dumped the green case down on the road, and began to unpack with feverish haste.

"In a subject like this," he remarked, as he screwed the camera on to the tripod, "what is required is atmosphere, softness and breadth. These I obtain by the use of the Scloppenhausen-Heimerdinger periplanatic polyplatystigmat, which gives a diffusion of focus so perfect as to completely obliterate all detail."

"But then you can't see what you've photographed."

"Of course not," exclaimed Merdle; "hence the delightful reticence of effect, which allows for the play of the imagination" — here he popped his head under the focusing cloth, and directed the muzzle of the lens at the sheep, who shouted defiance in a gurgling baritone.

"Not quite what I want either," Merdle remarked as he emerged presently with his hair all rubbed up on end. "There is plenty of softness and breadth, but perhaps a little lack of those crisp touches which give conviction and sureness. Perhaps the antichromatic holostigmat of Von Schafskopf would interpret my conception better."

He produced from the case a large brass tube with several milled screwheads, and substituted it for the discarded lens; then he retired once more under the focusing cloth.

"Beautiful! beautiful!" he exclaimed, as he peered at the focusing screen. "A most sympathetic rendering! Charming!"

"The antiscorbutic pantechnicon's done the trick, then," observed Brandon. But Merdle was still enshrouded, and heard him not.

"This will really be a masterpiece," exclaimed Merdle, coming forth from the focusing cloth with a crest like a cockatoo. "'Nature seen through a temperament,' as Zola says."

He fixed the shutter on the lens, introduced the dark slide, and extracting from his pocket an actinometer with a pendulum attachment, set the pendulum swinging, and counted the oscillations aloud.

"Fifteen," he observed at length; "there's nothing like being methodical, Brandon. Fifteen, now that gives, ha" — here he set the calculating circles of the instrument — "that gives $^{271}/_{864}$ of a second for the exposure." He set the lens-shutter to the nearest fraction, drew out the shutter of the dark slide, and arranged the focusing cloth over it.

At this moment the sheep turned and walked away.

Merdle gazed at its retreating figure for a few moments in silence, then turning to his companion, he said irritably: —

"I really wish you wouldn't do that sort of thing, Brandon."

"What sort of thing?" inquired the astonished painter.

"You see what has happened, don't you?" said Merdle.

"I see that the sheep has walked away."

"Precisely. And my picture is destroyed in consequence. It is really not considerate of you."

"What the deuce do you mean?" protested Brandon. "Why, I never moved nor spoke."

"Exactly," rejoined Merdle, with the air of a cross-examining counsel who has "got" his witness. "Now what could be more disturbing to a sensitive and excitable animal like a sheep than a silent and motionless figure. Pray be more thoughtful in future!"

"Oh, I'll dance a hornpipe and shout next time, if you think that will have a tranquillising effect," said Brandon. But to this offer, Merdle made no response, being busy re-packing his apparatus.

After this incident, the pair wandered about somewhat aimlessly for near upon two hours, Merdle somewhat disappointed and surly, Brandon on the look-out for something to sketch. The only result of these perambulations in the hot sun was a gradually increasing languor and a rather lively thirst, so that when a turn of the road brought into view a small alehouse (bearing the sign of "Ye Olde Spotted Dogge"), the two travellers simultaneously slackened their pace.

"What do you say to a glass of beer, Brandon?" asked Merdle, with unwonted cheerfulness.

"By all means," replied Brandon. "Perhaps we might get a snack of bread and cheese too."

They entered the little bar, and at their request there was set before each a mug of ale, accompanied by a trunk of bread and a slab of bright, yellow cheese.

"I see you have a parlour there," remarked Merdle. "Might we take our refreshments in and sit down?"

The landlady peered suspiciously over the counter at the green case.

"You ain't got a monkey, 'ave yer?" she inquired.

"A monkey?" exclaimed Merdle.

"Ah! a monkey," chimed in an old man, advancing from the back of the bar. "The last one as come along 'ere, 'e 'ad a monkey, 'e 'ad, and a mischievous little varmint it were. Eat up 'arf a basket o' wax fruit, it did, afore anyone twigged wot it wor up to; and then it knocked down two glass candlesticks and a china dawg afore they could catch it. My missus can't abide monkeys now."

"Why, what do you take me for?" gasped the astonished Merdle.

"I takes you for a organist," replied the aged man. "Ain't that a organ as you've got there?"

"Organ!" exclaimed Merdle indignantly; "that's not an organ, my good man. It's a camera. I'll show you."

He tore open the fastenings of the case, dragged out and unclamped the camera, and, with a flourish, drew out the bellows to their full extent.

"There!" he said haughtily. "Now do you see what it is?"

"Well, I'm jiggered!" keckled the old man. "Jest look at that, Mariar! I thought it was a organ, and, bust me, if it ain't a concertina! 'E's a wopper too, ain't 'e, Mariar? P'raps the young man'll give us a toon on 'im presently."

The exasperated Merdle shut up the camera, and having slapped it back into its case, commenced a lengthy explanation, while Brandon retired grinning to the parlour with the two plates in his hands.

He had just selected (after careful comparison) the thickest slab of cheese when he again caught the thread of the conversation.

"Now, how should you like me to take your portrait?" Merdle was saying, in persuasive tones, to the old man.

"How much?" inquired the latter cautiously.

"Oh, you don't understand!" spluttered Merdle irritably. "I am an artist, I tell you. I shan't charge you anything."

"Get out!" said the old man with a cunning leer. "You're mogueing, ain't you?"

"I tell you I will take your portrait for nothing," replied Merdle with offended dignity.

"Don't you let 'im, 'Enery," interposed the landlady. "That there face o' yourn'll break the machine, and then you'll 'ave to pay for it."

When the mirth provoked by this original sally had subsided, the old man, having admitted that he "didn't mind," was escorted by the entire household and a Windsor chair to the back garden, and Merdle rushed excitedly into the parlour to make his preparations.

"What a stroke of luck!" he exclaimed, "to get a model like that! Did you see his head, Brandon?"

"Distinctly," replied the latter.

"Well, what did you think of it?"

"Seemed pretty thick," replied Brandon, with his mouth full of cheese. "Precious little hair outside and precious little brains in."

"It seems to me," said Merdle severely, "that you landscape painters are sadly lacking in imagination. You appear to have no ideas beyond the mere literal rendering of bald realities."

"Well, as for that," replied Brandon, with a grin, "I should call that old man's head a tolerably bald reality."

"It is a head," Merdle went on loftily, "that Rembrandt would have loved. I shall call the picture 'A Village Patriarch,'" and, gathering up his apparatus, he departed for the garden.

Brandon tranquilly finished his bread and cheese and beer, assisting the process of ingestion by examining the pictures on the walls (which included the inevitable "Death of John Wesley," a portrait of her late Majesty, and a highly-coloured almanac); then he lit a pipe, and strolled to the window, where he commanded a view of Merdle and his victim — the former with his head buried under the focusing-cloth, the latter glued to his chair, rigid and staring, like a waxwork representation of Methuselah. In a few minutes Merdle re-entered the parlour with hair erect and face bathed in perspiration, but happy and elated.

"By Jove!" he declared. "It will be a masterpiece. Mark my words, and see if it isn't the picture of the year at the Royal."

In this jubilant frame he packed up his appliances, bolting his food and gulping down the beer in a way that was perfectly alarming, and as they trudged away along the sunny road, he talked incessantly of his anticipated triumph when the new masterpiece should be unveiled to the public gaze. They had travelled some three miles from the inn, Brandon making occasional ineffectual efforts to commence a sketch, and being invariably dragged away by his impatient comrade, when Merdle suddenly halted and clapped his hand to his forehead.

"Great Scott!" he ejaculated, fixing a stony glare upon his appalled companion.

"What the deuce is the matter?" inquired Brandon.

"Matter?" snorted Merdle. "I'll tell you. I never drew out the shutter of the dark slide!"

"Then you never took the old man, after all?"

"No. There was no plate exposed."

"How annoying, after all your trouble! I am awfully sorry, Merdle."

"Oh, it's all very well to say you're sorry, when the thing is done," exclaimed Merdle; "but you should really be more careful."

"*I*, more careful?" expostulated Brandon. "Why, what do you mean?"

"I mean to say," replied Merdle, "that in a supreme effort of intellect like this one should be — mind, I am not complaining; I merely state a fact — one should be free from all distraction."

"Do you mean that I distracted you?" asked Brandon.

"Since you ask me," replied Merdle, "I am compelled to admit — mind, I am not complaining; I merely answer your question — I am compelled to admit that you did."

"But I wasn't there!"

"*Pre*cisely," rejoined Merdle, "Now what could be more distracting than the — the — the unexpected absence of — er — of one who — er — who might have been present."

"Well, I'm hanged!" muttered Brandon, adding cheerfully: "However, it isn't too late. The old man is still there. Go back and do him again."

"No, no! One would look such a fool. Come along. It might have been, but the past is beyond recall," and he sullenly resumed his pilgrimage.

"Here's rather a good thing, Merdle," said Brandon presently, peering in at a cottage door. "See the old woman crouching over the fire — makes you sweat to look at her — and the black beams in the ceiling, and the old clock on the wall — quite a picture, isn't it? But I suppose it's too dark to photograph?"

"Light or dark is all one to the genuine artist," said Merdle loftily. "Why, the picture by which I made my reputation was taken in absolute darkness."

"Nonsense!"

"Fact," said Merdle impressively. "It was a wine vault. There was no window, and the door was shut. I gave an exposure of four hours."

"And how did it come out?" said Brandon.

"Well," replied Merdle slowly, "as far as the mere representation of the wine vault went, it didn't come out at all. In fact, there was nothing on the plate. But yet, with the aid of manipulative skill, a lucky chance, and, above all, *imagination*, a masterpiece was produced."

"Indeed! How?"

"I will explain. The negative was, as I have said, quite blank. Clear glass, in fact, excepting a few smears and stains. Now that blank negative was lying on my writing-table, when by chance I let fall on it a drop of ink. That drop of ink dried in a circular black spot. Here was an opportunity for an imaginative artist! I printed that negative — from the wrong side, of course — and obtained a most spirited rendering of a watery moon with a narrow halo. I enlarged it to four feet by three, printed it in blue carbon, and exhibited it at the Salon of the photographer-mystics under the title of 'Night.' It took the gold medal, and was the sensation of the season."

"Wonderful!" exclaimed Brandon, with unfeigned sincerity. "By the way, that's a charming little group — the old church among, those trees, the red outhouses, and that sunlit meadow with the sheep grazing on it. I think I'll just jot that down." And he began unstrapping his sketching bag.

"Nonsense, my good fellow," said Merdle. "Mere hackneyed, commonplace, literal rubbish. Come along." And he dragged the unfortunate painter away by main force.

It now began to dawn upon Brandon that his chances of making a sketch were receding to the vanishing point, especially as Merdle's plates lasted out so uncommonly well; and he began to revolve deep and crafty schemes for escaping from his bondage.

They had proceeded but a little farther when the group that had so taken his fancy presented itself from a fresh point with the addition of an ancient and highly picturesque barn.

And now it was that Brandon was suddenly inspired with a scheme of positively Machiavellian subtlety and cunning.

"Fine old barn that," he remarked.

"Very," said Merdle, without even looking at it.

"Speaking of barns," pursued Brandon, "it has often occurred to me how very few artists have had imagination enough to perceive the pictorial possibilities of barn interiors. There is Clausen's 'Golden Barn,' a most original and imaginative work, but I don't recall another example."

"Nor I," agreed Merdle. "The poverty of imagination among modern painters is most lamentable."

"I think, if you don't mind," said Brandon, "I'll just step across the meadow and have a look at that barn. I see one of the doors is only loosely fastened."

"Certainly," replied Merdle. "In fact, I'll step over with you."

They strolled across the meadow, and found, as Brandon had said, that one of the doors was so loosely chained that they could enter, one at a time, without difficulty.

"Wonderful!" exclaimed Brandon, groping about in the dark with his stick; "wonderful! Quite recalls Clausen's picture, doesn't it?"

"Entirely," replied Merdle (who, by the way, had never seen the picture). "How fine it is! So reticent; so full of mystery and suggestion."

He stepped back a few paces, and sat down heavily in a basket of swedes.

"This is where you photographers have the pull," remarked Brandon, as his companion arose, rubbed himself, and soliloquised hoarsely. "*I* should have to paint this from memory, whereas you could work direct from Nature."

"That is so," replied Merdle; "and if I were alone, I should certainly not let a chance like this slip."

"Why 'if you were alone?'"

"Well," said Merdle, "you see, this would require some two hours' exposure, and I could hardly trespass on your patience so long."

"Nonsense, my dear fellow!" responded Brandon cheerily. "Don't you consider me if you like the subject. What did we come out for?"

"True," replied Merdle gratefully, "but it's very good of you, all the same. Perhaps you could find something for your brush just to pass the time?"

"Perhaps I can," said Brandon. "I'll just take a look round when you've started."

In a few moments the camera was again set up, and Merdle with his paraphernalia vanished into the gloom. As he disappeared, Brandon broke into a broad grin, muttering "Peace, perfect peace."

Then selecting his pitch, he planted his stool, got out his sketch-block, and began to draw in his outline.

He had just finished pencilling in his subject, when Merdle came forth from the recesses of the barn.

"I've just taken the cap off," he said. "It will he two hours from now.

You're sure you don't mind?"

"Not at all, not at all," answered Brandon airily. "I'm quite happy with my colours." And as Merdle returned to the barn — round which he fidgeted like a dog that has hidden a bone — he got out his brushes, filled the dipper from his water-bottle, and reached into the bag for his colours.

"Where the deuce is that colour-box?"

He rummaged more and more furiously, and with increasing apprehension. Ah! where was it? The appalling fact soon burst upon him that, in the preoccupation of his mind by visions of Miss Merdle, he had forgotten to put the box in his bag before starting.

"Well," muttered Brandon, grinning with rage, "of all the confounded lunatics! And to think that I've got to sit here for two mortal hours, while that donkey photographs the invisible interior of a rotten old barn –" Here his soliloquy tailed off into incoherent and unpublishable fragments.

However, being on the whole a philosopher, he made the best of the situation, sharpened his pencil afresh, and proceeded to convert his rough outline into a finished pencil drawing, and so the time passed pleasantly enough after all. He was just putting the finishing touches to his drawing, when Merdle bustled up, and said in a brisk and cheery tone: —

"Nearly done, old man? Time's up, you know. I'm just going to put on the cap."

"Right," replied Brandon. "I'm just finishing," and as he spoke, Merdle passed through the narrow opening and vanished into the gloom.

But he was not long absent.

In less than a minute he reappeared, with great suddenness and a singular change of manner. His face was pale, his eyes very wide open, and his hand shaking.

"Here's an awful thing, Brandon!" he gasped as he came up.

"What is?" inquired the astonished artist.

"There's a bloodhound in the barn chained up right against my camera."

"A bloodhound!" ejaculated Brandon.

"Yes. An enormous beast. Looks as big as a calf and most ferocious."

"But we didn't see him when we were in there," objected Brandon.

"No, it was dark, you see; but when I went in just now to the camera, I heard the rattling of a chain, and struck a match to see what it was, and there was the great brute within a foot of me, crouching for a spring."

"'HERE'S AN AWFUL THING, BRANDON!'"

"It's very odd," mused Brandon.

"Odd, is it?" snorted Merdle. "Well, if you don't believe me, you can go in yourself, and see."

"Let us both go in," said Brandon cautiously.

"Very well," agreed Merdle a little reluctantly, and the pair made their way through the narrow entry. Brandon boldly leading the way.

They stepped slowly along the floor, treading delicately and listening intently; but not a sound disturbed the stillness.

About half-way down the barn they halted, and Merdle struck a match, and held it above his head. By its light they could just make out the camera standing gaunt and spectral in the gloom, and there, sure enough, within a yard of it, was the dim shape of the gigantic hound, half standing and half crouching, as Merdle had said.

Even as they gazed, the match went out, leaving a black darkness, and the moment after a heavy chain flew through a staple with a velocity only equalled by that with which the two men sprinted up the barn. They lingered awhile in the doorway (not willingly, but the opening being narrow and their arrival at it simultaneous, the traffic was for the moment somewhat congested), and when they had regained the meadow, held solemn council.

"What on earth is to be done?" groaned Merdle.

"I'll tell you," said Brandon. "We must find the owner of the barn."

"Of course," agreed Merdle. "Let us go to that cottage and ask where he lives."

They proceeded to the cottage, on the door of which Merdle thumped with his fist until it was opened by a shaggy-looking countryman.

"Can you tell us who is the owner of that barn?" inquired Merdle, indicating the building in question.

"The owner?" inquired the man drowsily.

"Yes. Who does it belong to?"

"The fact is," interposed Brandon, "that my friend has been taking a photograph inside the barn, and now he can't get his machine away because of a dog that is in there."

"A dawg?" repeated the man.

"Yes, a large dog — a bloodhound or a mastiff, I believe."

"Git out!" said the man incredulously. "There ain't no dawg there."

"But I tell you there is," said Merdle testily; "we've just seen him."

"Well, well," commented the rustic; "think o' that now! Ow'd 'e git in there? Must 'a strayed in."

"No, he couldn't have strayed in," said Brandon, "because he is chained up."

"Git along!" said the mail sulkily. "You been drinkin'! There ain't no dawg chained up there."

"But we both saw him," screamed Merdle. "A big dog, as big as a calf."

"Whereabouts was he?" asked the man, still unbelieving.

"Over in the further corner there, among a lot of baskets and rubbish."

The man stared at them blankly for a minute or more, scratching his shock head the while. Then, with remarkable abruptness, he turned about, and darted into the house, from which there presently issued sounds of smothered laughter.

In a few minutes an aged man appeared at the door, smiling blandly, and wiping his eyes.

"What's this 'ere as my boy's been a-tellin' me about that there dawg?" he asked.

"Oh, you know the dog then?" said Merdle anxiously.

"Oo, ay! *I* know 'im. What's 'e been a-doin' of?"

"Well, he hasn't been doing anything, but, you see, I want to take away my camera."

"And won't 'e let yer?"

"I don't know about that, but I should be glad if you could just step over and hold him while I remove it."

"Oo, ah!" said the ancient rustic, chuckling softly. "We'll 'old 'im — me and my boy will. You jest coot along over, and we'll be there as soon as you."

The two friends accordingly retraced their steps, and were soon overtaken by the countryman and his father, who passed them at a little distance with averted faces.

The whole party now entered one by one through the narrow opening, and groped their way along the barn. As they approached the farther end, the chain was heard to fly through its ring, on which the two artists scuttled hastily towards the door, and the younger rustic burst into undisguised guffaw.

"Tummas," said the old man severely. "be'ave yerself afore the quality. Don't be afeared gents; that's only the old hoss in the stable beyind there, a-rattlin' of his chain. Light the candle, Tummas."

Tummas thus adjured, struck a match, and having ignited a stump of tallow candle, held it out with a shaking hand, when its light revealed the fact that he appeared to he weeping copiously. But it also brought into view the gigantic hound, and a most singular hound he was, and of a strangely lethargic temperament — for he had not moved since they last saw him, but still remained half crouching and half standing. His marking too, was very curious, consisting of a number of circular blotches like those of an exaggerated Pomeranian.

"'E won't bite. yer see, gen'lemen," chuckled the old man. "'E's as quiet as a lamb, 'e is."

Here he stepped up to the dog, and rapped his knuckles smartly, on the animal's head, eliciting a curious hollow sound, but no sign of movement. A sudden suspicion flashed into Merdle's mind, and he strode towards the hound. Just then "Tummas" lowered the candle so that its light fell upon the box-like object on which the animal stood, and on this Merdle now perceived an inscription in faded gilt letters. It was almost illegible, but after careful scrutiny, he managed to decipher the words "Ye Olde Spotted Dogge."

As Merdle, without speaking, gathered up his camera, the old man broke into it flood of reminiscences.

"Oo ay! Know that dawg? I orter. I remembers 'im when I wur a boy. 'E stood over the door o' the poob up to the village. Main fine 'e wur too — all yaller, with big red spots, like as if 'e'd got the measles. But they took 'im down when they built the noo 'ouse, and 'ere 'e's been ever since. Thankee, sur; much obloiged to yer, and wish yer good-day."

Out in the meadow Merdle repacked his camera in silence, while Brandon stolidly arranged the contents of his sketching bag. When all was ready for the start once more, the latter asked:

"Which way now?"

"Station," said Merdle shortly.

And as they left the meadow, and "turned to take a last fond look," they could distinguish the forms of the two rustics leaning against the barn in attitudes suggestive of severe abdominal pain.

The Suburban Autolycus

THE HOUR of midnight had just been proclaimed by the cracked bell of the parish church. The announcement — to judge by the appearance of Constitution Crescent — was quite superfluous, for in the whole block of tall, stuccoed houses there was not a single light visible. Constitution Crescent was wrapped in slumber.

The last strokes of the bell, however, had barely died away when a solitary man turned the corner and walked slowly and somewhat stealthily along the pavement, looking up at the houses as he passed. Presently he stopped and examined the number on a door.

"No. 3. That's the 'ouse right enough," he remarked. "I wonder if she's been able to get 'old of that 'ousekeeper's key."

He stepped out into the middle of the road, and having looked first up the Crescent and then down, bent his gaze upon a second-floor window, and began to wave his arm.

"Dashed if they haven't left that ground-floor window open!" he muttered. "I 'ope they've told the coppers all about it. We don't want 'em knocking the housekeeper up just at the wrong time, and I can't undo the shutters to close it."

At this moment the second-floor window at which he had been gazing was softly raised, and a white figure, leaning out, flung down a small rag parcel tied up with string, which fell on the road with a muffled clink.

This object the man pounced upon greedily, and having untied the string with feverish haste, unrolled the rag and extracted a latchkey.

The upper window slid silently down, and the man, with another cautious glance up and down the Crescent, stepped up to the door of No. 3, inserted the key, and let himself in, closing the door quietly after him and putting up the chain.

A few minutes later the measured sound of footsteps was borne upon the still air in a gradual crescendo, and presently the guardian policeman of the district turned into the Crescent in company with an officer in plain clothes.

There had been several burglaries in the neighbourhood of late, and the plainclothes man had been commissioned to "look into the matter."

"There now, look at that," he exclaimed, in a tone of disgust, as he halted opposite No. 3. "Ground-floor window wide open. Why, it's just an invitation to cracksmen, nothing more nor less."

"Just what I told the old chap a night or two ago," said the pohceman.

"And what did he say?"

"Said it was his bedroom, and that he always slept with his window open."

"Did he? We'll just knock him up and give him another warning."

"He didn't seem to like being rowsted up last time," said the policeman dubiously.

By way of reply, the plain-clothes man strode on to the doorstep, and leaning over the railings, rapped smartly with his knuckles upon the window.

"Whozat?" droned a sleepy voice from within.

"Do know your window's open?"

"S'all right," replied the voice drowsily. "S'bdroom. Shutters inside. Good-night."

The plain-clothes man snorted impatiently, and and again plied his knuckles.

"Whas marrer?" inquired the voice.

The officer made no reply, but continued to bang away briskly at the window-pane.

"Tell you s'bedroom," protested the voice from within in a somnolent growl. "S'all right; thank yer, p'liceman. Good-night."

"I think you'd better shut this window, sir," said the plain-clothes man, still banging away like a demon drummer.

There was a sound of muffled anathemas from within. Then a faint glimmer of light appeared above the closed shutters, and presently, after much fumbling at the fastenings, these were thrown open, revealing a man in a dressing-gown, with his face tied up in a handkerchief, and bearing in his hand a lighted candle.

"Sorry to disturb you, sir," said the plain-clothes man, "but that open window isn't safe, you know, and there have been so many houses broken into lately just about here."

The disturbed sleeper made no answer to this, but slamming the window up and slipping the bolt, reclosed the shutters, and almost immediately the light was extinguished.

"That's all right," said the plain-clothes man. "Perhaps he'll shut his window another night. By the way, what is there at the back of these houses?"

"There's their own gardens," replied the policeman, "and then there's the fields belonging to the waterworks."

"Can you get into those fields?" inquired the plain-clothes man.

"Easily," replied the other. "Down at the bottom of that alley there's a wire fence. You get through that, and you're in the fields."

"High wall at the bottom of the gardens?"

"No wall at all. Just some low railings."

"I think I'll step round and have a look at them," said the plain-clothes man. "So long, Tom."

"So long," responded the policeman; and as he turned away to continue his round, his companion disappeared into the alley.

Now the two policemen had barely left the Crescent when there shot round the corner a jovial-looking elderly gentleman, tightly buttoned up in a dark overcoat. Augustus Pordle, Esq., the occupant of No. 3, Constitution Crescent, had just arrived by the late train. He had been dining with one of the City companies, and hence he moved with an elastic step and hummed a lively air as he went.

"I see they've shut my window," he observed as he stood on the doorstep, latchkey in hand. "That's that new housemaid, I suppose, confound her."

He introduced the latchkey with care and deliberation, and after several ineffectual attempts to turn it (for Mr. Pordle was somewhat of a mechanical genius, and had once effected a few trifling repairs on the lock), he felt the latch slip back, when the door opened a couple of inches, and was brought up short by the chain.

"Well," exclaimed Mr. Pordle. "Of all the infernal idiotic — and after leaving special directions too!" He closed the door softly and withdrew the key; then, looking up at the dark and silent house, he emitted a low whistle.

"This is a pretty state of things, certainly," he reflected, "and the question is, what's to be done? There's no knocker, the bell rings somewhere in the basement, which is all shut up, and the servants are asleep at the top of the house. I might ring till Doomsday. H'm!"

Suddely a most opportune idea presented itself. He had the back-door key in his pocket — at least, he had a key that he had made to fit the back door. He had put the finishing touches to it that very morning before breakfast. "I hope it will fit the lock," meditated Mr. Pordle as he stepped lightly down the side alley. "It's a pity I didn't finish it and try it yesterday. But there, the door may be bolted as well as locked."

He squeezed through the wire fence, and was just turning towards the end of his garden when there suddenly loomed up through the darkness the figure of a man, and that man was making his exit from the garden of No. 3 by the unconventional process of climbing the railings.

"Hallo!" said Mr. Pordle, crouching into the shade of an overhanging lilac bush, "I must just keep an eye on you, my friend."

The man, having climbed over the railings, backed into the field, and took a leisurely survey of the row of tall houses and their gardens, in the course of which his eye fell on the crouching figure of Mr. Pordle almost hidden by the shadow of the lilac.

"Hallo!" he exclaimed to himself, "you think I don't see you, my friend; but I do, and I'll just keep an eye on you."

To this end he strolled carelessly away to the corner of the high wall that enclosed the last garden of the Crescent. Turning the corner sharply, he made for a small elm-tree that stood hard by, and drawing himself up as straight as he could, took up a position behind it.

Meanwhile, Mr. Pordle crept stealthily along by the railings, like a puma stalking its prey, until he reached the corner, when he removed his hat and cautiously advanced one eye beyond the brickwork.

"Why, the fellow's gone!" he ejaculated. "He must have seen me, after all, and made a bolt for it as soon as he was out of sight."

He came forth from the shelter of the wall, and walked to and fro, peering into the darkness on all sides. He even walked round the elm-tree, but the man, noiselessly revolving round it, always kept the bole between his pursuer and himself.

"He was mighty smart in getting away," reflected Mr. Pordle; "mighty smart. I can't think where he can have got to."

Then his thoughts turned to his house, from which he had seen the mysterious stranger emerge, and he hastened towards it. Climbing the railings was no great task even for an elderly gentleman encumbered with an overcoat; it was soon accomplished, and then, having traversed the grass plot on tip-toe, Mr. Pordle made his way gingerly down the steps that led to the back-door in the basement.

"Now for the key," he exclaimed, extracting it from his pocket, and blowing into the barrel. It slipped into the lock without the slightest difficulty, and when Mr. Pordle began to turn it, it moved with equal facility — with too great facility, indeed, for it made a complete revolution without encountering any resistance.

"Hang!" ejaculated Mr. Pordle, turning the key round and round as if he were winding up an eight-day movement. "I must have made the wards too short; they don't catch at all. I'm afraid this is no go." He withdrew the key sadly, and stepping over to the scullery window, gave it an impatient shake. To his joy the sash moved slightly.

"Well now! isn't that just like a parcel of women?" he exclaimed. "To bolt me out of the house, and then leave the back of the house all unfastened for any burglar to walk in! For all I know, that fellow has ransacked the place already."

With some difficulty he slid up the lower sash, and prepared to enter. The window was small and its upper half obstructed by the sashes, and it was some little height from the ground. But Mr. Pordle was an active man for his years, and that window had to be entered, so placing his hands firmly on the sill, he sprang through the narrow opening, and turning a complete somer-sault, alighted in a sitting posture on a mound of tea-leaves in the sink.

Here he sat for a few minutes somewhat shaken and bewildered by his sudden transit, until he was abruptly recalled to consciousness by a curious creaking sound apparently proceeding from the pantry above.

"By Jove! there *is* somebody moving about up there!" he gasped, and slip-ping down from the sink and shaking the tea-leaves from his coat-tails, he stole softly out into the dark kitchen, and stood listening. Presently the creaking sound from above was repeated and accompanied this time by a faint metallic clinking; and then another sound caught the listener's ear — not from above, but from the scullery — the sound of a stealthy footfall approaching.

"Who's that?" he called out fiercely.

There was no reply, but the steps came nearer; out of the gloom emerged a dark shape, at which Mr. Pordle clutched, and the next moment he found himself lying on his back in the kitchen fender closely embracing and embraced by some wriggling and most obstreperous individual unknown.

The policeman had made the round of his beat, and once more entered Constitution Crescent. As he came opposite No. 3, he halted and surveyed the house, at first with languid interest, and then with rising curiosity, for his ear had caught a faint sound of hammering, as if a smith or tinker were at work in some part of the basement. At this moment the street door opened, and the man in the dressing-gown with his face still tied up, and with an unlighted candle in his hand, beckoned mysteriously.

"I say," he whispered, "I think somebody must have got into the house. Don't you hear a noise?"

"I should think I do," replied the constable, who had now entered the hall.

"Well, I think some thieves must have broken in, unless the place is haunted."

"If it's haunted," said the policeman with a grim smile, "it must be by the ghost of a boiler-maker. I never heard such a row in my life," and certainly a most terrific clatter was audible where they now stood, just at the head of the kitchen stairs.

"Will you just step down and see what's going on?" inquired the man in the dressing-gown suavely, unlocking the door of the kitchen staircase as he spoke.

"Cert'nly," replied the policeman, and having opened the slide of his lantern, he began to descend the uncarpeted stairs on tip-toe, thereby drowning all other sounds in the creaking of his boots.

About four stairs from the bottom his heel caught, and he dived forward into the darkness, shot through the open kitchen door, and finally arrived in the fender on his hands and knees, preceded at some distance by his helmet and lantern.

The door of the kitchen staircase then closed, and the key turned in the lock.

It was turned half-past one when Mrs. Dawkins, the housekeeper, awakening from her first sleep, sat up in bed and listened.

"He has come home then," she murmured, and lighting the candle that stood by her bedside, she drew her watch from under the pillow and held it to the light.

"Five and twenty to two!" she exclaimed in surprise. "He's very late, and what a noise he's making too — so unlike him. But there, at these City dinners I believe gentlemen do sometimes — he, he! — Still, I never knew him do so before."

She got out of bed, and taking the candle, softly opened the door and listened.

"Well, I'm sure," she muttered; "what can he be doing? He *must* have taken more wine than is good for him. Why, he seems to be talking to someone."

She continued to listen. A door was unlocked and opened. The voices ceased, and there was a loud sound of creaking boots. Then the door closed and the key turned, and almost simultaneously a dull crash was heard, followed by a muffled shout; and all the time, separate from and audible above these sounds, a kind of *obligato* accompaniment of smothered growls and clattering fireirons.

"Goodness gracious!" ejaculated Mrs. Dawkins, and leaning over the banister rail, she called out, "Is that you, Mr. Pordle?"

A sound of hurried movement in the hall met her ear, but no reply to her question, so she pattered back into her bedroom and hastily slipped on her dressing-gown; then snatching up the candle, she once more emerged, and began to cautiously descend the stairs.

She was halfway down the first flight when she heard a quick footstep in the tiled hall, and again she hailed the invisible Pordle, but still received no reply. Almost immediately after, however, she heard the front door close, and then all sounds ceased but the uncanny rumblings and clatterings from the basement.

A single glance into the bedroom on the ground floor showed her that Mr. Pordle was not there, and it was with a trembling hand and a thumping heart that she unlocked and threw open the door of the kitchen staircase. Out of the tangle of sounds that swept up it she was able to separate the familiar voice of Mr. Pordle huskily reiterating the word "Murder!" and, giving utterance to a prolonged and doleful scream, she stumped down the stairs to the rescue.

The light of the candle that Mrs. Dawkins carried revealed a confused heap of masculine humanity piled up on the hearthrug and wriggling violently. Rapid analysis showed it to consist of Mr. Pordle held firmly in the tenacious grasp of a large burly man, who in his turn was gripped as in a vice by a much dishevelled policeman with a black eye.

"Pretty goings-on, I *must* say!" observed Mrs. Dawkins severely, casting a withering glance upon the prostrate group. "Perhaps, Mr. Pordle, you will kindly explain what it means."

"I will when this ruffian lets me go," replied that gentleman hoarsely. The three men simultaneously released one another, and somewhat sheepishly rose to their feet.

"Good Lord, Tom!" exclaimed Mr. Pordle's captor, looking at the polceman, "who'd have thought it was you?"

"Ah! who would?" agreed the policeman sulkily, reaching down a fish slice and applying it tenderly to his occluded eye.

"May I ask who and what *you* are, sir?" inquired Mrs. Dawkins, addressing the big man with ineffable disdain.

"I am a plain-clothes constable, ma'am," replied that individual.

"And what do you mean by breaking into my house and assaulting me in this abominable manner?" demanded the indignant Pordle.

"How was I to know it was your house?" inquired the plain-clothes man in injured tones. "Gentlemen don't generally enter their houses in the middle of the night through the scullery window."

"Did you do that, Mr. Pordle?" asked Mrs. Dawkins incredulously.

"I did, madam," replied Mr. Pordle stiffly. "And why did I do it? I will tell you. Because some donkey had put up the chain of the front door."

"It wasn't up when I went to bed." said Mrs. Dawkins, "and I was the last to retire."

"I tell you it *was* up," screeched Mr. Pordle.

"I say it wasn't," persisted Mrs. Dawkins firmly.

"Well, I think you are mistaken. ma'am," interposed the policeman. "The chain was certainly up, for I heard the gentleman undo it when he let me in."

"The gentleman?" ejaculated Mr. Pordle and the housekeeper in chorus.

"Yes. The gentleman that called me in to see what the row was."

"What gentleman!" demanded Mrs. Dawkins and Mr. Pordle in increasing bewilderment.

"The gentleman upstairs," said the policeman impatiently. "Him that came to the window in the dressing-gown, you know," he continued, appealing to the plain-clothes man, who assented with a nod.

"There is no gentleman in this house, excepting Mr. Pordle," the housekeeper asseverated grimly.

"Certainly not," agreed Mr. Pordle.

Without another word the plain-clothes man snatched the candle from Mrs. Dawkins' hand, and made a rush for the stairs, up which he bounded, closely followed by the other three.

"There's nobody in the bedroom," declared the constable, with his head under the bed.

"No," agreed Mrs. Dawkins. "Stay! What's this — and that?" "This" was a billycock hat, greasy, battered, and disreputable; and "that" was a red-spotted handkerchief of portentous size and uninviting aspect.

"That's the handkerchief his face was tied up in," the constable affirmed; and then, at Mrs. Dawkins' suggestion, the party adjourned to the pantry at the end of the passage. Here the first thing that attracted their notice was an empty plate-basket, while Mrs. Dawkins became instantly conscious of the absence of the silver *entrée* dishes from their usual place.

"We've been done," said the plain-clothes man gloomily. "He just kept us amused while he hooked it with the swag. Reg'ler sell all round."

"What's in this bundle?" asked the constable, indicating the object with the toe of his boot.

"Oh, that," said Mrs. Dawkins; "that is a parcel of pies and things that I have had made and packed up for the Afflicted Orphans' annual treat."

The policeman gave the bundle (which was enclosed in a tablecloth) a suspicious kick, which elicited a metallic jingle. Then he unfastened a corner and peered in.

"Do the Afflicted Orphans eat their dinners off silver candlesticks?" he inquired sarcastically extracting an article of that nature from the bundle.

"Bless my heart!" exclaimed the housekeeper, and pouncing on the bundle she had it open in a twinkling, disclosing the missing entrée dishes, two silver candlesticks, a glittering collection of forks, spoons, salt-cellars, and other small articles, including Mr. Pordle's gold repeater, which he had prudently left at home on this festive occasion.

"Well, this is a regular snorter, this is!" observed the policeman. "He doesn't seem to have taken anything after all."

"Perhaps he was disturbed," Mr. Pordle suggested.

"He must have had pretty strong nerves if he wasn't," said the policeman, grinning and stroking his eye.

"'PRETTY GOINGS-ON, I *MUST* SAY!'"

"Didn't you say something about a bundle of pies or something, ma'am?" asked the plain-clothes man.

"Yes," replied Mrs. Dawkins, looking about the pantry with a puzzled air; "but I don't see it. Yet I know I put it down here the last thing before I went to bed, so that it might be ready for the morning. It's curious."

The plain-clothes man burst into loud guffaws.

"Don't you see what's happened, Tom?" he asked, slapping the policeman on the shoulder and wiping his eyes with his handkerchief. "That chap got bustled up at the end by the lady here, and he was in such an almighty hurry that he picked up the wrong bundle when he skedaddled. My eye! but isn't he using some language over those apple tarts by this time!"

A Woman's Vengeance

IN THE top-floor of a house in the Kentish Town Road a tall and comely young man sat on the edge of a bed reading a letter. The young man's appearance was not entirely congruous with his surroundings; for, in the matter of linen, clothes, and boots, he was as well turned out as a man need be who is not a professed dandy, whereas the room, though neat and orderly, as a well-bred man's bedroom should be, was an undeniable garret. He sat on the bed, not because there was no chair, but because experience had taught him that a chair with a defective hind leg is an unsuitable seat for a pre-occupied man. And Harry Sinclair was decidedly pre-occupied at the moment.

The letter which he held bore the superscription "44 Adam Street, Adelphi," and the signature "Polonius Turcival." It made a conditional offer of an engagement, and requested an appointment by telegram to "Magsulph, London." Sinclair was disposed to regard the telegram as unnecessary. He produced from his pocket a small pigskin purse and tipped its contents into his hand, and when he had counted the coins and shot them back into the receptacle he was quite certain that the telegram was unnecessary.

A few minutes later — at 8.35 A.M., to be exact — he might have been seen striding along the Kentish Town Road with a very shiny silk hat on his head and a neatly-rolled umbrella in his neatly-gloved hand. Quite a striking figure in that not very fashionable neighbourhood, and one by no means unnoticed by the younger members of the female population.

For a man whose entire pecuniary resources were under two pounds Sinclair was surprisingly cheerful. But, then, his state was not chronic. A week ago he had graduated as a Bachelor of Medicine; and you can't do that on nothing. Then, only the day before our introduction to him, he had paid five guineas for the privilege of putting his name on the Medical Register, and thought it mighty dear at the price; and a good many people will agree with him. So he had no cause for melancholy.

Nevertheless, it was not without a shade of anxiety that he entered the private office of Mr. Turcival, the well-known medical agent. It would be exceedingly inconvenient if he failed to get the engagement.

Mr. Turcival looked him over with a studious grey eye suggestive of old china and first editions, consulted a ponderous volume of the Doomsday Book type, and opened his mouth and spake: "I have a vacancy for a *locum tenens*, Dr. Sinclair, which ought to suit you. Eight weeks at five guineas. How will that do?"

Sinclair rapidly worked out a multiplication sum with a product of forty-two pounds, and decided that it would do very well indeed.

"Is it a town or country practice?" he asked.

"Hamblefield, Norfolk;" was the reply.

Sinclair started. For a moment he looked jubilant; then his face clouded. "What is the railway fare to Hamblefield?" he asked; and when Mr. Turcival replied "Nineteen and twopence," he performed a rapid subtraction sum, with a remainder of eighteen shillings. Turcival's fee was a guinea.

It was deuced awkward — embarrassing, too. He felt himself turning distinctly red, and when he looked up and met the speculative grey eye he blushed like a pickled cabbage.

Turcival recognised the symptoms. He had seen them before. Applying himself to the Doomsday Book, he coughed drily, and remarked: "You won't be paid till the end of the engagement, so perhaps you'd better settle with me when you come back, unless you're more flush than newly-qualified men are generally."

"I'm pebbly-beached, as a matter of fact," said Sinclair, "and it's awfully good of you."

"Not at all. Matter of business." Thus Turcival, as dry as a last year's walnut, and desperately afraid of being suspected of doing a kindly act. "Better catch the twelve-thirty from Liverpool Street, if you can," he added; and, shaking hands aridly, he buried his proboscis in the Doomsday Book.

Sinclair caught the twelve-thirty without difficulty. He even found time to drop into the telegraph office, and "bang went saxpence" in a telegram to Hamblefield, Norfolk. The reader will naturally suppose that the telegram was addressed to the doctor of whose practice he was going to take charge. But it was not. The address space was filled by the words "Miss Lucy Morris, Lavender Cottage, Hamblefield." And thereby hangs a tale.

Lucy Morris had been a student at the Slade School. Sinclair had been a student at University College Hospital. At one of the college dances they had become acquainted, and each had thought the other a quite exceptionally agreeable young person. But they were none of your cocksure sort. They gave themselves ample opportunities for reconsidering this opinion and testing its correctness, with the natural result — since their first impression turned out to be quite well founded — that they entered into certain mutual arrangements, which included the transformation of Miss Lucy Morris into Mrs. Harry Sinclair. But not yet. They were provident young people, and as poor as church mice.

Meanwhile, Lucy returned to her native village of Hamblefield, and, abandoning the charcoal point for the process artist's pen, and the agreeably rugged Michallet for prim-faced Bristol board, devoted herself to the art and mystery of illustrating children's books, sharing a cottage with an older Sladeite who drew fashion plates.

By the light of these facts the reader will have no difficulty in understanding the air of deep content with which Sinclair, reclining at his ease in a third-class smoker, consumed an inexpensive brand of tobacco in a ninepenny briar. He had not seen Lucy for many a long month, had not expected to see her for many a month more, and here he was, speeding to faraway Norfolk, where for full eight weeks he would have the daily chance of looking into her pretty hazel eyes, of hearing her well-beloved voice, and of whispering into her ear those persuasive utterances which were novel in the days of the mammoth and the cave-hyæna, and have remained novel ever since. Well might he look happy!

At Rugby he put out his head and acquired a Bath bun. By this time she knew he was coming. She might be, even now, devising some plan for a meeting; in fact, it was actually possible, though very unlikely, that she would be at the station. Remote as the possibility was, it occupied him at intervals for the remainder of the journey. And a very agreeable occupation, too.

But it was more than a possibility; it actually happened. Talk about the long arm of coincidence! There she was on the platform looking as pretty as a field daisy and as sweet as the lavender that gave her cottage its name. Unfortunately a trap was there, too, in charge of a chuckle-headed rustic. But Sinclair made short work of *him*. Pitching the Gladstone portmanteau into the trap, he said:

"I think I should like a walk after the railway journey. You go on with my traps and tell Dr. Gribble that I'll be with him in a jiffy."

The rustic jehu touched his hat. "Yezzir," he said. "You can't miss your way, zir; 'tis straight up the road from the station, zir." With which he drove off.

Now the exact duration of a jiffy, as determined, for instance, by a one-metre pendulum, has, I believe, not been satisfactorily settled. But in the present case its indefiniteness was atoned for by certain compensations.

Lucy, of course, as a local person, knew the way perfectly; in fact, she knew the very shortest cut, which took them zig-zagwise across several meadows, along a pretty rose-hung lane, and through a belt of wood. She was in great spirits, and made no secret of it, going so far as to execute a little dance on a piece of level sward in the lane, to the unmeasured surprise of a crow-boy, whose presence had not till then been observed.

"How did you come to hear about Dr. Gribble?" she asked, when she had recovered somewhat from the inopportune crow-boy.

"Turcival got me the job," replied Sinclair.

"He's a duck!" said Lucy. (Poor Turcival! If he could only have heard!) "And to think that you will be here for eight whole weeks!"

"Yes," he answered; "eight whole weeks. But they'll pass like a summer's night, dear little lady, won't they?"

"I'm afraid they will," she assented and for a while they walked on more soberly.

"I wonder," he said wistfully, "how long it will be before we can build our little nest, Lucy."

She looked up at him rather wistfully, too, and thought what a fine picture of wholesome, comely manhood he made, with his alert. intelligent face, his sinewy limbs, and smart, athletic figure.

"We could do with quite a little, you know," he continued. "You wouldn't mind if we had to spread the butter a trifle thin at first, would you?"

She slipped her hand through his arm and drew closer to him. "You are rather mixing your dear old metaphors," she said. "People don't spread butter in nests. But I mustn't be flippant. I don't feel so. And as to the mere discomforts of poverty, they would be nothing to me if we were together. The only question is as to what is practicable."

"The wise woman of Hamblefield," he chuckled. "But you are quite right, dear; a medicus can't live in a two-pair back — though, by the way, I know one who lives in a three-pair front, only he's a mere bachelor."

"It is early yet," said Lucy. "Why, you are only just fledged, in a professional sense. We mustn't be impatient and premature, though, of course, we don't want to go on waiting until we are old."

"You'll never be old, my dear," said he. "You will just go on getting sweeter and more lovely from year to year like, an everlasting golden pippin, though I should like to be near to watch the process of development."

"In case I should turn out a medlar, after all," she laughed.

Here they entered the wood, through which they walked hand-in-hand; a very necessary precaution, he being a stranger in the locality and due at Dr. Gribble's in a jiffy. It would have been a dreadful thing if he had lost his way.

On emerging from the wood they were confronted by an old-fashioned, red-brick house, which stood beyond a couple of meadows.

"That is Dr. Gribble's house," said Lucy.

"Hang Dr. Gribble's house!" said Sinclair. So they went back into the wood to say "Good-bye."

The practice at Hamblefield was not a disagreeable one to work. It was small, good class, and rather scattered. It could be worked in the saddle, which was better fun than sitting hunched up in a dogcart; and at present, "the weather being hot and dry," as the ballad says, there was not so very much to do. By judicious management, Sinclair found it possible on most days to chance to be in the vicinity of Lavender Cottage about tea-time. And very agreeable those improvised tea were; for the tea-things were providently set out in the little drawing room, whereas the hard-featured fashion-platist (which her name was Maggs — a professed Suffragist and a most inveterate match-maker, invariably found some engrossing occupation in the adjacent studio, which occupation she pursued to the accompaniment of loud humming. So there could be no possible doubt as to her whereabouts.

On these occasions the nest-building project was reviewed in all its bearings; minute computations were made of the compound interest on very small sums of money. Then, too, practical comparisons were made contrasting the velvety softness of the female countenance with the ruggedness of that of the porcupinous male; and so forth. It was all very agreeable. And so the time ran on.

But there was a fly in the ointment. We apologise for the metaphor, because the fly was a lady — which sounds nonsense, and is, in fact, absurd.

But that is the worst of embarking on figures of speech.

The lady was a young lady, and her name was Morris — a coincidence, since Lucy's name was also Morris. But, seeing that she was Lucy's first cousin, the coincidence was not so very remarkable. The fact of the relationship came to Sinclair's knowledge quite early, but there was another circumstance that he learned later and which is so relevant to the course of events herein set forth that it is necessary to mention it now. Daisy Morris was a young lady of means. Her considerable property was derived from an uncle (who was also an uncle of Lucy's), and it came to her subject to a certain condition, which was that, in the event of her dying without issue, the whole of it should pass to her cousin Lucy. Why the worthy uncle had not divided the estate between his two nieces no one could make out. But the ways of testators are inscrutable.

Sinclair made the acquaintance of the "fly" on the very day of his arrival. Gribble introduced her when handing over the practice. "Then there's a Miss Daisy Morris, cousin of your friend Miss Lucy." Sinclair had prudently mentioned his engagement by way of anticipating comment in the village. "You're sure to hear from her. Most unsatisfactory patient. Typical case of hysteria. Wants some thing to do. Damn nuisance. No sooner have you relieved one set of symptoms than she starts another. She's taken me through the whole Nosological index already, and when she sees you" — here Dr. Gribble glanced significantly at his handsome young deputy — "she'll start ringing the whole lot of changes over again."

"I suppose," said Sinclair, "if she sends for me I'd better go."

"Must," said Gribble. "Can't help it. If you don't, she'll swallow a hair pin and prosecute you for criminal neglect. You can't dodge a hysteric. You'll know that when you're my age."

Gribble's anticipations were realised within twenty-four hours. Sinclair was half-way through his first breakfast at Hamblefield, and had just inflicted a depressed fracture on his second egg, when the inevitable message arrived. "Miss Morris, of 'The Birches,' wished to see Dr. Sinclair. She was in great pain, and would he kindly go as soon as possible?"

Sinclair gobbled the remainder of his breakfast, gulped down a cup of tea, and started. "Pain" is a talismanic word. No doctor can afford to be sceptical of pain until he has seen the patient.

Miss Morris was "discovered," as the playwrights say, reclining gracefully on a sofa in a pleasant boudoir. Her bodily agonies did not appear to have inhibited the normal activities of the toilet; in fact, she was uncommonly well turned out, and was by no means a bad-looking young woman so long as her face was in repose. And in repose it was, most emphatically, when Sinclair arrived, for she was lying motionless with her eyes closed, and a general air of limpness suggestive of profound suffering, endured with heroic fortitude.

When Sinclair introduced himself she opened her eyes and took in her new medical attendant with some surprise and a good deal of approval. What a delightful change from old Gribble! (She didn't say this, of course. She only closed her eyes and breathed a patient sigh.)

Sinclair seated himself, and, after the manner of doctors, inspected the surroundings while the patient skirmished lightly round her symptoms. The constant relation between an organism and its environment makes the study of the latter highly instructive as to the former. And the present environment was very suggestive. It included a pile of novels from Smith's: *The Soul of a Woman, A Woman's Passion, The Master Woman, A Woman's Strength*, and others; a few more serious works such as *The Influence of Woman, The Power of Woman in the State, Woman in Art, Woman in Science*, etc., and some loose numbers of periodicals including *The Woman's Clarion, The Woman's Liberator, Modern Woman* and *Woman*.

Thus the environment furnished a working diagnosis. The patient was evidently suffering from an aggravated attack of the universal and everlasting ME.

Nevertheless her symptoms, picturesquely described, were sufficiently harrowing — to a person unacquainted with anatomy and physiology. Sinclair found them quite reassuring, and when he had made a slight and delicate physical examination he deeply regretted having bolted that second egg. However, regrets were useless, so, having administered a dose of valerian, which he had providently brought with him, he commenced to plan a strategic movement to the door.

Now there are several important subjects that are omitted from the ordinary medical curriculum, but the most important of them all is the art of escaping from the sick-room. It is a difficult art, but its acquirement is imperative or the day's work and the night's rest will alike be curtailed; and, like the cognate art of wrapping up a medicine bottle, its necessity is not suspected by the student until he emerges from the wards into general practice. Sinclair was as innocent of it as a baby. He rose from his chair and was made to sit down again. He rose once more, and was again begged to be seated. In fact, he continued to rise and sit down until he looked like a clock-work toy. He was introduced to the soul of a woman; he discussed — principally in the passive voice — the place of woman in contemporary politics, the influence of woman on art, and was even lured into an argument on love as it affects the two sexes — especially the female. When, two hours later, he walked up the garden path, the terms in which he soliloquized were calculated to curdle the milk in the neighbouring dairy-farm.

"So," said Lucy, when about four o'clock he looked in at Lavender Cottage, "Cousin Daisy has sent for you already."

"How on earth did you know?" he asked in astonishment.

"Know!" she repeated. "Everybody knows by this time. The proper study of mankind is man, and I can tell you that we carry that study to a finish here in Hamblefield. Why, I even know what you had for breakfast. You had eggs."

Sinclair glanced hastily at the front of his waistcoat. "That was just a shot," said he. "I shouldn't be likely to have parrots. But how did you know about Miss Morris?"

"Your housekeeper, Mrs. Stubbs, called to leave some strawberries from the garden. But do tell me what Daisy talked about. Did she hold forth on the mission of woman?"

"Never you mind, little gossip. A doctor's wife must learn not to be inquisitive about her husband's patients." Sinclair stated this maxim with becoming gravity until Lucy made a quaint little grimace at him, which made him laugh and spoilt the effect of the platitude.

"All the same," said she, "I wish there were more Daisies here — hundreds of them. Then you'd double Dr. Gribble's income, and he'd want to keep you as his assistant. And you wouldn't have to go away at all. How delightful that would be!"

She sat down by him on the little cane sofa, and laid a particularly soft cheek on his shoulder; and Sinclair, who had his ambitions, thought he would be willing to sink them all and "devil" for old Gribble *in perpetuam* if thereby he could avoid that "good-bye" that loomed eight weeks ahead. He stroked the soft chestnut hair that strayed so prettily from her brow and said cheerily, "We'll do better than that, little partner; we'll have a practice of our own —

a small one. I shall soon get a little money accumulated, and then I'll ask Turcival to find me a cheap nucleus. A very little one would do for a start."

She snuggled up closer to him and blushed with pleasure. "It *would* be glorious," she said. "And we could really do with a very small practice at first, because when people saw you they'd simply tumble over one another to get ill and be attended by you. And then there is my work. I could earn more than enough to pay the rent."

The prospect thus opened engendered further discussion, which, being conducted in increasingly-confidential tones, entailed increased proximity of lips and ears. Then Miss Maggs was heard approaching — very slowly — with the tea things, humming "Annie Laurie," and missing fire badly on the high notes. But she would not take tea with them. She couldn't leave her work. So she retired to the studio with her refreshment, and, no doubt, found a cup of tea and a plate of bread and butter useful aids to pen and ink drawing.

So day by day, as the weeks crept on, these two young mating birds would foregather to chirp hopefully of the nest that was to be builded. Or in the evenings, when the moon shamelessly got up in broad daylight, they would saunter through the lanes or by the wood and listen to other couples in the trees above telling the same story in twittering "songs without words." It is hard to be poor, no doubt, but it is good to be young, with the sunshine of love lighting up the rough places on life's highway. Who could pity them, but that, as the golden weeks ran out, they drew ever nearer to that desert of separation that lay between them and the nest that was to be builded?

But it was not all smooth running even at that. The fly — if you will pardon the expression — stuck fast in the ointment and even kicked feebly, but resolutely refused to come out. Miss Daisy Morris was still — as Sinclair coarsely expressed it to himself — "on the job." Gribble had not overestimated her powers. She rang the changes merrily, and her repertoire extended from the optic nerve to the vermiform appendix. It was of no use to discharge her as cured. That cat wouldn't jump. As surely as Sinclair struck her name off the visiting list, say, on Tuesday evening, so surely would an urgent message come up with the shaving water on Wednesday morning. And, to add to his exasperation, her symptoms began, about the third week, to assume especial virulence about tea-time, with the result that he was repeatedly prevented from making his afternoon call at Lavender Cottage.

Nor was this all. Modest as Sinclair really was, he could not be blind to the lady's manner towards him. It would have been a little embarrassing at any time. In the present circumstances it was excessively uncomfortable. There were other unpleasantnesses, too. The enthusiastic pursuit of "the proper study of mankind" by the Hamblefieldians set up certain eddies of rumour that — in a more or less attenuated form — reached both Lucy and Sinclair. There were the Misses Kiddle and old Mrs. Mumpton and Mr. Bodger, the curate — though he, poor man, contributed no more than a discreet cough — all were earnest students. As, for instance:

The elder Miss Kiddle (looking into the teapot and deciding not to add any more hot water until Mr. Bodger sends up his cup), "Well, people will talk. I don't suppose there's anything in it; though, to be sure, a substantial capital *is* very valuable — to a young medical man. But I'm sure it's all nonsense."

"Of course," said Miss Selina Kiddle; "it must be. He couldn't; under Lucy's very nose, too. Though he certainly does spend a deal of time at 'the Birches,' and, as you say, it must be a great temptation."

"I didn't say so," returned Miss Kiddle. "But since, you make the suggestion –"

"I don't," rejoined Miss Selina. "I merely understood you–"

"For my part," interrupted Mrs. Mumpton, "if I had to be attended in sickness I should *not* choose a doctor who was engaged to the woman who was waiting to step into my shoes."

"Good gracious!" exclaimed Miss Kiddle. "I never thought of that. You actually mean to say –"

"No I don't," said Mrs. Mumpton. "Nothing of the kind. Pray don't misunderstand me. I make no suggestion of any kind whatever."

There was a pause. Miss Kiddle filled up the teapot, and at that moment discovered that the curate's cup was empty. "How very dreadful," she murmured. "A most shocking thought — two lumps, I think, Mr. Bodger?"

"If you please; small ones," said the curate.

"Yes; a terrible thought. What fearful temptations a medical man may be exposed to! Don't you agree with me, Mr. Bodger?"

But the curate only coughed a discreet cough.

This was only a sample of the discussions that took place in the village of Hamblefield on the relations of the good-looking young doctor with his well-to-do patient. Of course, the matter of these debates did not reach the interested parties in a literal and unexpurgated form; but the air was charged with rumour and scandal, and the two young people could not fail to breathe in some of the poison.

Even here Sinclair's troubles did not end. As the weeks sped and the term of his stay at Hamblefield approached, an inverse transformation took place in the two cousins. In proportion as Miss Daisy's manner grew more confidential, more clinging, and more plainly affectionate, so did Lucy's cool off into something approaching stiffness. Sinclair made his afternoon calls at Lavender Cottage, when not prevented by unexpected and urgent messages, and was received not ungraciously, though with a new and discomforting reserve. He made his little appeals as of old, and was not actually repulsed; but though she suffered him to pet and even kiss her, and listened to the words that she had loved to hear, all the old responsiveness, which is the heart and soul of love, was gone.

Sinclair was profoundly puzzled. Something had clearly gone awry, but he could not imagine what. He tentatively sought an explanation, but was met by the impossible answer that there was nothing to explain. And meanwhile the dreaded day of parting drew near. Were they to say "Good-bye" with this mysterious cloud of misunderstanding between them?

The climax of unpleasantness for the unfortunate young doctor was reached less than a week before Dr. Gribble's expected return. He was cantering his horse homeward by a quiet by-road when he was overtaken by a perspiring youth on a bicycle. Miss Morris was dying! Would he go to "The Birches" on the wings of the wind?

Wearily he turned his horse's head and galloped away towards the too familiar bourne. Handing his steed over to the gardener, he tucked his emergency case under his arm and bounded up the stairs whispering profane objurgations. It was a quarter to four already, and Lucy would be waiting for him at four.

It was angina pectoris this time — a very severe attack. The symptoms were really alarming, and the more so because they were technically so very unorthodox. There was nothing like them in any of the text-books. It took Sinclair an hour and a half and two capsules of nitrite of amyl (of which he administered one in homeopathic doses, and, dropping the other on the carpet, trod on it to make a reassuring smell) before he could reduce the attack to manageable proportions. The pain was very severe (and all in the wrong place), and the emotional manifestations most remarkable, causing the patient to weep copiously, to fling her arms round her medical attendant's neck, and address him as "dearest." Sinclair fairly perspired with embarrassment.

At last she began to "come to" — very much "to," in fact. Then she made him sit by her on the sofa, and asked him penitently if he thought her very silly, which was an awkward question, because he did. But, of course, he couldn't say so.

"How kind you have been!" she exclaimed, tearfully. "How patient and sweet! And I so unworthy, too." (Sinclair inwardly agreed with her warmly.) "But I am a miserable wretch! Oh, if you only knew how miserable, how unhappy I am! You would forgive everything — you, so gentle, so tender-hearted, so — so — Oh, what shall I do: What *shall* I do?" She stared tragically at Sinclair, who, having no suggestion to make other than that she should stop playing the fool, preserved a diplomatic silence.

"What shall I, do," she repeated, "without you? When you are far away, and I am left alone with my sorrow? I can't — I can't let you go!" And here, to Sinclair's horror, she laid her head on his shoulder and began to sob.

"Oh, come," he said, in a matter-of-fact tone, "you'll be all right! Dr. Gribble will look after you — at half a guinea a time" (this was an unspoken "aside"). "He's much more experienced than I am."

Miss Morris snuggled closer to him. "I can't," she murmured, "I can't let you go out of my life for ever." Here she slipped her arm round his neck and whispered shyly in his ear: "Don't you understand? Have you never guessed? Oh. dearest! Don't think me unmaidenly and horrid. But I had to — I had to tell you!"

It was a devil of a position for the poor young man. The direct attack fairly "knocked him sideways," as the phrase has it; for he was only twenty-six. Now, if he had been forty-six or fifty it would have been different. A man of fifty who practises the art of medicine, keeping his weather eyelid elevated and his weather eyeball peeled — if you will pardon the colloquialism — takes a deal of surprising. But poor Sinclair was a green hand, and he was absolutely thunderstruck.

"It's awfully good of you, Miss Morris," he stammered, reaching tentatively for another nitrite of amyl capsule, "very flattering, and — er — and all that sort of — er –"

"Have I taken you by surprise?" she whispered. "But surely you must have guessed! You must have seen. And you do, don't you? Oh, say you do care for me just a little, only a little! But say it."

Sinclair wriggled in agony. "Of course," he spluttered. "I — er — I have the greatest regard — er — and — er — esteem and — all that sort of — er —"

"Esteem!" she exclaimed coquettishly. "As if I cared for your esteem, silly boy!" Then, with a sudden return to the tender manner: "Don't say esteem, dear one; say love! Say you love me, if it be only ever so little." The last words died away in a whisper, leaving Sinclair absolutely paralysed with horror.

"It — it's awfully good of you!" he gasped. "Should be delighted under other circumstances, but, you see, there's Lucy. You knew I was engaged to Lucy, didn't you?"

"Lucy!" was the disdainful answer. "Why speak of that absurd little scribbler. She is no match for you, and you know it. Now I — I should be proud of you. I should be ambitious for you. You should rise, you should soar. You should — but you know. You must know. Oh, say you know and understand!"

But the disrespectful reference to Lucy had stiffened Sinclair's back. He disengaged himself from her embrace, and said bluntly: "I can't listen to this, Miss Morris. Lucy is the one woman for me. Rich or poor, I want her and her only; and if I had to sweep a crossing to win her, I'd sweep it, and sweep it jolly clean."

He stood up, very red in the face, and began to gather up the implements of his trade.

Miss Morris sat bolt upright, pale and venomous, and as near to looking ill as Sinclair had ever seen her. Her appearance cut him to the heart. It is a hateful thing to have to humiliate a woman; and yet what else could he do?

"I'm most awfully sorry, Miss Morris," he said. And he was. And so would any man have been. When a woman dares, for love, to break the chains of convention every male heart is touched with a certain sneaking sympathy; though you understand the thing is quite wrong in principle.

But Miss Morris was quite equal to the situation. She sat on the sofa, rigid and white, breathing quickly and watching him, with a very devil of malice in her eyes, as he hastily packed his bag. For a few moments she was too angry to speak, but she soon recovered herself, and then said, with frigid self-possession: "I don't follow you at all. You seem to be putting a most extraordinary construction on my simple remarks. Anyone would suppose that I had been persuading you not to marry poor Lucy."

Sinclair opened his mouth like a newly-landed codfish, and felt rather like one, too. He had never met anything like this before. But, then as we have said, he was only twenty-six.

"I'm most awfully sorry, Miss Morris –" he began.

"So, I think, you remarked before," she interrupted coldly.

"Frightfully stupid of me to misunderstand you like that."

"Very," said Miss Morris, "unless you did it intentionally."

"You don't surely think –" he began to protest; but she stood up and interrupted him.

"I think we had better put an end to this ridiculous interview. Shall I ring, or can you let yourself out?"

He could let himself out, and he did, wondering meanwhile whether he was drunk, dreaming, or merely insane. He mounted his steed at the gate, preserving sufficient self-possession to get up with his face towards the horse's head, and surrendered himself to the guidance of that sagacious animal, who, considering the topography of the district in terms of oats, headed gleefully for the stable.

The remainder of that day Sinclair spent in profound cogitation. It was an astonishing affair. Deucedly unpleasant, too, though it had one redeeming element — she wouldn't send for him again. But even this circumstance appeared less gratifying when, in the course of the evening, he received a note from Mrs. Wingfield, the elderly relative who acted as Miss Daisy's companion and chaperon. The note was short and stiff. It informed him that his further attendance would not be required, and added the gratifying information that Dr. Gallibut, of Lynn, had been asked to take over the case. At the concluding clause Sinclair smiled grimly, and wished Dr. Gallibut joy of his attendance. But, all the same, it was no joke. Gribble would be furious. Miss Morris might be a "damn nuisance," as Gribble had said, but her yearly account must be something considerable. And the G.P. doesn't practise for fun.

Lucy's reception of the ill-tidings mortified him deeply. She had heard about it, of course; everybody had. She listened without comment to his statement that he "had given offence in some way." She agreed with his opinion that Gribble wouldn't like it, that Turcival would hear of it and write him down a duffer, but she offered no condolences. He felt her unconcern keenly. This was his first engagement, and he had made a mess of it, and she didn't seem to care a hang. Of course, she didn't know that it was not his fault; but the old Lucy would have taken that for granted.

It appeared from current report that Miss Morris was seriously ill. Dr. Gallibut had even asked for a second opinion, which might mean anything. But it didn't improve Sinclair's position. He thought about it a good deal in his intervals of leisure, which, by the way, were uncommonly few; for the unexpected had happened. He had taken it for granted that his dismissal from "The Birches" would throw him out of employment elsewhere. But the result was exactly the reverse; he was in universal demand. Elderly and middle-aged ladies, who had enjoyed uninterrupted good health for years, were taken ill by the dozen. It was a regular epidemic; and their symptoms were so much alike, too. In fact, they were identical. These good ladies "wanted to know, you know," as Mr. Tite Barnacle expresses it. Sinclair's language, as he rode from house to house, would have been indictable under the "Profane Swearing Act."

On the fourth afternoon, just after lunch, Sinclair was in the surgery spreading a belladonna plaster (Gribble was an old-fashioned man, and made his own plasters — didn't believe in the ready-made stuff that you buy in rolls like stair-carpet), when his occupation and gloomy reflections were interrupted by the appearance of the jovial and gigantic Chief Constable.

Sinclair looked up and laid down the spatula. "Good afternoon, Mr. Ratley," he said. "Just dropped in for a pick-me-up?"

The officer smiled uneasily. He stepped lightly to the door, looked out, closed it, and approached with a confidential air.

"The fact is, doctor." he said in a low tone, "I've come on a bit of very unpleasant business — unpleasant for you and unpleasant for me."

Sinclair looked at him sharply.

"Miss Morris," the officer continued, "has charged you with stealing a diamond from her dressing-table — there! Don't get in a fluster! We know it's all rot. But you've got to come and answer the charge before the justices. They are sitting in the courtroom now."

For one moment Mr. Ratley realised that he stood a first-class chance of having his head punched. Sinclair's face was crimson, and his eyes blazed. "It's no use getting shirty with me," said Ratley. And Sinclair realised that it was not. "You'd better search me at once," he said. "I insist on your searching me." He banged his keys down on the table and turned out his pockets one after the other. "Now take my keys and come upstairs."

Ratley accompanied him to his bedroom and made a very systematic search. But a diamond is a small thing. The most exhaustive search, even of a bedroom, might easily fail to discover it, especially if it wasn't there. But he had searched. That was the main thing. He could go into court and say so on oath with a clear conscience.

The Hamblefield bench was a cut above the ordinary. The chairman was a retired London solicitor, a very knowing old gentleman, who, as Sinclair entered the dock, red-faced and furious, glanced at him critically and decided that he didn't look like a petty thief. The charge was stated by a local solicitor who was retained for the prosecution, and the chairman looked critically at him, too.

"This charge," said the lawyer, "rests on the definite statement of the prosecutrix, Miss Daisy Morris, that she saw the prisoner take the diamond."

"Is Miss Morris present?" asked the chairman.

"No, your worship. She is very seriously ill."

"Is there any other witness?"

"Yes, your worship. There is Mrs. Wingfield."

"Did she see the prisoner steal the diamond?"

"No, your worship; but she saw the empty setting from which the diamond had been stolen."

"Has the prisoner been searched?"

"Yes, your worship," said Ratley. "I searched him at his own request, and his room also. I did not find the stolen property."

"Then," said the chairman, "the prisoner will be remanded until the prosecutrix can attend. He may be released on his own recognisance."

The ignominy, then, of confinement in a prison cell was at least deferred. The formalities complied with Sinclair took his way gloomily homeward; but the undisguised interest with which he was regarded by stray wayfarers told him the students of humanity were already in possession of the facts.

On arriving home his first act was to retire to the surgery and indite a letter to Lucy. He was a remanded prisoner charged with theft. If Daisy Morris was prepared to declare on oath that she saw him commit the theft, it seemed that there was no escape. A bare denial was all he had to offer. If he were convicted he was ruined, for his name would be erased from the medical register. And even if he were discharged, the stigma of that sworn statement would follow him through life. It was manifestly his duty to release Lucy from the engagement whether she wished it or not.

The letter was not a very long one. It set forth the facts of the case, and declared the engagement at an end. He had just signed it and was sitting staring at it, with a terrible lump in his throat, when he heard footsteps in the passage outside, and Lucy herself burst into the surgery. She ran to him, and, flinging her arms round his neck, laid her cheek against his.

"My poor darling!" she murmured; "what a fiendish thing this is. I have only just heard, and I ran up at once to beg your forgiveness."

"My forgiveness!" exclaimed Sinclair. "What on earth for?"

"For being a disloyal little cat," she replied. "For listening to calumny when I ought to have known better. But I know better now. I think I understand everything."

"What calumnies have you listened to?" Sinclair asked.

"That wretch Daisy," she answered viciously. "I called to see her that day when she was confined to bed with — what was it?"

"Gastric ulcer?"

"That was it. She was lying there with all her jewels spread out on the dressing-table. You had just left, and she was in great spirits for a person with gastric ulcer. She remarked on your insinuating manners, and told me how you stayed and chatted with her, so that she had the greatest difficulty in getting rid of you. In fact, she hinted that you were making love to her for all you were worth. She didn't pretend that you were in love with her; she professed to think that you merely wanted her for her money — the artful, lying wretch. And I actually took it all in."

"You must have been a silly little guffin," said Sinclair.

"I was a great deal worse than silly. But she was so circumstantial — the viper! Are you going to forgive me, Hal, dear?"

"Forgive you, my sweet!" exclaimed Sinclair, kissing her again and again, and forgetting all about his letter. "I'm only too thankful –"

"I want a token that you really forgive me," said Lucy, with a quick, nervous glance at the letter that lay on the table. "I want you to make me a promise."

"What is it, darling?"

"I'll tell you when you have promised."

"I don't like making promises with my eyes shut," said Sinclair, with masculine caution.

"Hal," she said earnestly, "I ask you to. Don't refuse. Trust me and say yes."

"Very well, I promise."

"It's really a solemn promise?"

"There's only one kind of promise, you know," Sinclair said bluntly. "Now, what is it?"

"You have promised," said Lucy, "that if they fix this ridiculous, trumped-up charge on you, and you have to go — to — to prison" (here her voice shook a little) "you will marry me directly you come out."

Sinclair started up. "Good Lord!" he exclaimed, "what a fool I am! I had just written you a letter –"

"Yes, I know," said Lucy. "I knew you would directly I heard. That is why I came here at once."

"But, my dear girl, it couldn't be. You must –"

"Rubbish," said Lucy. "She's not going to rob me of you that way. Oh — yes — I was going to ask you: what was it that you did to give her such mortal offence?"

Sinclair hummed and hawed. "I'm a tactless sort of fellow, Lucy," he said. "I'd rather not go into details."

"Did she make love to you?"

Sinclair gasped. These confounded women! "You oughtn't to ask me questions like that, Lucy" he said. "You know I shouldn't give her away if she had; but — er –"

Lucy laughed. "Very well, you dear old innocent. You needn't give her away — any more. I think I know pretty well what happened. But I don't care. She shan't part us; and I don't suppose anyone will believe this diamond nonsense."

Whether this was so or not, the practice suddenly went as flat as a punctured tyre. The ladies all re-covered simultaneously. For now they knew all about it, or thought they did. Which answered their purpose as well.

Besides, you can't repose confidence in a medical man who is admittedly a snapper-up of unconsidered trifles from the dressing-table. It would not be safe, and it certainly would not be proper.

It is needless to say that Sinclair avoided the vicinity of Lavender Cottage, He was unclean; a social leper, whose presence was a contamination. But the cottagers weren't going to have that. They revolted in a body. And when repeated and urgent invitations proved unavailing, the forbidding Maggs marched boldly into the surgery with a warlike air and a large smear of Indian ink on the side of her nose, and led him, a protesting captive, to the cottage, where he was given more tea than was good for him and as much petting as two loyal-hearted women could contrive. And we all know what they can manage at a pinch.

On the fourth day after the first hearing. Sinclair duly surrendered to his bail and took his place in the dock. There was a profound hush in the court, though every available place was occupied. The magistrates looked preternaturally solemn, and the face of the jolly chief constable wore an expression of gloom. The case was reopened by the solicitor for the prosecution in tones of portentous gravity.

"Since the prisoner was first charged four days ago," he began, "a very terrible thing has happened. The prosecutrix, your worship, is dead. She died this morning at half-past eleven."

The magistrates were profoundly shocked; the spectators, who had all known Daisy Morris, were still more profoundly shocked; and as to Sinclair, he was thunderstruck. Dead! Could it be that those symptoms of grave disease at which he had inwardly scoffed were, after all, genuine? That he had held this poor woman's life in his hands and negligently let it slip? It was an awful thought. His present peril was forgotten for the moment in the horror of that hideous possibility. He looked up with a haggard face and met the eye of the chief constable watching him curiously.

Here the chairman turned to the solicitor and asked: "Were any depositions taken?"

"Yes, your worship. I have them here. They were taken in the presence of witnesses a few hours before the death of the deceased lady."

"When the depositions were taken was the deceased aware that she was dying?"

"No, your worship, she was not."

"Was she told by the doctors that she was dying?"

The solicitor hastily consulted a gentleman who sat by him at the table, and then replied:

"No, your worship, she was not."

"Then," said the chairman, "it is unnecessary for me to tell you that those depositions are not admissible as evidence."

Apparently the solicitor was aware of the fact. He laid down his papers and said:

"In that case, your worship, the prosecution falls through. The evidence of the other witnesses is merely corroborative."

"Exactly," said the chairman. "There is no case. The prisoner must be discharged."

Sinclair stepped out of the dock in a state of bewilderment, which did not, however, prevent him from perceiving clearly that he was by no means cleared of the charge. But he had no time to reflect on this unsatisfactory circumstance, for hardly had he left the dock when the chief constable approached and touched him on the shoulder.

"Harry Sinclair" said the officer, "I arrest you on the charge of the wilful murder of Daisy Morris, and I caution you that anything you say will be used in evidence against you."

Sinclair gazed at the officer in utter stupefaction. The caution was unnecessary. He was speechless with amazement and horror. Before he could recover himself he had been hustled back into the dock.

The chairman looked sharply at Sinclair and from him to the chief constable.

"What is this case?" he asked.

"The prisoner, Harry Sinclair, is charged, your worship with the wilful murder of Daisy Morris, spinster, of 'The Birches,' Hamblefield."

A murmur of amazement arose from the body of the court. A faint shriek was heard, and a woman was borne insensible out through the open doorway. The woman was Lucy Morris.

"I propose," said the officer, "merely to offer evidence of arrest."

"But," said the chairman, "is it a known fact that the deceased died from other than natural causes?"

"No, your worship; but the circumstances are very highly suspicious."

The chairman briefly consulted with his colleagues; then he said:

"We can't accept evidence of arrest only. You will have to make out a *prima facie* case against the prisoner."

The officer bowed, and proceeded to outline the case.

"In the first place, it appears that the prisoner had a distinct interest in the death of the deceased."

"We won't go into that now," said the magistrate. "Let us have the actual facts."

The officer bowed again, and continued: "On the fourteenth instant the prisoner was in attendance on the deceased, and is known to have administered certain medicines to her with his own hand. Later on, the same day, the deceased dismissed the prisoner for reasons which are not clearly known, and called in Dr. Gallibut in his place. Dr. Gallibut called in Dr. Horner in consultation, and the two medical gentlemen continued in attendance on the deceased until her death. Dr. Gallibut is in court now."

"Let him be sworn," said the chairman; and Dr. Gallibut entered the witness box. Having taken the oath, and made the usual preliminary statement, he gave a brief account of the circumstances of his attendance. The case had been a very puzzling one, the end was rather unexpected, and he had not felt justified in giving a certificate of death. The symptoms were anomalous throughout, but rather suggested the effects of an irritant poison.

"Did you observe anything that led you to suspect foul play?" the chairman asked.

"Nothing beyond the peculiar nature the symptoms."

The chairman pursed up his lips. "The arrest," he said, addressing the Chief Constable, "seems to have been rather precipitate. It would have been better to wait until the cause of death had been ascertained. However, the prisoner must now be remanded in custody. When is the inquest to be held?"

"To-morrow, your worship," said the Chief Constable.

The hours dragged out their weary length. Night melted into dawn, dawn brightened into day, the sun climbed aloft and shot its golden beams into the gaunt little room, lighting up the dusty volumes of police records on the shelves and heralding the approach of noon. At length the Chief Constable entered, and Sinclair stood up expectantly.

"Now, doctor, if you are ready we will go down," said the officer; and captor and captive went forth together.

The inquest was being held in a room in the courthouse. It was a large room, but none too large, for the whole of Hamblefield seemed to be crowded into it. Lucy and Miss Maggs had chairs near the table, and both nodded cheerfully to Sinclair as he entered with his custodian. Three of the magistrates, including the chairman, sat immediately behind the coroner, and the two doctors from Lynn, with Mrs. Wingfield and the deceased woman's solicitor, sat at the far end of the table. When Sinclair entered the jury had already been sworn, and had just returned from viewing the body. They now took their seats, and the first witness, Dr. Gallibut, was called.

He had taken the oath and made the preliminary statements when the coroner interposed. "I think, doctor," said he, "before you give your evidence in detail, there is one question that the jury would like to have answered. Have you ascertained the cause of death?"

"Yes, I have," was the confident reply.

"Have you ascertained it beyond doubt?"

"Yes; the cause of death is perfectly clear. There can be no doubt whatever."

"What was the cause of death?"

Dr. Gallibut felt in his waistcoat pocket and drew from it a small packet. He opened the packet and took from it a pill-box, which he handed to the coroner.

"The cause of Miss Daisy Morris's death, sir," he said, "is in that box."

There was a deathly silence in the room. The coroner raised the lid of the box, peered in, and then turned it upside down, when a small, sparkling object dropped on to the table.

"Bless my soul," he exclaimed, looking up at Dr. Gallibut, "it's a diamond!"

"Yes," said the witness, "it is a diamond. I may add, sir, that it is *the* diamond — the one which is supposed to have been stolen. Mrs. Wingfield identified it in my presence, and I myself tried it in the empty setting and found that it fitted."

"Astonishing!" exclaimed the coroner. "And are we to understand that the deceased — ah –"

"Swallowed the diamond?" said Dr. Gallibut. "Certainly. There can be no doubt whatever about that; and appearances suggest that she had already swallowed it when she sent for me."

There was very little more evidence given after this. The facts were as plain as anyone wished them to be and a charitable verdict of "Death from Misadventure" brought the proceedings to a close.

As soon as the verdict was given the three magistrates conferred briefly, and the chairman beckoned to the Chief Constable. The officer approached with his prisoner. "I suppose, your worship," he said, "Dr. Sinclair may now be released from custody?"

"Certainly," was the answer, "And if you, doctor, will step into the courtroom with me and my colleagues and the coroner, we will formally dismiss the charge and place the circumstances on record."

A few minutes later Sinclair went forth escorted by Lucy moist-eyed but radiant, and the faithful Maggs; and a great success the escort was — so much so that he determined to retain it permanently, and does so even unto this day. Lucy, of course, had to get rid of the ill-omened name of Morris, but Maggs is still Maggs.

Ruth

S TEPHEN CORFIELD was an artist. Some would have described him merely as a workman, by virtue of the fact that he was employed at a weekly wage — of two pounds — by a maker of stained glass windows. But we need not quarrel about names. Workman and artist are not mutually exclusive terms; and if Stephen sometimes worked at the glass itself, and even soldered the leads, his time was chiefly spent in the making of drawings from artists' designs, and in looking forward to the time when other craftsmen should execute designs of his own.

Two pounds a week is not a lordly income. But a thrifty middle-class man with ambitions generally contrives to live within his income, no matter how small it may be. Corfield was the son of a country curate, and had grown up with a full appreciation of the value of small change. The mouldy little studio with bedroom attached stood him in nine shillings a week, and answered his purpose completely. The hinterland of Albany Street is not a fashionable locality, but then Corfield himself was not a man of fashion.

Here he sat in the gloaming of an evening early in May, smoking a highly meditative pipe, and looking critically round his domain. It was not a luxurious apartment, but it was clean and tidy. Besides the two easels and the range of shelves its furniture comprised a couple of wheel-back Wycombe chairs, a table, a big cupboard, a Yorkshire dresser (for which he had "swapped" a picture), which displayed his modest outfit of crockery, and a four-fold screen painted by himself. If you had impertinently looked behind the screen you would have seen a gas ring on a shelf, a frying pan, a saucepan, a kettle and, in fact, a miniature kitchen, from which you would have gathered that Corfield's cookery, like his painting, was characterised by a broad and simple technique.

As to the subject of his meditations, an acute psychologist would have guessed easily — and guessed wrong. The "R.A." had been open a week, and in Room IX hung a decorative painting signed Stephen Corfield. It was his first exhibit at Burlington House, and he might well have been supposed to be speculating on its destiny. But he was not. His mind was occupied — and very actively, too — by an exhibit in the sculpture gallery, a little gesso panel bearing the initials "M. de W.," which inscription the catalogue amplified into "Muriel de Walden." It was but a small work, some eighteen inches by twelve, but it had captivated him at the first glance. Simple and naive, its simplicity was informed either by profound knowledge or by that infallible intuition that comes from genius alone. The exquisite pose and balance of the single, lightly draped figure, the suavity of line, the perfect spacing and setting in the background, and the fitness and beauty of the border that framed the composition, had all delighted him in turn. But it was not these alone, not only the fine sense of the convention of the material — though this appealed to him profoundly — not the masterly sureness of handling. Above and beyond its quality as a piece of faultless decoration, was a subtle emotional quality as perfect as the other. The relief showed the figure of Ruth at that moment, when far from home and kindred —

"She stood in tears amid the alien corn."

And from the little panel there exhaled a sense of sorrow and loneliness that spoke eloquently to the young artist, himself a stranger in a great city, living a lonely life in the heart of a multitude.

From the work itself his thoughts travelled — not for the first time — to its creator. The artist was a woman. Now platform folk may cackle as they will about "sex jealousy," but the fact is that for some thousands of years men and women have been very good friends, looking on one another with instinctive sympathy and kindliness: and probably the tendency is incurable. At any rate Corfield liked to know that this little masterpiece was the work of a woman. Its tenderness and grace were the more tender and graceful for the knowledge. There is nothing strange about the woman artist. A lady surgeon may be a little alarming. A lady engineer or channel pilot would be more so. But from time immemorial, pretty fingers have held the brush and modelling tool, have wielded the persuasive quill, have "waked to ecstasy" the throbbing string of lute or viol, of harp or virginal. The woman artist is an entirely gracious personage.

So Stephen Corfield, who was something of a poet, meditated on the unknown Muriel de Walden with a sentimental interest that was growing by degrees into actual tenderness. The charming mental pictures that he drew of the fair unknown had even crystallised into a number of delightful charcoal sketches (which came in very usefully later), and if, in lucid intervals, he had realised the possibility of a stout, middle-aged lady with a complete suite of double chins, he had let the interval pass, and made another yet more fascinating sketch.

Suddenly, he sprang up. A new idea had seized him. The modest price of the panel was only ten guineas — he had looked it up in the list at his last visit. Ten guineas was a good deal to him, but surely, to live always with that lovely work near him — her work — was worth — Yes, he would do it. From the shelf on which he kept his powder colours he reached down a jar labelled "Raw Umber." There were two jars with that label. This one was his bank, quite a secure one, too, for no burglar or marauding charwoman would want to steal raw umber.

He shot the contents of the jar out on the table, and counted the miscellaneous coins. Eight pounds sixteen shillings and sixpence. That represented a quarter's rent, a prospective suit of clothes and a pair of boots; and it was not enough. He swept the coins back into the jar with a grunt, replaced the jar on the shelf and retired discontentedly behind the screen to fry a mutton chop for his dinner.

On the following day, during his dinner hour, he made his customary pilgrimage to the Academy. The glass works were in Soho, near by, and a little French restaurant furnished him with a lightning repast that occupied barely a quarter of an hour. So, making use of his exhibitor's ticket, he had a full half hour in the galleries every day.

As he entered the sculpture room he perceived a lady standing before that object of his workshop, and regarding it with an air of deep reflection. Now the fact is that Corfield had kept a very sharp eye on the lady visitors to this room, conceiving naturally that the fair Muriel would surely pay her child an occasional visit to see how it fared. True, the catalogue gave her address as care of a picture dealer at Portsmouth; but still, human nature is human nature, and there are such things as railways. So he approached warily with an inquisitive eye on the lady.

She was deeply interested and very thoughtful. That would be quite natural. And she might naturally have chosen the quiet luncheon hour that she might not be observed looking at her own work. Still, there was no evidence that she was Muriel. The thing was there to be looked at and she was looking at it. Nevertheless Corfield watched her furtively — for it might be she, after all

— noted her fine profile, her stately figure and rather proud carriage; estimated her age at twenty-eight; and observed that her dress was rich to the verge of extravagance. The last item he noted with considerable distaste; and immediately — and most unreasonably — decided that she was not Muriel at all.

At this moment he caught her eye. She gave him a steady, supercilious look, and then moved away from the panel to transfer her attentions to the portrait bust of a bishop. Rather abashed by the haughty glance, and acutely conscious of his own shabby exterior, Stephen slunk through the doorway into Room IX mentally noting, however, that the proud lady did not seem to care two straws for the bishop. In Room IX he ventured to take a bashful peep at his own picture, and then browsed round, thinking of the lady in the next room. Presently, when his wanderings brought him opposite the doorway, he glanced furtively into the sculpture room, and was thrilled by the discovery that the unknown lady had returned to the panel, and was once more absorbed in its contemplation. Upon which he decided, quite unreasonably, that this must really be Muriel de Walden, after all.

It was a preposterous conclusion, and it comforted him not at all. As he hurried back to the works, with the mental picture of a rather over-dressed lady standing entranced before her own work, he was sensible of a keen disappointment. He would have scorned to stand staring at his own picture, and he disliked such egotism equally in a woman, forgetting, with absurd inconsistency, that he had made this very quality the touchstone of identification. Moreover, this superfine lady was a very different creature from the Muriel of his dreams and his charcoal sketches.

But "absence makes the heart grow fonder," and "distance lends enchantment to the view." As time went on, the chilling effect of the rich apparel and the haughty bearing faded by degrees, and only the fine profile and the graceful figure remained in his mind. By the time he had cooked his supper, and settled himself for his evening meditation, the new Muriel had fitted herself quite comfortably into the aerial castle of which he was the industrious architect. After all, he was not a mere futureless artisan. Presently his abilities would gain him a position, and then he would be a fair match for the finest of fine ladies. And meanwhile, he was keener than ever on possessing the little masterpiece that her patrician fingers had wrought.

At last came Saturday afternoon and the weekly wage. Joyfully did Stephen enter the counting house and, spreading his savings before the astonished cashier, demand and obtain a cheque for ten guineas. At headlong speed he raced down Shaftesbury Avenue, watched by suspicious policemen, and, taking the stairs three at a time, breathlessly entered the central hall of the Academy galleries. The official in charge of the price book was engaged at the moment with an elderly lady, and Stephen unavoidably heard what passed.

"Number 1647," the lady was saying — "a small gesso panel."

Stephen's blood ran cold. With a thumping heart he watched the official turn up the number, and heard him impassively state the price. Then he held his breath to listen to the words of doom.

"Ten guineas," exclaimed the lady. "It's rather a high price for such a small thing. I must just speak to my friends." She walked across to a lady and gentleman who stood by the turnstile.

It was not time for delicacy. Stephen strode up to the table and said bluntly: "I wish to purchase Number 1647, a panel by Miss de Walden."

The official hesitated and glanced at the lady.

"It isn't sold, you know," said Stephen. "My name is Stephen Corfield, and if you will oblige me by forwarding this cheque to Miss de Walden, the transaction will be closed."

With a grim smile the official entered Stephen's name against the number, but declined the cheque. "You must send that to the artist yourself," said he. "The entry in the book is evidence of purchase."

Stephen drew a deep breath, and sneaked away towards the sculpture room, and as he looked back he caught a venomous glance from the elderly lady, who had just returned to the table.

The solitary life in the mouldy little studio was not what the young artist would have chosen. But his ambitions and social prejudices kept him from making intimate of his fellow workmen; and other friends he had none. With one exception — and a very odd one. At the shop where he bought his drawing materials was a youthful apprentice, a tall slip of a girl who wore her hair in pigtail, and her skirts in an abridged edition — that was when he first met her. Since then the pigtail had changed into a bun, but the skirts still afforded a fairly complete view of a pair of shapely ankles. She was, in fact, in that stage of adolescence implied by the word "flapper."

But she was a very superior flapper. Grave and demure, and even a trifle motherly — as well-disposed flappers are apt to be towards presentable and well-behaved young men — she represented the brains of the establishment. When he asked her for charcoal paper she never advised him to try at the oil shop, as one of the older women did; nor did she offer him gilt J pens as an improved substitute for Gillot's "303." She attended to his wants intelligently, and gave him motherly advice on the subject of cheap materials. In short, Stephen decided that she was a "nice child" (he being a hoary veteran of nearly twenty-four) and patronised her accordingly — when she wasn't patronising him; and many a sheet of the Michallet that she sold him came afterwards to bear a recognisable presentment of her rather wistful face and her lissome, maidenly figure.

She lived somewhere at Kentish Town — Stephen had met her tripping homewards with a little bag, and had even on occasions obtained a cautious permission to walk a little way with her, when he would carry her bag and enrich her mind with pearls of wisdom and she would steal an occasional glance of girlish admiration at the breezy, honest young fellow by her side.

Now it befell that on the day following that of the momentous purchase; Stephen having effectually broken the Sabbath by a morning's work at his easel, fortified himself with half a loaf (which is a good deal better than no bread, if you take it all at once) and a hunk of cheese, set forth with his sketch-book for the heights of Hampstead. Joyful, though insolvent, he strode northward, recalling his letter to Miss de Walden, in which, suppressing an impulse to address her as "Dearest Muriel," he had called her merely "madam," and "begged to tender his cheque" in payment for her delightful panel, and reflecting gleefully that that priceless work was now his own. Thus, in due course, he arrived at the Vale of Health, and there, looking around with a figure-draughtsman's interest at the groups of holiday-makers, his attention was attracted by a girl who sat limply on a seat in an attitude suggestive of utter weariness. The pose was so expressive that he drew out his sketch-book and was preparing to take a flying note, when the girl turned her head — and behold! it was the flapper.

She was very pale (or "white about the gills," as Stephen expressed it to himself), and looked tired and faint, but she greeted him with a wan smile of recognition. He smuggled the sketch-book out of sight, and approached deferentially.

"You look very ill," he said.

"I'm not, " she answered. "I'm only tired. I thought I would have a day in the country, and I suppose I have walked too far — that is all."

Stephen looked at her suspiciously. He was not entirely ignorant of women's ways.

"What did you have for dinner?" he demanded.

"Well," she said, evasively, "I had some biscuits in my pocket."

Stephen snorted. "Now, isn't that like a girl — to try to do a whole day's tramp on a few biscuits."

She smiled apologetically. "I suppose it is. But girls are rather apt to be like girls, and I didn't tramp on the biscuits — I ate them."

He grinned at the retort, but persisted: "You're faint for want of a square meal. No, won't you let me take you to the 'Spaniards," and get you some tea? I wish you would."

"It's very kind of you," she said, gratefully," and I *should* like some tea — if you would let me pay for myself." At which Stephen grimaced slightly. But he saw that the girl was right — they were virtually strangers — and he agreed without demur.

So they crawled up the hill to the inn, and had a very substantial tea in the coffee-room in company with a rather wheezy piano and a very bald stuffed leopard. And the flapper revived amazingly, and became as sprightly as consisted with her habitual quiet dignity. Then they went forth and sat under Constable's firs and looked into the west. And Stephen discoursed learnedly, and the flapper listened and egged him on to talk more. Then he grew more confidential. He told her about the glass works, and his ambitions and his picture in the Academy, of which she insisted on being told the catalogue number, and then — he had only meant to coast very cautiously round the subject of his romance, but before he knew what he was saying, the cat was out of the bag. For the flapper had a very neat, feminine knack of hooking out items of information that interested her. And this interested her very much.

"What's her picture called?' she asked, innocently. But Stephen was now on his guard.

"I mustn't tell you that," said he, adding: "you see she's never heard of me, and — and, of course, it's all nonsense. I'm a sentimental idiot."

"You're not," she replied, indignantly. "It's very nice and romantic of you. Most people are so deadly prosaic and literal nowadays." She spoke as a person of experience reviewing an illimitable past.

"I think I'm rather a fool," said Stephen, "but I'm glad you don't. My only excuse is that she is a kindred spirit, and that, artistically speaking, I'm not worthy to polish her boots."

And Stephen stared into the western sky, and his companion looked at him long and thoughtfully.

A long and delightful evening they spent roaming about the Heath together, for they were really very nice young people, and very much bent on making themselves agreeable. It was only when, from the flagstaff, they had watched the sun wink into the west that they turned reluctantly homewards, to exchange ceremonious adieux in the vicinity of Chalk Farm, and go their respective ways thinking their respective thoughts.

As to Stephen, he found himself wishing that the proud Muriel had been a little more like the sweet-faced flapper, with her gentle voice, her kindly manners and her obviously clever brain. And the flapper herself walked soberly homewards thinking a little about Stephen's romance — but not very much, for she had just discovered that she had a little romance of her own to attend to.

The following Saturday was a red-letter day for Stephen, for the morning post brought him a letter at which he could only gasp in delighted amazement. It was from a wealthy manufacturer, who was building a large house, the principal rooms of which he wished to have decorated with wall paintings. "I propose," he said, "to spend fifteen hundred pounds on the walls, and, having seen your charming work in the Academy, I offer you the commission. Part of the work will have to be executed in gesso-duro, and I should like to know if you can undertake this also."

The latter question offered a difficulty for his experience of modelling was small. He ruminated on it during the morning's work in the drawing office, and when he was free, hurried away to Burlington House to study his newly acquired treasure and consider the difficulties of the medium. On his way to the sculpture galleries he called in at Room IX to glance at his own picture, which now had a new interest for him. A lady was standing before it, studying it intently — a young lady, slim and graceful, and dressed with a simple elegance that he thought very charming. As he sidled up, she stepped back a pace and looked at him, and he uttered an exclamation of surprise. It was the flapper! Only she was really a flapper no longer. The ample skirt had made an end of that stage. Now she was an elegant and rather distinguished-looking young lady, and, realising this, Stephen became uncomfortably aware of his own shabbiness.

"You didn't tell me what a lovely thing your picture was," she said.

Stephen blushed, and mumbled that "he was glad she liked it."

But she not only liked it. She entered into detailed appreciation. And thereby Stephen got a new surprise. For there is, in the speech of persons who know, an incommunicable something that is instantly recognised by others who know. Humbugs try to imitate it, and fail miserably. Now the flapper's appreciation was expressed in terms of unmistakable knowledge — not ostentatiously displayed, but unconsciously suggested. And it gave Stephen considerable food for thought.

When they had exhausted his picture she turned to him and asked in a wheedling tone:

"Won't you show me the — other picture? *Her* picture, I mean. You can trust me to respect your confidence, can't you?"

Stephen hesitated. But the thought of his changed fortunes gave him new confidence. He was not any longer a mere artisan. "Come along, then," said he, and he led her through into the sculpture room. Halting before the little panel — now his very own, for he held the agent's receipt for his cheque — he gazed at it entranced. In impassioned language he descanted on its beauties, and on the knowledge, the skill, the genius and the delightful fancy of its creator, until, chancing to look up at his companion, he stopped in confusion. The flapper's cheeks were scarlet, her eyes were downcast, and she was obviously greatly agitated. With a sudden fear that he had said something that ought not to be said before a maiden, he looked at her in dismay.

"Is anything the matter?" he asked.

"No," she answered: "at least — isn't this room rather hot and close?"

"Perhaps it is," he agreed. "Shall we go out into the air?" And, as she acquiesced, he led the way towards the entrance. In the hall she turned aside to look at the price book. He watched her with surprise as she eagerly turned over the leaves, wondering what she was seeking. Suddenly she shut the book, and walked straight to the exit. Following quickly, Stephen was astonished to perceive that her eyes were full of tears, and, as they descended the stairs, he heard her choke back a little sob. She was a most unaccountable girl.

Out in the street she recovered somewhat, but was still a little agitated and distraught; wherefore, Stephen, recalling the miraculous effect of tea on a former occasion, decided on a further trial of the remedy, and led her unresisting into the shady recesses of a tea-shop. But even here she was silent and abstracted.

"We are getting quite old friends," Stephen said, cheerfully, pushing the teapot towards her. "And," he added, "it's a ridiculous thing, you know — you have only just learned my name from the catalogue, and I don't know yours even now. Do you might telling me your name?"

She was an extraordinary girl. It was an innocent enough question, but it covered her with confusion. Once more her cheeks "were like the red, red rose," her eyes were cast down, and the bosom of her dress rose and fell with tell-tale rapidity. Stephen looked at her in amazement, and watched her with growing curiosity as she opened her little wrist-bag, took from it a card-case, drew out a card, and pushed it across the table to him. But this was nothing to his astonishment when he held the little pasteboard slip in his hand; for, legibly written on it was the familiar name, "Miss Muriel de Walden."

"So this is actually your work!" he gasped, at length.

"Yes, " she answered: "and I wanted to give it to you, but it is sold." And once more her eyes filled.

The rest of this veracious history may be briefly summarized in an extract from a letter from Sir Andrew Bing, Bart., to Mr. Stephen Corfield.

"I want to tell you how perfectly delighted I am with the charming decoration that I owe to you and your talented wife (whose father, the late Lieutenant de Walden, I may say, I had the pleasure of knowing slightly). You will be pleased to know that your joint work is universally admired by all my visitors."

Which goes to show that Stephen Corfield was not a sentimental idiot after all.

The Great Slump

IT IS not enough for the scrupulous man to practise all the virtues himself: he should inculcate the principle, "Go thou and do likewise." For just as jolly John Falstaff, though witless himself, was often "the occasion of wit in others," so a man of the strictest probity may, under unfavourable circumstances, become the occasion of dishonesty in others. Of which general truth my dealings with that rascal Phipson accord a melancholy instance.

Phipson and I together formed the complete and perfect rogue. We were the complementary parts. Phipson had the roguery, but not the wits, whereas I had the wits without the roguery. Separately we were perfectly harmless, but united we should have been a formidable ruffian. And the regrettable fact is that, in all innocence, I allowed this undesirable union to take place.

Phipson was something in the city; I don't know what, but I do know that he dabbled extensively in stocks and shares. And that was how the mischief arose.

We were talking speculation on the Stock Exchange, when I happened to remark, apropos of gambling in general: "This sort of thing is a mystery to me. A game of chance is an absurdity. You have no control over the result. You may win, or you may lose."

"Exactly," said Phipson. "That is speculation. But what's the mystery?"

"The mystery," said I "is that a man should accept the chance of losing. He doesn't want to lose, does he?"

"No, I'm blowed he does!" replied Phipson.

"Then why does he? Why does he leave the result to chance? He knows what he wants, and your gambler is not usually a man of nice scruples. Why doesn't he exercise a rational control over the results of his actions?"

"Because he can't, I suppose," said Phipson.

"Then," I replied, "he must be a fool!"

And the conversation languished for a time, while Phipson smoked his cigar and eyed me speculatively. Presently he reopened the subject.

"When you speck of exercising control," said he, "I don't quite see what you mean."

"I mean that a gambler who stands to win if a certain thing happens would take measures to ensure that it should happen."

"But," exclaimed Phipson, "how the deuce could he? Give me an example."

"Well, take this rubber boom. The prices of rubber shares may go up, or they may go down. Now supposing you sell a thousand or so, and then you arrange a slump so that the prices go down to half what they were when you sold — you'd clear fifty per cent, wouldn't you?"

"Of course you would," Phipson agreed. "Any blooming juggins can see that. Only how could you arrange that slump? It's easy to talk, but it's a mighty difficult thing to do, let me tell you."

"I don't see any difficulty in it at all," said I. "Plenty of simple plans suggest themselves. Of course, I am speaking only of what an unscrupulous gambler might do. To you and me there would be the insuperable moral difficulty. The proceeding would be dishonest, and therefore unthinkable."

"Exactly — exactly!" said Phipson. "Couldn't be thought of in practice. But — er — speaking theoretically and — er — academically, so to say — er — how do you suppose the thing could be managed?"

I leaned back in my chair, and, placing my finger-tips together, commenced oracularly:

"I take it that our intellectual jeremy-diddler would first consider the factors that determine the price of rubber. There are three. First, there is the possession by rubber of a valuable set of properties peculiar to itself; second, the great demand for a substance having those properties; third, the limited supply. Disturb any one of those factors and down goes the price of rubber immediately."

"M'yes," said Phipson. "I see that."

"Diminish the demand, increase the supply, or produce a substance of identical properties, and the rubber boom is at an end."

"M'yes," said Phipson. "I see that. But you couldn't do it, you know."

"I think you could," said I. "In fact, I am sure you could. Quite easily."

"The deuce you could!" Phipson exclaimed eagerly. "Tell me how, old chap. How would you set about it?"

"I shouldn't set about it at all." I said severely. "I hope you haven't such a poor opinion of me, Phipson."

"No, no; of course," Phipson broke in hastily. "I know you wouldn't do such a thing. I meant the other chap — the gambling covey. How do you suppose he would go about it, just as a matter of — er — academic interest, you know?"

"Well," I said, "assuming a person entirely devoid of the higher moral sentiments. I imagine he would first obtain the ear of someone connected with the daily Press. To that someone he would communicate the discovery of a perfect rubber substitute about to be patented and put on the market."

"Lord bless you," said Phipson, "the Press man wouldn't rise to that bait! It's been done a hundred times."

"And then," I continued, "he would produce samples of the new substance."

Phipson was deeply disappointed.

"My dear fellow," said he, "that has been done a thousand times. These rubber substitutes are as dead as Abraham. They're hopeless failures every time."

"I think, Phipson," I said quietly, "you are misunderstanding me. The substitute that our ingenious and immoral friend is producing is not for industrial purposes. Its functions are purely financial."

"But the Press chappie would spot the sample. He'd see that it wasn't anything like rubber."

"Excuse me Phipson," said I, "he would see nothing of the kind. The samples that our really intelligent friend would submit would be practically indistinguishable from rubber of the best quality."

"Oh!" said Phipson. "And how would you — I mean, how would he — manage that?"

And that was how the mischief began. I assure you it is a most dangerous thing for a man of high ethical principles to allow his subtle intelligence to be made use of by a person of doubtful morals In the innocence of conscious integrity, I made that fatal mistake. I answered Phipson's question.

"He would make his samples of rubber substitute of a substance that bore the closest possible resemblance in physical properties to rubber."

"Naturally," said Phipson, "but can you name any such substance?"

"Well, Phipson," said I, "I think you will agree with me that, of all the known substances in the universe, there is none that resembles rubber so closely as — rubber."

Phipson stared at me, like the fool that he was, for quite a long time; but when at last he saw the point, he dropped his cigar into the fender, and stood up with a guffaw that made the windows rattle.

"By Jove, Fox, I never thought of that! Well, I — am — jiggered!"

After that he became socially impossible. He strode up and down the room laughing like an idiot and talking incessantly about rubber, whereas I would have dismissed the subject and turned to more intellectual topics. At last, when I could stand him no longer, I cleared out.

I saw no more of Phipson for a day or two. Then, one morning, he appeared at my rooms in a state of great excitement and giggling nervously.

"I say, Fox, old man," he said, "I've got a rare bit of sport on, and I want you to come and see the fun, and lend a hand, if you will."

"What is it?" I asked a little suspiciously.

"Oh, it's just a little practical joke! Yes, I know you don't approve of practical jokes in general, but this is quite a harmless one, and it will be so deuced funny. You see, I've got a chappie who thinks he knows absolutely all there is to know about rubber, and I've pitched him a yarn about a substitute. He says all substitutes are all bosh — can't be done; but, all the same, he's coming round to my rooms tonight to hear more about it and see the samples. I thought it would be a howling joke to try him, as you suggested, with some bits of real rubber, and hear what he says. You will come and see the fun, won't you?"

I was strongly inclined to refuse. Practical jokes are anathema to me, and this looked rather a poor joke. On the other hand, the expert's remarks might prove highly entertaining, and Phipson might make an amusing ass of himself. In the end I was persuaded to go and look on at the sport, and thus, in the innocence begotten of habitual rectitude, put my head into the noose.

"And I say, Fox, old man," Phipson added as an afterthought, "I wish you'd get the samples and prepare them. You're such a neater-handed chap than I am."

In my innocence, I even agreed to this, making, however, one stipulation.

"I must have your promise that your friend shall be undeceived when you have had your little joke. There must be no permanent deception."

"Oh, that's all right, dear boy!" said Phipson. "You leave that to me. I shall see him tomorrow, and then I'll let him know how his leg has been pulled."

Here Phipson lugged out his watch, and sprang to his feet, exclaiming that he must really be off. Which made me suspect that, for some reason, he was anxious not to pursue this question further.

I carried out my promise to Phipson with my customary thoroughness. A small fount of rubber-faced type that I keep by me enabled me to produce a stamp that read: "Gullamite. Fidge's Patent." Then I went forth and purchased a Walker motor tyre, which I cut into four pieces. Two of these bore the name of Walker; the other two I stamped "Gullamite," after having given them a wash of dilute, indelible green ink. I also obtained a few large rubber bands, a finger-stall or two, a length of garden-hose, and one or two blocks of artist's rubber, all of which I treated with the green ink. excepting the finger-stalls, which were black, and the artist's rubber, which might have to be cut up, and stamped on them the magic word "Gullamite." Then I bestowed them in separate envelopes, and betook myself to Phipson's rooms.

"He hasn't come yet," said Phipson, gleefully relieving me of the 'samples' and stowing them away in a drawer, "but I'm expecting him any moment. His name is Stoggles."

"What is he?" I ventured to ask.

"He's — er — he's in the city, you know — merchant — er — corn and coals, and that sort of thing, don'tcher know." The resemblance between corn and coals was not very obvious to me, but discussion was prevented by the arrival of Mr. Stoggles himself, a strenuous and eager gentleman in spectacles, who came to the point with disconcerting promptness.

"I've been awfully interested in Phipson's account of this new rubber substitute. DO you know anything about it? Has he shown you any samples?"

"Oh yes!" said I. "I've seen the samples. Of course, I'm not an expert, but to me those samples look and feel exactly like rubber?"

"Do they indeed?" said Stoggles. "Well, I hope they may be. About half my income goes on motor tyres, so I should welcome an efficient substitute if it would bring down the prices. I should like to see those samples. I flatter myself I know something about rubber."

Here Phipson opened the drawer, and, selecting one of the pieces of motor tyre, pitched it on the table.

"What do you say to that?" said he.

Stoggles pounced on the strip of rubber, stared at it, turned it over, stared at it again, and then looked up at Phipson.

"Why," he exclaimed, "this is a piece of Walker tyre!"

"Looks like it, my boy," said Phipson, "looks like it. I could hardly tell the difference myself."

"Well, I can," said Stoggles. "This piece has got 'Walker Tyre Company' stamped on it. How's that?"

Phipson turned purple.

"Oh, I've given you the wrong piece!" he spluttered, "that one was put in for comparison. This is our stuff." And he produced one of the green stained pieces stamped with the name 'Gullamite.'

Stoggles took it from him and glared at it, comparing it with the undeniable 'Walker.'

"Gullamite, eh?" said he. "I see you've adopted the Walker pattern. Shouldn't have done that. Not that it matters. It's an excellent imitation. Best substitute I've seen. Although, mind you" — here he glared at me owlishly, and wagged the Gullamite to and fro between his fingers — "no one who really knows rubber could be deceived. To the touch of an expert finger there is, in genuine rubber, a certain something — I can't exactly say what — but something that is quite unmistakable. No expert, for instance, could possibly mistake this" — holding up the Gullamite — "for that" — holding aloft the admitted Walker.

I glanced at Phipson, who was mercifully, behind Stoggles at the moment. His face was the colour of a beetroot, and his eyes appeared to be starting from his head. Phipson was not without a sense of humour. Still, it wouldn't do to let him give the show away by laughing. Stoggles was so very amusing.

"I think," said I, "some of the other samples are more striking. Hand out some of those elastic bands. Phipson, and some of the other things."

Phipson produced the rest of the samples, and laid them before the expert, who, I could scc, was deeply impressed. H stretched the bands, put on the finger-stall, and pinched and twisted the artist's rubber.

"Surprising," said Stoggles. "To anyone but an expert it's almost like the real thing. Is it expensive to produce."

"Lor' bless you, no!" replied Phipson. "Costs next to nothing."

"And I see you've got it protected. Patent quite sound?"

"Rather!" said Phipson.

I looked at him meaningfully.

"I thought there was some little hitch about the patent," said I "and that was why we were keeping so dark at present."

Phipson looked puzzled, but murmured that "he hoped it would be all right."

"So do I," said Stoggles — "for your sake, not for my own. If this stuff could be made by anyone, the market would be flooded with it, and I could get my tyres for next to nothing. By the way, I suppose you couldn't let me take one of these samples to show our — edit — er — a friend of mine who's interested in rubber?"

Phipson looked at me quickly and rather queerly, I thought.

"Remember the patent, Phipson," said I. "If Mr. Stoggles takes a sample, he must keep it dark. No analysis or expert opinion, you know."

"I won't show it to a soul," said Stoggles, "excepting our — my friend. And I'll swear him to secrecy."

On this understanding he was allowed to cut a lump off one of the blocks of artist's rubber, and having pocketed this, he rose.

"You're going to make it bad for the rubber growers," he said, as he shook hands with Phipson.

"Rather," was the cheerful reply. "I fancy so. Hope you haven't got any shares in rubber."

Stoggles looked startled.

"N-no," he said, "I haven't. But it might be worth while to — er — to –"
He didn't finish the sentence, but, shaking hands with me abstractedly, walked out of the room in deep thought.

"He gorged the bait properly," Phipson remarked gleefully as the street door slammed.

"Yes, he has," I agreed. "But it hardly seems fair to let him go away possessed with this delusion. Shall I run after him and undeceive him?"

"Lord no!" gasped Phipson. "You'd upset all my — all my — spoil the joke, you know. You leave it to me, dear boy; I'll see him in the morning. That'll be all right. Have a cigar? Have some whisky? Glass of Port, Chartreuse, Benedictine?"

I've never known Phipson to be so hospitable.

I took a cigar, and then I took my leave to walk home and smilingly recall the expert pronouncements of Mr. Stoggles. It had been very amusing, though it was hardly kind of Phipson to pull the poor fellow's leg to that extent. And at this point I began to have misgivings. Was Phipson really acting on the square, and would he fulfil his promise to undeceive Stoggles?

At intervals during the night these misgivings recurred and kept me wakeful; in the morning they revived, and were with me as I shaved, took a bath, and breakfasted. Finally, they became so acute as to impel me to withdraw from my despatch-box a sheaf of securities representing my entire capital of three hundred and twenty pounds, and hurry away Citywards with the whole bundle in my pocket. My stockbroker, Mr. Edmondton Abbott, resided in Adam's Court, and oddly enough, chance or blind instinct led me almost to his very door. Almost, but not quite, for as I turned into the court a gentleman emerged from Abbott's doorway and stopped to light a cigarette — a gentleman in spectacles. Stoggles, by the living Jingo!

I stepped back into Broad Street, and let him pass out of the court. Then I returned, and boldly entered the office.

When I stated my business to Mr. Abbott, he was astonished.

"What! Another!" he exclaimed.

"Another what?"

"Another philanthropist who wants to make some poor jobber a present of two or three hundred pounds. I've just finished with one, and he'll lose his money. So will you. Rubber shares are steadily rising. It's madness to sell just now."

"I don't care," said I, "I'm going to sell. And I'd like the deal settled now. I'll leave these securities with you for cover."

Mr. Abbott rubbed his hair until his silvery forelock stood up like the crest of a white cockatoo. He was very disapproving. But he stowed my securities in his safe, and consented to walk round with me to the house, outside which I waited while he transacted the deal. Presently he reappeared, putting out his cheeks and shaking his head, to announce sadly that the deed was done.

"I've sold a thousand at the highest point they have yet touched, but you will probably lose heavily if the rise continues at the same pace. By the way, do you propose to deliver the shares or carry over?"

"Oh," I said, "I shan't carry over!"

Whereupon Mr. Abbott breathed a sigh of relief, and left me.

In the smoking-room of my club — the members of which are mostly retired Civil Servants — the conversation had, for the last few weeks, focused itself on the subject of rubber to an extent that had maddened me. And so it was on this eventful afternoon. Those wretched men — every one of them with a good fat pension — could think and talk of nothing but their miserable, sordid investments. Suddenly there danced into the room a small, puffy, elderly man, very pale as to his face, and grasping in his trembling hand a copy of *The Evening Comet.*

"Great Caesar!" he gasped. "Have you seen the news?"

There was an expectant silence, and he continued:

"There's a new rubber substitute just going to be floated; a perfect substitute — just like the real thing, and cheap as dirt; and rubber shares are dropping like a burst balloon!"

With one accord the smokers leaped to their feet. There was a wild stampede to the door. I sauntered out into the hall, and a moment later the men flew past me with hats awry, wriggling into their overcoats as they went. A hansom stood at the kerb, and as the leading fugitive sprang in I heard him shout to the cabby to drive like the devil to Throgmorton Street.

I only saw Phipson once in those four days, and then he didn't see me, for his eyes were glued to a couple of posters outside a newspaper shop. One of the posters bore the words "The Great Slump," and the other, "Collapse of the Rubber Boom."

I did not call on Abbott until the day before the account. He met me with a foxy smile and a faint trembling of the left eyelid.

"I shall write your cheque to-morrow," said he. "Three thousand six hundred and fifty. The labourer is worthy of his hire." (I don't know what he meant.) "Is there any other little commission I can execute for you?"

"Yes, there is," said I. "My capital is now a little more substantial than it was. I think of investing it in a bull. A large bull. An Assyrian bull. A bull of Bashan!"

"Rubber?" inquired Abbott.

"Rubber!" I replied.

Again his left eyelid quivered, and he reached down for his hat.

"You'd like the transaction completed now, I suppose?" he suggested; and as I replied that I should, we set forth together for the House.

And as I left the vicinity of the Stock Exchange I was conscious of a warm glow of satisfaction. I had bought three thousand shares at "bed-rock" prices. But it was not that which caused the glow. Not at all. What really filled me with elation was the thought that I was about to make restitution. It was clear to me that Phipson had failed to keep his promise. He had not undeceived Stoggles after all. Hence this disastrous slump.

But Stoggles should be enlightened. I had been an innocent party to the fraud; on me lay the duty of applying the remedy. And that duty I would faithfully discharge.

My suspicions led me to the office of *The Evening Comet*, and there, sure enough, I found Stoggles, writing furiously on a pad. He was rather preoccupied at first, but I soon secured his attention. In fact, at the word "hoax" he nearly fell off his stool.

"I should like to have a few words with Mr. Phipson," he said viciously, when I had laid all the facts — all the important facts, that is — before him.

"Well, you know where he lives," said I.

"I know where he lived," Stoggles corrected. "His landlady told me this morning that he had gone abroad for a week or so."

"At any rate," said I, "you have the facts now, and you have a bit of Gullamite to analyze if you want to. Your duty to the public is obvious."

"I know," groaned Stoggles. "But I shall look such an infernal fool!"

It was about a week later that I encountered Phipson, prowling disconsolately down Throgmorton Street. I was inclined to be stiffer.

"Look here, Fox," said he, "I've had enough of you!"

"Indeed!" said I.

"Yes. You're a clever chap in your way, I dare say; in fact, you're a sight too clever!"

"Why, what's amiss now?" I asked.

"I'll tell you," he replied savagely. "On the strength of what we told Stoggles — knowing him to be on the *Comet* — I sold four thousand shares."

"Well," said I, "it was very dishonest of you. But you must have made a good sum on the differences — didn't you?"

"Of course I did," he almost blabbered.

"But look at the prices now! They've bounced up higher than ever. And they're still rising!"

I stared at Phipson in amazement. For a moment I was unable to fathom his meaning. Then his stupendous folly dawned on me.

The idiot had sold his four thousand, raked in the differences at the settlement, and then — oh, incredible imbecility! — had carried over instead of closing while there was a profit.

I cleared about eight thousand over that deal. As to Phipson, he shortly afterwards "went through the hoop."

Essays and True Crime

The Art of the Detective Story

THE STATUS in the world of letters of that type of fiction which finds its principal motive in the unravelment of crimes or similar intricate mysteries presents certain anomalies. By the critic and the professedly literary person the detective story — to adopt the unprepossessing name by which this class of fiction is now universally known — is apt to be dismissed contemptuously as outside the pale of literature, to be conceived of as a type of work produced by half-educated and wholly incompetent writers for consumption by office boys, factory girls, and other persons devoid of culture and literary taste.

That such works are produced by such writers for such readers is an undeniable truth: but in mere badness of quality the detective story holds no monopoly. By similar writers and for similar readers there are produced love stories, romances, and even historical tales of no better quality. But there is this difference: that, whereas the place in literature of the love story or the romance has been determined by the consideration of the masterpieces of each type, the detective story appears to have been judged by its failures. The status of the whole class has been fixed by an estimate formed from inferior samples.

What is the explanation of this discrepancy? Why is it that, whereas a bad love story or romance is condemned merely on its merits as a defective specimen of a respectable class, a detective story is apt to be condemned without trial in virtue of some sort of assumed original sin? The assumption as to the class of reader is manifestly untrue. There is no type of fiction that is more universally popular than the detective story. It is a familiar fact that many famous men have found in this kind of reading their favourite recreation, and that it is consumed with pleasure, and even with enthusiasm, by many learned and intellectual men, not infrequently in preference to any other form of fiction.

This being the case, I again ask for an explanation of the contempt in which the whole genus of detective fiction is held by the professedly literary.

Clearly, a form of literature which arouses the enthusiasm of men of intellect and culture can be affected by no inherently base quality. It cannot be foolish, and is unlikely to be immoral. As a matter of fact, it is neither. The explanation is probably to be found in the great proportion of failures; in the tendency of the tyro and the amateur perversely to adopt this difficult and intricate form for their apprentice efforts; in the crude literary technique often associated with otherwise satisfactory productions; and perhaps in the falling off in quality of the work of regular novelists when they experiment in this department of fiction, to which they may be adapted neither by temperament nor by training.

Thus critical judgment has been formed, not on what the detective story can be and should be, but on what it too frequently was in the past when crudely and incompetently done. Unfortunately, this type of work is still prevalent; but it is not representative. In late years there has arisen a new school of writers who, taking the detective story seriously, have set a more exacting standard, and whose work, admirable alike in construction and execution, probably accounts for the recent growth in popularity of this class of fiction. But, though representative, they arc a minority; and it is still true that a detective story which fully develops the distinctive qualities proper to its genus, and is, in addition, satisfactory in diction, in background treatment, in characterization, and in general literary workmanship, is probably the rarest of all forms of fiction.

The rarity of good detective fiction is to be explained by a fact which appears to be little recognized either by critics or by authors; the fact, namely, that a completely executed detective story is a very difficult and highly technical work, a work demanding in its creator the union of qualities which, if not mutually antagonistic, are at least seldom met with united in a single individual. On the one hand, it is a work of imagination, demanding the creative, artistic faculty; on the other, it is a work of ratiocination, demanding the power of logical analysis and subtle and acute reasoning; and, added to these inherent qualities, there must be a somewhat extensive outfit of special knowledge. Evidence alike of the difficulty of the work and the failure to realize it is furnished by those occasional experiments of novelists of the orthodox kind which have been referred to, experiments which commonly fail by reason of a complete misunderstanding of the nature of the work and the qualities that it should possess.

A widely prevailing error is that a detective story needs to be highly sensational. It tends to be confused with the mere crime story, in which the incidents — tragic, horrible, even repulsive — form the actual theme, and the quality aimed at is horror — crude and pungent sensationalism. Here the writer's object is to make the reader's flesh creep; and since that reader has probably, by a course of similar reading, acquired a somewhat extreme degree of obtuseness, the violence of the means has to be progressively increased in proportion to the insensitiveness of the subject. The sportsman in the juvenile verse sings:

I shoot the hippopotamus with bullets made of platinum
Because if I use leaden ones his hide is sure to flatten 'em;

and that, in effect, is the position of the purveyor of gross sensationalism. His purpose is, at all costs, to penetrate his reader's mental epidermis, to the density of which he must needs adjust the weight and velocity of his literary projectile.

Now no serious author will complain of the critic's antipathy to mere sensationalism. It is a quality that is attainable by the least gifted writer and acceptable to the least critical reader; and, unlike the higher qualities of literature, which beget in the reader an increased receptiveness and more subtle appreciation, it creates, as do drugs and stimulants, a tolerance which has to be met by an increase of the dose. The entertainments of the cinema have to be conducted on a scale of continually increasing sensationalism. The wonders that thrilled at first become commonplace, and must be reinforced by marvels yet more astonishing. Incident must be piled on incident, climax on climax, until any kind of construction becomes impossible. So, too, in literature. In the newspaper serial of the conventional type, each instalment of a couple of thousand words, or less, must wind up with a thrilling climax, blandly ignored at the opening of the next instalment; while that *ne plus ultra* of wild sensationalism, the film novel, in its extreme form is no more than a string of astonishing incidents, unconnected by any intelligible scheme, each incident an independent "thrill," unexplained, unprepared for, devoid alike of antecedents and consequences.

Some productions of the latter type are put forth in the guise of detective stories, with which they apparently tend to be confused by some critics. They are then characterized by the presentation of a crime — often in impossible circumstances which are never accounted for followed by a vast amount of rushing to and fro of detectives or unofficial investigators in motor cars, aeroplanes, or motor boats, with a liberal display of revolvers or automatic pistols and a succession of hair-raising adventures. If any conclusion is reached, it is quite unconvincing, and the interest of the story to its appropriate reader is in the incidental matter, and not in the plot. But the application of the term "detective story" to works of this kind is misleading, for in the essential qualities of the type of fiction properly so designated they are entirely deficient. Let us now consider what those qualities are.

The distinctive quality of a detective story, in which it differs from all other types of fiction, is that the satisfaction that it offers to the reader is primarily an intellectual satisfaction. This is not to say that it need be deficient in the other qualities appertaining to good fiction: in grace of diction, in humour, in interesting characterization, in picturesqueness of setting or in emotional presentation. On the contrary, it should possess all these qualities. It should be an interesting story, well and vivaciously told. But whereas in other fiction these are the primary, paramount qualities, in detective fiction they are secondary and subordinate to the intellectual interest, to which they must be, if necessary, sacrificed. The entertainment that the connoisseur looks for is an exhibition of mental gymnastics in which be is invited to take part; and the excellence of the entertainment must be judged by the completeness with which it satisfies the expectations of the type of reader to whom it is addressed.

Thus, assuming that good detective fiction must be good fiction in general terms, we may dismiss those qualities which it should possess in common with all other works of imagination and give our attention to those qualities in which it differs from them and which give to it its special character. I have said that the satisfaction which it is designed to yield to the reader is primarily intellectual; and we may now consider in somewhat more detail the exact nature of the satisfaction demanded and the way in which it can best be supplied. And first we may ask: What are the characteristics of the representative reader? To what kind of person is a carefully constructed detective story especially addressed?

We have seen that detective fiction has a wide popularity. The general reader, however, is apt to be uncritical. He reads impartially the bad and the good, with no very clear perception of the difference, at least in the technical construction. The real connoisseurs, who avowedly prefer this type of fiction to all others, and who read it with close and critical attention, are to be found among men of the definitely intellectual class: theologians, scholars, lawyers, and to a less extent, perhaps, doctors and men of science. judging by the letters which I have received from time to time, the enthusiast *par excellence* is the clergyman of a studious and scholarly habit.

Now the theologian, the scholar and the lawyer have a common characteristic: they are all men of a subtle type of mind. They find a pleasure in intricate arguments, in dialectical contests, in which the matter to be proved is usually of less consideration than the method of proving it. The pleasure is yielded by the argument itself and tends to be proportionate to the intricacy of the proof. The disputant enjoys the mental exercise, just as a muscular man enjoys particular kinds of physical exertion. But the satisfaction yielded by an argument is dependent upon a strict conformity with logical methods, upon freedom from fallacies of reasoning, and especially upon freedom from any ambiguities as to the data.

By schoolboys, street-corner debaters, and other persons who are ignorant of the principles of discussion, debates are commonly conducted by means of what we may call "argument by assertion." Each disputant seeks to overwhelm his opponent by pelting him with statements of alleged fact, each of which the other disputes, and replies by discharging a volley of counter-statements, the truth of which is promptly denied. Thus the argument collapses in a chaos of conflicting assertions. The method of the skilled dialectician is exactly the opposite of this. He begins by making sure of the matter in dispute and by establishing agreement with his adversary on the fundamental data. Theological arguments are usually based upon propositions admitted as true by both parties; and the arguments of counsel are commonly concerned, not with questions of fact, but with the consequences deducible from evidence admitted equally by both sides.

Thus the intellectual satisfaction of an argument is conditional on the complete establishment of the data. Disputes on questions of fact are of little, if any, intellectual interest; but in any case an argument — an orderly train of reasoning — cannot begin until the data have been clearly set forth and agreed upon by both parties. This very obvious truth is continually lost sight of by authors. Plots, i.e. arguments, are frequently based upon alleged "facts" — physical, chemical, and other — which the educated reader knows to be untrue, and of which the untruth totally invalidates conclusions drawn from them and thus destroys the intellectual interest of the argument.

The other indispensable factor is freedom from fallacies of reasoning. The conclusion must emerge truly and inevitably from the premises; it must be the only possible conclusion, and must leave the competent reader in no doubt as to its unimpeachable truth.

It is here that detective stories most commonly fail. They tend to be pervaded by logical fallacies, and especially by the fallacy of the undistributed middle term. The conclusion reached by the gifted investigator, and offered by him as inevitable, is seen by the reader to be merely one of a number of possible alternatives. The effect when the author's "must have been" has to be corrected by the reader into "might have been" is one of anti-climax. The promised and anticipated demonstration paters out into a mere suggestion; the argument is left in the air, and the reader is balked of the intellectual satisfaction which he was seeking.

Having glanced at the nature of the satisfaction sought by the reader, we may now examine the structure of a detective story and observe the means employed to furnish that satisfaction. On the general fictional qualities of such a story we need not enlarge excepting to contest the prevalent belief that detective fiction possesses no such qualities. Apart from a sustained love interest — for which there is usually no room — a detective novel need not, and should not, be inferior in narrative interest or literary workmanship to any other work of fiction. Interests which conflict with the main theme and hinder its clear exposition are evidently inadmissible; but humour, picturesque setting, vivid characterization and even emotional episodes are not only desirable on aesthetic grounds, but, if skilfully used, may be employed to distract the reader's attention at critical moments in place of the nonsensical "false clues" and other exasperating devices by which writers too often seek to confuse the issues. *The Mystery of Edwin Drood* shows us the superb fictional quality that is possible in a detective story from the band of a master.

Turning now to the technical side, we note that the plot of a detective novel is, in effect, an argument conducted under the guise of fiction. But it is a peculiar form of argument. The problem having been stated, the data for its solution are presented inconspicuously and in a sequence purposely dislocated so as to conceal their connexion; and the reader's task is to collect the data, to rearrange them in their correct logical sequence and ascertain their relations, when the solution of the problem should at once become obvious. The construction thus tends to fall into four stages: (1) statement of the problem; (2) production of the data for its solution ("clues"); (3) the discovery, i.e. completion of the inquiry by the investigator and declaration by him of the solution; (4) proof of the solution by an exposition of the evidence.

1. The problem is usually concerned with a crime, not because a crime is an attractive subject, but because it forms the most natural occasion for an investigation of the kind required. For the same reason — suitability — crime against the person is more commonly adopted than crime against property; and murder — actual, attempted or suspected — is usually the most suitable of all. For the villain is the player on the other side; and since we want him to be a desperate player, the stakes must be appropriately high. A capital crime gives us an adversary who is playing for his life, and who consequently furnishes the best subject for dramatic treatment.

2. The body of the work should be occupied with the telling of the story in the course of which the data, or "clues," should be produced as inconspicuously as possible, but clearly and without ambiguity in regard to their essentials. The author should be scrupulously fair in his conduct of the game. Each card as it is played should be set down squarely, face upwards, in full view of the reader. Under no circumstances should there be any deception as to the facts. The reader should be quite clear as to what be may expect as true. In stories of the older type, the middle action is filled out with a succession of false clues and with the fixing of suspicion first on one character, then on another, and again on a third, and so on. The clues are patiently followed, one after another, and found to lead nowhere. There is feverish activity, but no result. All this is wearisome to the reader and is, in my opinion, bad technique. My practice is to avoid false clues entirely and to depend on keeping the reader occupied with the narrative. If the ice should become uncomfortably thin, a dramatic episode will distract the reader's attention and carry him safely over the perilous spot. Devices to confuse and mislead the reader are bad practice. They deaden the interest, and they are quite unnecessary; the reader can always be trusted to mislead himself, no matter how plainly the data are given. Some years ago I devised, as an

experiment, an inverted detective story in two parts.[1] The first part was a minute and detailed description of a crime, setting forth the antecedents, motives, and all attendant circumstances. The reader had seen the crime committed, knew all about the criminal, and was in possession of all the facts. It would have seemed that there was nothing left to tell. But I calculated that the reader would be so occupied with the crime that he would overlook the evidence. And so it turned out. The second part, which described the investigation of the crime, had to most readers the effect of new matter. All the facts were known; but their evidential quality had not been recognized.

This failure of the reader to perceive the evidential value of facts is the foundation on which detective fiction is built. It may generally be taken that the author may exhibit his facts fearlessly provided only that he exhibits them separately and unconnected. And the more boldly he displays the data, the greater will be the intellectual interest of the story. For the tacit understanding of the author with the reader is that the problem is susceptible of solution by the latter by reasoning from the facts given; and such solution should be actually possible. Then the data should be produced as early in the story as is practicable. The reader should have a body of evidence to consider while the tale is telling. The production of a leading fact near the end of the book is unfair to the reader, while the introduction of capital evidence — such as that of an eye-witness — at the extreme end is radically bad technique, amounting to a breach of the implied covenant with the reader.

3. The "discovery," i.e. the announcement by the investigator of the conclusion reached by him, brings the inquiry formally to an end. It is totally inadmissible thereafter to introduce any new matter. The reader is given to understand that he now has before him the evidence and the conclusion, and that the latter is contained in the former. If it is not, the construction has failed, and the reader has been cheated. The "discovery" will usually come as a surprise to the reader and will thus form the dramatic climax of the story, but it is to be noted that the dramatic quality of the climax is strictly dependent on the intellectual conviction which accompanies it. This is frequently overlooked, especially by general novelists who experiment in detective fiction. In their eagerness to surprise the reader, they forget that he has also to be convinced. A literary friend of mine, commenting on a

---

[1] "The Case of Oscar Brodski."

particularly conclusive detective story, declared that "rigid demonstration destroyed the artistic effect." But the rigid demonstration was the artistic effect. The entire dramatic effect of the climax of a detective story is due to the sudden recognition by the reader of the significance of a number of hitherto uncomprehended facts; or if such recognition should not immediately occur, the effect of the climax becomes suspended until it is completed in the final stage.

4. Proof of the solution. This is peculiar to "detective" construction. In all ordinary novels, the climax, or denouement, finishes the story, and any continuation is anti-climax. But a detective story has a dual character. There is the story, with its dramatic interest, and enclosed in it, so to speak, is the logical problem; and the climax of the former may leave the latter apparently unsolved. It is then the duty of the author, through the medium of the investigator, to prove the solution by an analysis and exposition of the evidence. He has to demonstrate to the reader that the conclusion emerged naturally and reasonably from the facts known to him, and that no other conclusion was possible.

If it is satisfactorily done, this is to the critical reader usually the most interesting part of the book; and it is the part by which he — very properly — judges the quality of the whole work. Too often it yields nothing but disappointment and a sense of anti-climax. The author is unable to solve his own problem. Acting on the pernicious advice of the pilot in the old song to "Fear not, but trust in Providence," he has piled up his mysteries in the hope of being able to find a plausible explanation; and now, when he comes to settle his account with the reader, his logical assets are nil. What claims to be a demonstration turns out to be a mere specious attempt to persuade the reader that the inexplicable has been explained; that the fortunate guesses of an inspired investigator are examples of genuine reasoning. A typical instance of this kind of anti-climax occurs in Poe's *Murders in the Rue Morgue* when Dupin follows the unspoken thoughts of his companion and joins in at the appropriate moment. The reader is astonished and marvels how such an apparently impossible feat could have been performed. Then Dupin explains; but his explanation is totally unconvincing, and the impossibility remains. The reader has had his astonishment for nothing. It cannot be too much emphasized that to the critical reader the quality in a detective story which takes precedence of all orders is conclusiveness. It is the quality which, above all others, yields that intellectual satisfaction that the reader seeks; and it is the quality which is the most difficult to attain, and which costs more than any other in care and labour to the author.

The Cleverest Crime in Fact or Fiction: Foiled by a Hat

SINCE the mere killing of a human being usually presents little difficulty and demands but little ingenuity, the cleverness of a murder must be judged by the efficiency of the measures taken by the murderer to conceal his connection with the death. Of such measures, the most effective are those which conceal the fact of the murder; which produce the appearance of death from natural causes. For thereby are avoided, not only the almost insuperable difficulties of disposing of the body, but also the incalculable possibilities of an inquest in a case of murder.

It is difficult to judge how far in real life these conditions of safety have been fulfilled. The murders which are recorded are the murders which have been recognized as such, and in most of them the criminals have been discovered. But murders, like other human achievements, cannot be fairly estimated in terms of their failures. A perfectly successful murder would pass unrecognized and unrecorded; and when we recall the numerous cases, characterized by the crudest and stupidest methods, which have only, at long last, been brought to light through idiotic repetitions, we cannot avoid an uncomfortable suspicion that many an innocent-looking grave guards the secret of an unrecorded murder.

Of the murders actually recorded, few would satisfy the most modest demands of the detective story-writer, who must needs invent his own crimes owing to the incapacity of the real criminal. The sensational murder trial, which thrills the newspaper public, would read but flatly if translated into fiction. The methods even of famous murderers are commonly crude and even foolish, and the gross and palpable traces that they leave can be followed by the most obvious and commonplace means. Indeed, on the whole of my reading — with some experience as a prison medical officer — I have met with but a single case which seemed to be worth using as fiction; the one upon which was founded my story of "The Case of Oscar Brodski." And

335

even this case was selected less for its ingenuity of plan than for the excellent opening that it offered for the medico-legal investigation. The following is a summary of the case, "Reg. *v.* Watson and Wife" (Notts Lent Assizes, 1867).

The prisoners, who inhabited a cottage abutting on a railway line, planned to murder a man named Raynor and to conceal the crime by means of a fictitious railway accident. Accordingly, the victim was enticed to the cottage and there murdered by manual strangulation — throttling. Then, just before the time at which a train was due to pass the house, the body was dragged down to the railway, lifted over a gate, and laid across the rails.

So much for the plan; and, simple as it was, if it had been completely carried out it would almost certainly have succeeded. All of the traces of the murder — the finger-marks on the throat and the conditions of the heart, lungs, and brain — would have been obliterated by the mutilation that the train would have produced in passing over the body.

What actually happened was what usually does happen. The murderers had sketched out the crime, but had not filled in the details. They had "gone nap" on the one chance and had made no provision against its failure; and in their haste they had forgotten, until too late, to place the victim's hat on the line. But the main chance failed. The expected train was late, and in the interval the body was seen by a porter and removed. Then, of course, the murder was out; and a smear of blood on the top bar of the gate, marks of dragging and recognizable foot-prints in the soft clay, connected the body with the cottage. There, bloodstains and other traces of the crime were discovered, including the charred remains of the missing hat. And thus the Providence which watches over murderers — with no benevolent eye — intervened once more to play upon the murderer's calculations the trump card of the incalculable.

The Peasenhall Mystery

HE DIFFICULTY of attempting to solve the "unsolved mysteries" of the past is that you have to work from the facts recorded; and they are usually the wrong facts. But they are all you have. You can't cross-examine a law report.

A criminal trial is not an inquiry into the whole set of circumstances. It is concerned with the specific issue: "Was this crime committed by the prisoner at the Bar?" And if the verdict is that it was not, and no one else is charged, the problem is left in the air with no recorded facts but those that were found insufficient to solve it.

The Peasenhall Mystery illustrates this. Several of the crucial facts are not available. The recorded evidence is concerned with the guilt or innocence of the prisoner at the Bar. No other issues are dealt with, and the facts bearing on those issues have to be inferred.

The case was concerned with the death of Rose Harsent, the pretty and attractive maid-servant of a most respectable couple named Crisp, who lived in an ancient dwelling known as Providence House, in a Suffolk village named Peasenhall. The maid's quarters were, in effect, a self-contained tenement, for her bedroom was over the kitchen and communicated with it by its own little staircase. A door led from the kitchen into the rest of the house, but at night, when that door was shut, the maid's premises were quite isolated.

It was a bad arrangement, for the back door of the house opened into the kitchen; so that the maid could receive nocturnal visitors without fear of disturbance. And this is what she appears to have been in the habit of doing, as was made evident in the course of the trial. Nor did her proceedings pass unsuspected, for, long before the date of the tragedy, the village of Peasenhall seethed with gossip and scandal concerning her and her lovers.

Thus the stage was very effectively set for the tragedy that was presently to be enacted. The curtain was rung up on a certain Saturday afternoon at the end of May, 1902, when Rose received a letter in a yellow envelope beating the postmark of a neighbouring village and a date of the same day. Its contents were as follows:

"Dear R. — I will try to see you to-night at 12 o'clock at your place. If you put a light in your window at ten for about ten minutes, then you can put it out again. Do not have a light in your room at 12, as I will come round the back way."

Let us follow events in the order of their occurrence. It is known that the signal light appeared in the girl's window about ten o'clock that night and, after a short interval, was extinguished; and it is noted that a violent thunderstorm was raging at the time. The noise of the rain and thunder roused Mrs. Crisp from her sleep, and amid the din of the storm she thought that she heard, faintly and indistinctly, what seemed to her like the sound of a fall, accompanied by a cry, and the breaking of glass. Shortly afterwards she heard the church clock strike twelve.

On the following morning — Sunday — Rose's father, William Harsent, who was a milk roundsman, came to the kitchen door to deliver the milk. He knocked several times, and then, getting no answer, looked in at the window. To his horror, he saw his daughter lying on the floor.

Thereupon he ran round to the front of the house and battered on the door until Mr. Crisp came down. On hearing the news he, with Harsent, hurried through the house to the kitchen, and there they found the girl lying dead at the foot of the bedroom stairs. She was in her nightdress, which was partly burnt. On the floor, which was flooded with oil, lay the fragments of a broken lamp, an overturned candlestick, a broken medicine bottle, and a newspaper.

The bottle bore a label on which was written: "Mrs. Gardiner's Child." And mingling with the oil on the floor was a pool of blood which had flowed from a wound in the girl's throat and from an irregular, jagged wound in the breast.

The inquest seems to have thrown little light on the mystery. The cause of death was obvious enough, and the time of it was judged to be about midnight on Saturday.

Wilful murder was assumed from the first, but the question was: Who was the murderer? It was ascertained that the girl had had several lovers, two of whom volunteered the information. But the police investigations showed at once that they could all be eliminated as suspects.

As none of the known lovers could be suspected, the police looked round eagerly for a possible murderer, and eventually fixed upon an eminently respectable master-craftsman named William Gardiner. It seems to have been entirely a matter of guess-work; for Gardiner was a man of excellent character and reputation, was happily married and a good father to several children. However, there was no one else, so the police proceeded to prosecute.

Eventually, at the Suffolk Autumn Assizes, 1902, he was brought to trial before Mr. Justice Grantham. The leader for the Crown was Mr. Henry Dickens, K.C., and the counsel for the defence was Mr. Ernest Wild, whose great reputation may be said to have been founded on his brilliant conduct of this case.

The evidence produced by the prosecution was undeniably formidable. That the signal light in Rose's window could be seen from Gardiner's house was proved by a witness who stood talking with the accused at his cottage door about ten o'clock on the night of the murder and had seen the light.

A gamekeeper named Morris who had passed Providence House after the storm deposed to having seen footprints leading from the kitchen door to the road that passed Gardiner's cottage. The footprints showed the impressions of rubber soles similar in pattern to a pair in Gardiner's possession.

There was the evidence of the bottle with Gardiner's name on the label, a blood-stained knife found by the police in his house, and the fact that the envelope of the letter making the assignation was of the same kind as those used by the firm who employed the accused. The handwriting of the letter was also said to be similar to his, but this was not clearly proved.

The theory of the prosecution — largely built up on conjecture — was this: They suggested that the accused had compromised himself badly with this girl and, as she was now pregnant, grave scandals loomed ahead. The only way out was to get rid of her, and it was to this end that he had made this assignation. On the fatal Saturday night he had set forth taking with him the knife, the bottle filled with paraffin, and the newspaper with which to start a fire. This theory was supported by the evidence, and a deadly case against him seemed to have been made out.

But as the defence disposed of one after another of the items of incriminating evidence, this theory became untenable. There was no evidence of any improper relations between the accused and the deceased. The bottle was one which had contained some liniment which the prisoner's wife had given to deceased. The knife had been used by her to gut some rabbits for the Sunday dinner.

The newspaper had been in the prisoner's possession on the Sunday morning. And, finally, at the very time of the tragedy, the prisoner was sitting — according to his wife's statement — in the bedroom, nursing an ailing child. There was a complete alibi.

In the end, the jury disagreed. There was a second trial, and again the jury disagreed; and, as public opinion was by this time strongly in favour of Gardiner, the Home Secretary decided against a third trial.

Thus, the accused was innocent, and as no one else was even suspected, the mystery remained, and still remains, unsolved. What really happened on that stormy night in the kitchen of the old house is a matter of speculation to this day.

Is it possible to construct a reasonable theory? A definite conclusion is impossible since certain vital facts are lacking. We can only re-examine those which are available. When the body was found it was instantly assumed that the girl had been murdered. No alternative seems to have been considered. But was she murdered? Long afterwards a clergyman suggested the possibility of an accident. Let us see whether the known facts will bear that interpretation.

We now that a little before midnight this girl, either in response to a signal or in anticipation of the arrival of her visitor, came down the little flight of stairs to the kitchen. We have seen those cottage staircases, with their steep, narrow, twisting stairs enclosed in a sort of high cupboard, and no hand-rail.

As she came down she carried in one hand a lamp and in the other a lighted candle, and, in addition, she was carrying the bottle and the newspaper. She was thus inconveniently burdened; and if we bear in mind the storm — the lightning and the alarming crashes of thunder — and the fact that it was the dead of night, and that she was on an unlawful errand, we may feel sure that she was considerably agitated.

Now let us suppose that as she was descending those break-neck stairs with both her hands full something happened to startle her. It might have been a sudden crash of thunder or, jammed up as she was in the narrow stairway, the candle might have set fire to her nightdress.

In any case, she might easily have slipped. Then as she fell with a scream headlong down the stairs, she flung away the lamp to free her hands and came down on the shattered fragments or on the broken bottle, the jagged edges of which inflicted the wounds that were found. If her nightdress was not already alight, the overturned, lighted candle would probably have ignited the paraffin which had splashed up from the shattered lamp.

How does this suggestion square with the known facts? There seems to be considerable agreement. We can only argue the probabilities; thus:

1. Were the wounds such as might have been made by broken glass, or were they characteristic knife wounds? Now, the wound in the breast was described as irregular and jagged. This is strongly suggestive of a broken bottle or lamp chimney. But if one wound was a glass wound that establishes a probability that the other was, too.

2. Was the kitchen door fastened? If it was, that would seem to exclude the possibility of a murderer having entered; for he could not have bolted it after him when he fled. But the behaviour of William Harsent suggests that it was bolted. For, surely, when he saw through the window his daughter lying on the floor, he would have rushed in to see what had happened to her if that had been possible. Instead of which he ran round to the front of the house and battered on the door until Mr. Crisp came down; suggesting that the front door also was fastened.

3. Were there any muddy footprints on the kitchen floor? If there were not, that is strongly against anyone having entered. For it was stated that the roads were deep in mud. But from the other evidence we may fairly infer that there were none. For there was considerable conflict of evidence concerning footprints said to have been seen leading from the door to the road. But if there had been footprints inside the kitchen any outside would have had little significance.

Thus the known facts seem to be quite reconcilable with the theory of accident, and no other explanation has ever been offered. Whether the unknown writer of the letter came to keep his tryst, or whether he was kept away by the storm, we shall never know. But the evidence concerning the footprints outside suggests that he did come. And if he did, the events of that night must have been somewhat thus.

The Unknown came to the door just before midnight, made the signal and stood in the pelting rain awaiting the response. He sees a glimmer in the bedroom window As the girl lights her candle.

It disappears; and then, looking in through the window he sees it reappear on the staircase. Suddenly — perhaps coinciding with a crash of thunder — he hears a cry, a heavy fall and the sound of shattering glass, and then, by the light of the blazing nightdress, he sees the girl lying on the floor and a stream of blood mingling with the spilt paraffin. Stunned by the fall, she seems to be dead.

What is he to do? He cannot, even if he dared, enter by the bolted door. And he dare not stay. So, with a last horrified glance at the motionless figure, he turns away and vanishes into the darkness.

Meet Dr. Thorndyke

MY SUBJECT is Dr. John Thorndyke, the hero or central character of most of my detective stories. So I'll give you a short account of his real origin; of the way in which he did in fact come into existence. To discover the origin of John Thorndyke I have to reach back into the past for at least fifty years, to the time when I was a medical student preparing for my final examination. For reasons which I need not go into I gave rather special attention to the legal aspects of medicine and the medical aspects of law. And as I read my textbooks, and especially the illustrative cases, I was profoundly impressed by their dramatic quality. Medical Jurisprudence deals with the human body in its relation to all kinds of legal problems. Thus its subject matter includes all sorts of crime against the person and all sorts of violent death and bodily injury: banging, drowning, poisons and their effects, problems of suicide and homicide, of personal identity and survivorship, and a host of other problems of the highest dramatic possibilities, though not always quite presentable for the purposes of fiction. And the reported cases which were given in illustration were often crime stories of the most thrilling interest. Cases of disputed identity such as the Tichbourne Case, famous poisoning cases such as the Rugeley Case and that of Madeline Smith, cases of mysterious disappearance or the detection of long-forgotten crimes such as that of Eugene Aram; all these, described and analyzed with strict scientific accuracy, formed the matter of Medical jurisprudence which thrilled me as I read and made an indelible impression.

But it produced no immediate results. I had to pass my examinations and get my diploma, and then look out for the means of earning my living. So all this curious lore was put away for the time being in the pigeon-holes of my mind — which Dr. Freud would call the Unconscious — not forgotten, but ready to come to the surface when the need for it should arise. And there it reposed for some twenty years, until failing health compelled me to abandon medical practice and take to literature as a profession.

It was then that my old studies recurred to my mind. A fellow doctor, Conan Doyle, had made a brilliant and well-deserved success by the creation of the immortal Sherlock Holmes. Considering that achievement, I asked myself whether it might not be possible to devise a detective story of a slightly different kind; one based on the science of Medical jurisprudence, in which, by the sacrifice of a certain amount of dramatic effect, one could keep entirely within the facts of real life, with nothing fictitious excepting the persons and the events. I came to the conclusion that it was, and began to turn the idea over in my mind.

But I think that the influence which finally determined the character of my detective stories, and incidentally the character of John Thorndyke, operated when I was working at the Westminster Ophthalmic Hospital. There I used to take the patients into the dark room, examine their eyes with the ophthalmoscope, estimate the errors of refraction, and construct an experimental pair of spectacles to correct those errors. When a perfect correction had been arrived at, the formula for it was embodied in a prescription which was sent to the optician who made the permanent spectacles.

Now when I was writing those prescriptions it was borne in on mc that in many cases, especially the more complex, the formula for the spectacles, and consequently the spectacles themselves, furnished an infallible record of personal identity. If, for instance, such a pair of spectacles should have been found in a railway carriage, and the maker of those spectacles could be found, there would be practically conclusive evidence that a particular person had travelled by that train. About that time I drafted out a story based on a pair of spectacles, which was published some years later under the title of *The Mystery of 31 New Inn*, and the construction of that story determined, as I have said, not only the general character of my future work but of the hero around whom the plots were to be woven. But that story remained for some years in cold storage. My first published detective novel was *The Red Thumb Mark*, and in that book we may consider that John Thorndyke was born. And in passing on to describe him I may as well explain how and why he came to be the kind of person that he is.

I may begin by saying that he was not modelled after any real person. He was deliberately created to play a certain part, and the idea that was in my mind was that he should be such a person as would be likely and suitable to occupy such a position in real life. As he was to be a medico-legal expert, he had to be a doctor and a fully trained lawyer. On the physical side I endowed him with every kind of natural advantage. He is exceptionally tall, strong, and athletic because those qualities are useful in his vocation. For the same reason he has acute eyesight and hearing and considerable general manual skill, as every doctor ought to have. In appearance he is handsome and of an imposing presence, with a symmetrical face of the classical type and a Grecian nose. And bore I may remark that his distinguished appearance is not merely a concession to my personal taste but is also a protest against the monsters of ugliness whom some detective writers have evolved. These are quite opposed to natural truth. In real life a first-class man of any kind usually tends to be a good-looking man.

Mentally, Thorndyke is quite normal. He has no gifts of intuition or other supernormal mental qualities. He is just a highly intellectual man of great and varied knowledge with exceptionally acute reasoning powers and endowed with that invaluable asset, a scientific imagination (by a scientific imagination I mean that special faculty which marks the born investigator; the capacity to perceive the essential nature of a problem before the detailed evidence comes into sight). But he arrives at his conclusions by ordinary reasoning, which the reader can follow when he has been supplied with the facts; though the intricacy of the train of reasoning may at times call for an exposition at the end of the investigation.

Thorndyke has no eccentricities or oddities which might detract from the dignity of an eminent professional man, unless one excepts an unnatural liking for Trichinopoly cheroots. In manner he is quiet, reserved and self-contained, and rather markedly secretive, but a kindly nature, though not sentimental, and addicted to occasional touches of dry humour. That is how Thorndyke appears to me.

As to his age. When he made his first bow to the reading public from the doorway of Number 4 King's Bench Walk he was between thirty-five and forty. As that was thirty years ago, he should now be over sixty-five. But he isn't. If I have to let him "grow old along with me" I need not saddle him with the infirmities of age, and I can (in his case) put the brake on the passing years. Probably he is not more than fifty after all!

Now a few words as to how Thorndyke goes to work. His methods are rather different from those of the detectives of the Sherlock Holmes school. They are more technical and more specialized. He is an investigator of crime but he is not a detective. The technique of Scotland Yard would be neither suitable nor possible to him. He is a medico-legal expert, and his methods are those of medico-legal science. In the investigation of a crime there are two entirely different methods of approach. One consists in the careful and laborious examination of a vast mass of small and commonplace detail: inquiring into the movements of suspected and other persons; interrogating witnesses and checking their statements particularly as to times and places; tracing missing persons, and so forth — the aim being to accumulate a great body of circumstantial evidence which will ultimately disclose the solution of the problem. It is an admirable method, as the success of our police proves, and it is used with brilliant effect by at least one of our contemporary detective writers. But it is essentially a police method.

The other method consists in the search for some fact of high evidential value which can be demonstrated by physical methods and which constitutes conclusive proof of some important point. This method also is used by the police in suitable cases. Finger-prints are examples of this kind of evidence, and another instance is furnished by the Gutteridge murder. Here the microscopical examination of a cartridge-case proved conclusively that the murder had been committed with a particular revolver; a fact which incriminated the owner of that revolver and led to his conviction.

This is Thorndyke's procedure. It consists in the interrogation of things rather than persons; of the ascertainment of physical facts which can be made visible to eyes other than his own. And the facts which he seeks tend to be those which are apparent only to the trained eye of the medical practitioner.

I feel that I ought to say a few words about Thorndyke's two satellites, Jervis and Polton. As to the former, he is just the traditional narrator proper to this type of story. Some of my readers have complained that Dr. Jervis is rather slow in the uptake. But that is precisely his function. He is the expert misunderstander. His job is to observe and record all the facts, and to fail completely to perceive their significance. Thereby he gives the reader all the necessary information, and he affords Thorndyke the opportunity to expound its bearing on the case.

Polton is in a slightly different category. Although he is not drawn from any real person, he is associated in my mind with two actual individuals. One is a Mr. Pollard, who was the laboratory assistant in the hospital museum when I was a student, and who gave me many a valuable tip in matters of technique, and who, I hope, is still to the good. The other was a watch- and clock-maker of the name of Parsons — familiarly known as Uncle Parsons

— who had premises in a basement near the Royal Exchange, and who was a man of boundless ingenuity and technical resource. Both of these I regard as collateral relatives, so to speak, of Nathaniel Polton. But his personality is not like either. His crinkly countenance is strictly his own copyright.

To return to Thorndyke, his rather technical methods have, for the purposes of fiction, advantages and disadvantages. The advantage is that his facts are demonstrably true, and often they are intrinsically interesting. The disadvantage is that they are frequently not matters of common knowledge, so that the reader may fail to recognize them or grasp their significance until they are explained. But this is the case with all classes of fiction. There is no type of character or story that can be made sympathetic and acceptable to every kind of reader. The personal equation affects the reading as well as the writing of a story.

Sources

DETECTION AND MYSTERY
"The Dead Hand" [*Cassell's*, October 1912 and November 1912]
'The Sign of the Rarn" [*Everybody's Weekly*, May 20,1911]
"The Mystery of Hoo Marsh" [*Pearson's*, March 1917]
"The Mystery of the Seven Banana Skins"
   [*Everyman*, December 1, 1933 and December 8, 1933]

BILL JAKINS STORIES
"Caveat Emptor"' [*Cassell's*, August 1900]
"Victims of Circumstance" [*Cassell's*, February 1901]
"The Great Tobacco 'Plant'" [*Cassell's*, March 1902]
"Beyond the Dreams of Avarice" [*Cassell's*, May 1902]
"A Bird of Passage" [*Cassell's*, July 1904]
"The Sleuth-hounds" [*Nash's*, August 1909]
"The Free Trip" [*Nash's*, January 1910]
"The Comedy of the Artemis" [*Nash's*, November 1910]

OTHER SEA STORIES
"The Resurrection of Matthew Jephson" [*Cassell's*, September 1898]
"A Signal Success" [*Royal*, September 1900]
"The Ebb Tide" [*Cassell's*, February 1903]
"By the Black Deep" by R. Austin Freeman and Ashdown Piers
   [*Windsor*, April 1903]
"A Question of Salvage" [*Cassell's*, September 19161

COMEDY AND ROMANCE
"Under the Clock" [*Royal*, July 1901]
"The Costume Model" [*Cassell's*, January 1902]
"Ye Olde Spotted Dogge" [*Cassell's*, April 1904]
"A Suburban Autolycus" [*Cassell's*, November 1904]
"A Woman's Vengeance" [*Pall Mall*, October 1912]
"Ruth" [*Ladies' World*, December 19121
"The Great Slump" [*Red Magazine*, November 15, 19121]

Sources

ESSAYS AND TRUE CRIME
"The Art of the Detective Story"
  [*Nineteenth Century and After*, May 1924]
"The Cleverest Murder — In fact or Fiction" [*Strand*, January 1927]
"The Peasenhall Mystery" [*The* (London) *Evening Standard* , November
  1, 1934 as "The Fate of the Girl with Several Lovers."]
"Meet Dr. Thorndyke" [Meet the Detectives, 1935]